Fic SCHOENBERGER
Schoenberger, Susan.
A watershed year /

A Watershed Year

A Watershed Year

a novel

SUSAN SCHOENBERGER

amazon publishing

Copyright © 2011 by Susan Schoenberger
First edition published by Guideposts in 2011.
Amazon Publishing edition published in 2013.
All rights reserved.

Printed in the United States of America.

Published by Amazon Publishing

PO Box 400818
Las Vegas, NV 89140

ISBN-13: 9781477848012
ISBN-10: 1477848010

To my wonderful parents,
Joyce and John

one

The tawdry mermaid painted on the inside of Harlan's front door wore a bikini top made of undersized clamshells. A crude wave curled over her neon-green tail, and the door's peephole left the impression of a third eye in her forehead. Lucy had recommended that Harlan repaint the door or ask his landlord to do it, but Harlan had decided the mermaid would be a great conversation starter at parties.

Parties he had never had.

Lucy lingered by the door, looking for bits of mermaid paint to flake off with a fingernail as she waited for Harlan to emerge from the bedroom, where he was speaking on the phone to one of his doctors. Lucy had spent the afternoon with Harlan, and she had already said good-bye when his phone started ringing. She should have let herself out, but she hated being separated from him. She sensed that he was slipping away, leaving her before she was ready.

"Go," Harlan said when he returned to the living room. He nudged Lucy gently through the door, and she could hear him twist the bolt lock into place with a rusty scrape. She was still standing on the welcome mat, ruffling its artificial grass with one of her clogs, when the bolt scraped in the direction of forgiveness. But Harlan only cracked the door wide enough to force her saddlebag purse through the opening.

"Five more minutes," she said. "Then I promise I'll leave you alone."

He dropped the purse, and it fell like a bag of rocks, keys clattering onto the tile floor.

"I know you mean well, but it's my decision," he said, before closing the door again.

Lucy could picture him slumped against the mermaid: heavy lids blinking behind glasses so thick they left his face a blur; shadow-rimmed eyes peering out from the sallow skin that made him avoid mirrors. The same mirrors had once framed his thick, dark hair; the confident set of his shoulders; the well-defined lines of his jaw. All these, now gone. She knew his eyes were failing, his feet were numb, and he could barely taste or smell his food anymore. The experimental treatments had been ineffective, but she wanted him to give it more time.

"You're thirty-three," she said, crouching to speak through the mail slot. "No one dies at thirty-three."

"Think about it, Lucy," he said from his side of the door. "They do."

She snatched up her purse and keys, then stumbled down the hallway toward the stairs, reviewing the argument she never seemed to finish with him: You don't give up at thirty-three. You fight until you can't stand up anymore, because science might, at any moment, catch up with your disease. And medical miracles happen. She didn't make them up, she saw them on *Dateline* at least three times a year. What about the orthodontist who lived on sun-dried tomatoes and watched an eight-pound abdominal tumor shrink to nothing? "The results astounded even me," the orthodontist had said, patting his taut midsection with both hands and turning sideways as if posing for an "after" picture in a weight-loss ad.

She drove to her own one-bedroom apartment on campus. Ellsworth College was highly respectable, but she found that it drew an odd mix of students to Baltimore: Midwest churchgoing valedictorians reared on beef, and East Coast vegetarian burnouts with high SAT scores.

The moment she entered her apartment, she kicked off her clogs in the direction of the coat closet and unzipped her jean skirt, undressing as the room's cluttered quality struck her anew. Plaster saint figurines were everywhere—on top of the television and perched on the windowsills, adorning the used bookcases and lining the kitchen counter—all mementos of her PhD research. What would happen if she got tenure? Would she stop cramming her saints inside the broken microwave and under the bed whenever she had to host the religion department's monthly wine-and-cheese gathering? Were there any sins more shocking among her peers than a little spirituality?

Harlan, who taught early European history at Ellsworth, once pointed out that impoverished Chinese factory workers—most likely atheists—had produced most of her little statues. But that didn't bother her; it wasn't the statues that mattered but what they represented. What could it hurt to ask for intercession, she had told Harlan more than once, as long as you weren't careless about it, as in "Please, let there be enough mustard for my hot dog."

Standing in her underwear, she had a sudden impression of her life post-Harlan, which involved hours of sitting in chain-bookstore cafés, sipping lattes in absurdly large cups, in the vague hope that someone would find that her long dark hair, her deep-brown eyes, and her genuine smile made up for her thick ankles, the unfortunate legacy of the Sicilian farming stock on her mother's side of the family.

She sat down at the computer in a small alcove of her bedroom to e-mail Harlan, apologized for pushing the experimental drugs, and signed off as Mary Magdalene, patron saint of repentant sinners.

"You and your saints," he responded. "Want to know how I feel?"

"Yes, I do."

"I was in a movie theater once when the film broke, and they couldn't fix it, and they sent me home with a coupon. That's how I feel."

"Like the film or the coupon?" she wrote back. "Are you the coupon?"

Ten minutes passed with no response, and Lucy thought she had pushed him too far with her belief in the healing power of humor. She pulled a long T-shirt over her head and brushed her teeth, checking and rechecking for a new e-mail.

"Okay," he finally wrote. "I'm the coupon. But I get folded up, put in your pocket, and thrown in the wash. I never get redeemed."

"Is anyone truly redeemed?" she wrote back.

"Only in cartoons. Meet me for lunch on Thursday at Artie's. Around noon. I'll buy you some crab soup."

...

THAT THURSDAY, Lucy shifted her wire-mesh chair into the shade of the restaurant umbrella and thought of Elijah the Prophet, who was said to help motorists and might save Harlan a parking spot so he wouldn't have to walk far in the midday sun of an unusually warm November day. Since the soles of his feet had gone numb, Harlan walked like an arthritic senior citizen, planting a cane before placing his weight on feet that were perpetually asleep.

A few months before, she had gone with him to the medical-supply store to buy the cane, and they had wandered horrified among the prosthetic limbs and geriatric toilet seats until a saleswoman in a maroon velour sweat suit steered them to a whole room full of canes, identified by a sign as the Largest Selection on the East Coast.

The saleswoman let Harlan try out the specialty canes, including one that carried five brandy flasks inside the wooden shaft, one that concealed a twenty-three-inch stainless-steel sword, and one that converted into a pool stick with blue chalk inside the knobbed handle. Then she recommended a cane with a derby-shaped marble handle on an extralong walnut shaft, which Harlan tested, thumping around the store. Lucy remembered what he'd said as he yanked the price tag off his cane on the way out the door: "A good sales pitch is a rare and beautiful thing."

Lucy waited at the restaurant for an hour, drinking free refills of strong iced tea until her veins throbbed with anxiety and caffeine and her ankles swelled. She called Harlan's apartment, but his answering machine picked up, with its complicated beeping and voice mailboxes and instructions, and she hung up. Just as she was dialing the Johns Hopkins emergency room, Harlan's red Saturn lurched into a parking space on the other side of the street. He emerged slowly, grabbing his cane and a bottle of water and shuffling toward her, not looking either way for traffic.

He looked decades older than thirty-three, with untrained wisps of gray hair growing from the nape of his bald head and just over his ears. He couldn't stand up to his full six feet anymore; the treatments had softened his bones. At one point during early rounds of chemotherapy, he had lost fifty pounds and looked frail, but he had gained a bit of it back. Still, there was something awkward about him, as if his skin no longer fit correctly. A young boy at a nearby table stared as Harlan sat down.

"What happened?" Lucy said, her voice rising. "You are *never* more than forty minutes late."

He shrugged and took a swig from the water bottle. His hands, she noticed, now seemed too small for the rest of his body, while his neck looked swollen. The proportions were all wrong, reinforcing her long-held belief that Harlan's illness had been visited on the wrong person.

"I'm having trouble swallowing solids," he said. "I tried to eat some Cheerios for breakfast, and I almost had to give myself the Heimlich. But that's not why I'm late."

Harlan leaned his cane against the table and tilted his head back to catch the sun on his face. Still waiting for his explanation, Lucy noticed he was wearing a hooded sweatshirt on a day when it had to be at least seventy-five degrees.

"I was about to leave when I checked my calendar—out of habit—for doctors' appointments and realized I didn't have any. Then I flipped the page to January—it's one of those calendars for procrastinators that gives you an extra month in the next year to buy a new calendar—and it was empty. Completely empty. Nothing but clean white squares. I do have an appointment in December to have my teeth cleaned, but I guess I can cancel that. It kills me to think about all that dental work I had two years ago."

The waitress approached abruptly, took a pen from over her ear, and wrote down Lucy's order for crab soup and chicken salad, barely glancing at her. In better days, Harlan would have chatted with the waitress and cracked her brittle exterior with a smile, but in the past few weeks, illness had drained away his social skills, as if the niceties of human interaction now seemed pointless. He told the waitress he would have the soup if they could make it extra hot. She scribbled something on her notepad and left.

"I just stared at the calendar for maybe half an hour," Harlan continued. "Then I snapped out of it and drove over. I probably shouldn't be driving anymore."

When his crab soup arrived, Harlan leaned over the bowl and let the steam float up around his cheeks, warming his face and condensing into tiny drops on his chin. Then he picked up his spoon, stirred it around in the bowl, and left it there, as if he had forgotten what to do with it. Lucy watched him as she ate her soup, the Old Bay spices and the sweet crab mingling on her tongue. She felt, oddly, as though she were eating for two, though not in the way she had always hoped.

"I'm planning to die at home," he said. "Would it be too much if I asked you to be there? Just to sit with me."

Lucy probed her chicken salad with a fork, as if the walnuts and raisins would give her an answer. "Give me a minute," she said, blinking hard at the crab-shaped napkin holder.

She knew very little, really, about how he was dying, though it seemed to her like small footsteps toward the grave—two forward, one back. But she knew why he needed her. His other friends had swarmed at first, suffocating him in their need to comfort themselves. But after more than a year of procedures and hospital stays and days on the brink, the calls came only once or twice a week. Even then, Harlan sometimes complained, they probably had "call Harlan" written in their planners, right up there with "clean gutters." Emotionally, he said they had already chosen the suits and dresses they would wear to his funeral.

He could have called his mother in Florida, who thought he was in remission, but she would have fussed at him mercilessly with her antibacterial spray and her pillow plumping and her fluttering hands. His father had died in a car accident when Harlan was twelve. As Harlan's illness had progressed, the circle of friends and family around him had grown smaller and smaller.

In the end, he had only Lucy.

"Do you have to . . . ?" she said. "There must be some alternative."

She had loved Harlan from the time they met in graduate school three years before, but he had been engaged then, and she had kept it to herself, guiltily, like a shoplifter. She had put off telling him for so long that it didn't seem right to spill it now. She had almost stopped wondering whether he returned her feelings; she knew it was all he could do to get through another day.

He cleared his throat as the waitress took his uneaten bowl of soup. His friend at the hospital, he said, would bring him a syringe. He only needed Lucy there for moral support.

"I'd rather not be alone."

"What if it doesn't work?" she said.

"Trust me, it'll work."

"But why can't you hold off for just—"

"The alternative, since you asked, is one organ failing after the other, nurses mopping up the fluids as they leak away. It could take months. Is that more comfortable for you?"

She looked down at the table, reminding herself that he wasn't annoyed with her, only with the universe.

"I'm sorry," he said. "I'm having one of those days angry about the whole thing. It comes and goes."

He blew his nose on a crumpled white handkerchief and stood up unsteadily. She pulled some cash from her wallet, left it on the table, and followed him as he crossed the street, leaning heavily on his cane.

"Tell me what you need," she said. "I can do this."

"Would you mind coming over Saturday?" he said. He slid the cane into the backseat of the car and then folded himself stiffly into the front.

"I'll be there first thing," she said.

"Thanks. I have a few things I'd like to take care of first, and really, I shouldn't be driving," he said before pulling away.

...

ON SATURDAY, Lucy knocked on Harlan's door, balancing a cardboard tray of hot coffees and cranberry muffins. She pushed on the door, which was open, and walked into a room that seemed too bright, overexposed, like a roadside bar before noon. The curtains and shades were gone, shedding an unflattering light on the mermaid as Lucy closed the door behind her.

Three-quarters of the living room had been emptied—going out of business—with the exception of a few unconnected wires scattered on the floor. The dining-room table was still there, and Harlan, inexplicably wearing suspenders, sat at one end, hunched over like an aging accountant, surrounded by stacks of papers and books.

"Hey there," he said, his voice light with decisions made. "Come help me give away my money."

She set the cardboard tray on the table, kissed him on the cheek, and handed him a coffee, which he cradled with both hands. He pulled off the plastic lid to let the steam drift out and held the cup in front of his nose as if to recall, at least, the olfactory memory. In the center of the table was a foot-high plastic statue of Saint Apollonia, which Lucy had given him as a joke a few years before when he was having his wisdom teeth removed. Apollonia was the patron saint of toothaches because she had been tortured for her beliefs by having all her teeth pulled out.

"I'm closing out the old checking account," he said. "After funeral expenses and the final bills, my net worth is about eight thousand dollars. I'm returning it to the neighborhood."

Harlan wrote a check for $500 to Best Dry Cleaning, whose Korean owner called him "Har-LAN." The letters on the check slanted in both directions, unsure of themselves. Harlan seemed to have trouble holding the pen.

"My mother doesn't need it," he said, in answer to a question Lucy hadn't asked. "And I never could bring myself to make a will, so probate might tie it up for years."

He wrote another check to his barber, for $1,000, and asked Lucy to find the address in the phone book.

"This guy cried when my hair fell out," he said. "He actually shed tears over it. I couldn't go back when the gray hair came in."

She wrote down the addresses as Harlan made out checks to his landlord, the mailman, and the single mother next door, who once baked him a loaf of banana bread. Lucy suggested including a short note with an explanation, and Harlan spent half an hour on the wording, which finally read: "Please accept this small gift from someone who appreciated your kindness." On the landlord's note, he also added, "If you want my opinion, the mermaid should stay."

He removed his thick glasses and massaged the puffy skin around his eyes. Lucy watched him and wondered how it would feel to know—*Holy Mary, Mother of God, pray for us sinners*—the hour of your death.

"Anything here you want?" he said. "I gave it all away, except for my bed, this table, my laptop, and my books. It was all junk anyway, except the table, which belonged to my Cajun grandmother, who broke her nose in a banjo accident. I keep meaning to tell you that story—I know you'd like it—but I always get choked up when I think about my grandmother, and there's nothing worse than seeing a grown man cry. It's genuine rosewood. I was hoping you'd take it."

Lucy didn't answer but gathered up the envelopes and affixed the stamps. Though Harlan wasn't gone yet, loneliness was already converging into a small point inside her chest, as if she had swallowed a tack.

"Let's go drop these off at the post office," she said. "What else is on your list?"

"I did want to show you something," he said. "I'll explain when we get there."

A light rain began falling as they dropped the letters off at the post office drive-through, but Harlan left his window down. He tilted his head out and let the fine mist plaster the gray strands of hair to his head. If Lucy hadn't been driving, she would have closed her eyes and pretended she was sitting next to the precancer Harlan: the political junkie, the sports fan, the man who once drove to Boston overnight because he had a craving for Legal Sea Foods clam chowder. Like no one else their age, he had enjoyed a good game of bridge.

"Here's some more saint trivia," she said, needing to hear a voice inside the car. "Saint Jude was often mistaken for Judas after Jesus died. He had to pull out all the stops to help people so that he could build his own reputation. That's why he's the patron saint of lost causes."

"You don't say," Harlan replied, blowing his nose into his handkerchief. "Turn left here."

He led her outside the city to a small cemetery in the western suburbs. She parked the car and followed him as he plodded up a small hill, breathing heavily, his cane sinking into the soft brown soil in spots where the grass had been cut away. The rain, which had grown heavier, ran down behind his ears, though he seemed not to notice.

"This is it," he said, stopping at a plot marked with yellow string. "I hope you don't mind seeing it in advance."

She stopped halfway up the hill.

"There's a statue," he said. "Where is it?"

He wandered around the gravestones until he found it, a two-foot-high white stone Virgin Mary. He leaned forward and cupped his hand on the statue's head, bending down to stare into the crudely carved eyes.

Lucy pressed her fingers to her nose to stifle tears and nodded, but she stayed on the hillside. She had the sense she had been there before, standing in that very spot, as though she had dreamed of it as a child, and the place, the idea of it, stretched as far into her past as it would into her future.

Harlan picked his way back down the hill, leaning on gravestones, and followed her back to the car.

On the way home, he told her about the suit hanging in his closet, the one inside the dry-cleaning bag. He dug around in the glove compartment for a pen and an old envelope to write down the name of the funeral home director with whom he had made all his arrangements. Lucy pulled up to Harlan's apartment building and walked him up the stairs, holding his elbow.

"You should call your mother," she said.

"I will. You go home. I'll see you tomorrow."

"You sure you'll be okay tonight? I could stay here."

"I'll be fine."

He looked pale and feeble, no color to his lips, like a young boy with a high fever. Though he had aged in appearance, he had somehow become more childlike in the past few months: careless about grooming, closer to nature, prone to saying whatever was on his mind.

"Lucy?" he said.

"Yes?"

"I love you."

She was surprised to hear the words, and yet they had become so close during his illness, she simultaneously wondered why he hadn't said them before. She had a fleeting impression that he had rehearsed this moment in his mind.

"I love you, too," she said, embracing Harlan and pressing her forehead into his chest. "Are you sure you don't want me to stay?"

"I'll be on the phone for hours. Go home and get some rest."

. . .

THE NEXT MORNING, Lucy pulled into Harlan's parking lot at eleven thirty. An ambulance was parked at the bottom of the apartment-building stairs, but its lights were off. The paramedics were shutting the doors.

"Who's in there?" she asked them, wishing sickness or death on someone else.

"Guy who lived on the third floor. Neighbors said he had cancer."

Her legs folded underneath her. One of the paramedics ran over with a blanket and wrapped it around her shoulders.

"No one dies at thirty-three," she said, sobbing into the blanket. "Thirty-four, thirty-five, maybe. But not thirty-three."

They nodded and sat with her until she stopped crying, then gently took the blanket back and drove off in the ambulance without turning on the siren.

Later that night, Lucy turned on her computer and found a message from Harlan, which he'd written and sent early that morning.

Lucy,

I just want you to know that I tried with the saints. To be honest, I begged. It just wasn't meant to be.

I also realized how unfair it was that I asked you to sit with me. I decided I couldn't leave you with that image.

Don't forget the dining-room table. It's yours.

I love you very much.

Harlan

She read the e-mail again and ran the cursor gently over the letters in his name, caressing each one—H-a-r-l-a-n.

t w o

Lucy's love for Harlan had always been consigned to a box, like a piece of inherited jewelry—authentic, precious, burdened with history, and underinsured. When the paramedics took Harlan's body away, it was as if the box disintegrated, and the love became a broad kind of yearning that radiated from deep within her core and colored everything around her a faint purplish blue. Her family seemed to sense this and tried to help during Christmas Eve dinner in Towson, the Baltimore suburb where Lucy had grown up.

"Maybe you should take a class," Rosalee, Lucy's mother, said during the meal, an ordeal of fish and pasta dishes in the Sicilian tradition. The air in her parents' dining room smelled like the seashore after a hard rain.

"But I teach," Lucy said, a forkful of cod halfway to her mouth. "The last thing I want to do is sit in another classroom."

"No, I mean something social, like a cooking class. That's where I learned to make the bûche de Noël. Wait till you see it. It's got little candy mushrooms and bark and everything, exactly like a log."

Lucy took a sip of eggnog, which tasted so thickly of optimism she had a hard time swallowing. Her family just wanted her to be happy, she knew that. But she questioned the obligation of happiness. Was there some ratio out there, some secret happiness-to-misery index by which everyone else measured their life and decided whether or not it was worth living? The McVie family—just as Irish as it was Sicilian—seemed particularly intent on passing happiness down through the generations like a small business. But it wasn't as though happiness could be trapped and sustained. Consider the saints she studied. They were celebrated for their unfortunate circumstances, their torture, their untimely deaths. Did anyone measure their happiness?

Her nephew Jack, who was sitting on her right, was pushing tiny clam bits around his plate with a fork and pretend-firing at them with one of the small Lego men he always seemed to be carrying.

"Can I have dessert now?" he asked Lucy.

She studied the curve of his cheek, still downy at ten, still full and soft and vulnerable, needing protection. Here was the crime of Harlan's death. In the last stages of his illness—as Lucy's midthirties became her late thirties—she came close to telling him how much she wanted a child. But, from Lucy's perspective, they always had it backward: no sex, all commitment.

"You better ask your mother," Lucy said. She looked across the table toward her sister-in-law, Cokie, who was pouring another glass of pinot grigio. When Cokie had married Lucy's brother, Paul, they had all been astounded at the quantity of alcohol such a thin-wristed woman could consume without falling over.

Jack appeared to change his mind about dessert and left the table instead. Paul and Cokie's other children, Sean and Molly, seemed to take Jack's departure as a signal, and they drifted off as well, leaving their plates on the table. Lucy noticed that her father was rubbing his belly as though it needed encouragement. Her great-grandmother, Mavis, seemed to be dozing at the other end of the table.

"Let's open some presents," her mother said, standing up. "Just leave all this. I'll get it later."

The rest of the family ignored her, grabbing plates and glasses to deposit in the kitchen. Paul stacked several plates and tried to pick up four wine glasses at once. When he dropped a glass on the table, Mavis woke up, peering at everyone as if they were strangers. Lucy pulled Mavis's wheelchair away from the table and steered her into the living room, parking her next to the Christmas tree, which seemed to shimmer in a haze of blue. Mavis looked at the tree.

"And how are you, dear?" she said before her head began bobbing again, searching for a place to rest as though her neck had given up trying to support it.

The kids rummaged among the presents, each of them pushing the others' hands out of the way, wanting to be first, determined to win, competition bred in their mid-Atlantic, lacrosse-obsessed bones.

"Here, Aunt Lucy," Molly said, handing her a small package. She had clearly wrapped it herself. "We picked this out for you."

Lucy looked at it, embarrassed. She had gotten everyone bookstore gift cards this year, having no enthusiasm for trips to the mall or the toy store. She had more or less managed to tune out Christmas altogether, until this small tape-tortured package with reindeer wrapping paper landed in her lap. She opened it, even though her mother was still audibly rinsing plates and bumping about in the kitchen. It was a Word of the Day calendar.

"We know you like words," Molly said, and Lucy did. She liked their elegance, the shapes they made on paper, the musical way they could sound, the subtlety of meaning. She favored some words over others, leaning toward three-syllable words with forceful meanings like "kinetic" and despising mushy two-syllable words like "cuddle."

"Give us one," Molly said. "Maybe we'll know it."

Lucy opened the box and looked at the first page—January 1, 2003. "Providence," she read.

"I think it's in Rhode Island," Molly said.

"True," Lucy said. "But it also means: 'one, the foreseeing care and guardianship of God over his creatures; two, God, especially when conceived of as exercising this; and three, a manifestation of divine care or direction.'"

"What's the next one?" Sean asked, but Lucy didn't answer. She stared at the word: "Providence." She felt the density of the calendar's pages in her hand—as if she were holding the days themselves—and it seemed to her suddenly that 2003 would be a watershed year. She had no evidence for this, only the conviction that all her yearning would latch onto something eventually. It had to.

...

ON THE FIRST DAY of classes in the new year, Lucy found a prominent place for her Word of the Day calendar on the kitchen counter and tacked the "Providence" page on her small bulletin board to remind her that guidance might arrive when she least expected it. She brushed her long hair into a low, serious ponytail and applied enough lipstick to make it look as if she had pulled herself back together, which somehow made her feel as though she had.

With her book bag over one shoulder, she took the stairs down two floors and left her apartment building—only one step up from living in a dorm—and followed the narrow path between the arts center and the gymnasium, passing a rusted iron sculpture that had always looked to her like some kind of weird urban cactus. The sharp smell of the rusted iron, the bite of cold dry air, and the evidence of frost on the ground surprised her. It was winter now, as if the seasons would go on changing just as they always had, without any regard for Harlan's passing.

She crossed the main quad and nodded at the freshmen running past her, late to class. A year from now, those same freshmen would either schedule later classes or walk in with a coffee after class had started, nodding casually to the professor, and new freshmen with different faces but the same expression would run past her. The cycle of academic life.

Lucy's small book-lined office in the Arts and Humanities building was on the second floor. She felt fortunate to have the type of office designated for assistant professors in line for tenure, which meant that it had five shelves instead of four and a chair for students in addition to the one behind the desk. The short-term-contract professors had offices that were little more than closets, and the adjunct professors hired to teach individual classes didn't have offices at all. But as she put down her book bag, she wondered if she deserved that fifth shelf, which was so crowded with books that it looked as if it might collapse under the weight.

She made a silent vow to redouble her research efforts and crank out at least one notable work of original thought before the end of the school year. She picked up the phone and began dialing Harlan's number—he had a way of helping her clarify her research ideas— when it struck her again, with fresh pain, that he was gone. It seemed, at times, that her need was great enough to bring him back. Who else would let her rattle on about saints or shake her shoulders when she started feeling sorry for him or for herself?

After Harlan's death, there had been days so dark they ran into each other like flickering silent movies. The anticipation of missing him, the thumbtack inside her chest, had turned out to be nothing like the real thing, which was an anvil of terrifying weight that seemed to restrict her breathing.

She sat down at her desk, every muscle aching as the anvil pressed down on her. She heard a knock at the door.

"Lucy?"

Angela poked her head in, then rested it against the door frame.

"Hi," Lucy said, surprised at her ability to speak with so much weight bearing down on her body.

"You're back," Angela said.

In the days after Harlan's death, Angela, who worked in the admissions office, had insisted on coming to see her. She was one of those people who could never seem to sort out her own problems but seemed to enjoy untangling other people's messy lives. It had been Angela who told her the dean was worried about her, concerned that she had stopped publishing, had sidelined her own career. It had been Angela to whom Lucy had confessed her deep desire to have a baby, her anguish and guilt at the thought of the time that had slipped by as she took care of Harlan; Angela who had rubbed her back with a circular motion that made her feel dizzy, imparting these words: "Somehow these things work out, Lucy. It's all part of the ride."

And now it was Angela passing on more condolences. More "I'm sorrys" from the dean, colleagues, students, friends.

How many times had she heard those two words in the past few weeks, spoken with the same sincere tone? She could fill a swimming pool with the sorrow other people felt for her grief, but then what? Was she expected to immerse herself, dive to the bottom, and then rise up through their offerings, becoming whole again? She wished she knew how it was supposed to work. Her vision, which had become briefly blurred, returned when she focused on the dark skin on Angela's smooth forehead.

"I'm sorry, too," she said, though it came out in a cracked, strangled voice she didn't recognize. Angela nodded and closed the door.

Lucy took a deep breath and opened her laptop, trying to decide if she could teach her ten o'clock class without bursting into tears. She had called up her e-mail, hoping to be distracted by the task of deleting spam, when she saw a subject line that said "A Message from Harlan."

Her heart began to thump in a frightening, arrhythmic way. The e-mail had been sent from an address she didn't recognize. She checked the date, assuming it had somehow been held up for months in some shadowy Internet limbo. It had been sent that morning. She then assumed it was a cruel joke, or a perverse spam message that had copied a frequently used name from her old e-mails. A sudden palsy in her hand made it difficult to open the message.

Dearest Lucy,

First off, I'm not talking to you from the grave. I had my old friend from MIT set up a program that sends e-mails on specified dates in the future. I'm writing this in November, but if it works, you won't see it until January. I debated about sending the first one earlier, but I thought it might be cruel to hit you with this too soon after my death. By now, I hope you will have forgiven me.

So why am I sending this at all? Maybe it's only a selfish impulse to leave something of myself behind: I won't have any children, I never wrote that book on the Crusades, I made nothing with my own two hands that will stand the test of time. But I hope it's more than that. I hope it gives me a chance to explain why I chose to leave the way I did, to document the journey of the past year, and to let you know how much you mean to me. Yes, I could have told you face-to-face, but I was afraid I'd make a mess of it. I needed to write my drafts, see the words, and make them right. That's what I'm trying to do now as much as my energy allows.

I remember so clearly the night I told you about my diagnosis and how you refused to believe it. Even I didn't quite believe it then, although a small voice was already telling me to accept the inevitable. So strange that we were locked out on your balcony that night. In a way, that set me up for what was to come: peering inside at the warm and comfortable place I want to be but having no way to get there.

They had a catheter pumping chemo drugs into my chest just a few days later, and you refused to leave, punishing the doctors with questions based on your Internet research. You sat beside my bed with your laptop and a notebook, drilling me on my symptoms and test results as if you could turn yourself into an oncologist in a matter of days if you tried hard enough. You came close, too.

I didn't really mind that first chemo treatment. I had a few days of nausea, but I was distracted by all the cards and letters and friends. Remember when I was the popular sick man? The nurses used to joke that I needed an auditorium for all my visitors. But you kept them moving, ushering them in and out, telling them not to tire me. And when my mother came to visit from Florida, you sat with her and muted her hysteria and made sure she didn't tuck too many pillows under my head. That's all she seemed able to do.

This may sound strange, but I had a dream about you one night back then, and you were you, but you were also Eleanor of Aquitaine, one of my favorites from the Crusades. You were riding off to the Second Crusade in your armor, on a white horse, young and fierce and determined to help your husband, Louis VII, as he battled the infidels. Technically, Eleanor didn't even like her husband, and she ended up *dumping him after the Crusades. Later, she married a man a decade younger, who became King Henry II of England, bore him a pack of children, and then turned against him along with three of her sons. But the point is, I've never had such a literal dream: you in armor, ready for battle.*

I never told you this, but in my third round of chemotherapy, when the visitors had dwindled to one or two a day, I woke up from a nap, and you were gone from your chair next to my bed. I don't think five minutes went by before I started to panic—shortness of breath and everything. I even called the nurse, but you walked in with a cup of coffee before I could start drilling her on your whereabouts. I should have told you then, but I didn't, so I'm telling you now: I couldn't have survived the past year without you.

You have no obligation to receive these e-mails, Lucy. I realize this may upset you so much that you won't want them. If that happens, just click on the link below to disable the program. You can do that any time. It just made me feel better to think that we could talk somehow, beyond the end of my life, that I could preserve my presence in some small way. And I haven't told you everything I should have. I wasn't finished yet, at least where you are concerned.

So, if it's okay, you'll receive an e-mail once a month, another part of my story, your story, our story. I can't guess what will happen to you, Lucy. Your life surely will take some unexpected turns; you will adopt a whole new frame of reference. I believe that somehow you're destined for motherhood (Eleanor, who lived into her eighties, had ten children, just so you know). We never talked much about it, but you seem to me like a natural mother. Clearly, you're someone who knows how to give, and that's what good mothers do.

Find out what most fulfills you, Lucy, and go after it. It may not be my place to tell you, but you sometimes deflect the obstacles that come your way instead of racing ahead of them to chart your own course. If I can play some small part in nudging you toward something wonderful, then it won't be as if two-thirds of my life evaporated. You'll take me along on your ride.

If you click on the link below, a prompt will ask if you're sure you want to disable the program. If you click "yes," there's no going back. It's up to you.

Otherwise, look for my message on the tenth of the month.

Love,

Harlan

Lucy rubbed her eyes as if that might make the whole thing disappear. On an impulse, she called up the link at the bottom of the e-mail, and a window popped up asking if she was *sure* she wanted to delete the program. She moved the cursor to "Yes" because she didn't want to plunge into the depths of grief every month; she moved it to "No" and then back to "Yes" because she hated the idea of waiting a month at a time to hear what Harlan could have told her when he was alive. But she clicked on "No."

It was as if she had blinked, and everything she thought she knew about the past year had changed. Had it been that obvious that she wanted to be a mother? She couldn't remember talking about it. Had he caught her staring at babies in strollers? And his dream of her as Eleanor of Aquitaine? She seemed to recall that Eleanor got herself into loads of trouble. She flushed at the idea of Harlan imagining her on a white horse.

It was true, though, that she had wanted to fight the battle for him. She often cut him off when he started to talk about dying, in the belief that he needed to stay positive. All the articles had said a positive attitude helped in healing.

She read the message again. *And I wasn't finished yet. At least where you are concerned.*

Now she would second guess every interaction, browbeat herself for not telling Harlan she loved him from the moment her car had rear-ended his car in the parking lot at Rutgers when they were both graduate students. She'd been feeling around on the floor of her car for a Chapstick that had fallen out of her purse, and her foot had slipped off the brake. Harlan had gotten out of his car to assess the damage and stood there, arms crossed, looking half-annoyed, half-amused. She had opened her window and apologized extravagantly—flustered, disheveled, dry-lipped—but he had only laughed and told her it was nothing to worry about, just one more scratch among many. He was nice enough looking, tall and dark haired, with broad shoulders, a sincere smile. But it was his laugh that drew her in, made her want to touch the traces of childhood freckles on his face.

They had exchanged phone numbers because, Harlan had joked, he might experience delayed whiplash. She had called him that night to check on him and to apologize again for her Chapstick obsession.

"I'm addicted," she had said. "I can't go more than two hours without it."

"I'm like that with cheese."

"Cheese?"

"I lived on a dairy farm when I was a kid. It was a small one, in Tennessee, but you can't take the cheese out of me."

"So maybe we could go out for fondue sometime."

The hesitation in his response, that one long second of dead air, had left her mortified, wishing she could reach into the phone and retract what she had just uttered. She had no balance in this regard, alternately saying what shouldn't be said and not saying what should be said, a social affliction for which there was no cure.

"My fiancée probably wouldn't be too happy about that," he had said.

"Got it," she had assured him. "Say no more."

"You said you were getting your PhD in religion though, right? Maybe we could get together to talk about the Crusades. That's my specialty."

They had met now and then over coffee or a beer, exchanged e-mails, debated aspects of the Crusades. She had forced herself not to think about him on quiet nights—erasing his image from her mind as from a chalkboard—but when they were hired by the same small college, she had every reason to hope, to imagine that iridescent moment when he would tell her that Sylvie had dumped him, or vice versa. But Sylvie had the kind of smile often described as "winning," and she had won, scheduling herself into Harlan's weekends, brightening his apartment with decorative accessories from Crate and Barrel, advertising their future together with strategically placed and tastefully framed snapshots, until they broke up right before Sylvie learned about his diagnosis.

Lucy glanced up and saw that her ten o'clock lecture was due to start in a few minutes. She closed the e-mail and walked to class, slightly stunned but fairly sure she wasn't going to cry. The students followed along with their new-semester attentiveness as she delivered a smooth lecture on Aristotle. Then she strode back to her office to see if she had imagined Harlan's e-mail.

It was still there, the words unchanged, and she read it for a third time, seizing now on one phrase: *my story, your story, our story.* Now that the initial shock had passed, she realized that he was trying to give her answers to questions she had always wanted to ask. That meant he knew those questions were there, radiating between them like sound waves that could only be heard at the right frequency. She decided to view it as a blessing of powerful measure. At a time when Harlan had every right to gather his resources toward the center, to pull inward, he had reached out, thought of her instead. She thanked every saint she could think of for bringing Harlan—in his own inimitable way—back into her life.

three

With the advent of Harlan's messages, the anvil of grief pressing down on her either weighed less or Lucy had learned to balance it more effectively. She had lost weight—her ankles seemed almost normal—and she noticed in the pearly light of the bathroom mirror that her face had acquired a new maturity during her period of virtual hibernation. Still, she was rusty on living. She had a hard time making conversation with casual acquaintances like Harlan's dry cleaner, to whom she took a big armload of clothes that had accumulated in the bottom of her closet.

"Morning, miss," the dry cleaner said. "You friend of Har-LAN. So sad."

"Yes, very sad," she said, not knowing whether to put the clothes on the counter or stand there holding them. It seemed wrong to follow "very sad" with "What do you charge for sweaters?" So she waited, nodding her head, until the dry cleaner—square jawed and muscular, clearly the outgoing son in the family business—reached out his hands.

"What you got?"

"A lot," she said. "I've been putting this off for too long."

"Ah," he said, as though detecting some hidden meaning in her words. "I fix everything."

He sorted quickly through the clothes and filled out a slip, letting her write in her name, address, and phone number. She glanced up at the dry cleaner's bristling hair, which reminded her of Harlan when he cut his hair short in the summer.

Then the dry cleaner handed her a business card, which listed the hours of operation. On the flip side was another business with the same address but on the second floor. It said U-Bet Adoptions— Arlene Kim, Proprietor.

"U-Bet," the dry cleaner said, noticing that Lucy had turned over the card. "My mother find best babies. Top quality."

She read the card again and thought of Harlan's message, his certainty that she was destined for motherhood. *Your life surely will take some unexpected turns; you will adopt a whole new frame of reference.*

"You pick up Thursday," the dry cleaner said.

"A baby?"

"Clothes," he said, laughing. "Clothes ready Thursday. Babies take six, seven month."

"Of course they do," she said, trying to laugh along. She stuffed the dry-cleaning slip and the business card into her wallet. "See you Thursday."

She walked slowly back to her car, glancing at the battered storefronts: Ferdie's Franks 'N Stuff, Charm City Shoe Repair, the House of Foam. She had been living in Baltimore for a year and a half now but never failed to wonder at how the whole messy conglomerate of package stores and check-cashing joints, Italian bakeries and cramped bars, Greek restaurants and sticky-floored sandwich shops managed to function without devolving into chaos. She swore the whole place was held together with fryolator grease and old habits.

In sections of the city, vandals had stolen all the copper pipes from deteriorating row houses; in others, whole blocks had been abandoned. But the city bottled its own brand of charm. It all but dared people to love it, to embrace its dark alleys and its crab-fixated, tourist-plagued waterfront, its overly earnest street performers and its mumbling homeless. It was a place that attracted the kind of entrepreneur for whom success was all about defying the odds:

when a tailor went bankrupt near the college, a twelve-seat sushi bar wedged itself into the narrow storefront and regularly turned people away.

Lucy rested her purse on the car's hood and took out the dry cleaner's business card. She had turned thirty-eight the day after Thanksgiving. The statistical probability of a woman with a PhD finding a spouse after thirty-five had been well documented and was something in the neighborhood of bowling a perfect game. Even by optimistic calculations, she would be well into panic mode by the time she met someone new, forced him to propose, and tried to get pregnant.

The adoption side of the card had slightly raised lettering, and she ran her fingers over the braille-like surface.

She wondered how she had reached this moment in her life. There had been near misses and long-term disasters—in her midtwenties, there was even a marriage proposal from an old boyfriend who was drunk at the time but half meant it. Then time had slipped by in its insidious way, and Harlan had gotten sick, and next thing she knew she was thirty-eight and single without even a long-shot prospect.

Before Harlan's death, Lucy had certainly lived under the false premise that she had all the time she would ever need to speak fluent French, finally learn to do a cartwheel, write a book, get married, have a couple of children. The day after his funeral, she had glimpsed the end of her life in the distance like a boat on the horizon that might swing toward land at any time: only so many Christmases, only so many birthdays, only so many unfertilized eggs, their numbers dwindling as her body rejected one every month, the little futures of those that remained fraught with invasive testing.

She looked at the card again. U-Bet Adoptions was a frightening thought. The agency could be legitimate, but aside from sharing a business card with the dry cleaners beneath it, the name alone gave her pause. She seemed to remember a chocolate syrup called "U-Bet." There were other adoption agencies, of course.

She got into her car to head home but changed her mind and drove south past block after block of hundred-year-old row houses with white marble steps. Finally, she rose on a highway ramp above the thick columns of industrial smoke and past the city's harbor, with its vast containerships and its complex web of cargo-lifting cranes. The ramp soared over the parallel lines of row houses until it descended gently, unfurling into the western suburbs, deliverance of a sort that only highways can give.

Lucy had been to Harlan's grave several times since his death, always on a rainy day in the depths of her gloom. This time it was the start of a new year, with the slight swelling of hope that things might be different. She knelt in front of the polished gravestone and traced the carved letters with her finger. HARLAN MATTHEWS (1969–2002). Harlan's mother had wanted to bury him in Florida near her home, but he had already purchased the plot, and the funeral director wouldn't be swayed.

"He had his own map of the cemetery," the director told Harlan's mother the day before the funeral. "He requested southern exposure."

And so the grave was facing south, just above where she stood when Harlan had showed her his plot. She faced the granite.

I miss you, Harlan. Terribly. It's awful to admit, but I even miss going to the hospital, where all the nurses and doctors treated me like I was your girlfriend. I never told you, but I liked that . . . I never told you a lot of things . . . So, anyway, I had this idea about adopting a baby. Maybe it's not what you meant, but it would be a new frame of reference, wouldn't it? And you did say you thought I was meant to be a mother. I hope you're well, Harlan, or at peace. I'll be back again soon.

She stood up and brushed wet leaves from her jeans, then circled several gravestones before finding the stone statue of the Virgin Mary. It wasn't quite hip high, so she had to bend down to look into the eyes, which stared back. Harlan had been so charmed by the statue, maybe assuming it would comfort her as it stood there spreading holiness across the hillside. But it gave her no comfort. The opposite, in fact, with its empty eyes and inscrutable face. Very unsaintlike. She felt an urge to knock it down the hill. She gave it a little shove and was surprised to find that it moved slightly on its pedestal. She left it that way, an inch off center.

Back in the car, she decided to head home and start researching adoptions on the Internet. She passed beneath the stone archway that marked the cemetery entrance, noticing how the bare trees in the distance appeared to have only two dimensions against the flat and patient dove-gray sky, as though they were etched on ceramic tile.

...

YULIA DOLETSKAYA wore a polyester slacks suit in navy blue, her white shirt tucked inside the elastic waistband. Lucy glanced at the dandruff gathered on the jacket's shoulders but tried not to look at the wiry hair that stuck out from a mole on Yulia's left cheek. Her breath smelled of breakfast meat and strong coffee, and the top of her outdated computer monitor was crowded with dusty Beanie Babies. On the plus side, she had a firm handshake.

Lucy sat down, knees together, hands folded, toward the edge of a worn couch draped in some sort of tweedy pumpkin-colored slipcover. She had been to five other adoption agencies within the first week after visiting Harlan's grave, and all of them told her she needed at least $25,000, which was a problem. She had $10,000 in a savings account from when her great-aunt Paloma had died, and a money-market account with another $9,000 or so—her new-car fund—but she had no idea where she'd get the rest. It didn't seem wise to start out with loans on top of an empty savings account. In addition to that, two of the agencies had frowned on single-parent adoptions. One woman had handed her a stack of paperwork as thick as the Baltimore phone book, with a request for eight personal references. Lucy wasn't sure she knew eight people she could ask to vouch for her moral character.

At first the roadblocks had only made her more determined, but increasingly, she had episodes of fevered anxiety. She combed through adoption Web sites and read message boards. She called friends who knew friends who had adopted. She filled out applications and waited for the phone to ring. Then she spotted a tiny ad in the *Baltimore Sun* classifieds: Doletskaya Adoptions. The agency, which handled Russian and Ukrainian adoptions, had seemed a little more relaxed, and now she knew why. The office had a secondhand feel to it, like a used-car dealership. She imagined the orphans with "JUST REDUCED" stickers slapped on their tiny-footed pajama-onesies.

"So," Yulia said, sitting down behind her desk. "I have important question: Do you want infant or older child?"

"I'm pretty sure I want a baby," Lucy said.

"Most people want infant, but older children do very well. You say on the phone you have small apartment?"

"Yes, but I can move to a two-bedroom duplex on campus. I'm on the waiting list."

"This is good," Yulia said. "Social Services will want separate bedroom."

Lucy shifted as the coarse fibers of the pumpkin couch began to prick her skin through her black tights. She had worn a conservative black skirt to look motherly. She cleared her throat.

"What kind of time line would we be talking about, assuming everything works out?" she asked.

Yulia glanced out the window, then looked down and worked at the skin around her fingernails in the manner of someone waiting in a long line at the post office.

"Russian system is very complex, some regions more demanding than others. Then we have also requirements from state and federal Bureau of Citizenship and Immigration Services. You could go to Russia over summer, depending on region. Many areas require two trips, but some can do entire adoption in one."

Lucy nodded, pleased that she might be able to travel over the summer when she wasn't teaching. She wondered if she could manage a little field research on a saint she had always found fascinating: Savvati of Solovki, the patron of bees. Yulia interrupted her thoughts.

"You have work, Miss McVie. You must arrange child care and support services. You must examine everything you do. You must be like nervous bride who tends to every detail before wedding," she said, leaving her chair and circling the desk to stand in front of Lucy.

"I can do that. You'll never see a more nervous bride," she said, smiling.

Yulia ignored this and handed her a dingy manila folder that looked as if it had been sent home with other prospective parents and returned more than once. Lucy rose from the pumpkin couch and shook Yulia's hand again, feeling dismissed by her brief and less-firm handshake.

"Cost is outlined in first section," Yulia said. "Call when you decide."

"It'll just take me a day or two to go over this information," she said. "You'll be hearing from me soon."

The adoption process, as complicated and nerve-racking as it was, had given Lucy a sense of purpose, had lifted her from the mourning sickness that might, strangely enough, produce a baby. If she had to deal with Yulia and her bacon breath, well, it would be worth it to feel the weight of a small warm head on her shoulder.

She flipped open the folder in her car and ran a finger down the cost estimates. Total: $22,000, which included travel expenses. She could swing it with a small loan, or maybe no loan at all. It seemed important that she didn't overreach financially. A single mother needed to have the kind of fiscal restraint that told her to put back the Ben and Jerry's and buy the store brand instead.

...

THE SMALL STATUE of Saint Jude on Lucy's kitchen counter served to remind her that almost nothing in life could be ruled out. She called her mother.

"Don't flip out," she said when Rosalee picked up the phone. "I'm thinking about adopting a baby."

"It's about time," Rosalee said.

"I'm sorry?"

"Your brother's kids are practically grown."

"But I'm not married, Ma. I thought you'd be shocked."

"Why? It's not like when Mavis came here from Sicily, sweetheart. Now we do what makes sense."

Lucy turned the Saint Jude statue around on the kitchen counter. It seemed, to her, to be questioning her judgment.

"At first I didn't think I could manage it, but then I found a Russian adoption agency. Their fees are pretty reasonable. I still have to fill out all the paper work and get approved and all that. If I decide to go ahead, I'd probably go to Russia over the summer."

"I can see it now. A little Russian baby with enormously round cheeks."

"Enormously . . . round . . . cheeks," Lucy said, pretending to write it down. "I'm adding it to my application."

"This is a good thing, Lucy," Rosalee said. "You'll make a wonderful mother. I'm calling all my friends."

"Maybe you should wait until I get approved, but put Dad on."

Rosalee yelled for Bertie without covering the receiver, but Lucy couldn't hear what he yelled back.

"I'll have him call you later," Rosalee said. "He's rototilling the front garden."

"In the middle of winter?"

"We lost our big rhododendron last year, and he's convinced that the soil is too packed. Retirement has turned him into a home-improvement fanatic. I'd get him for you, but he's renting the rototiller by the hour."

"Rototillers don't come cheap."

"You're telling me."

"Ma?"

"What?"

"You always said Nana Mavis refused to die until I got married, but maybe I'll never get married."

"She's a hundred and one, doll. She'll go when she goes."

When she hung up, Lucy realized she'd been secretly hoping that her mother would protest and tell her she'd surely find someone and have her own children before long. It was now obvious that everyone—including her own mother—had given up on that fantasy. So she'd be a mother anyway, celibate and devoted. She might call it a trade-off, but what was she trading in? Had she missed the boat in the year she had devoted herself to Harlan, or maybe even before then?

She went to bed that night and dreamed of Russian babies with round cheeks, twenty or so in an oversized playpen, all holding out their arms to her.

...

HARLAN CALLS. His voice sounds pebbly, grainy, thick with something Lucy can't identify.

"Do you mind if I come over?" he says.

"I'm reading Aristotle. You know how I get when I read Aristotle."

"That's okay. Advice is what I'm looking for."

Twenty minutes later, he knocks softly and she answers the door. As he walks inside, she notices that the skin around his eyes looks irritated, as if he's been rubbing it.

"Are your allergies acting up?" she says. "You look a little drained."

"It's that image of the plane hitting the second tower. I see it every time I close my eyes. Why do they keep showing it on TV, over and over and over?"

She gestures toward the secondhand couch, and he sits down. The seat is too low for him, and his knees point awkwardly away from each other. She walks to the kitchen and opens the refrigerator.

"Okay, these are your beverage choices: Amstel Light, grapefruit juice, or half-and-half. Oh, wait, here's a root beer in the vegetable drawer. I also have some cottage cheese and a jar of pickles, if you're hungry."

She smiles over the refrigerator door.

"My refrigerator's better than yours," he says. "I have four different kinds of cheese and a gallon of maple syrup I bought two years ago in Vermont. Oh, and a papaya."

"A papaya?"

"From Sylvie. She thinks I should try new fruits."

Lucy returns with two beers and sits on her only other piece of legitimate furniture, a high-backed armchair she rescued at a yard sale. She had felt the chair was trying hard to be noticed, to retain a certain dignity despite sitting lopsidedly on its previous owner's weed-plagued lawn. Harlan's mention of Sylvie irritates her, as it always does, her name like a burr, like a bad taste. She shifts in her seat.

He takes a sip of his beer.

"I have a question I need to ask you," he says.

She assumes he is talking about the twin towers again.

"They keep showing that image because they have nothing else. No way to put it into perspective."

"It's not really about that . . ."

"I've been waiting for a nightmare, but I haven't had one. Maybe I can't go there at night because I'm immersed in a bad dream all day. It's like everything's reversed. Know what I mean?"

"I do," he says. "For once, I know exactly what you mean."

...

SUNLIGHT SEEPED through the blinds, sending narrow stripes across the bedspread. Lucy peered at the light through reluctant eyelids until something in the back of her consciousness found its way to the front. She remembered that she had never picked up the dry cleaning she had dropped off several weeks before.

When she walked into the shop later that morning, the dry cleaner stretched out his arms, practically touching the walls of the small storefront.

"Hey, where you been?" he asked.

"I'm so sorry," she said. "It's almost your fault, in a way. Remember that business card you gave me? It actually got me thinking about adoption."

The dry cleaner smiled. "So happy for you," he said before he walked toward the back of the shop, she assumed, to get her clothes. A few minutes later, he emerged with an infant, perhaps three months old, in his arms.

"I think I gave you the wrong impression," she said nervously. "I'm working with another agency. I hope I didn't—"

"No," he said. "This one mine. You try. For practice."

The dry cleaner walked out from behind the counter and placed the infant in her arms, holding the back of the baby girl's head until Lucy could support it.

"She's beautiful," Lucy said. "What's her name?"

"American name, Lola."

Lucy stared at the placid eyes and smooth skin, examined the miniature fingers and toes. There it was in front of her: every trip to the pediatrician and every school play, every tantrum and every report card, every forgotten lunch bag and every broken heart. And Harlan had missed it all. She smiled idiotically, fighting the urge to cry. Grief rose inside her until it focused itself inside her throat. She took a deep breath through her nose as a prayer from Blessed Julian of Norwich came to her. It was a maddeningly bland prayer, so nonspecific that it bordered on the useless; yet somehow it always made her feel better.

All shall be well, and all shall be well, and all manner of thing shall be well.

The baby squirmed and began to frown, so Lucy handed her back to the dry cleaner. Children, it seemed to her, came so easily to some—too many, sometimes, as if through an open faucet. For others, like her, they were like precious gems that could only be obtained at great expense and after many months of window shopping and filling out loan applications.

"Babies," the dry cleaner said, as his daughter took in a breath to let out a wail. "Happy one second, crabby the next . . ."

"Aren't we all?" Lucy said.

The dry cleaner left his daughter with someone in the back and returned with Lucy's clothes, a foot-thick row of hangers.

"New life starting for you," he said, running her credit card through the machine. "Good to have clean clothes."

She laughed and lugged her dry cleaning outside, wishing she had parked closer to the door.

...

ON LUCY'S NEXT TRIP to the adoption agency, Yulia presented her with a picture of a little boy, probably three or four, with deep-brown eyes, full lips, a wide forehead, and wheat-colored hair with several cowlicks. His cheeks were round, though not enormously so.

"Little Azamat," Yulia said. "Tell me what you think."

The photo was smudged, its corners bent. She tried not to look at it.

"Didn't we agree to look for a baby?"

"Let me tell you about this boy, though, because he is special. He has been with parents until recently. He was dropped at orphanage in Murmansk after his mother died, very young. His father could not care for him alone. This is not unusual in Russia."

Lucy sat down on the pumpkin couch with the photo. The cowlicks made her want to reach into the picture to smooth the boy's hair, but she had pictured herself singing a small baby to sleep in her great-grandmother's cane-backed rocking chair. Just the day before, she had purchased a pair of miniature white socks while buying shampoo at Target. The socks were still in her purse.

"But wouldn't it be a hard transition for him? I was really kind of set on a baby who wouldn't remember anything about the orphanage."

"Of course," Yulia said. "Everyone wants baby. But Azamat is strong, healthy. He waits for someone to choose him."

Lucy pictured a retail store with the orphans on shelves, one for babies propped up in bouncy chairs, and others for each year, progressively less crowded, until the shelf, up high, for the four-year-olds, who sat swinging their legs, poking each other, and sticking out their tongues. What would she do with a four-year-old?

"This is good," Yulia continued. "You would have to find day care for infant, but this boy is almost ready for school. And such a sweet face."

Yulia's voice, though it seemed strangely animated in comparison to her first visit, faded. The more Lucy looked at the picture, the more those deep-brown eyes pulled her in. She wasn't often impulsive—except when she was overtired and spoke sharply to telemarketers—but this seemed like the kind of decision she would either have to make quickly or torture from every angle and never make at all. The picture had to mean this boy was available, that a word from her would radically alter the course of his life—change his citizenship, his language, his socioeconomic status, everything but his genes.

"I must know today," Yulia said.

"Today?"

"Russian agency will go elsewhere if we do not answer."

"I'm still working out the money issue."

"For older child, there is small discount. Twenty thousand."

Lucy took this in. If she could do the adoption for twenty thousand, she might not have to take out a loan. And Yulia was right, it would eliminate years of day-care issues for her. She had to keep her job, didn't she? But a baby would be more malleable, less marked by what had come before. What if this four-year-old had a hard time adjusting?

Logically, she knew she should give herself some time to consider Yulia's offer, weighing the pros and cons of adopting an older child, but the tangle of grief and longing inside spoke for her.

"What would I have to do next?"

"We submit I-600A to Bureau of Citizenship and Immigration Services, complete state papers and home study. FBI does fingerprints and background check. Then we plan trip to Russia."

"You'll come with me, right?"

"No, but we have facilitator in Murmansk. Very easy."

"So I'm about to become a mother?" Lucy said. An emotion she couldn't identify filled her chest, something with enough power to push the anvil of grief aside. She put a hand over her mouth, unsure of how to process the excitement, the terror, the joy, the finality of the moment. She looked at Yulia, who gave her a rare smile.

"In Russia, we say *mama*."

. . .

AS A TEENAGER, Lucy would dread being kissed by her great-grandmother's wet, quavering lips, already so wrinkled they had lost their definition from the rest of the face. But now she enjoyed spending time with Mavis, who could be counted on to forget anything Lucy told her. She liked stroking the delicate meringue of white hair, which had been wiry at one time but now felt as soft and fine as a toddler's. Mavis couldn't say what year it was, but she sometimes talked about what milk cost in Sicily when she was a girl.

"How is she today?" Lucy asked the receptionist on duty in the front lobby of the nursing home.

"Lovin' life," the woman said. "Just told me I needed a breath mint. She don't hold back."

This was true. Whatever mechanism prevented people from saying what they thought had worn out for Mavis. She opened fire and then blew on the gun without a trace of guilt. Lucy found her propped up in her wheelchair in front of the television, watching, of all things, *I Love Lucy*.

"Hi, Nana," she said, kissing the top of Mavis's head.

"Well, how are you, dear? Did you see that? She just lit her nose on fire," Mavis said.

"I thought I'd take you out for ice cream," Lucy said.

"As long you're paying."

She signed Mavis out, and a male nurse arrived to help Lucy take her great-grandmother out to the car. Mavis weighed no more than eighty pounds and couldn't have been more than five feet tall, but she retained the vocal power of her younger years, when she was a full-figured woman who always wore heels.

"Look at this mess," Mavis said loudly as the nurse buckled the seat belt around her delicate bones, which Lucy knew would snap like balsa wood under the slightest pressure. "Wadded-up tissues, wrappers, coffee cups. I'm so sorry, dear. If I'd known it was this much of a disaster, I would have suggested we take your car."

"This *is* my car, Nana."

"It is? I could have sworn mine was blue."

"You haven't had a car for fifteen years."

"Wait, it was aquamarine. A Pontiac with automatic windows. I used to drive it down to the . . ." Her voice trailed off, then she looked at Lucy as if seeing her for the first time, which made Lucy wonder whether Mavis perceived the passage of time as a forward motion anymore.

At Friendly's, Lucy parked the car and then helped Mavis into her wheelchair, relying on passersby to help her push it over the curb and through the heavy glass doors. Harlan, whose upbringing compelled him to open doors for Lucy, had taught her over the years that accepting help was a form of giving. "It's a greater gift than the opening of the door," he would say. "It takes a strong person to accept assistance."

Inside Friendly's, the hostess showed them to a booth, helping park Mavis on the open end.

"Two Fribbles, please," Lucy said when the waitress arrived. "One chocolate, one vanilla."

"Chocolate gives me gas," Mavis told the waitress.

Lucy held a water glass up to Mavis's mouth and tipped it past her dentures. She hoped Mavis would be able to handle a straw.

"Guess what," Lucy said, wiping Mavis's mouth with a wad of paper napkins. "I'm going to adopt a little boy from Russia."

"A Commie?" Mavis said, frowning. "Mean, those Commies. Heartless."

"No, a little boy. He's almost four. His name is Azamat, but we'll call him Mat. Want to see his picture?"

Lucy took the worn photo from her purse and smoothed it out on the table. Mavis's nose almost touched it as she examined the face and began, suddenly, to cry.

"Looks just like my dear Willard. Oh, I do miss him," she said, weeping loudly, though without tears.

"Who's Willard, Nana?"

"What's that?" She had stopped crying.

"Who's Willard?"

"Who?"

When the Fribbles arrived, Mavis demonstrated what she could do with a straw, sucking up the blended ice cream with more power than Lucy could muster, and Lucy realized that she'd probably been sucking her meals through straws for the past ten years.

"So I'm going to be a mother," Lucy said, smiling at Mavis as she drained the last of her Fribble.

"It's not all it's cracked up to be," Mavis said.

"What does that mean?"

"And you're still not married, so you'll be all by yourself. A boy needs a father."

Lucy was surprised to hear such doubts from Mavis, who, she assumed, had been only half listening.

"I know it won't be easy, but I can help him," Lucy said. "I can save him from a place where he'd have no future. I can give him a better life."

Mavis raised her eyebrows, then went back to her Fribble without another word.

On the way back to the nursing home, Mavis fell asleep, slumping against Lucy's arm as she drove. It reminded her of Mavis's one hundredth birthday party, an absurdly elaborate affair at the Sheraton. Mavis's hair had been teased into a froth infused with tiny sparkles. Her nails had been painted bright red, and she wore a purple satin pantsuit Rosalee had purchased in Macy's preteen department. The band played Sicilian folk songs, and the mayor of Towson danced with the children.

But before the cake had been cut, Mavis fell asleep in her wheelchair and missed all the speeches. Rosalee and Bertie had to wheel her back to the hotel kitchen because Molly had cried, thinking she was dead. Harlan was at the party too, just after his first round of chemotherapy. He spent most of the evening talking sports with her uncles. He still had most of his hair then—though he kept touching his head as though he thought it might fall out publicly and all at once—but he didn't have the energy to dance.

four

Lucy had been waiting for Harlan's e-mail, anticipating it for days, and yet when it came, she still felt a chill at seeing his name appear in her in-box as she ate an English muffin and drank her coffee before class.

Dear Lucy,

I don't know about you, but February was always one of the hardest months for me. The holidays are long past; it's drab and gray, with spring still months away. Back in my teaching assistant days at Rutgers, the students would get into a funk where they started debating every grade. "But according to the rubric, this is really a B-minus, not a C-plus."

February was also the month my father died, and I get a little melancholy when I imagine how my life would have been different if an eighty-five-year-old driver hadn't crossed the center line. I was only twelve, and I had to watch my mom turn into a basket case as Dad's coma stretched on for weeks. I wish I could say that I grew up then, matured enough to care for my mom, but I didn't. I just resented her for losing it, because I was only a kid who didn't want anything to change.

Did I ever tell you what I was thinking when you rammed me in the parking lot at Rutgers? I glanced into my rearview mirror and saw this terrified woman with her hand over her mouth, her crazy hair filling up the rest of the mirror, and I wanted to kick you into next week. Careless driving, for good reason, is a pet peeve of mine. I don't even turn on the radio when I drive because I'm afraid I'll become distracted and cause the same kind of accident that took my father from me.

But when I got out of the car and saw how sorry you were, it all disappeared. You were going on about insurance and how you'd never hit anything before, and all I could see was your absolute sincerity. It's there in your face, along with your intelligence, and you can't do anything to hide it. I knew you would be part of my life. I knew it with absolute certainty, the way you know right away which students will get A's as soon as you meet them. I just didn't know how important you would become.

Sylvie didn't like you, although you probably knew that. When I look back, I realize that she redoubled her efforts to get me to set a date soon after I mentioned your name. When you and I both got hired at Ellsworth, she would show up for the weekend with her plans and her presents and her paint-by-number canvas of our future together. Then, suddenly, I wasn't sure any of it mattered, because that long, untroubled road I assumed I had ahead of me suddenly turned into an intersection with a stop sign, and I didn't know if or when I'd be allowed to continue.

The doctors really tried to provide a future for me; I want you to know that. They even talked to me about infertility before my treatments started, but I didn't see any reason to bring children into a world that allowed such suffering. I almost laugh when I think about it now, because my suffering had only begun. That was right around the time of your great-grandmother's one hundredth birthday party, which had a strange effect on me. I started to think that maybe I was the lucky one, that maybe it would be better to die than to see what other torture life had in store for me, or to live to the point where I didn't recognize my own relatives or my own face in the mirror.

I tried to hide it from you, though. I didn't want you to know that I sometimes succumbed to my own drowning thoughts, when you were trying so hard to keep me on the surface. It's funny, but I've heard you complain about your own mother's relentless cheerfulness and how *annoying it can be, and yet you* are *cast in her mold, showing up with your Junior Mints and your clipped-out comics and your forced smile. But when that first depression lifted, I loved you for it. I knew you wouldn't let me sink all the way to the bottom, and that's what kept me going as they stuck me with needles and took my blood and scanned me and probed me and pumped me full of toxic chemicals. It kept me from ending it back then, when I first thought about it.*

I find myself hoping that you've started a new life, one that involves less sacrifice and more joy. Take a few moments this month to do something for yourself. Don't get me wrong, teaching overprivileged teenagers about religion and philosophy is important, but it's not the end of the world if you don't get tenure. Maybe it's just not worth it if it means confining yourself to a library carrel for months at a time.

It's hard for me to remember what it feels like to wake up without pain, but I know I'd appreciate it in a completely different way now. So maybe you can do that for me; appreciate what you have every right to take for granted.

Love,

Harlan

Lucy's coffee grew cold as she read the e-mail over and over, floored by her own ignorance. Of course he had been depressed, for legitimate reason, and yet she had tried to talk him out of it, to pretend it wasn't happening. Had she hauled a drowning man to shore, over and over, when he didn't want to be saved?

His comments about his father and mother surprised her as well. He had rarely talked about his family, and she had never really stopped to think about how lonely he must have been as a child. On the outside, he had been so outgoing, so well adjusted, but his losses weren't your everyday losses. His mother had never been able to cope with his illness, just as she had apparently abandoned him after his father's death. Lucy had projected the warmth of her own family onto Harlan's, almost unable to imagine a childhood devoid of tender care.

What struck her, finally, were his revelations about Sylvie, and strangely, the fact that Sylvie hadn't liked her. *Who wouldn't like me?* she thought, before acknowledging some small satisfaction that Sylvie had seen her as a threat after all.

She wondered, then, about her great-grandmother and tried to imagine herself in Harlan's place. Would she want to live more than one hundred years if ten or fifteen of them were spent in a cloud of confusion? Would it be better to have only fifty, if every day were appreciated in the way Harlan was talking about? It was a good thing, she decided, that few people were given a choice.

...

A FEW DAYS after Harlan's February e-mail, Lucy checked her phone messages and found one from the faculty housing department telling her she could move into the two-bedroom duplex on March 1, much sooner than she had hoped. This is what Harlan wanted, wasn't it? She was taking charge, moving ahead with the adoption in the name of love and life, and putting her work second. She only wished she could tell him she was listening.

She took stock of her place and realized she could pack and move most of it herself, with the exception of Harlan's rosewood dining table, which she would have to pay to have moved for a second time. She would start her packing with the saints.

Lucy picked up Saint Gregory the Great, the patron of teachers and students, who had been pope in the sixth century and had founded a number of monasteries. She had called upon Saint Gregory a few times during her first few classes, when the students had looked at her as if she were an abstract painting, squinting their eyes and tilting their heads in an effort to gain perspective. Back then, she had a tendency to begin a sentence without knowing where it was going, and her lectures, she told herself gently, were a little bumpy. Now she looked at Saint Gregory, the plaster chipped from the end of his nose, and wondered how she would explain her fascination with the saints to a child. To her son.

She couldn't convey in words why she had connected more with the saints themselves than with the Catholicism in which she had been raised. She had always been drawn to the saints—how they lived up to impossible standards in ways that most humans couldn't fathom—and by the specific needs each had come to shelter. Maybe it was even more basic than that. Categories had always made her happy, from the time she was in preschool, grouping the blocks in descending order of size. And wasn't it nice to know there was a saint who looked after fugitives, and one who might help if your contacts felt too dry?

There were saints for accountants, knife grinders, longshoremen, circus workers, and lighthouse keepers; others who might protect you from kidney stones, procrastination, shipwrecks, or rheumatism; some took care of whole towns or countries, while others focused on particular situations, such as parents separated from children or crop failures. Thousands of categories. She liked to think of it as a vast coatroom with outerwear to cover any and all suffering. Whether or not she actually benefited from saintly intercession seemed less important than the comfort of knowing where to ask for it in an emergency, like having a doctor in the family.

She had put down Saint Gregory and had decided instead to start with her many unused kitchen gadgets—all gifts from her sister-in-law—when her doorbell rang. She assumed it was her neighbor Louis, since he was the only person who came to visit without calling first, now that Harlan was gone. She was right.

"I'm deep into Aquinas today," Louis said, following her into the small kitchen and sitting on a stool. "I really need your take on the five ways to prove the existence of God."

"Sorry, I can't today," she said. "Want to help me pack? I'm moving into a two bedroom in a couple weeks. I'm adopting."

"It's not one of those freshmen boys in your Bible course, is it? They'd love for you to adopt them."

"No," she said, laughing. "It's a four-year-old boy. From Russia." She felt a surge of affection for Louis, not having laughed out loud for some time.

"A four-year-old." Louis whistled, replicating the sound of a bomb being dropped in the distance. "That's a huge commitment. When does he get here?"

"If everything goes well, I'll go to Russia this summer to pick him up."

Louis picked up Saint Gregory from the kitchen counter. Lucy set down a box holding a never-used apple-peeler-corer-slicer and stood next to Louis. The statue had come from one of her favorite gift shops in Rome, near the Vatican. It sold only plaster pieces with hand-painted details.

"Saint Gregory kept getting drawn into all these ecclesiastical disputes," she said, rubbing her finger along the chip in the statue's nose. "But all he really wanted to do was stay in the monastery and write."

"I can relate," Louis said. "I had a chance to go out Saturday, and I stayed in to read *Summa Theologica*. So, what's his name? This four-year-old."

"I'm calling him Mat." She showed Louis the worn photograph.

"Is the dean giving you some time off? I asked him for a day off about a month ago, and he told me PhD students are indentured servants who don't get paid to take vacations."

She moved a few kitchen gadgets into a box and realized that she hadn't really thought any of this through: how she would care for a child and continue working full time; whether or not she could expect to get tenure; if she would ever again open the musty pages of a book in some half-forgotten monastery.

"I'll work it out," she told Louis, who had hopped off the stool to go. She admired the way his limbs moved. There was something athletic about him, though she had never seen him exercising.

"I have no doubt," he said on his way out the door. "You're just one of those people."

"One of what people?"

"You know. The ones who take care of sick people, adopt orphans from Russia. The rest of us just want to know when it's time for dinner."

...

"SO WHAT'S your question?" Lucy says, tucking one foot underneath her in the chair.

Harlan stares up at the ceiling for a moment, gathering his thoughts from the four corners. He rubs his hands on his splayed knees.

"I'm not sure how to put this."

"What?" she says, worried.

He stands up, with more effort than she would have thought necessary, and takes his drink to the kitchen counter. He pulls out a stool, maybe to stretch out his knees. She notices that he looks pale, tired, under strain. It's a look that reminds her of the day at Rutgers when he told her that she couldn't leave messages on his home answering machine because Sylvie didn't understand their friendship. She wonders if he's here to say good-bye, to tell her that Sylvie is moving to Baltimore for good instead of staying with him only on weekends, or that he's moving back to New Jersey to be with her. Maybe they've set a date for the wedding. Her stomach clenches.

"When the planes hit   " he says. "I passed out."

"Passed out?"

"I guess you could call it fainting, although that sounds so feminine."

"You lost consciousness?"

"I've been feeling a little off lately, but this was different. My mother called me from Florida and told me to turn on the television. One minute I was looking at the footage of the second tower, and the next minute I was waking up on the floor."

"Have you seen a doctor? I don't think that's a normal reaction."

She's even more worried now; waves of uneasiness travel along the backs of her thighs. Her capacity for worry is as vast as the ocean. It's one of the reasons she thinks she would make an excellent mother.

"I finally went for a checkup," he says. "Do you have another beer?"

She untucks her foot, but he motions for her to stay where she is. He circles the counter and opens the refrigerator. As he does, she turns on the lamp next to her chair. The lightbulb pops and goes out.

"Want to split the last one?" he says. She notices the pebbles in his voice again, the rippling of uncertainty.

"It's all yours," she says. "What did the doctor say?"

He looks at her then, a look that is the equivalent of a phone call in the middle of the night.

...

LUCY MADE some hummus to bring to her brother's house and then spent the rest of the afternoon tracking down documents she would need for the agency that would conduct her home study. For $1,200 of her $20,000 fee, a social worker would walk her through the paperwork, visit her home, and interview her at least twice. Yulia had told her that the process had two sides: first, to educate the adoptive parent on what to expect before and after the adoption; and second, to make sure the parent wasn't dealing drugs, stealing cars, or possibly worse, taking antidepressants.

Lucy found her birth certificate in a folder in the bottom drawer of her bureau, underneath some old bathing suits. A copy of the apartment lease was shoved in a basket of papers underneath her desk, and her latest W-2 form was in a magazine rack that she sometimes used to organize her tax returns. The exception was her passport, which she kept in a plastic bag in the refrigerator at the insistence of her mother, who had read an article about identity theft and convinced Lucy that it was the only safe place if, God forbid, someone broke in. "Do you know what the terrorists would pay for your passport?" she had said. "A dark-haired American girl?"

That evening Lucy dressed in jeans, boots, and a thick turtleneck for dinner, because Paul and Cokie kept their house at sixty-three degrees to save energy ever since Paul's software business had dried up. She mildly dreaded seeing them. Paul and Cokie, it turned out, had a relationship that centered on a joint interest in purchasing the latest technology. When the flat-screen television came on the market, they pored over issues of *Consumer Reports* and talked endlessly about which models offered the best features. Then the money dried up, and they couldn't afford one. The tension had been rising ever since.

"Aunt Lucy's here," Cokie yelled over her shoulder as she opened the door and stuffed some used tissues into the pocket of her belted sweater. "Come on in, little mother."

She took one of the tissues out again, blew her nose, then gave Lucy a hug, whispering into her hair, "What have you done?"

Before she could answer, Paul came out of the kitchen, wiping his hands on a barbecue apron.

"We're making pizza," he said. "Gotta use that bread maker for something. Hey, congratulations."

She thought Paul looked a little thicker around the middle, but maybe it was the apron. It still surprised her a little to see him as a suburban father. To her, he would always be the brother who let her fold his newspapers and follow him on his route as he darted through the neighborhood on his bike. Or the brother who had talked one of his baseball teammates into asking Lucy to the junior prom when she had already given up hope.

"Kids," he yelled into the family room. "Aunt Lucy's here."

As usual, she found herself slightly unnerved by the cavernous two-story foyer, with its elaborate chandelier, which seemed to rise above them like the lobby of an office building. Beyond Paul, on the wall behind the sweeping staircase, was something new: an enormous painting, six feet high at least, a Degas-like scene of ballerinas in a gold-painted frame.

"Holy cow," Lucy said, nodding in the direction of the painting.

"That's how Paul's latest client paid his bill," Cokie said, blowing her nose again. "You love it, right? Because I love it. We all love it."

"Don't start," Paul said.

Cokie shrugged and went toward the kitchen as her children trooped into the foyer. She touched each of them along the way, a light skim across their foreheads as if she needed to verify that they were real, hers, still fresh and lovely. Sean was the only one to protest.

"Hey, Mom, you have a cold or the plague or something," he said, yelling into the kitchen. "Don't touch that pizza dough either."

Molly and Jack hugged Lucy around her waist. Sean stood off to one side and seemed to be looking for something in his pockets.

"Will you let me babysit, Aunt Lucy?" Molly said, grabbing Lucy's arm. "Please? I'm taking this babysitting class in school, and then I get this certificate. I'd be totally responsible."

"I'm sure you would, Mol," Lucy said, gently peeling Molly's hand from her arm. "Let me go get the hummus. I left it in the car. I'll meet you guys in the kitchen."

Paul turned on the front porch light and walked outside with Lucy.

"So how's everything?" she said, meaning it almost literally: Cokie, the bills, the business, what it was like to face middle age, and all the angst in between.

"Lousy," he said with a smile. "But we have our health."

"Cokie looks tired," she said.

"She has a cold. Nothing serious," he said. "I've got a client on the fence. If I can nail a decent contract, we'll be solvent again. But don't say anything, okay, because the kids don't know."

"They don't know?"

"They think we've gone green, conserving energy and reusing aluminum foil."

"So how are you paying for the braces and the piano lessons and the mortgage, Paul?"

"Home-equity loan, credit cards. We're coping. And I'm looking for a job in case this client doesn't come through. The mailman told me they need an assistant manager at T.G.I. Friday's."

"Good for you, keeping your sense of humor," Lucy said, opening the car door to retrieve the hummus. Paul waited until she turned around and handed him the ceramic bowl.

"I'm dead serious," he said, and she could see by his half-sick expression that he was. "Cokie would die, but we gotta pay the bills. Do you know what a new lacrosse stick costs?"

"Not really," she said. "I guess I'm about to find out."

"Yes, you are. Jumping right on the roller coaster, poor girl."

Paul laughed a little too loudly at his own remark, and she found herself in the odd position of being worried about him. She was accustomed to being the one people worried about, with her excessive schooling and lack of a boyfriend.

They walked back with the hummus and found Cokie in the kitchen with the kids, rolling pizza dough. Lucy always thought of their kitchen as a little too antiseptic, with its stainless-steel center island and its gleaming KitchenAid mixer squatting on the counter near the sink. A medieval-style pot rack hung above the six-burner Viking range, and a glass-fronted hutch displayed Cokie's collection of tiny enameled boxes.

Cokie rubbed her nose with the back of her hand to prevent a sneeze, leaving traces of flour across her right cheek and eyebrow. She rinsed her hands and took a box of cold tablets from the cabinet near the sink, washing two of them down with a swig of Amstel Light. By the set of her shoulders, Lucy could tell that she would rather be in bed watching *Entertainment Tonight*.

"So tell us about your baby," Cokie said. "What's his name?"

"I'm calling him Mat," Lucy said. "He's four, and if everything works out, I should be going to Russia over the summer to pick him up."

Jack was sitting at the counter, quietly creating something robotic looking out of Legos. Sean, having been sent to the refrigerator to get some presliced pepperoni, threw an elbow as he walked by, sending

Jack's Lego robot to the floor. Jack slipped off the stool, stood behind Sean, who was sorting through the cold-cut drawer in the refrigerator, and punched him in the kidney.

"Mom, did you see that?" Sean said. "Jack just punched me for no reason."

Cokie turned a glazed eye toward the refrigerator. "Out of my sight," she said.

"Both of us?" Sean said.

"All of you," Cokie said. "I need to speak to Aunt Lucy privately."

The boys and Molly left for the family room to watch TV as Paul put the pizzas on their browning stones in the oven. Cokie sat down on a stool and ran her hands through her multicolored hair.

"I just want to say, Lucy McVie, that you astound me," she said, looking up at Lucy, who was dipping a carrot in hummus. "Don't you think you should have called me *before* you made this life-altering decision?"

"Here we go," Paul said.

"Stay out of it, Paul," Cokie said. "I'm just telling my sister-in-law that it might have been wise for her to consult with someone, a close and caring relative, before she decided to bring a child into this world."

"He's already in this world," Lucy said, nervously biting the carrot. She tried to think of a reason to leave before the pizza was out of the oven.

"I mean *this* world," Cokie said, exasperated. "I mean the world of Cub Scout fund-raisers and kindergarten homework and going to three, yes, three sporting-goods stores to find the regulation mouth guard for lacrosse camp. Do you have any, *any* idea what you're getting yourself into?"

"She didn't check with Mom," Paul said, "so why should she check with you?"

Lucy became aware, instantly, that her decision had prompted a flurry of phone calls, probably hours spent discussing her situation and whether this was "wise" from the perspective of people who had "been there." She could imagine them all, eyes lifted to the ceiling: "What does she know about sitting up all night with a kid who keeps throwing up on the bedspread?"

"It's what I want. I thought you'd be excited about it," Lucy said.

"I just think you need to open your eyes," Cokie said.

Lucy could see that Cokie needed to have her say. She decided to get it over with.

"Enlighten me . . ."

"Let me just give you a little rundown of my week," Cokie said, slurring slightly, the cold tablets kicking in. "On Monday, I got up at six, made coffee, three lunches, five breakfasts, cleaned the kitchen, packed a snack and a water bottle for each kid, spent ten minutes looking for Jack's sneakers, which turned out to be in the laundry hamper, found Sean's overdue library book, and dropped the kids off late at three different schools, which prompted a call from Molly's principal, whose helpful suggestion was that I leave the house just a few minutes earlier, because my kid was missing valuable instructional time.

"Then I went to work, where I listened to the dentist complain about the car insurance on his fully loaded BMW. I worked until three, came home to find the house full of Sean's hockey friends, who were also kind enough to empty the refrigerator, which meant I had to go grocery shopping, drop Molly off at Irish step, come home, clean up, run back to pick up Molly, cook dinner, clean up, help everyone with homework, do two loads of laundry, bake cupcakes for the chess-club bake sale, and clean up again. Do you see where I'm going with this?"

"Of course," Lucy said. "But I don't think —"

"And that was Monday," Cokie continued. "That was a *good* day. By Friday, I am completely incapable—"

"Incapable," Paul agreed.

"—of putting dinner together. I just can't face it, cooking and setting the table and begging them to eat broccoli, just to dump half of it in the garbage and clean up for the fiftieth time this week.

And this never ends. The seasons change, the mess may look a little different, but it's always there. Twenty-one meals a week, and since no one in this house likes the same food, you can at least triple that. Week in, week out, that's thousands of meals a year I have to plan for. And if I don't do it, I'm a bad mother. Check the pizzas, Paul."

A wisp of smoke escaped from the oven door as Paul opened it and took out one pizza with a paddle.

"The edges are burned," Cokie said. "Sean won't even touch it. Check the other one."

The other pizza emerged unscathed. Cokie threw back her head and finished the Amstel Light, then grabbed a pizza wheel and divided the pizza with startling efficiency.

"I don't want to scare you, Lucy. I just want you to go into this with your eyes open," she said more calmly, as if cutting the pizza had purged her frustration. She called into the family room. "Pizza's ready."

The kids sat down and began to eat pizza, telling jokes as they drank root beer.

"Aunt Lucy," Sean said. "Spell *pig* backwards, and then say 'pretty colors.'"

Lucy complied, glad to be talking to anyone other than Cokie. "G-I-P pretty colors."

The three root-beer drinkers laughed until they gagged, as Lucy smiled indulgently. Cokie, meanwhile, stood by the sink, rubbing her eyes. Lucy came over and squeezed Cokie's shoulder. "You okay?" she said.

"That was good," Cokie said, laughing convulsively. "You should have seen your face."

five

Dear Lucy,

It should be March now, almost spring. If I were you, I'd get on that beat-up Schwinn you have and take the loop around the reservoir. Remember the day you got your skirt caught in the bike chain and fell off near the library?

I loved it that you didn't need the latest gadget or the newest clothes. You had a way of making the right choices for yourself, like with the saints. I'm not saying I always got it, but it was right for you. See how tolerant I've become in my old age?

Last March, as I recall, you spent three or four nights sleeping in a waiting-room chair at the hospital when I had my first close brush with mortality. It's not surprising that I developed pneumonia, but I remember being shocked, even in my fever-induced haze, that this might be the end. You can mourn your own mortality with every birthday, but it really doesn't hit you until you can't breathe without forcing yourself to think about inhaling and exhaling.

You finally talked them into letting you in the room, but you were wearing so many layers of paper and latex, I didn't know you at first. Then you took my hand, and I saw your eyes, the only part of you left uncovered. You were pleading with me, willing me to stick around with the force of your stare. It wasn't a conscious decision, but I think I got better because you made me.

My mother never even made it to the hospital that time. She told me later that she tried to get her doctor to prescribe some Valium so she could fly, but he was out of town, so she got in her car instead but had a flat tire in Georgia. She told me you called her when the crisis passed, and she was so drained by the whole experience, she went back home to Florida. I know I've told you before, Lucy, but you have no idea how lucky you are to have the parents you have. They have their faults, sure, but they'd do anything for you. Anything.

Writing these notes is getting harder and harder. I can't guess where you are, who you're with, what your life is like. I worry that I'll seem pathetic to you. I also worry that I'll say something to hurt you, and I won't be around to make it right. Let me issue a blanket apology, right here, right now. The last thing I want to do is hurt someone who always had my best interests at heart. Someone I loved.

Until April,
Harlan

Lucy had been awake since six thirty, unpacking boxes of books in the new duplex in between checking her e-mail every ten minutes. Harlan's first and second letters had clocked in at precisely 8:00 a.m., and this one arrived at the same time, just as normally as the ones from people presumably living. She wondered how long Harlan had spent on this project of his, tapping away at his keyboard for hours at a time, ticking off the months, the seasons, maybe even the years of her life with a story she couldn't read ahead to finish. She couldn't decide if she was deeply touched or terribly saddened that he would spend so many of his final hours thinking not of his own death but of her future.

The day he was admitted for pneumonia had been one of the most frustrating of her life, because the doctors had put Harlan in isolation and wouldn't give her any information because she wasn't a relative. But she had gleaned from the nurses that he might not recover, and so she had slept in the waiting room under the protection of a night-shift supervisor who felt sorry for her.

Days had passed in the pitiful way they do in hospitals, until they agreed to let her see him, maybe just to make her go away. She knew, though, when she saw him that he wasn't going to die. She could tell that he hadn't given up. What he had interpreted as her willing him to live had been her certainty that he would.

She read the e-mail again.

Someone I loved. But in what way, Harlan? In exactly what way?

It could have meant that he loved the way she wore hats, or her uncanny memory for birthdays. It could have meant, "Should you ever require dialysis, count on me for rides." It could have meant, as he had said, "I respect and admire the choices you've made." Or it could have meant, "Would you mind if I kissed you?" There were categories of love. You couldn't just throw the word out there without placing it in some sort of context, and though he was gone, she still needed to know. *Someone I loved.*

She glanced at the clock. She threw on an old pair of jeans and a fleece jacket, ran a brush through her hair, nearly poked out her eye putting on a quick coat of mascara, and then headed for the car. The radio had nothing to offer but drivel—cheesy advertisements, pop songs by those big-breasted women who couldn't sing, oldies that were carved into her brain so deeply, she couldn't bear to hear them again. She switched off the radio and watched the trees go by, allowing herself to replay her favorite immature fantasy: Harlan shows up at her door and tells her that the past year was all a dream. He's been away, in the Brazilian rain forest, where they've discovered a cure. Long embrace. Fade to black.

Inside the IHOP, plates and utensils clinked and scraped. Her parents were already sitting in a booth, drinking coffee. Bertie got up and hugged Lucy, then sat down next to her, leaving Rosalee the extra room.

"Ah, you're a sight for sore eyes," said Bertie. "Your mother's after me with the Atkins. But when you're in a pancake house, I say you order the pancakes. Or the waffles, depending on your preference."

Lucy glanced down at her father's belly, which ballooned over his pants, the legacy of forty years with a cook who thought of mozzarella as a food group. She found that people with potbellies tended not to be overly critical of others, as if the belly itself was a repository of sympathy. It reminded her of the time she had come home from second grade, upset because she had gotten a spelling word wrong on a test. She had been reading since she was four, and she had become accustomed to perfection. Her mother had brushed it off, but her father had picked her up and hugged her. "So, my little genius, you're human," he had said, kissing her hair. "I'm relieved."

She turned over her coffee cup for the waitress to fill. "So how'd that rototiller work out for you?"

"Like angels singing the 'Hallelujah' chorus," said Bertie. "Cuts through the ground like butter."

"And straight through the hose," Rosalee said.

"Which shouldn't have been where it was," he said under his breath, winking at Lucy.

"Never mind about the rototiller," Rosalee said, brushing the dark bangs from her wide forehead. "We wanted to talk to you about the adoption. My friend Patty says you should check out any adoption agency with the Department of Consumer Protection. Just make sure everything's on the up-and-up."

"You think I should be worried?" Lucy asked.

"Patty says some of them give false information about the children: disabilities, wrong birth dates, things like that. It's just wise to check."

"Cokie thinks I should call it off," Lucy said flatly.

She felt the discomfort of minor guilt, knowing this pronouncement would bring her parents to her defense. They had no idea she had already picked out the color she would paint Mat's bedroom, already purchased a Tonka dump truck and a stuffed penguin to place on his bed, already anticipated the way his brown eyes would widen when he saw his own small bathroom decorated with the fish wallpaper she had ordered from a catalog. They clearly thought her toes were in the water, when she had already jumped into the lake.

"Call it off?" Rosalee said. "Did she really tell you to call it off?"

"Basically, yes."

"That's just the stress talking," she said. "The woman is too thin. It's a little-known fact, but stress is actually absorbed by fat cells. It gets diluted."

"On that note," Bertie said, "I'll be having the tall stack of pancakes with a side of bacon."

When the food arrived and Bertie had tried out all six varieties of syrup, Lucy remembered something she had wanted to ask her mother.

"Ma, who's Willard? I showed Nana Mavis a picture of Mat, and she started crying over someone named Willard."

Rosalee put down her fork. "To think that she remembers."

"Remembers what?"

"He would have been my brother, but he died before I was born. He was your Gram and Gramps's firstborn, Mavis's first grandchild, and she came to see him every day, or so I've been told. He died when he was three, and I was born five years later."

"Poor Mavis," Lucy said. "So why is this the first time I'm hearing this?"

"You know why, Lucy. You cried when Aunt Bonnie threw out her old sewing machine because you couldn't stand to see it abandoned. Why should you suffer over something that happened long before you were born, before even I was born? And besides, it just never came up. I don't remember Mavis ever talking about Willard. Gram and Gramps, rest their souls, only mentioned him once a year, on his birthday in April."

Lucy took this in. She certainly felt for Mavis, but she wasn't going to cry about someone who died more than a half century ago. Her mother, evidently, couldn't separate the sensitive child she had been from the pragmatic adult she had become. She pushed her annoyance aside, given what Harlan had said in his e-mail. She smiled at her mother.

"Just so you know, I don't take on everyone's pain anymore. I've reformed."

"Of course you do, hon. It's what makes you special."

Lucy shrugged and distributed the whipped cream more evenly across her Belgian waffle. The air in the pancake house suddenly felt too warm, and the waffle tasted too sweet, or maybe she could only learn so much about herself in one morning.

...

BACK AT THE DUPLEX, Lucy saw Louis outside her door, arms crossed, sitting in a frayed folding lawn chair that had been left on the tiny front porch when she moved in. She was a little startled to see him, realizing he must have trekked all the way across campus. He appeared to be dozing, but he opened his eyes as soon as she approached.

"I've never been down here before," he said, getting up and stretching. "It looks like they built this place in about three weeks."

"I know," she said, running a finger over the white porch railing. "I'm already worried about Mat picking up splinters."

"You were out early for a Sunday," he said. "I thought you might be running or something."

"I had breakfast with my parents," she said, opening the door. "Is there something you need help with? Aquinas?"

"Not really," Louis said, following her inside. "I just miss having you around. Some poet moved into your apartment. He leaves his door open and walks around with a baseball hat on."

She went back to the first part of what he said. He missed her. He came all this way to tell her so. She couldn't decide if this was something she should encourage, so she jumped to the second part.

"You're complaining about a baseball hat?"

"*Just* a baseball hat. We're chipping in to buy him a robe."

She laughed and found herself a little sorry she had moved to the other end of the campus. They wouldn't run into each other by chance anymore.

"I brought you a book," Louis said. "From the library sale."

She picked up the narrow volume, which had a blank red cover, and opened to the title page: *The Life and Times of Saint Blaise*. So thoughtful. Most people seemed a little put off by her interest in saints.

"Do you know anything about Saint Blaise?" she said. "He was this Armenian doctor in the third or fourth century who healed a boy with a fish bone stuck in his throat. So he's the patron saint of sore-throat sufferers."

"I thought you'd like it," he said, straightening some mail on her kitchen counter. "You and your saints."

She sat down at Harlan's rosewood table, which fit snugly into the small dining space opening onto the kitchen, and pressed the heels of her hands into her eye sockets. She knew it wasn't rational, but she had some weird sense that Louis was trying to take Harlan's place. And what if he did? Would he get sick too?

"Thanks for coming by, and thanks for the book," she said, standing up again. It seemed important to be friendly yet brisk until she could sort out whether she wanted his attention.

"Hey, I was thinking," Louis said, turning on the threshold. "Ellen Frist is letting me borrow her class to practice my lecture on Aquinas, and I was hoping you'd come. Then maybe we could get some lunch when it's over. I'm afraid the students will give me the same reaction my parents do—the 'Why-am-I-supposed-to-care?' look—when I get going on my research."

"I know that look. I'll have to check my schedule and let you know," she said, rubbing her forehead. She found herself looking at his arms, which were thin but muscular. An emotion long buried flickered for an instant but went out. She had poured so much into her grief, which could still pull her under like a riptide, and into the idea of becoming a mother. The reservoir felt close to empty.

When Louis left, Lucy took out her photo of Mat and smoothed it on the edge of the kitchen counter. The boy in the photo was wearing a white T-shirt, thin-looking pants, and round-toed sneakers that looked too big for him. He was looking at the camera, but his body was turned, as though he were being asked to abandon a ball or a tricycle to say "cheese," or the Russian equivalent. Soft light-brown hair framed his broad face. His lips, opened slightly, were red and full, and Lucy could make out a few tiny white teeth. His eyes drew her in, just as they had in Yulia's office, deep and brown and mystical, holding some secret longing. Boys like this, she realized, would be hugged more often than they wanted. Already she loved him. Already she anticipated how he would resist that love, struggle for his independence, keep her at arm's length. It seemed inevitable.

She crawled back into bed with her jeans and sneakers on, though it wasn't yet noon, exhausted by images of her relationship with Mat, who, in her mind, had already left home at sixteen to join a cult or a band or a cult-inspired band. But she couldn't sleep. Harlan's voice poked and prodded her. *Don't forget the dining-room table. It's yours . . .*

She got out of bed and went to the dining room. On one end of the table were the home-study papers, which she had to complete before the end of the week. Next to the home-study papers were stacks of her students' essays that should have been graded days ago. Near the essays were piles of newspapers, the *Baltimore Sun* and the *New York Times*, which she had never even scanned: the United States was on the verge of invading Iraq, and she hadn't been keeping up with the news. The table was waiting for her, offering space for her to plan her future, just as it had been Harlan's workplace, where he had planned his own exit and where she imagined he had composed his monthly e-mails to her.

The student essays came first. When they were finished, she opened the home-study folder, which she had started three or four times before but never finished. At the end of the first section, she read that the home-study process could take up to three months, after which she would be given a child referral. But she already had a child referral, didn't she? What was Mat's picture if not a referral for this specific child? She called Yulia's cell phone and left a message: "Yulia, this is Lucy McVie, and I need to speak to you right away."

She flipped through the stacks of newspapers, nerves exposed, until the phone rang.

"Lucy? Yulia. Is something wrong?"

"The home study says I'll receive a child referral once everything's complete, after I get all my approvals, but I already have one, don't I? Is there a chance I wouldn't get Mat?"

Yulia didn't speak for a few moments. Lucy hadn't known Yulia long, but she knew her well enough to sense she wasn't going to like the answer when she finally received it.

"Remember I told you Azamat is special boy?"

"Yes."

"Well, I was waiting for right time, but . . . he is, you see, my nephew."

"Your nephew?"

"It was my sister who died. A car accident. When I heard his father sent him to children's home, I decide to find someone here to adopt him because this is my business."

Lucy could breathe, but with a shallowness that made her dizzy. Her eyes fell on a newspaper photo of a young Iraqi boy selling batteries. A trickle of sweat ran down the side of his thin face.

"So were you planning to take him back once he got here?" she asked, hearing an echo of her own voice.

"He will be yours, yours alone, unless you think he needs his aunt Yulia now and then. This is good for little Azzie. This is why I give you special price."

Lucy held the phone away from her face and tried to absorb what Yulia had just told her. She could hang up now and stop the whole process, and her rational side told her she should. Yulia had lied to her, and she might have to deal with "Aunt Yulia" long past the final paperwork. She should start over or maybe even forget about adopting altogether, just throw Mat's picture away.

But then Mat—whose photo alone already had absorbed so much of her yearning—would not come to live in her second bedroom, would not learn to ride a bike on the college quad, would not draw pictures for her lonely refrigerator. He might never be adopted at all, or he would go to someone else and draw pictures for a refrigerator in a house that could be anywhere on the map.

"I'll be at your office at ten on Tuesday, and we'll discuss this," Lucy said in even tones.

"I understand," Yulia said. "I'll see you at ten, Tuesday."

When she hung up the phone, Lucy contemplated calling her parents and asking for advice but decided against it. Her mother clearly thought she was overly sensitive, couldn't accept reality, needed to be protected from the world. If she was going to be a mother, she had to prove to herself that it wasn't true. She filled out as much of the home study as she could and wrote out a list of questions she would have to be prepared to answer.

No matter how much she worried about trusting Yulia, she couldn't face going back to the other agencies. And she knew that if Mat didn't come to live with her, she'd spend the rest of her life worrying about where he had ended up. For a moment, she wondered if the beautiful little boy in the photo even existed. Maybe Yulia would just take her money and disappear, leaving her with a gaping hole in her heart. She had no way to assess the risk.

...

LUCY DRESSED in the black pantsuit she had worn to Harlan's funeral. Normally she was drawn to long skirts, gauzy scarves, clogs, and dark tights; wide-legged jeans and embroidered cotton tops; and she owned more than one vintage leopard-print coat. This suit was different. It was expensive and fitted and had a board-meeting look to it, and she had chosen it to keep her pulled together during the funeral, believing that the actual fabric would hold her emotions inside and allow her to stand upright. But the suit was looser than before; anxiety spilled from the gaps.

Standing on the miniature porch of the duplex with her coffee cup, she took in the morning light, which had some true warmth to it. It would be one of those mid-March days that felt like the middle of spring, despite the calendar. Baltimore was like that. In addition to an early spring, it offered summer days in May and a freakishly warm day or two well into November. It was ideal, she thought, if you could stand the furnace blast of July and August and the cinder-block gray of winter.

Her view took in other duplexes with identical miniature porches, some of which had been personalized with hanging plants or nylon kites or wind chimes or, in one case, several empty beer kegs. Hard to the left, Lucy noticed for the first time that the bell tower of the college library could be seen through the trees. The spire, spiking the sky, gave her evidence of something outside the stultifying sameness of the duplex world.

She drove to Yulia's office, sitting with her back straight, not even touching the car seat behind her, absorbing the residual power of her black suit. When she arrived at the office building, she didn't see Yulia's car in its usual place in the parking lot. She took the elevator to the third floor, then wound her way down the narrow corridors, whose walls looked as if they could be punctured with a sturdy fork. The door to Yulia's agency was locked. She looked at her watch: 9:59. A slight growl escaped from the back of her throat as she dug through her purse, looking for a scrap of paper on which to write Yulia an extremely unpleasant note. But just as she was testing pens to find one that worked, Yulia came huffing down the corridor, clutching her chest.

"You are early," she said, plastic and canvas bags flying around her.

"No, I'm on time," Lucy said. "If you don't already know this, I'm habitually punctual."

"I got stuck on beltway, some kind of accident. I had to drive on shoulder and take back road."

Still breathing heavily, Yulia unlocked the door with bags hanging from her wrists, and Lucy walked inside, straightening the hem of her jacket.

"Nice suit," Yulia said. "I will make coffee."

"Thanks, but no," Lucy said. "I'd like to discuss my situation."

"Of course," Yulia said. "Please sit down."

Lucy started toward the pumpkin couch but stopped. Sitting down would give Yulia a position of superiority. She crossed her arms and turned.

"I'd rather stand. Now, please explain to me what's going on. If Mat is your nephew, why can't you take him?"

"I considered, of course. But I have three children already. My husband has bad back and cannot work. I hear from friends in Russia that Azamat's father has new girlfriend, but they still leave him at orphanage. He deserves chance to live better life. I owe this to Mitya."

"So I'm supposed to believe all this?"

"Wait," she said. "I have something."

Yulia tore through the plastic bags she had left in a clump by her desk and took out a videotape. Lucy surrendered to the pumpkin couch as Yulia inserted the tape into a small television with a VCR. On the screen, a small boy pushed a Matchbox-style car along the ground, making motor noises and smiling at the video camera. The camera followed him to a pile of sand, where he sat down and dug with a small shovel. He seemed to forget the camera at one point and began to sing a little song.

"Can you turn up the volume?" Lucy asked. "What's he singing?"

Yulia rewound the video and turned it up so that Lucy could hear Mat's voice. Some of the words were garbled, but she caught most of them.

"'Twas brillig, and the slithy toves
Did gyre and gimble in the wabe;
All mimsy were the borogoves

And the mome raths outgrabe."

As the video went on, the little boy repeated the same verse over and over, sometimes in a high voice, sometimes in a lower one. A chill traveled down Lucy's spine as the two-dimensional Mat of her worn picture became three-dimensional, took on sound and personality, acquired a beating heart.

"It's 'Jabberwocky,'" Lucy said. "He must have seen the Disney version of *Alice in Wonderland*."

"Mitya bought many Disney movies for him. As you can see, he has excellent memory. He is good boy. Very healthy. You take him. Please."

"What happens if I don't take him?" she asked.

"Maybe he gets adopted by someone else, though this is less likely because he is no longer a baby. Maybe he grows up in orphanage—this is stigma in Russia—and trains for job. Maybe he never leaves Murmansk."

Lucy leaned back, her sharp jacket askew. It was obvious that Yulia knew she was hooked, that she wouldn't jeopardize her chances of getting Mat, so what was the point of pretending? She hated that her emotions were always too close to the surface, behind a flimsy veil that could be swept aside when she least expected it.

"No more surprises, Yulia," Lucy said, one hand pressing her forehead. They had crossed some barrier now, beyond polite business talk. They were, for all practical purposes, about to be related by a small Russian boy obsessed with *Alice in Wonderland* as interpreted by Disney. Nothing had prepared her for that.

When Lucy went home, she found her copy of Lewis Carroll's *Through the Looking Glass* and looked up "Jabberwocky," which Alice had read by viewing the backward text in a mirror.

"Beware the Jabberwock, my son!

The jaws that bite, the claws that catch!

Beware the Jubjub bird, and shun

The frumious Bandersnatch!"

Lucy was amused to read that Alice said the poem was a bit hard to understand, at which point Lewis Carroll added this aside: "You see she didn't like to confess, even to herself, that she couldn't make it out at all."

six

"You're an intelligent girl, Lucy," Paul said, taking a sip of his Sprite. "But you're missing the point. Springsteen doesn't sugarcoat the truth."

She looked at him, then glanced at the large pieces of romaine in her Caesar salad. She would have to cut them with a knife and fork.

"I still say 'You ain't a beauty, but, hey, you're alright' is the harshest lyric ever written," she said.

"You're forgetting what comes next: 'And that's alright with me.'"

"Like that takes the sting out of it."

Paul had called her right after her meeting with Yulia to tell her he had taken the job at T.G.I. Friday's. His client had fallen through.

"This could be worse," she said, putting an arm around his shoulder as he stood at the bar. "It could be Taco Bell."

Paul laughed, but she regretted the joke. She hated to see him in a place so clichéd, with its dim interior lighting and its unnecessarily large hamburgers. Even the name, with its partial acronym, seemed to mock his situation. It couldn't always be Friday.

"I still haven't told Cokie," he said, suddenly serious. "She thinks I'm working late to nail a new client."

"But Paul, you have to tell her."

Paul's head slumped forward, and she could see that the bald spot on the crown of his head had grown in a matter of weeks. The skin looked slightly pink.

"It's such a colossal mess. We don't even talk about it anymore, and I've been sleeping on the couch for months because she says I've been tossing and turning too much. I feel like she despises me for letting the business go down the toilet."

"She doesn't despise you, and you didn't cause the entire country's economic downturn."

"You don't see her face before she's had coffee in the morning. But I have to tell her about the job before someone rats me out. Sean's lacrosse coach came in yesterday, and I had to hide in the bathroom."

"If you need a little money, I could come up with something."

"Absolutely not. I know you need it for the adoption. And this will tide us over for a little while. I just don't want to lose the house."

"What about Mom and Dad?"

"You didn't tell them, did you?"

"No, but . . ."

"I can't have them finding out. They'll be driving over with casseroles every day like somebody died."

Lucy saw his point. Their parents had been nervous about Paul starting his own company. Their sympathy, in lasagna form, could be too much to bear. Paul tore the paper off a roll of wintergreen Life Savers and stuck three in his mouth, crunching them with his back teeth.

"I can't take the food here; it's killing me," he said, burping. "Thanks for coming up."

"It'll all work out, Paul," she said, though she sounded unconvincing even to herself. "This is temporary."

"It better be, or Cokie will wring my neck. Luckily," he said, looking around, "our friends wouldn't be caught dead in this place."

She gave Paul a hug and paid her bill, stopping on the way out to examine an old-fashioned bicycle hung on the wall. It had an enormous front wheel with a tiny one in back and appeared physically impossible to ride.

Wow, she thought. *What a long way down.*

...

LUCY GRABBED THE STACK of graded essays on the dining-room table and brought them to her Friday-morning philosophy class, during which twelve of her best students sat around a table arguing in voices made thin by sucking in too much stale library air. She wasn't trained as a philosopher, but few universities had need for a full-time hagiographer. She had developed a course based on the teachings of some of the greats—Aristotle, Socrates, Sartre, Nietzsche, Kant—and threw out ethical dilemmas the class had to solve using one or several of their arguments.

"I don't get all this 'God is dead' stuff," said her youngest student, a nineteen-year-old from St. Louis. "I mean, who or what killed him off?"

A senior girl with a nose ring and greasy hair spoke up. "Nietzsche said, 'God is a thought who makes crooked all that is straight.'" She was scribbling stars on her notebook. "I think that says it all right there."

Lucy intervened. "You don't need to agree with it, Peter; you just have to remember it. Maybe you'll like Euripides better. He said, 'The way of God is complex, He is hard for us to predict. He moves the pieces and they come somehow into a kind of order.'"

Peter wrote down the Euripides quote, nodding. Nietzsche never appealed to the Midwestern students, Lucy thought. They hated to think that God was dead or even under the weather.

After class, she saw Angela walking down the hallway from the admissions office. She had an enviable walk, a way of holding her shoulders that implied confidence and training in dance.

"You're all scrunched up," Angela said. "You look like a hobbit."

"Thanks, and yes, I'm fine," Lucy said, pulling her shoulders down and back. "I'm actually feeling marginally good today."

"How's the adoption going?"

"A few bumps in the road, but it's progressing. Did I tell you I picked out some wallpaper for Mat's bathroom?"

"Yuh-huh, some kind of fish," Angela said, looking at her nails. "Why don't you start coming to the single mothers' group? I try to go once a month before we get into the admissions crush. Lets out all those toxins."

Lucy imagined the single mothers in a circle around a life-size voodoo doll in the shape of an ex-husband. Each had a frozen daiquiri in one hand and a large pin in the other.

"I'm not even a mother yet," Lucy said. "I've still got forms to fill out."

"We'll be there when you need us. And you will need us," Angela said, continuing down the hall. "Good luck with that wallpaper."

As Angela left, Lucy suddenly remembered Louis's Aquinas lecture. She had never gotten back to him. The class had started at noon, so she knew she could probably get there in time to hear the second half of the lecture and provide a friendly face. She hurried across the quad, dodging clumps of students, her book bag walloping her thighs with every stride. She burst through the double doors of Wyman Hall and ran down the main corridor to the lecture room on the first floor, sliding a bit along the high-schoolish gray and white floor tiles before taking a breath and opening the door. Louis's voice emerged, then surrounded her.

"That brings us to Aquinas's fourth way to prove the existence of God, the argument from degrees and perfection," Louis said. "Aquinas argued that two objects may be compared in terms of beauty; for example, two paintings. One can be said to be more beautiful than the other, possessing, then, a greater degree of beauty. Aquinas reasoned that there must be a standard of perfection from which we measure degrees of beauty or goodness or kindness. And that standard, that perfection, he said, is contained in God."

About thirty students sat in the middle of the sloping lecture hall. Some scribbled down every word or typed on laptops; others nodded along as though they knew where to find the information online. Louis was standing at a lectern to the left of a broad screen, which, at the moment, showed a Renaissance painting of Saint Thomas Aquinas.

Lucy entered the room and sat down in the back, though Louis didn't appear to see her. She noticed that he was wearing a shirt and tie with khaki pants and a leather belt, which she would have assumed he didn't own. He looked quite comfortable up there, changing slides with a remote control.

"The fifth, and final, way to prove the existence of God, Aquinas said, was the argument from intelligent design. It's just common sense, according to Aquinas, to believe that the universe was created by an 'intelligent designer'; in other words, God. The order of nature, the beauty of the stars, the clever way it all fits together had to be arranged by such a designer and not by chance. Just look around you, Aquinas was saying; examine the perfection of a tree or an insect or a child and tell me there isn't a God."

As Louis continued, Lucy directed her attention to Ellen Frist, who sat off to one side in a chair, watching Louis give his lecture. Lucy noted that Ellen was wearing a shortish skirt and high heels, not her usual teaching attire.

When Louis finished, the class applauded as Ellen took the lectern to remind them of their reading assignments. Lucy waved her hand to catch Louis's eye as the students gathered their things to leave. Her cheeks felt slightly warm. She was forced to admit, if only to her most inner self, that it made her happy just to see him. He smiled and motioned for her to wait.

"No one applauded my first lecture," she said as he came up the aisle. "You're surprisingly good."

"No, I'm not," he said, tugging on his tie. "Wait a minute. Why 'surprisingly'?"

"Because you're what, twenty-nine, thirty? Most people need a few years to get the hang of it. You looked like an old pro up there," Lucy said.

"I had a tree stump in my backyard growing up. I practiced by lecturing to squirrels."

"Which have notoriously short attention spans," Lucy said.

"Not if you talk about acorns... I'm almost thirty-two, by the way."

She smiled and shouldered her book bag. Louis stepped aside to let her pass in front of him, and they both walked out through the doors of the lecture hall.

"I'm so sorry I was late," she said. "This week turned out to be insane, and then I completely forgot until . . ."

A student came up to Louis and stood nearby, waiting for her to finish. She was about twenty, evenly browned as though just back from a week in Cancún, with buoyant breasts that couldn't be ignored. Lucy stopped talking and pretended to look for something in her book bag.

"Professor Beauchamp?" the student said, with a distinctly Maryland accent that flattened the long "o" sound. "I just wanted to ask a quick question."

"I'm not really a professor yet, so it's just Louis. What can I do for you?" Louis said, his voice rising slightly.

Lucy waved and slipped out the front door of Wyman Hall. She started back across the quad, deciding to pick up a sandwich in the faculty cafeteria and eat it at her desk. But a minute into her walk, Louis came running up behind her.

"I thought . . ." he said, panting slightly. "Maybe lunch?"

"What did she want?"

"Who?"

"You know who."

"Oh," Louis said, flushing. "She just wanted to know if I taught any courses she could take."

"Your first devoted follower."

"Right," he said. "Hey, let's go to the grill. I'm starving. I was too nervous to eat breakfast."

"Sorry, I can't," she said, running ahead, her book bag hitting her thighs for the second time that day. "I've got too much work. And Mat's wallpaper is coming in today."

"Okay," he yelled toward her. "Maybe some other—"

She looked back as a student trying to catch a Frisbee ran between the two of them and hit Louis in the shoulder. But she turned away again. She didn't want to see Louis's face because it might confirm that she, Lucy McVie—scholar of useless information, unmarried thirty-something, failed vegetarian, pseudo-Catholic—embodied the standard by which disappointment was measured.

...

HARLAN OPENS his second beer and drains half of it. He doesn't usually drink much. He told her once that alcohol makes him feel disoriented, bringing back memories of a childhood bout with vertigo. Her worry multiplies.

"I still need to ask you a question."

She nods, but he remains silent. She tries to wait as he finishes the beer, but she's compelled to fill the void.

"I fainted once. In high school. I was giving blood for the first time. When they brought me over to the cookie table, I slipped out of the chair and slid right underneath the feet of my trigonometry teacher."

She smiles at the memory, though she suddenly wonders if it ever happened. It sounds like the story of a friend or something she saw on an after-school TV special. She doesn't like to doubt her own recollections. It makes her feel old and unsafe.

For unknown reasons, her story brings Harlan back to the planes.

"Have you noticed, with the planes," he says, "how quickly the disbelief evaporates? Just a few weeks later, and now it seems ridiculous that we never anticipated this—"

"I know," she says, nodding.

"Because we should have seen it coming. Why didn't we understand the threat?"

"Fanaticism is a great motivator," Lucy says. Harlan looks restless, as though this can't be the answer.

"I'm sick," he says. "The doctor says I'm sick."

...

"DID YOU CHECK OUT the agency?" Rosalee asked over the phone, which had been ringing when Lucy walked into her office back in the Arts and Humanities building. "I've been waiting to hear."

"I did, and it's all fine," Lucy said as she unpacked her book bag and cradled the phone with her shoulder. She had, in fact, made sure no complaints had been filed against Yulia's agency, though she knew her mother would have been appalled to hear how Yulia had lied to her.

"You're absolutely sure?" her mother said.

"How're Cokie and Paul?" Lucy asked, willing to go into uncharted territory to avoid talking about the adoption.

"Well, now that you bring it up," Rosalee said. "I'm very concerned. Paul's acting strangely, and Cokie won't even talk to me on the phone anymore. She just covers the mouthpiece and gets Paul."

Lucy murmured her sympathy, expecting her mother to continue. Instead, she heard a long pause.

"You were there not too long ago," her mother said. "What's your take on it?"

"I have no take on it," she said, finding it surprisingly easy to avoid the truth. "I'm sure they're just going through a rough patch."

"Well, I hope that's all it is."

"Me, too. Nice talking to you . . ."

"Lucy," her mother said. "You'd tell me if you thought something was wrong, wouldn't you?"

"You mean like you always do for me?"

"I see your point," Rosalee said. "Good-bye, honey."

"Bye, Ma."

...

IT WAS LUCY'S BELIEF that chocolate-covered peanuts were a gift from a higher power. She might even have to tell Louis to include it in his presentation as the sixth way to prove the existence of God. Arnold's, a drugstore just down the street from the campus, had bins of loose candy that could be scooped into little white paper bags for the purpose of spiritual renewal. She hadn't visited this altar of comfort since Harlan died, but the bruises of the week—and the fact that she had never managed to eat lunch—put her in the mood for the walk. She left her office and strode down the hill toward the small strip of commercial businesses that catered mainly to students and college employees.

Arnold's was a throwback, probably one of the few drugstores in Baltimore still owned by a family instead of a corporation. Lucy appreciated the meticulously organized shelves rising from pine floorboards worn thin and soft, their grains compressed by eighty years of foot traffic. She passed through the air-freshener and cleaning-fluid section, getting a whiff of Mr. Clean before entering the candy aisle, which smelled of chocolate and salt and sugar, with overtones of Maalox. She stood in front of the chocolate-covered-peanuts bin, which was nearly full, but she scanned the other choices, as always: Gummi Worms, chocolate raisins, Red Hots, M&M's, Gummi Sharks, chocolate caramel peanut clusters, and the dietetic candy, which no one ever seemed to touch.

She took the metal scoop and filled half of a tiny white bag with chocolate-covered peanuts. Angela came up behind her as she was paying for them.

"Candy is not a substitute for a man," Angela said, eyeing the bag.

"Thanks for the advice," Lucy said.

"You think that sugar and fat and salt is just as good?"

"As a matter of fact, I do."

Lucy opened the bag, and Angela grabbed a handful of chocolate-covered peanuts with her right hand. She picked out two with her left hand, ate them delicately, then threw the rest into her mouth.

"These are evil," she said.

"Get your own bag," Lucy said.

Angela paid for her sugar-free gum and took another handful of peanuts from Lucy as they walked back to campus.

"You know what I hate most about being single?" Angela said. "Kix cereal."

Lucy said nothing, knowing Angela needed to talk.

"Breakfast is the most important meal of the day, right? But I cannot be bothered to cook an egg for just one person, and Vern won't touch anything but Kix. So that's what I eat, too. Kix. These bland little corn balls. And I'm a vegetarian, so I could use the protein."

"So get over it and make yourself some eggs."

"The loneliest sight in the world—the whole entire world—is just one egg in the frying pan."

"So make two."

"Too much cholesterol."

They walked the rest of the way up the hill, discussing cholesterol and how you couldn't eat anymore without wondering if the food would kill you. Lucy briefly thought about Harlan's cancer, the cause of which would never be known. Memories of Harlan had become less painful, she noticed, since she had started receiving his e-mails. He hovered now, returning to her thoughts sometimes in vivid flashes, but more often just coloring the air, resting on her skin, infiltrating her hair. As Angela explained the philosophy behind her new obsession with protein, Lucy wondered if Harlan perceived being there at the same time, and in the same way, that she sensed it.

She left Angela at the administration building on her way to Arts and Humanities to collect some papers to grade, work she would fit around decorating Mat's room. In her mind, the room had to represent all she could offer to a small child; it had to convey, the first time he saw it, that he would be cared for, comforted, loved, even spoiled to a degree. Even in its strangeness, it had to communicate that a place had been saved just for him. It had to be a room he couldn't imagine ever wanting to leave. It had to be perfect.

...

THE PACKAGE CONTAINING Mat's wallpaper was on her porch when Lucy got home. She opened it and stretched out several feet of the roll, admiring the glossy, sparkling fish on the deep blue background. She had never tried wallpapering before, but it was a small bathroom, and she had purchased a book at Home Depot promising step-by-step instructions.

The next morning, she had a quick cup of coffee and a bowl of cereal, thinking of Angela's Kix, and then started in on the bathroom, spreading her supplies across Mat's bedroom floor: tape measure, yardstick, pencil, paste, brush, wallpaper, X-Acto knife. She saw that she could fit two full sheets of paper from floor to ceiling on the wall opposite the door. Then she would have to piece the rest together around the toilet and the mirror and sink. She scanned the first page of the book and then stretched out her roll, piling books on one end to prevent the paper from curling.

She brushed the back of the first long piece with paste. But when she stood up, she realized that she wasn't tall enough to reach the top of the wall. She stepped on the edge of the tub and tried to paste it up from a slight angle. The top was more or less straight, but a large bubble appeared in the middle, and she couldn't seem to smooth it out. She pulled that piece off the wall and wadded it up, tossing it in the corner.

An hour and a half later, she realized that she couldn't do this by herself. Not only was she apparently incapable of cutting a straight line, but she couldn't hold both ends of the paper and smooth it at the same time.

"They should have a label on the front of the book: two people required," Lucy told Angela on the phone. "I ruined so much of the paper, I'm not sure I have enough to finish."

"Okay if I bring Vern?"

"Sure," she said. "But won't he be bored?"

"He's got a Game Boy. He's never bored," Angela said. "I'll be there in a half hour. Have to find my tools."

Lucy waited for Angela and Vern at the dining-room table with her feet on another chair. She took in the living room, with its miniature gas fireplace, wondering why she never sat in front of it. Would that change, she wondered, when there were two people living here instead of just one? For a moment, she felt a twinge of panic about how she was barreling along on the path toward this adoption, knowing full well that Yulia wasn't following the normal protocols. But she had to believe that Yulia knew the system intimately enough to make it work; after all, hadn't she handpicked Lucy to become her nephew's new mother? Before Lucy could take the other side in her own argument, Angela came in with her large pink plastic tool kit, and Lucy didn't see Vern at first, because he was right behind Angela, looking down at his Game Boy as he walked.

"Hey, is that Vern, coming in on little cat's feet?" Lucy said. She stood up and noticed, suddenly, that Louis was a few feet behind Vern. She admired his resilience, considering her last conversation with him on the quad.

"He actually does have little cat's feet," Louis said. "I've seen them. Must be hard to find shoes for him, Angela."

"Yeah, it's hard, but they're more like rhinoceros feet. Boy wears double Ds."

Vern seemed not to hear any of it. He parked himself on the couch, never taking his eyes from the tiny screen.

"What are you doing here?" Lucy asked Louis. He was wearing an old T-shirt and a pair of paint-spackled sweatpants.

"I was picking up some window shades, and I saw Angela at the hardware store. I told her I'd help, if that's okay," he said.

"You're saving me," she said. "I am a complete failure at home improvement. I'll show you the damage."

She led Angela and Louis upstairs and showed them the bathroom, which was sticky from floor to ceiling with wallpaper glue. Wads of rejected wallpaper lay strewn around the bedroom floor like a Christmas morning gone horribly wrong.

Angela looked at the wallpaper still on the roll and determined that enough remained to complete the job if they didn't waste any.

"Tell me again how you know about wallpaper?" Lucy asked.

Angela opened her toolbox, which contained every tool Lucy could name and several others she could not.

"My mother was a flipper. Fixed up old houses and sold them for a profit. My sister Paula specialized in the wallpaper, but I used to help her. I never told you how we lived in twelve different houses growing up?"

"Never," she said, and then, turning to Louis: "What's your story?"

"I just like to watch the home-and-garden channel."

"Which explains nothing."

"Don't be so sure," he said, stretching out a roll of wallpaper. "I'm a visual learner."

Lucy sat on the floor as Angela and Louis measured and cut. They brought in a chair to reach the ceiling and added water to the paste, and when the job was under control, they let Lucy help by holding one end of the wallpaper. At one point, Vern came in to ask for a snack, and Angela draped his arms with wallpaper sections. In two hours, the entire job was done. Angela packed her toolbox and snapped it shut.

"Pizza on me," Lucy said. "You deserve it."

"Thanks, hon," Angela said, "but Vern's got tai chi at five."

Louis was picking up bits of scrap wallpaper and stuffing them into a plastic bag. He absentmindedly ran a gluey hand through his long hair.

"Sorry," he said. "I'd really like to stay but—"

"He has a date," Angela said.

"More like coffee with a friend," Louis said, giving Angela a look that made Lucy think they had discussed this before.

"Who?" Lucy asked. She was genuinely curious, slightly jealous, and somewhat annoyed that she had been left out of the loop.

"Ellen Frist," he said quickly. "Well, that was fun. See you later."

Louis let himself out as Angela checked the couch cushions for tiny Game Boy cartridges.

"What's going on with you two?" Angela asked.

"Absolutely nothing's going on with me," she said. "I just can't figure out what's going on with him. Ellen Frist is old enough to be his very young aunt."

"She's your age," Angela said.

"There you go."

"Don't give me that. He likes you, and you know it."

"No, he doesn't. It's just one of those little attractions academic people get when they admire another academic's work. Happens all the time."

"Please," Angela said. "I'm going home."

"Bye, and thanks again. Bye, Vern," Lucy said. "I owe you a pizza."

Vern looked up from his Game Boy.

"When you get your son, can I teach him to play baseball?"

"Of course, Vern. That would be great," she said. She had assumed that Vern had been dragged to her house and made to sit for hours without even knowing why.

Angela put her arm around her son and kissed the top of his head. "Tai chi," she whispered, pushing him through the front door.

seven

*M*y *dear Lucy,*

Strange as it may sound, there is some small sense of relief in dying young. What I mean is, I won't disappoint anyone by failing to reach my full potential; I won't have to see those brown splotches appear on my skin; I won't spend years in a nursing home without knowing my own name. It's not that I want to die, but since I don't have a choice, I sometimes try to look at the upside.

I also try to think about September 11, and how those people working in the World Trade Center and the Pentagon, or the people getting on planes, couldn't have anticipated dying when they did. I've had time to prepare. There are moments when I find enough emotional distance to realize I just got dealt a bad hand. At least I had thirty-some fairly nice and productive years.

One of the hardest times for me this past year was having that brief remission, after my bout with pneumonia. I started feeling better, and the tests showed the tumors in my lymph nodes were shrinking, and yet I couldn't enjoy it. I had this powerful sense that it would never be over, and you tried to talk me out of it. You dragged me to movies and plays—all with a message of hope, as if you thought I wouldn't notice. You replaced the navy-blue towels in my bathroom with bright yellow ones. You drove me all the way out to New Market to look at antiques, as if to say, "Last, Harlan, last, just as long as these pieces of furniture. I insist *that you last."*

When my other friends stopped showing up, when my mother couldn't overcome her fear of flying and had one excuse after another for not visiting, you were there. On the outside, you're such a gentle person, Lucy, almost too passive sometimes. But your core is made of titanium, or at least it is where I'm concerned.

I think you need to tap into that strength in your own life. Sometimes I wonder about your fascination with the saints, whether you truly believe in the possibility of intercession, or if it's just an excuse to step back, to recede a bit from a challenge. I'm not saying I have the answers, but sometimes I wonder about it.

April is when the tulips bloom in that beautiful garden near campus. I remember seeing you there once, when I was still with Sylvie and she came to visit. You turned away, as if you didn't want us to see you. I brushed it off at the time, but for some reason, I keep coming back to that image: you reading on a stone bench surrounded by flowers, pretending not to be there.

Don't think I haven't noticed that you gave up most of your social life to spend time with me over the last year. I hope that's changed, now that I'm gone. I'm sorry I wasn't strong enough to push you away.

Go see the tulips for me,
Harlan

When Lucy finished reading, she was grateful to be at home at the computer in her bedroom, because she needed to throw herself down on the bed and cry just long enough to feel sorry for herself again.

She had driven Harlan crazy, tortured him with her need to keep him alive. Even during his brief remission, she had insisted—insisted—that he refuse to backslide. The part about the saints didn't surprise her; he had often made the observation that she had no business throwing problems into the hands of dead people who had mostly likely been brainwashed or delusional. He had never really understood her fascination with the persistence, century after century, of saintly petitions. But how could she, who knew so many of their stories, have ignored them when it cost so little—under dire circumstances—just to try?

She returned to the chair in front of her computer, sitting now as though her spine had wilted. She was never one to spend much time documenting her life, but now she regretted not having a photo album with pictures of her with Harlan. She could have flipped through the pages—supplanting all this new information with a carefully edited mirage of good hair days and boisterous laughter.

She scrolled through the e-mail again.

Dealt a bad hand. She so admired his ability to distance himself from something that couldn't be more personal. And that last part: *I'm sorry I wasn't strong enough to push you away.* He had always been honest about how much he needed her, and she had never regretted the time spent rubbing his back as he vomited or reading the newspaper to him in a hospital room. He had been the strong one, in accepting her help, in allowing her to see him as vulnerable. She had always been glad he hadn't pushed her away until the very end.

What stung, though, was the part about her attempt to disappear in the garden. She had never known how to react when she saw him with Sylvie, who had a way of looking at her as if she had something in her teeth, whose silk camisole she had found in Harlan's laundry basket days after their breakup and had thrown away, stuffing it deep down inside his kitchen garbage with the orange peels and coffee grounds.

She went downstairs to the kitchen, washed down a piece of dry toast with a swallow of cranberry juice, grabbed her book bag, and attempted to tap into the titanium core Harlan said she had. Yulia had pulled some strings to move the adoption forward a bit, but she wasn't sure she could wait until June, given a recurring nightmare that involved Mat falling out of a plane without a parachute. He would tumble down in slow motion like a character from *Alice in Wonderland*, singing his little "Jabberwocky" song, and she would run around on the ground below, arms outstretched, trying to guess where the air currents might take him.

Less than an hour later, she sat on a cold metal bench outside the federal building and flipped through her new Russian adoption guidebook. Around her, lawyer types walked briskly to and from the federal building, with its dark, monolithic slabs. She peered up, noticing the building was virtually windowless. A chill crept through the plaza, seeping, it seemed, out of the concrete itself. Small bursts of wind sent bits of gravel into motion around her feet. The sky, the benches, the walls, the ground all merged into shades of gray, with the exception of a large stone container filled with half-dead daffodils in one corner of the plaza. She walked toward the daffodils, drawn to their struggle, as Yulia walked into the plaza from the other direction and caught up with her. She put down several plastic bags, pulled a pack of cigarettes out of her coat pocket, and lit one.

"I didn't know you smoked," Lucy said.

"Not so much," Yulia told her, sucking on the cigarette like it was an oxygen mask. "No lecture, please."

"It's your life," she said. "What time do we have to be inside?"

"Five or ten minutes."

Lucy looked up at the building again, trying to imagine what it would be like to work in a windowless building every day, never seeing the sky, always out of sync with the weather. "So tell me something about your kids."

Yulia leaned back against the planter, took another drag from the cigarette, and exhaled. "They go to school," she said, picking a tiny shred of tobacco from her tongue. "Oldest is seventeen, from first marriage. Younger two—fourteen and twelve—from my husband's first marriage. They stay with us on weekends, holidays."

Lucy nodded. Yulia, clearly, was a big-picture person, someone for whom the troubling intricacies of blended families or tax codes wouldn't much matter. As someone who found God in the details— or at least in the categories—it worried Lucy.

The metal detector inside the federal building scanned Yulia's plastic bags and Lucy's purse. A security guard checked their IDs and filled out temporary badges, directing them to the fourth floor for fingerprinting. Once in the elevator, Lucy thought of Saint Blaise, who might relieve the tightness in her throat from the cigarette smoke, and Saint Basil the Great, the patron of those facing court appearances. The fingerprinting wasn't really a court appearance, but it felt like some kind of judgment would be made. On the other hand, she couldn't think of anything the FBI might find, except for an unpaid parking ticket from a trip to Boston twelve years ago. She still felt guilty about it.

"Relax," Yulia said. "You press fingers. Boom. Done. How is home study?"

"It's going well," she said, deciding not to tell Yulia that the social worker had knocked on her door while she was arguing over the phone with her mother, who had accused her of hiding Cokie and Paul's financial troubles. It turned out that T.G.I. Friday's wasn't beneath Bertie and his Thursday-morning golfing buddies. The social worker, luckily, had seemed more interested in whether Lucy kept a fire extinguisher in the house and where the household cleaners were stored.

The waiting room in the fingerprinting office was packed with people, all flipping through magazines. The ones in chairs seemed to anchor themselves more deeply as newcomers arrived. Lucy leaned her back against the wall in a small space near a magazine rack. Yulia followed and dropped her bags.

"What's in all those bags anyway?" Lucy asked.

Yulia brightened a bit at the opportunity to explain.

"This one, knitting. I took course at community college. This one, hair dye and rubber gloves. I thought I might have chance for touch-up. This one, laptop, which needs to be fixed, and files. And this one is bathing suit to return. Too small."

"Why didn't you leave all that in your car?"

Yulia shrugged. "I took bus. Car is in shop."

They finally found seats, then waited another fifteen minutes until Lucy was called in. She let the fingerprint technician place her hand on a glass plate, which took a computerized scan. She was grateful it wasn't ink, but she still felt like a criminal. She walked back into the waiting room to find Yulia knitting what looked like a striped afghan. As they walked back down the corridor, Lucy realized that she could have done this on her own.

"You really didn't need to come," she said as they waited for the elevator. "Don't you have other cases to work on?"

"A few," Yulia said. "But this one is most important. I hate to mention, but my brother-in-law is . . . *sobaka*. Dog."

Lucy's heart stopped for several beats.

"What are you saying, Yulia? Could he interfere, could he stop the adoption?" she said. The six or seven other people on the elevator looked toward Yulia.

"Well . . ." Yulia said. "This is very unlikely."

Lucy took a deep breath as they left the building. Between Harlan's e-mail that morning and Yulia's commentary on her brother-in-law, she felt as if her seams might come apart again, and she wasn't wearing her black suit to keep everything in. When they were back out on the concrete plaza, she grabbed Yulia's forearm.

"You need to tell me if the rug might be yanked out from under me. I'm not sure I could take another loss right now."

Yulia put down her bags and wrapped a thick arm around Lucy's shoulders.

"He is meant to be with you. I feel it. I came to America ten years ago, when Mitya was just a girl. I do this for her."

And the way she said it, the utter conviction in her voice, allowed Lucy to move one foot in front of the other. She dropped Yulia off at her office and went back to campus, alternately terrified and resigned that she couldn't predict how all this would turn out. From her computer at work, she read Harlan's e-mail again and decided that she would see the tulips on Saturday. And she would stand there in the midst of the beauty that Aquinas said was evidence of God's existence, and she would pray.

...

PAUL SQUASHED a paint-filled sponge on the wall and turned to Lucy. "It's a little too regular," he said. "I'm too type A for this. You need a random touch."

Lucy took a step back from the wall in Mat's bedroom, which they were sponging in sunrise yellow over an off-white background.

"I hate it," she said. "Why don't we just get some rollers and make it all yellow?"

"Sounds good to me," he said. "I never took you for a sponge painter anyway."

"It was Angela's idea. Since she helped me so much with the wallpaper, I thought I should take her suggestion. But this looks like creamed corn thrown against the wall."

"Cokie likes the sponge effect," Paul said. "But only when it's professionally done."

"Anything new on that front?" she asked. She had been waiting for Paul to bring it up.

"We've reached détente. She works, I work, the kids do whatever it is they do, and we're not going to lose the house, for now. But I'm bringing bologna sandwiches to work, and Cokie brings cheese and crackers. She actually clipped a coupon the other day."

"You're lying."

"She figures she can afford to go back to the hairdresser if she saves fifty bucks at the grocery store. And she's putting in a few more hours at the dentist's office. He says she's the best receptionist he's ever had."

"I have to say, I'm pretty impressed she's handling it so well."

"She took the news better than Mom and Dad. And she's loving the casseroles because she doesn't have to cook."

"Has she mentioned anything more about the adoption?" Lucy asked.

"Let's not get into that," Paul said, pulling his sweatshirt over his head. They walked down the stairs. "Cokie's not objective about it."

"Just tell me what she's saying."

"Only if you promise not to tell her I told you."

"I promise."

"Well, she thinks you're adopting this boy because you lost Harlan. She's worried that you're trying to replace one with the other."

Lucy crossed her arms and gazed at the ceiling.

"She's not completely wrong," she said, looking back at Paul. The truth of it couldn't be ignored, though it pained her a little to think that Cokie had perceived it. "That might have had something to do with it, at first. But I still think it's a good thing, for both of us."

"Makes sense to me," he said. "But as Cokie often says, what do I know?"

...

EIGHTY THOUSAND TULIPS. They were categorized by color into defined spaces called beds, though nothing had ever seemed more awake, more alive. Lucy sat down on a stone bench across from a bed of frilly-edged white flowers with red and yellow stripes. A small green sign stuck in the grass identified them as Tulipa Carnival de Nice. She loved the order and precision of the place, imposed by garden-club ladies with wide-brimmed straw hats. She thought about the whole culture of gardening, about which she knew absolutely nothing except that Saint Fiacre, an Irish-born monk, was the most commonly cited patron saint. He was a healer, too, and the patron of cab drivers.

She settled in with her book, the one Louis had given her about Saint Blaise, and read for twenty minutes until the garden began to murmur, and she realized the place was now filled with couples and joggers and mothers pushing strollers. She looked up toward the central gazebo and saw Louis standing there with Ellen Frist. They were examining the trellises and speaking in low voices. Lucy ducked her head and turned on the bench to face in the other direction. She made herself as small as possible, hoping, as she did that day with Harlan, that motionlessness was the first cousin to invisibility.

"Lucy!"

Louis ran over in his T-shirt and jeans and flip-flops. His hair looked as though he had combed it with his fingers just after getting out of bed. The remnants of sleep lingered around his eyes. He stood there, hopping up and down a few times against the morning chill, staring at her expectantly.

"Hey there," she said. "You picked a great day."

"This place is unbelievable," he said. "Ellen showed up at my door this morning and dragged me over here."

She noted certain words: *This morning. Dragged me over.*

Ellen, who had stopped to examine the Carnival de Nice tulips, walked over and stood next to Louis in a manner Lucy interpreted as girl-friendly.

"Lucy," she said. "Lovely to see you."

"Lovely to see you, too." Lucy had always been powerless to avoid repeating British turns of phrase. Ellen was holding an expensive-looking camera with a long lens. Lucy noticed the precision of her short blond bob. Someone must have used a ruler to cut it.

"You're reading *Saint Blaise*," Louis said. "Anything new in it?"

"I really just started," Lucy said. "I'm going to sit here and enjoy it. Don't feel like you have to keep me company."

Louis sat down on the bench and stretched out his legs. "I could use a rest. Sit down, Ellen."

"I'd rather not, actually," she said, holding up the camera. "The light is brilliant just now."

"Okay, then I'll catch up with you in a minute," Louis said.

Ellen turned slowly and walked down the stone pathway, adjusting her newsboy cap. Lucy noticed she was wearing riding boots with jeans, and she forced herself not to ask Louis where the crop was.

"That was rude," she said when Ellen was out of hearing.

"No more rude than being forced to wake up at eight thirty on a Saturday morning."

"Maybe," Lucy said, considering this as she turned slightly toward Louis. She suddenly became aware of the fine hairs on the back of her neck.

"Would you mind if I sat here a minute?" Louis said. "She's totally obsessed with that camera. Writes down the exposure for every frame. She wanted me to carry the notebook, but I refused."

Lucy laughed and rubbed the back of her neck. She could have listened to him complain about Ellen all day.

"I don't know why, but the British like to document everything," she said. "I had this friend in London who had a collection of gum wrappers. He wrote down on the back of each wrapper what he was doing while chewing the gum and then pasted all the wrappers in a scrapbook. They would say things like 'Saw *Evita* in West End. Wrigley's Spearmint.'"

As Lucy talked about the gum wrappers, Louis leaned back on the bench and closed his eyes. She wasn't sure if she was boring him with her story, but he looked content. A slight smile lifted the corners of his mouth, as if he had just lain down on a warm beach after a long winter.

"I had a friend a lot like that, only he's not English," Louis said, opening his eyes. "He lived next door to me growing up in New Hampshire. He was obsessed with gum too, only it was those flat pink sticks that came inside baseball cards. For years he wrote down all the cards that came in the pack on the actual piece of gum, in tiny print with a ballpoint pen, and kept them in one of those magnetic photo albums. But then the gum started to disintegrate, and his mother made him throw the whole album away. I was never much of a collector. Just books."

When Louis finished his story, he reached over the back side of the bench and picked a red tulip, down toward the leaves. Lucy looked around to see if any of the wide-brimmed hats were in sight.

"You can't pick those," she said. What would she do if he gave her a flower, with Ellen right there, probably watching them through her telephoto lens?

"I guess you're right," he said, trying to stand the flower back up among its leaves. It leaned awkwardly against another tulip. "It seemed like a good idea for a second."

She remembered, then, why she had come to the garden. She was supposed to be praying for the safety of her future son and honoring the memory of her beloved friend.

"Ellen's coming back," she said, though this wasn't true. "I better go."

"Okay, well . . ."

Lucy threw the book in her purse, then hurried through the garden, hoping absurdly that Louis would come after her. It wasn't right, though. He was too young, too sure of himself, too annoyingly attractive with his careless hair and his narrow hips and his academic obsessions. She just couldn't see it working out. And she should stay focused on the adoption; she couldn't afford to divide her attention. Louis was resilient; she had to give him that. But certainly, there would be one rejection that would end his efforts, and for all she knew, this had been the one.

eight

There were times when Lucy felt almost transparent, insubstantial, as though her body would offer no resistance if the wind chose to lift her into the sky. At such times, she wished she had a small brick house to call her own, something earthbound and solid that could keep her from getting swept away like the seeds of a dandelion.

She had considered herself a rare exception to the laws of gravity ever since she was a child. Paul would be down the street playing kickball with his friends, and she would be hiding inside the branches of an enormous copper beech in her front yard, climbing as high as she dared and then sitting on a narrow branch that would bend under her slight weight. She felt closer to nature there, without her feet on the ground; not above it all, exactly, but within, enfolded in the arms of a benevolent spirit.

But one night, when she was nine, she had a dream that she had flown up to the ceiling in her room and woke to find herself perched in the copper beech on a branch fifteen feet above the ground. She had been a sleepwalker as a preschooler but hadn't done it in years. Shaking, she had climbed cautiously down the tree. She was almost there, about four feet from the bottom, when her bare feet slipped and she hit the ground with a thud. She crept back into the house with a sore shoulder and a bruised knee and went back to bed, never telling her parents. For the next year, she slept with a jump rope tied to her wrist. It ran under the covers and looped around a bedpost. She told her mother she was afraid of being kidnapped.

The week after the tulip garden, that feeling of transparency returned. Mat's adoption was held up in some bureaucratic tangle that Yulia described as "typical" but had Lucy in knots, Nana Mavis had developed pneumonia, and the United States was fighting a war that left her bewildered and saddened.

Then Cokie showed up on Lucy's doorstep.

"I'm thinking of leaving Paul," Cokie said, bursting into tears as she came in the door.

"You don't mean that," Lucy said. They sat down on the couch in front of the tiny fireplace. She patted Cokie awkwardly on the back.

"Do you have any tissues?" Cokie said. "I used up the ones in my purse on the way here."

Lucy ran to the kitchen and found a small box of Kleenex.

"This might not be enough," Cokie said, bleating again. "I'm sorry. I'm a complete wreck. I just don't know what to do anymore."

"Take a deep breath and start from the beginning," Lucy said. "We're going to talk this out until you can think clearly."

Cokie drew in a gallon of air and let it out in one long, flattened sigh. Her head bowed, she spoke softly to her knees.

"It's not that I don't love Paul, because I do. I'm really fairly sure that I do. But I totally resent the house—why did we ever think we needed five bathrooms?—and I hate the bills and the cooking and the cleaning and the fighting over the remote control. I must be a terrible mother. I can't stand to be around my kids anymore."

"You're not a terrible mother," she said, handing Cokie another tissue. "You've just reached a breaking point."

"That's just it. A breaking point. Paul comes home every day smelling of beer and fried calamari. I bet those waitresses come on to him, too."

"Cokie, even if they did . . ."

"I just feel like my life has turned into some kind of joke. I'm clipping coupons, pouring unused cereal back in the box, letting my hair go. I haven't had a facial in six months."

"Maybe I should try to reach Paul," Lucy said.

"No, no. Don't call him. I'll be fine. I'll be good. I'm leaving." Cokie stood up, but Lucy stopped her.

"You're not going anywhere. Stay here for a day or two until you can sort things out. You can have Mat's room."

"Who's Mat?"

She refused to answer, so Cokie went on.

"But who'll feed the kids and take them to practice and get their lunches ready?"

"Paul will have to rise to the challenge. Or maybe he'll call my moth—"

"He has to promise not to call her, or I'll get on a plane and never come back."

"Just sit down, and we'll figure this out."

Lucy went to the kitchen to make Earl Grey—because tea seemed like what you should drink if your marriage only appeared to be falling apart but really wouldn't—and arranged the cups on a tray with some Scottish shortbread someone gave her two Christmases ago. Cokie, in the meantime, had put her head down on a pillow and closed her eyes, so Lucy set down the tray and went upstairs to call Paul, who told her he'd be there in an hour.

Cokie woke up a half hour later. She was still agitated but less so, and she apologized for dumping her problems on Lucy's doorstep.

"I can't talk to my other friends," she said. "They're all in the same boat, but they won't admit it. But you, Lucy, you have a chance to save yourself. You really are the smart one. You don't have to answer to anyone but yourself."

"The grass is always greener, Cokie," she said.

"But I don't think you really understand what it's like," Cokie said, her voice rising again. "Yesterday, Luke called me a nag. 'You're such a nag, Mom.' And he's right. That's all I do, morning, noon, and night. 'Did you finish your science project?' 'Did you pick up your room?' 'Why can't you ever screw the cap back on the toothpaste?' That's who I am now. The nag."

While Cokie talked, Lucy straightened up the kitchen and tuned her out as best she could . . . *blah, blah, blah, air freshener floating in the bathtub . . . blah, blah, blah, drink cups everywhere, in every room, like they're reproducing when my back is turned . . . blah, blah, hamster in the linen closet . . . blah, blah, blah, ketchup all over my nice clean blah, blah, blah.*

By the time the doorbell rang, Cokie was just about talked out. Lucy answered the door, and Paul stood there, kneading one hand with the other. When Cokie continued to sit quietly on the couch, he came in and kneeled in front of her.

"Why don't you stay here for a few days?" he said, looking hopefully at Lucy. "I can handle the kids."

"I can't possibly do that. Molly has a dentist appointment, and Jack's book report is due soon, and he hasn't even started it, and . . ."

"I'll take care of it. All of it," he said. "The important thing is for you to feel better."

Lucy mumbled something about needing to get to a class and left Paul and Cokie to sort out their mess. She walked toward the center of campus, thinking about how you move along, day by day, collecting dirt on your shoes, until one day, you can't put those shoes on anymore. They're beat-up, out of style, and you can't, for the life of you, imagine why you bought them in the first place.

Harlan had brought up the topic once that most people are creatures of routine, but they resent it at the same time. What they don't realize, he had said from his hospital bed, is that routine doesn't look so unappealing when it's snatched away from you. Then you're all about routine, getting it back, craving it like a drug. You're desperate to get the oil changed, read the comics, talk about the weather. He knew all about that.

When Lucy reached the central quad, she noticed a large group of students lying on the street in front of the main administration building. From a distance, she saw Louis, who stood there with a heavy backpack slung over one shoulder, bunching up the sleeve of his T-shirt in a way that struck her as unbearably beautiful. She came up behind him and tapped him on the shoulder, unsure of whether he would want to see her.

"What's going on?" she said.

"Oh, hey," he said, slightly flustered. "I think they're protesting the war, but no one seems to know for sure. How have you been?"

"Oh, I've been busy with the adoption, and my great-grandmother's dying and my sister-in-law is having a breakdown and so on and so on. How's Ellen these days?"

Louis grabbed her hand, pulled her away from the crowd toward the quad, and threw his backpack down underneath a tree.

"Sit down, right here, and don't say anything," he said.

She sat down on her book bag, and Louis sat on the ground, arms around his knees. Behind him, increasing numbers of students were joining those on the street. From a distance, she could see the campus security guards converging. Louis ran his hands through his hair and looked at her with eyes the same blue as the robe painted on her favorite Saint Jude statue.

"Ellen is a nice person. I respect and admire her. But I'm not interested in her. The person I'm interested in keeps dodging me, and I'm close to giving up. If this person isn't interested back, I'd like to know before I make more of a fool of myself."

Lucy wanted to look away—her eyes were tearing from the sun—but she didn't.

"This person," she said, "is several years older than you."

"So what?" he said. "How is that relevant?"

"And this person is adopting a child, which will change her life, and not just a little. I mean it will change everything."

Louis sighed.

"Lucy, do you know what happens to me when I meet people outside our department? Eventually they want to know what I do, and I have to tell them I'm writing my thesis on Thomas Aquinas.

And then their eyes glaze over, and that's the end of it, unless I'm willing to pretend that my work isn't important to me, that it's just work. Seriously, Lucy, who else values what we know? This country is full of religious people who don't care about the history, the facts. They just want it to mean what they've already decided it means. But you get it. You get why it matters. And it goes beyond that . . ."

The campus police began pushing through the crowd surrounding the protesters. Lucy looked down at her watch, saw the time, and realized that her seminar should have started five minutes before.

"My class," she said. "I'm already late."

Louis stood up and helped her to her feet. She grabbed her book bag and stood looking at the soft hollow at the base of his neck where it disappeared into his T-shirt. She wanted to inhabit that space, to curl up and go to sleep there. Their hands brushed.

"I'll call you later," he said. "Can we maybe just have dinner tonight?"

"I'll try," she managed to say and turned to go. Was it fair? Was it unfair? Did it matter anymore? She sensed the water spilling down on either side of a concrete divide: her wall of choices, her watershed year. She walked toward the Arts and Humanities building and glanced back at Louis, who was standing there watching her go. This time he didn't look quite as disappointed. Behind him, on the street, the campus police apparently had decided to let the students have their way. The crowd had thinned, and the students lying there were starting to look uncomfortable. She wondered how long they would stay.

. . .

"SICK WITH WHAT? The flu? The flu could make you faint," Lucy says.

He swallows audibly, looks down, then puts a palm to his forehead, rubbing it hard. She doesn't want him to say anything now, because if the wrong words emerge, they will change him, and she loves him just as he is. She begins to hum softly, stalling, flicking the switch on the dead lamp as if it might come back to life, but now he looks desperate to get it out, to confront the fear, to name it.

"Cancer," he says. "I have cancer."

She looks past him, not understanding the words, although they release images: a bald head, a hospital bed, bags of fluid hanging from an IV pole. A dryness starts in her throat, along with a faint hum in her ears. She feels as though she isn't quite sitting on the chair anymore but hovering just above it. The backs of her thighs go numb with fear.

"How is that possible?" she says. "You're young, you're healthy."

"Young, yes," he says. "Healthy, apparently not. I've had some symptoms, but nothing I couldn't explain, and then I fainted when the towers fell. I even ignored that for a week or two, but then I found this lump, and I knew it wasn't good. I haven't been to the doctor in years, and I didn't have one here, so it took me a few days to find one. I had all kinds of tests. I'll spare you the details, but it's everywhere, including my bone marrow. They want me to start intensive chemo right away."

She says nothing. The international drama of the past few weeks has left her feeling pummeled, but this hits her in a new place, a place she can't protect.

Harlan begins to peel the label off his beer bottle.

"They're not that hopeful, actually. I don't have a good chance to survive this."

She shakes her head. People survive cancer all the time. Years from now, among scores of survivors on a cancer walk, they'll look back at this conversation and smile with hard-won wisdom. "Remember how you felt back then? Like the world was ending?"

He explains the terms: anaplastic large cell lymphoma, stage four. He describes the experience of entering the doctor's office, hearing the diagnosis, sitting on his hands to stop them from shaking. The doctor had been reluctant to give him the odds, but Harlan had pressed. Thirty percent.

"Thirty percent die?" she says.

"No, thirty percent survive," he says. "For five years or more."

She stays in her chair, unable to move, although she feels strongly that she should do or say something uplifting. Instead, a question forms.

"Was Sylvie with you in the doctor's office? Was she there?"

He looks uncomfortable, and she wishes she hadn't asked.

"I haven't told her yet," he says. "She's coming down this weekend. I don't know how she'll take it."

"She'll be devastated, Harlan," she says, "but she'll help you through this. So will I."

A manic laugh escapes him.

"I'm not prepared for this," he says, looking down. "It definitely throws a wrench into my retirement plans."

...

"THIS IS IT for Nana Mavis. I'm just . . . I can't . . . Call me."

Lucy returned home in the late afternoon to find a message from her mother on the answering machine. The strangled "call me" acknowledged all that was to come: the bedside vigil, the funeral arrangements, the luncheon, the burial, the distribution of Mavis's belongings, the final yard sale, the end of a century.

Bertie answered the phone when she called back.

"Dad, I just got the message. Where's Mom?"

"She's with Mavis. My heartburn started acting up, so she sent me home."

"I'll go keep her company."

"She'll be happy to see you, hon."

Lucy ran a brush through her hair and went to tell Cokie about Mavis.

"Should I come with you?" Cokie said, looking up from a fitness magazine she must have brought with her. Lucy was grateful for the offer, even if she could tell that Cokie was hoping she'd say no.

"I'll call if you need to be there," she said. "I left an extra set of house keys on the dining-room table."

Lucy drove to the nursing home, more worried about her mother than Mavis. Rosalee knew Mavis couldn't have asked for a longer life, wouldn't have wanted to live with tubes up her nose or needles in her arm. But that didn't make losing her any easier. Mavis had been one of Rosalee's closest allies, her connection to European tradition and an authentic marinara. Rosalee was on her knees, saying the rosary, when Lucy entered the softly lighted room. She stood up with effort, bracing her hands on a small chair near the bedside. Lucy hugged her, pressing her face into her mother's soft shoulder. Then Mavis shifted slightly, letting out a barely audible sigh, and they both turned toward the bed.

"You know her real name wasn't Mavis," Rosalee said. "It was Rosalia, which means 'melody.' I was named after her."

"But everyone called her Mavis."

"She took it as her American name. It was popular back then, and she wanted to fit in."

"She never seemed like a conformist to me."

"Oh, we all conform. But you're right. She developed independence with age. By the time she was eighty-five, nobody could tell her what to do."

"How much longer?"

"I'm not sure, but you can say good-bye."

Lucy kneeled, took Mavis's hand, and thought of Joseph, Jesus's father and the patron of happy death. Mavis's breath was almost inaudible, but Lucy could feel that her hand was still warm, pulsing with the same energy she had carried through more than a hundred years inside a frame that had been thin but muscular as a child, sturdy and straight as a yardstick during her childbearing years, thinner and slightly stooped after menopause, and now brittle, almost weightless, a husk of her former self. Her skin felt powdery.

Lucy rested her forehead on Mavis's hand, hoping Saint Joseph would lead her to a better place, a place where she could reunite with her dear Willard. Lucy could sense that Mavis was fading, life not draining away, as Harlan feared, as much as running its course, nearing the finish line. But then she heard footsteps and, through the open door, saw Paul run-walk down the hall as the three kids ran-walked behind him. Mavis's breath resumed at a shallow but steady pace.

"I'm here, Ma. She's not gone, is she?" Paul yelled before he was even to the door.

"Keep it down," Rosalee said in a brusque whisper as Paul filled the frame of the doorway. "What if she can hear you?"

Sean, Molly, and Jack found places on the bench seat along the windowsill. Sean took out earphones and wedged them into his ears.

"Put that away," Paul said. "Show some respect."

"Just let me hear the rest of this song," Sean said.

Paul walked over and yanked out the earphones.

"Take it easy, Dad."

"Watch your mouth, young man."

Rosalee came over and put her arm around Paul.

"I'll take them to the cafeteria," Rosalee said, shooing the kids toward the door. "You spend a little time with Nana."

Paul went to Mavis's side, made the sign of the cross, and stood with his head bowed. He couldn't stay still for more than a few seconds.

"So what's Cokie telling you," he said. "Why isn't she here?"

"Paul," Lucy said. "Let's worry about Nana Mavis, okay?"

"She's a hundred and one," Paul said, pinching the bridge of his nose. "I'm sorry. I just can't take this with Cokie. Is she leaving me or what? I don't know what to tell the kids."

"She's not leaving you," Lucy said, although she had no idea what Cokie planned to do. "I think she needs to see someone, a therapist, and talk things out."

"My medical insurance doesn't kick in until the first of May."

"Look, let's just give it a couple days and see what happens. Maybe she'll realize what she's missing and turn things around on her own."

"Well, she picked a fine time to lose it. We're starting a new menu and a dessert promotion next week, and I'm up to my butt in ad copy. Did I tell you they made me the manager?"

"No, when?"

"Last week. The old guy took a transfer to a T.G.I. Friday's in Silver Spring. You wouldn't believe it, but this place is a gold mine, Luce. I'll have it doubling its profits in under a year."

Paul sat down in a chair near the bed and seemed to see Nana Mavis for the first time.

"She looks so small," he said quietly. "So frail. When we were growing up, I thought she was a giant. A giant in orthopedic shoes. Remember those big black shoes she always wore? With that rubber tread on the bottom like a waffle iron?"

Lucy nodded. Rosalee brought the three children back into the room and asked each one to say a quick prayer for Mavis. Sean stood quietly at the foot of Mavis's bed, looking chastened.

"Where's Cokie?" Rosalee suddenly asked.

The kids looked at their father, who looked at Lucy, who made the sign of the cross again and turned back to Mavis.

"She's out with some friends," Paul said. "Away, actually, for a few days."

Rosalee looked puzzled, but the doctor came in before she could ask any questions. She asked everyone else to wait outside. Ten minutes later, she opened the door and waved them all into the room.

"It seems her heartbeat is slowing, but she's hanging on," Rosalee said. "It could be another day or two."

Paul bit his lip. "I'd better get the kids home," he said.

"I'll stay, Ma," Lucy said.

"No, you go, honey. I want to spend some time with her alone. I'll call you if anything changes."

Back at home, Cokie was asleep, and Lucy's answering machine gave her nothing but a blank stare. Louis had said he would call, but maybe he already regretted approaching her. That would be a first. Normally she had a first date before the phone call that didn't come.

...

THE NEXT MORNING, Lucy came downstairs to find that Cokie had fixed her breakfast: toast, an omelet, juice, coffee. Cooking tools she had never used—when had she acquired a whisk?—littered the limited counter space, contributing to the air of neediness that Cokie had brought with her. Once used, these tools would have to be cleaned, returned to their places, recognized for their efforts.

"I hope the eggs in your fridge weren't too old, because they looked a little gray," Cokie said in an oddly cheerful way.

"You didn't have to do this," Lucy said, trying to remember when she last bought eggs. "I thought you needed a break from taking care of other people."

"I guess I don't mind messing up someone else's kitchen. Now eat before the omelet gets cold."

They sat at one end of Harlan's dining-room table, which Cokie had set with place mats and the china Lucy had inherited from the same great-aunt who had left her $10,000. Cokie did all the talking.

"So I sat there thinking, *What's really going on here?* and then it hit me. It's not the money or the kids or Paul. It's my energy. I've been on a low-carb diet, and it's just sapping the strength right out of me. This is the first piece of bread I've had in eight weeks, and let me tell you, it's like water in the desert."

"Did anyone call for me last night?"

"Good thing you asked, because I forgot to write it down. The first time, he didn't leave his name. The second time, we had a nice conversation. He seemed to know who I was. I think his name was Louie."

"Louis."

"Is he one of your students? He sounded like a teenager."

Lucy buttered her toast and took a bite, ignoring her. It embarrassed her, somehow, to imagine what Cokie would think of Louis, who looked even younger than his thirty-two years.

"Oh, and there was another call," Cokie said. "From a woman with a strange accent. She said she'd call you back today."

"Yulia?"

"She didn't say."

"I better run," Lucy said. "Thanks for breakfast."

It was raining, so she threw on a long black raincoat and a beret to keep the water off her hair, which was sure to inflate to the size and texture of a toy poodle. Her hair had always functioned as a fairly reliable psychrometer, expanding and retracting along with the relative humidity. She left the house in a blur, with Cokie standing at the kitchen sink, scrubbing a frying pan. She made it to class just as her students were walking in and got them started on a discussion of the Iraq War, knowing it would tie them up for at least fifteen minutes; then she ran down the hall to her office to call Yulia.

"It's Lucy. What's going on? My sister-in-law said you called last night?"

"Good news," Yulia said. "We move ahead. All paperwork is okay. You go to Murmansk in June."

"That's great. How'd it happen so fast?" she said, her breath coming in small bursts. Emotions pummeled her—fear, excitement, love, confusion—in quick succession, leaving her with the stomach-clenching feeling that she had just jumped from a great height.

"I have connections," Yulia said. "And so you know, I use name of colleague on paperwork."

"What does that mean?"

"Well, technically, I should not be involved in adoption of relative. I have another call. We talk soon."

Lucy heard a dial tone before she could even say good-bye. She went back to her students, who were having a heated debate, even though they all seemed to be on the same side. She tried to follow the arguments but kept drifting away on a tide of what-ifs. What if Yulia couldn't pull this off? What if her brother-in-law interfered? What if Lucy went all the way to Russia only to find out that Mat wouldn't be coming home with her? Would it be like losing Harlan all over again? Could she shoulder another anvil, or would it crush her completely?

"Professor McVie?"

"Yes?"

"I think we're out of time."

She looked at her watch. "I guess you're right," she said. "Check your syllabus for the next reading assignment." The students shuffled out of the room as Angela walked in carrying a pair of frog-shaped rubber boots.

"Nice boots," Lucy said with a sigh.

"Vern actually tried to wear these to school today. They're two sizes too small, and I just about had to cut them off his feet. I thought they might fit Mat in a few years."

"Assuming the adoption goes through," she said, packing up her book bag.

"Why wouldn't it?"

"It's a little complicated."

"You've been walking around in a daze for weeks. Just give me the story. You know you want to."

Angela sat down at the large central table and folded her arms, waiting. Lucy paced, telling the story from the first meeting in Yulia's office to the last phone call.

"You can't go through with it," Angela said.

"You don't understand," she said. "I've seen him, seen him playing and heard him talking, and now I can't start over. I think about him all the time, in that children's home, eating gruel or whatever they feed them. He needs me, Angela. Not some couple in Boise with a tire swing in the front yard, but me. I can't explain it, but I have this connection to him. I can't just write him off and pick some other child. What if someone asked you to trade in Vern? Just say good-bye and start over with another kid."

Angela looked at the rubber frog boots. "This isn't a good day to ask me that question," she said, standing up to go. "I hear what you're saying, but I'm still worried." Then she paused. "Heard from Louis lately?"

Lucy flushed and began rooting around in her book bag for some Chapstick.

"Tell me," Angela said, sitting back down. "Tell me, tell me, tell me. Everything."

"You're embarrassing me," she said.

"Oh, get over it," Angela said, an edge to her voice. "Grow up and look at what's in front of you. That man won't wait around forever."

"I know," she said, her temples pulsing. "I'm going to call him right now."

"You do that," Angela said as she left the room. "Chocolate-covered peanuts don't keep you warm at night, and they're lousy at conversation. Take it from someone who knows."

...

ON THE DOOR of Lucy's office was a note from Dean Humphrey's secretary.

"The dean would like to see you in his office at ten thirty. Cheryl."

Lucy threw down her book bag, dialed Louis's number, and got his answering machine. She hated leaving messages—always wanting to edit and rerecord what she had blurted out—but she didn't want him to think she was avoiding him.

"Hi, it's Lucy. My sister-in-law didn't tell me about your call until this morning. She's a little wrapped up in her own problems right now . . . Oh, and my great-grandmother's dying. Did I tell you that? That's where I was last night, at the nursing home . . . and I'm just not sure—"

The machine cut her off.

She thought about calling back, but she couldn't be late for her meeting with the dean. Dean Humphrey had been known to lock his door and leave if his appointments didn't show up on time.

...

THE DEAN'S OFFICE usually smelled of drugstore aftershave and decaying books, but this time she detected something that reminded her of cows. The dean motioned toward his new leather couch, which squeaked as she sat down on it and every time she shifted, as if it were some kind of primitive lie detector.

"Lucy, Lucy, Lucy," he said, looking back down at some papers on his desk.

"Dean, Dean, Dean," she replied. Dean Humphrey's first name was, in fact, Dean, which she and Harlan had always found hilarious.

"I know you've had a rough time this year," he said, "but you haven't published in quite some time, and your tenure review will begin soon. You know how it is, Lucy. The committee will insist on it."

"You're right. I know that. I had every intention of writing an article this year and updating my thesis to submit to a publisher next year."

"Good plan."

"Yes, except that things have come up and . . ."

The dean waved his hand, making it obvious that he didn't need to know any more.

"I don't usually do this, but I'd like to see an article ready to submit for publication on my desk by the end of the semester, or I'm afraid you'll be looking elsewhere. If your student evaluations were outstanding, that might take the pressure off the publishing a bit, but they're just average. Frankly, you're still here because of your recent troubles and because we like you. You've got great potential, Dr. McVie, but it's not showing. Do you read me?"

"Very clearly. I won't disappoint you."

"I hope not, Lucy. You have an original mind. Now use it."

nine

Lucy soaked in the bathtub, hoping that a research topic would offer itself to her like a gift. She couldn't lose her job before Mat's adoption was final, and certainly not after. But she had a full course load this semester, and she couldn't be traipsing around in dank cathedral basements or whitewashed monasteries. She sank a little lower in the tub, letting the warm water close around her. She took her wet washcloth and laid it across her collarbone, trapping the warmth, protecting her heart.

Searching for her research topic would be like searching for a forgotten name, something she couldn't think about too directly, or it would elude her. She felt as though the sharp edges of her mind had been scraped dull with worry. But she knew something was there, some fragment she had come across in her reading on the granting of sainthood, something on which she could frame an argument.

Cokie rapped loudly on the door. "Hey, are you just about done? Because I'm meeting a friend for dinner, and I'd like to take a quick shower."

Lucy stuck her head under the water and didn't answer, but now she had soap in her eyes. Another knock startled her as she was rinsing shampoo from her hair.

"I'll be done in a minute, Cokie," she yelled.

"You have a visitor," Cokie said. "I told him you were taking a bath, but he wanted to talk to you anyway."

"Who is it?"

"Lucy, it's me."

She sat up at the sound of Louis's voice. Water sloshed over the side of the tub and onto the floor. Even with the closed door between them, she felt exposed, as if he could see her through the soapy water.

"Cokie, can you give us a minute?" Lucy said.

"Sure," Cokie said, sounding reluctant. "I'll go for a walk or something."

Lucy shivered in the tub, realizing she had left her robe in the bedroom. She could get out and wrap herself in a short towel, but she wasn't ready for Louis to see her all pink and splotchy, hair plastered to her head. Instead, she let some water out of the drain and added a slow stream of hot water.

"Hi, Louis," she yelled through the door. "What can I do for you?"

"I just want to talk to you. Preferably face-to-face."

"Just give me a couple minutes, okay?"

Lucy intended to get out of the tub, but something held her there. She didn't want to see Louis just yet, and the water was so warm, so comforting. "I had a meeting with Dean Humphrey today," she yelled through the door again. "He says I have to hand in an article by the end of the semester. He says my tenure's at risk."

"Seriously?"

"No lie. Did you get my message?"

"That's why I'm here. You said you weren't sure."

She slid back down into the warmer water, noticing the blue veins that ran across her skin. How could anyone be sure if starting a relationship was a good idea? This would affect Mat and her plans to be celibate and devoted. And though it shouldn't matter, there was Harlan, who was gone but not gone. Somehow, she felt disloyal to him.

"I just don't know . . . I'm confused."

"Tell me one thing. Aren't you even a little bit curious?"

She didn't answer right away. Some soap had worked its way into her eye again, and she was feeling around for the washcloth. Then she heard the phone ring and Cokie say hello.

"I'm leaving now," Louis said.

She sat up in the tub. "Stay," she whispered. He couldn't have heard her through the door, but when the knob turned slowly, she wondered if he had changed his mind.

It wasn't Louis who peered around the door, though. It was Cokie, holding her palm over the phone.

"It's Mavis, Lucy," she said quickly, looking down at the floor. "She's gone."

Despite the warmth of the water, she went cold. It shouldn't have shocked her that Nana Mavis was gone, but it did. "No," Lucy said.

"I'm so sorry, Lucy," Cokie said. A beat of silence passed between them before Cokie turned to leave, closing the door behind her.

Lucy got out of the tub, slid on the watery floor before catching her balance, and hurried into her bedroom, her conversation with Louis now blurred into her feelings of loss.

Cokie came in as Lucy pulled on a T-shirt and struggled into a pair of jeans. Her legs were still wet.

"Should I go with you to see Rosalee?" Cokie asked.

"That might be nice," Lucy said, pulling on some socks. Her face burned, but she had a chill from staying too long in the bathtub. "Oh, by the way, I told my mother you were going away for a few days with friends. But now, I guess, you're back."

"What?"

"I'll explain on the way. Let's go."

...

THE DYING SUN colored the underside of the stratus clouds a vivid pink as they drove to the nursing home. Lucy had a hard time keeping her eyes on the road and kept glancing up through the windshield, somehow seeing Nana Mavis in that final burst of beauty at the end of a very long day.

When they parked, Cokie refused to go inside.

"You don't understand," she said. "I hate these places. They reek of death. I thought I could handle it, but I can't."

"Fine. Stay here then, but I have no idea how long I'll be," Lucy said, disgusted. She wondered sometimes if Cokie's children would grow up before she did.

She ran through the lobby and pushed the elevator button impatiently, glancing at the front-desk nurse, who gave her a sympathetic nod. Lucy ascended one floor and made her way through the maze of wheelchairs parked in small conversational groups, mainly for looks. One woman, who might have been twenty years younger than Mavis, sat with a rolling IV line next to her wheelchair and stared at a blank white wall.

Was that what it came down to, she couldn't help but wonder, if you were lucky enough to live to old age? Finding paint more interesting than people? Maybe, by that time, you'd had enough of people. Or maybe you needed to empty the brain again, tabula rasa in reverse. At the end of the hall, nursing aides removed boxes from Mavis's room. Rosalee followed them out into the hallway, her head low, carrying an armful of clothes and shoes. Lucy hugged her over the clothes.

"Which do you think?" Rosalee asked. "The lavender slacks suit or the maroon linen dress? I'm thinking it's spring, so maybe the lavender."

"I like the lavender. She wore that to Molly's First Communion. It's probably too big now, though; they'll have to take it in."

"Help me with the jewelry," Rosalee said, heading back into Mavis's room and opening her jewelry box. "Find something for the funeral—maybe a necklace with some matching earrings—and tell me if there's anything you might want."

Lucy picked up a few interesting pins, enameled Christmas trees and one shaped like a gardening hat. She opened an inside pocket of the jewelry box and ran her hand inside, feeling only paper—a letter, in fact, with her name on the front in crooked handwriting. Rosalee was in the closet, foraging for the lavender-dyed shoes, so she folded the letter and slid it into her back pocket.

About ten minutes later, they had assembled the outfit Mavis would wear for the rest of time—forever in lavender because she had died in the spring. Then Paul arrived.

"Grab a box, sweetie," Rosalee said. "We've got to clear out of here by tomorrow. There's a diabetic in assisted living who's been waiting for the corner room for two years. Where are the kids?"

"They're home," he said, packing up Mavis's pile of romance novels and her back issues of *Reader's Digest* in large print. From under the bed, he pulled out a stack of old racing forms.

"Are they okay on their own? At night?"

"Ma, Sean's fourteen. I put on a movie. They'll be fine."

A few minutes later, Cokie arrived in the doorway.

"I thought you were away," Rosalee said, looking from Cokie to Paul.

"Where are the kids, Paul?" Cokie said. "Did you get Maureen to watch them?"

"Maureen was out. But they're fine. They're watching TV."

"You left them alone?"

"Cokie, just help pack," Paul said, throwing Mavis's medications into a plastic bag.

Cokie began to complain of a headache, but Paul handed her a suitcase and told her to fill it. They all worked in silence for the next half hour, sorting and folding, packing what little was left of Mavis's life. Lucy wondered what had happened to all the merchandise any one person buys in the course of a lifetime. The cars, the furniture, the pots and pans. The books, the coats and sweaters, the rugs and the bed linens, the lighting fixtures and the kitchen appliances. The humidifiers, the drapes, the napkin rings, and the dried flower wreaths. How had a century of acquisition been reduced to one room?

Bertie came in a few minutes later with a handful of plastic bags for the clothes that would be donated to the Salvation Army. When they were done cleaning the room, they all stood, arms crossed, at the entrance to the nursing home. The sky was dark and all was still except for the hum of a large central air-conditioning unit nearby. The lights of the parking lot cast dim halos on the cars, each in its designated slot. In this place, Lucy realized, death was all part of an orderly process. It hardly caused a ripple.

"So when's the funeral?" Cokie asked, breaking the silence.

"Tuesday morning," Rosalee said. "At ten, Saint Joseph. Lunch at my house after the cemetery."

"She'll be cooking all weekend," Bertie said, putting an arm around Rosalee, whose shoulders suddenly seemed narrower.

"I'll get the anise cookies," Lucy said. "Those were her favorite."

"Call me, Ma," Paul said. "Tell me what else you need."

He took Cokie's hand and led her to his car, although she seemed to hesitate for a moment. Maybe they were pretending for Rosalee and Bertie's sake, Lucy thought. Or maybe Paul would drop Cokie off at her house later. But Lucy hoped they would pull themselves together, at least until after the funeral.

When the others drove off, she sat in her car, turned on the overhead light, and opened the letter she had found in the jewelry box. It was dated July 14, 1994.

Dear Lucy,

I've been thinking about you and the rest of the family. I will list my thoughts:

1) You're a special girl. Very very smart with the books.

2) You got a lovely face. Do something with that hair.

3) You're too sensitive. Get over it.

4) Tell your mother you can take care of yourself.

5) What's all this with the saints?

6) Don't hide in the library. Boys like a girl with some sun on her face.

Love and good fortune,

Nana Mavis

...

THE NEXT MORNING, Lucy took out Mavis's letter and read it again as she ate half a bagel at the dining-room table. Why hadn't she sent the letter? Maybe she had decided it was too blunt . . . but then she had saved it. Had she hoped Lucy would find it, or had she just forgotten about it? Either way, Lucy couldn't help but notice that she had two people communicating with her after death. How many people could say that?

Whatever Mavis's intentions, the letter somehow made her industrious, gave her energy. She called Yulia and arranged to meet her for lunch near her office. She also left a message for Louis, telling him she would call after the funeral. Then she called her mother, who was surprisingly upbeat.

"Wait till you see the flowers from Uncle Stan and Aunt Velma. Gorgeous. And Cokie just stopped by with a huge box of anise cookies. The good ones from Pescatellos," Rosalee said.

"But I told you I'd get those when we were all standing in front of the nursing home. Cokie heard me too," Lucy said.

"You did, didn't you? Well, maybe she didn't know what to do. And she's been having a tough time lately."

"And I haven't?"

"You've been telling me everything is fine," Rosalee said. "Is everything not fine?"

"No, I meant . . . forget it. I'll pick up some napoleons, and I'll see you at the funeral."

Lucy met Yulia for lunch at a small Indian restaurant in Federal Hill, a neighborhood that had the kind of carefully renovated brick row houses and charming narrow streets that made Lucy want to own real estate. They ordered after Yulia quizzed the waiter on the lactose content of every entrée on the menu. Then she spread out some papers in front of Lucy.

"Most adoptions need two visits: first to meet child and attend court hearing; second, after approvals, to take child home. In

Murmansk, only one trip with accredited agency. Two-hour flight from Moscow. Two good hotels."

"It all seems to be happening so fast," Lucy said, breaking off a piece of naan. "You wait and wait and wait, and then wham! Is that how it usually works?"

"Well, I grease tires a bit. I also need some of your fee for next phase."

"For what?"

"So paperwork goes to top of pile."

"How much?"

"Two thousand."

"Are you sure this is necessary? I don't mind waiting a few extra days in Murmansk. I can always do some research."

"Very necessary," Yulia said, starting on a samosa. "Documents get lost. Very important to pay people."

Lucy tried to block out sudden images of dark alleyways and back doors and envelopes of cash. It wasn't in her nature to distrust people; she always assumed they had basically good motives, even if she couldn't always see them. But the whole adoption process was steeped in the mist of the unknown, and as hard as she tried, she couldn't see to the bottom of the unfathomably steep hill Yulia was barreling down, pulling her along behind. She pressed her napkin to her forehead, which was damp from a combination of curry and nerves.

"I have something to show you," Yulia said. "This came in mail."

The construction-paper card had a roughly drawn blue heart on the cover. Inside were squiggles that might have been water and a sun with green rays poking out. An adult hand had written a name in Russian letters in the lower right-hand corner. Yulia handed the card to Lucy.

"Mat made this himself?" Lucy said. "Can I keep it?"

"Of course," Yulia said.

She realized Mat hadn't made the card specifically for her, but it made him real in a way the picture, and even the video, did not. She could imagine him sitting at a low table, coloring the heart, trying to stay inside the outline, and then the sun, choosing the crayons that weren't already broken or small nubs. And then a caregiver—some adult who was paid to keep the children occupied—would have taken it from him. Written his name. Cleaned up the crayons. No more time for coloring. Lucy would let him color for hours if he wanted to.

Yulia spoke, bringing Lucy back to the present as their meals arrived.

"So, you have a boyfriend, Lucy?"

"The social worker already went over my love life during the home study."

"I am asking as friend. And this, of course, will affect Mat as well."

"Well, you have nothing to worry about. Someone very special to me died last year, though he was never my boyfriend. There might be someone new, but it's very early, so I can't really tell you where that's going."

Yulia stopped eating her *biryani*, a sign that she was exceptionally interested in the topic. She rested her broad chin on a closed fist.

"So this man you loved who was never boyfriend? He was married?"

"No, it wasn't that. We just didn't talk about how we felt. He was engaged when we met, and then he was diagnosed with cancer. I just didn't think it was fair to tell him how I felt."

"So nothing?"

"Nothing . . . Except for one night. But I'm not even sure that happened."

Yulia put another fist under her chin, as if it needed two for proper support.

"Tell me."

"It was just a kiss, or at least I think it was."

"And you never talk about this?"

"Never. Maybe I dreamed it."

"But this is not something you forget."

Yulia was right, of course. A kiss, you don't forget. Her confession had taken a third seat now, in front of the plate of naan. It was a source of embarrassing intimacy, binding them together like a pilfered diary.

"And now?" Yulia said. "Other man?"

"He's a little younger than I am," she said. "I can't see him taking on the father role just yet, so I don't see how it'll work out."

The smell of curry and the weight of the Indian food in her stomach made Lucy feel sluggish. She pulled out a twenty, said good-bye, and left Yulia to finish the naan. On the way out, she regretted running at the mouth about her love life. But as she walked down the sidewalk, slowing to let a woman with a stroller go by, she realized it had given her some clarity. She had loved Harlan in a way that never quite fit with the reality of their lives. But with Louis, the potential was there for substance, for more than just stories she told herself inside her head.

...

HARLAN IS RELATING someone else's experience, Lucy's sure of it. The doctor is confused. They'll find out that the test results were swapped, meant for an elderly man from Tacoma Park who had emphysema anyway. They'll call him tomorrow with the news, and his wife will cry.

On the off chance that Harlan's diagnosis is accurate, she wants to mention a few saints he might consider studying for inspiration. His beliefs, she knows, are agnostic at best; he's like most of her academic friends, too research bound to allow for the mystery of grace. But she tries anyway.

"Do you know why I'm so fascinated by the saints?" she asks.

"I can't say that I do."

"Because they take me out of my small frame of reference and force me to think about the scope of human history, not just whether my library books are overdue. If you want to know what the human spirit is capable of doing, read about the life of a saint."

"I'll take your word for it," Harlan says, which means he must be tired. He rarely passes up the chance for a good didactic argument.

"Let's go outside," she says. "I need some air."

She pulls open the cheap sliding-glass door, and he follows her onto the small balcony, which she has furnished with an outlet-store lounge chair and a folding metal chair. She's only on the third floor, so they don't get much of a view, just a long line of anemic pine trees. No moon at all.

She gives him the lounge chair, which has cushions on it. She balances on the folding chair, bringing her knees up to her chin. She closes her eyes and feels as if she is in a play, waiting for the curtain to open, memorized lines at the ready. The dialogue is new, strange in her mouth, and has an air of unreality about it. But it's Harlan's turn to speak. She's waiting for her cue.

The night air is still, as if it's holding its breath, waiting for Harlan's next words.

"When I was a kid in Tennessee," Harlan says, "I used to imagine that someday I would have my own house, and it would have a special room just for playing cards, because my parents played cards all the time. I would invite my friends over, and we would play cards all night, and they would never refuse, because I had this special room. Just for cards."

"Just for cards," she says.

"It had a bar in it, too."

"Of course."

"And a soda machine."

She nods, and they both look up, searching for the moon instinctively, though it's nowhere to be seen.

"People don't play cards anymore," he says. "Not like they used to."

"I'm a little cold," she says. "I'll be right back."

She slides the door open and finds a fleece pullover and a chenille blanket and brings them outside, sliding the door back into place. She hears an unexpected click and tries the door again.

"It's locked," she says. "Help me try it."

Harlan gives the door a good tug, but it holds. He tries again but fails. They look around below the balcony, but there are no signs of movement. It's dark, silent, and cool, a good night for sleeping.

...

LUCY ARRIVED a bit early for Mavis's funeral Mass, knelt down in an empty pew, and prayed that her great-grandmother would find a new life beyond this one, one where she would be healthy and upright again. No more orthopedic shoes. No more arthritis. Rosalee and Bertie arrived, followed by Paul and Cokie and the kids. The rest of the mourners—mostly Rosalee and Bertie's friends and neighbors—sat behind them.

The priest spoke movingly—dust to dust—and told a few anecdotes about Mavis's life: about her arrival in New York City with nothing but a pocketful of seeds from her family's vegetable garden in Sicily; about her years as a seamstress in Brooklyn, making ladies' undergarments; about her successful efforts in the 1960s—something Lucy had never heard before—to prevent the government from taking her home in New Jersey by eminent domain for a highway.

Lucy left the funeral with an entirely new view of Nana Mavis, who had been so old throughout Lucy's life that Lucy never imagined her having a youth.

At the cemetery, the soft April sunshine warmed her back as she placed a white rose on Mavis's casket and saw another white stone Mary a few graves away. Harlan's funeral came back to her with a vividness that wasn't there on the day itself, and she was grateful for the friends who had spoken about him with so much wit and warmth, since she had been barely able to speak at all without sobbing. She wondered if the Mary near his grave was still off-kilter, the way she had left it.

On the way back to her parents' house, Lucy stopped at the bakery to pick up the napoleons. By the time she arrived at the house, she had to walk an entire block past all the parked cars. She balanced the white cardboard bakery box on one knee while trying to open the front door. To her right, she could see that the garden had been stripped of its large rhododendron, rototilled, and then replanted with bushes that weren't doing well. They looked as if they hadn't been watered in days, in the way that the exterior of a house sometimes must defer to what's happening inside. And inside was a carnival.

Mavis, she found out, was something of a legend in the nursing home. She had been there only nine years—a short tenure compared to some—but had managed to charm and insult everyone connected with the place. And funerals, apparently, were big occasions for the residents. Rosalee's house was teeming with the superannuated, lurching awkwardly across the carpeting in wheelchairs or being shuttled to the bathroom by nursing aides. The home must have bused them in. Add to that all of Rosalee and Bertie's friends, and the friends of Rosalee's deceased parents, and the result was an undulating sea of teased hair, in many bluish tones of gray, through which bobbed the occasional bald head.

Lucy suddenly felt young, flexible, brimming with health. It seemed as if she were back in school, walking among the relatives as she collected checks for her various passages of life: First Communion, confirmation, graduations, birthdays. She gently touched sloping shoulders—*may Saint Anthony of Padua protect you*—and inched toward the dining-room table, where three cakes on the sideboard spelled out 1-0-1, as if this were Mavis's birthday.

Lucy stood in the dining room, remembering birthdays capped by Rosalee's exceptionally dense homemade cake, as her childhood selves filed in. In their own way, each had a relationship with Mavis and had come to say good-bye. There was the four-year-old Lucy asking Mavis to braid her hair, make it red, and give her freckles; the seven-year-old Lucy crying on Mavis's knee because she couldn't do a cartwheel; the nine-year-old Lucy singing "Delta Dawn" into a fork for Mavis, who told her she was good enough for the radio; and the twelve-year-old Lucy, standing with her arms crossed in front of her emerging breasts, not wanting to grow up and make Mavis feel even older. They all offered condolences to the thirty-eight-year-old Lucy, who wished she could give each of them a napoleon. Instead, she poured herself a glass of red wine and downed it on an empty stomach, because the food all around her looked too perfect to be eaten.

The dining-room table was invisible under Rosalee's weekend efforts: antipasti glistening with red roasted peppers, artichoke hearts, and olives; vast bowls of couscous; piles of oranges and lemons; trays of cannoli; and an enormous tuna, with the head on, on a platter at the center of the table. On the sideboard, to the left of the cakes, sat Lucy's plaster-of-paris model of Sicily's Mount Etna. Rosalee or Bertie must have dug it out of the basement. Did she make that in third grade or fourth? Back then, she wouldn't have known anything about Sicily's Saint Agatha, wouldn't have suspected that a human being was capable of surviving imprisonment and torture before dying on a bed of hot coals. But Mavis would have known about her, maybe even have seen Saint Agatha's veil carried in processions to prevent the volcano from erupting. Lucy wished she had asked her more about Sicily when she was alive.

Inside the kitchen, clutches of women in shapeless black dresses stood arranging food on platters and sipping ginger ale, smiling with their too-perfect dentures. Rosalee towered above them with her dark puff of hair as Lucy reassessed her place in the world, as people do at funerals, and realized that the kaleidoscope had twisted—she was no longer a kid, and her mother fit in with the older crowd. Rosalee hesitated as she bit into a piece of celery, Lucy noticed with sadness, closing her lips around it as if her teeth weren't strong enough to be trusted.

But there was someone else in the room who stood above the rest, someone bending an ear toward a cheese-plate organizer with a riot of bobby pins protruding from a wispy bun on the back of her head; someone whose youth pulsed even more than Lucy's, but who nevertheless looked comfortable amid the deafness and the humped backs and the inelastic skin all around him, drooping from necks and arms and earlobes. It was someone Lucy hadn't anticipated seeing at her great-grandmother's funeral.

ten

The shrine of the unintended consequence. This was where Lucy led Louis after discovering him in the kitchen. Her old bedroom was now a gallery for Rosalee's inadvertent collection of vintage lunchboxes. It was the only room in the house with a lock on the door, besides the bathroom, which was being monopolized by dozens of people with bladder-control problems. The room had no furniture. Bertie had purchased white plastic cubes, two feet high, which were stacked in various configurations to display the lunchboxes. A low-pile Berber covered the floor, and track lights cast a fluorescent glow on the white cubes. The room had a reverential feel to it, as if the lunchboxes were just placeholders for the real art that was to come.

Lucy closed and locked the door, shutting out the funeral-party din. She had no plan, just a need to be alone with Louis. He looked around the room.

"Somebody likes lunchboxes," he said, bending to examine a Roy Rogers in mint condition.

"You'd think so, wouldn't you?" she said. "My mom got one for a present about five years ago, and she faked her enthusiasm so effectively that everyone gives her lunchboxes now. Then she got caught up in the buying and the selling and realized she was good at it. She has at least one for every year between 1950 and 1985. You wouldn't believe what some of them are worth. That one you're looking at, the 1953 Roy Rogers, is worth almost a thousand."

"Dollars?" he said, moving back to where Lucy stood near the door. He put his arms around her and bent his head down until his forehead gently touched hers.

"I can't believe you're h—" she said, swallowing the "here" as Louis covered her mouth with his, pressing her up against the door. They slid down to the floor. The sounds of the funeral faded as they faced each other, kneeling.

"So you do like me," Louis said, brushing her hair away from her face.

"I do," she said.

"And you won't send me away? Even if your life is complicated?"

"I won't send you away," she said.

Louis put a hand on either side of her head and kissed her for a long time. She had almost forgotten what it was like to be kissed that way. It seemed to eradicate all the doubt, all the second-guessing. It seemed like the only logical thing that had happened to her in months and months, and now that the fences were down, she wondered why she had thrown them up in the first place.

Then Louis, shifting on his knees, accidentally kicked one of the plastic cubes, knocking several lunchboxes to the floor. The din of the party ceased. Someone came to the door and rapped on it loudly.

"Who's in there? What's going on?" Rosalee said.

"It's me, Ma. Everything's fine," Lucy said. "I just tripped."

She and Louis sat with their backs against the door, waiting for the talking to resume. They both looked straight ahead until Louis threaded his fingers through hers, which she took to mean they were together in this, equally awkward and equally elated. A few minutes later, she stood up, unlocked the door, and left, leaving Louis to sneak out after her. Rosalee had moved away but must have had her eye on the door. She walked over, took Lucy's arm, and whisked her into the master bedroom.

"Who is that young man?" Rosalee asked. "He said he was a friend of yours, but I've never heard you mention him."

Lucy could feel the redness creeping down her neck. "He *is* a friend. I work with him, sort of. But I'm sorry about the lunchboxes. We were just—" she started, but Rosalee stopped her.

"Never mind all that." She turned toward the mirror on her bureau and straightened her necklace. "I need to check on my lunchboxes."

"I understand." Lucy sat down on the bed, sinking into the too-soft mattress, and pulled her hair around her neck. Rosalee hadn't left yet. As she rearranged her bangs in the mirror, Lucy saw her expression soften.

"Oh, doll," Rosalee said, coming back to sit down on the bed. She could tell that her mother was in some way grateful to know that Lucy was capable of sneaking a man into a room and locking the door. It meant she was putting her grief behind her.

"Lunchboxes can be replaced. They can," her mother said. "I want you to be happy. Look at me, Lucy. That's all that really matters. So why didn't you tell me about him before?"

"There wasn't much to tell," she said. "Honestly."

Rosalee gave her a look of disbelief. She stood up to go, then turned back.

"He's not one of your students, is he?"

"He's thirty-two, Ma," Lucy said, flipping over to bury her face in the mattress.

"I'm sorry; he looks like a boy. Now go out there and talk to some of these deaf people. I'm already hoarse from shouting."

Lucy sat on the bed for another five minutes until the redness receded. Then she straightened her own hair in the mirror and left the bedroom. As she walked down the hallway, she could see Louis putting on his coat near the door. He left with the muted wave of a co-conspirator, and now she only had to get through the rest of the afternoon, which she did by deciding that Mavis would have forgiven her. *You're too sensitive. Get over it.* It had been right there in her letter, a reminder that we all humiliate ourselves from time to time. But then we move on.

...

FOR THE NEXT WEEK, Lucy and Louis spent every day together, blocking out the world. They ate meals together, watched old movies on television, and sat on Lucy's couch reading the newspaper, their legs intertwined. Then the pressure of her precarious job status intervened.

With only a month before the end of the semester, she had to come up with a topic, research it, and write an article, a task on the order of reading the complete works of Shakespeare in a week. Louis offered to let her use his data on the study of gender differences in religious devotion, but she refused.

"I can't take your research," she told him.

"But I haven't written it yet. It's just the raw numbers," he said.

"It's not even my specialty."

"But if it means your job, don't you think that takes precedence?"

"I just can't do it that way."

Finally she withdrew to the library to gather data on Pope John Paul II's extraordinary rate of beatification. This papacy, she decided after reviewing the numbers, was Saints-R-Us. You still needed to be a martyr for the faith, or live a life of sacrifice, plus have your miracles verified after death. But John Paul II had lowered the requirement from four verified miracles to two and had dropped the Devil's Advocate appointed by the Vatican to argue against sainthood. She would compare it to an earlier era of church history.

After three days of seclusion in the library, she called Louis and asked him to come over for dinner. She was chopping carrots for a salad when he arrived.

The rhythmic slicing, the thunk of the knife on the cutting board, kept her mind from wandering. Louis opened a can of seltzer and sat on the stool, watching her chop.

"What can I do?" he said, and she glanced up from her carrots to see a look on his face that was unmistakable: the gratefulness of belonging. The knife dropped from her hand, then she walked over and placed her forearms on Louis's shoulders.

He tucked a few strands of hair behind her ear.

"Poor thing," he said. "Those saints must be torture."

"Some people say anyone who makes it to heaven becomes a saint," she said.

"Sometimes I get the feeling you believe it yourself."

"Not all of it, of course. Some saints aren't even based on real people."

"So you don't believe in them. You don't pray to them."

"Technically, you're supposed to pray *with* a saint, although I don't think of it that way. I guess I just leave open the possibility of intercession because there's so much genius in the idea that these humans somehow created pathways to God based on the way they lived their lives. If you'd done the research I have, you might be swayed. Some of the miracles are impossible to explain."

"Give me an example."

"Well, there are a few studies that show greater improvement among sick people who were prayed for. No, I'm serious. You can look it up. And if you want a specific case, a woman was cured of leukemia in 1978 after asking for the intercession of Saint Marie Marguerite d'Youville. Doctors testified at the Vatican. They called it miraculous."

"But how does that prove anything? It just means they don't understand it yet. There could be a hundred scientific explanations."

"How were you raised?" she asked.

"Roman Catholic. But I never made my confirmation."

"Why not?"

"Because I thought it was all bunk by the time I was twelve."

The real miracle, she wanted to tell him, was the life of a saint. Marie Marguerite d'Youville had persevered with everything against her: a husband who died early, extreme poverty, the loss of four of her six children in infancy. But she who had nothing found it necessary— *necessary*—to be charitable. Every setback only renewed her need to serve the poor. How could anyone hear about her and the Grey Nuns of Montreal and fail to be moved? And what about the pervasiveness of the saints in modern society?

Most Christian churches and schools were named after saints; they were immortalized in books, movies, songs. Beyond that, small groups devoted themselves to particular saints, supporting shrines and societies that offered hope to people who couldn't live without it. And those people came week after week, even day after day, to petition, say novenas, move rosary beads swiftly through practiced fingers. They didn't make the news, even if their prayers were answered, but that never stopped them. Lucy could accept the argument that it was all a human construct, but it couldn't be called bunk.

None of this came out of her mouth. She wasn't up for the inevitable debate that would follow.

"Will you miss me when I go to Russia?"

He let out a long breath.

"I've been thinking about that," he said, talking to the ceiling. "I was wondering if I could come with you."

"Come with me?" she said. "Why?"

"I don't know. I've never been to Russia."

"It's not exactly a vacation."

"I don't like the idea of you being there all by yourself, with all those Russian men wearing black."

"I'll be fine," she said, touching his cheek. "Not that I wouldn't like the company."

"I understand," he said.

"You do?"

"I do," he said. "But tell me if you change your mind."

She nodded but felt somehow that he didn't understand. He hadn't thought any of this through—any more than she had—hadn't truly acknowledged that she would have a child soon, who might need her more than anyone could anticipate. Louis wanted to help her; she felt his sincerity. But Mat was still just a mysterious boy in a photo who liked to draw hearts. She wouldn't know what to expect until she brought him home.

...

HARLAN'S MAY E-MAIL ARRIVED in the midst of an avalanche: Lucy's frantic work on the research paper, her planning for the trip to Russia, and her deadline to grade a stack of philosophy term papers, one of which was titled "Kant Get(s) No Satisfaction."

Dear Lucy,

The school year must be winding down for you by now. I had a chat with Dean Dean the other day. He called, I think, to see if I was still alive, and the discussion turned to you. He told me you were one of his "rising stars." I probably wasn't supposed to pass it along, but what's he gonna do about it?

I had a good cry this morning, just bawled like a baby. I don't do that often, but it seems to help release the stress, and let me tell you, dying this way is stressful. The doctors hold out hope, almost literally, dangling it there in front of you on a pole so that you'll dive for it, strive for it, and yet you can't do anything but curse the cells in your body that are responsible for making you sick and hope they'll respond to the treatment. Even if they do, you spend every day knowing your cells could turn on you again. As stupid as it sounds after all this time, you just want to know: Why does it happen? What evolutionary purpose does cancer serve? And more important, the inescapable cliché: why me?

The second time I almost died wasn't quite as bad as the first. I remember feeling feverish, and then a little nauseous when you were driving me to the hospital. After that, I was completely out of it until the next day, and when I came to, a bunch of doctors were standing around my bed looking at you, asking if I wanted a priest for last rites. Poor thing, you looked completely horrified, not only by the thought of me dying but by the idea that you would have to make that decision— you, who were neither my wife nor my girlfriend nor my sister nor my mother, though you were all of those, Lucy, the closest person to me on this earth.

You shook your head, of course, but I could see that it was tearing you apart. You wanted someone to send me off to the hereafter with a freshly scrubbed soul. Then the infection subsided, and I surprised them all again by not dying. But not dying, I feel compelled to point out, is not quite the same as living.

Have you visited my grave? I'm sure that you have. It's not like I'll have any perception of you being there, but it seems to comfort me that there's a place that represents me. And then there's Mary, looking over my little hillside, and that should help you, too. You know, I always found the saint thing a little off-putting, but sometimes, I can see it more from your point of view. Why not allow for the possibility?

I also hope you're enjoying my grandmother's table. It's an inspiration to me, how she got her life back together after the banjo accident. It's just one more example of what I mean when I tell you to ignore all the aggravation that life throws your way, because none of it means anything in the end.

Love, as always,

Harlan

"Unbelievable," Lucy said aloud, though no one was around to hear.

That day in the hospital had been a tornado of phone calls and running doctors and crying and praying. She had been so drained by the time they asked her about last rites, some very small part of her was relieved that Harlan wouldn't have to fight anymore. He had mistaken her exhaustion for anguish.

She had been the closest person on this earth to him. The closest one. After that crisis, he had given her medical power of attorney, but she thought it was because his mother never seemed to arrive in time. Really, though, it was because she knew him—and what he would want—better than his own mother. Better than anyone.

She closed the e-mail and went to the dining room to stretch her arms around Harlan's grandmother's table and to wonder about the banjo accident, which must have been worse than it originally seemed. Hadn't he mentioned a broken nose or something? Now it sounded more ominous. She wondered if Harlan would ever spill the whole story and was struck by the strange nature of the very thought. When someone died, weren't you supposed to stop anticipating new information? Didn't you take the old information and sum it up, complete the picture, an estimate of that life?

But here she was, trying to guess what else Harlan would spring on her some tenth of the month in the future. Of course, others before Harlan certainly wrote letters—like Nana Mavis—or wrote in diaries that couldn't be released until years after their death. It suddenly occurred to her that she might not be Harlan's only e-mail recipient. Maybe he did this for his mother, or another friend? Somehow, though, she knew she was the only one. She also began to recognize his effort, the gathering of energy in those final weeks, because she was gathering energy herself from pockets deep inside that she never knew existed.

She was due to meet Yulia for a final checking of paperwork and to apply for her visa. Later she would have to begin packing for her trip, which involved a long shopping list, clothes for her and for Mat, and gifts for the orphanage. Her classes were over for the semester, but she still had to complete her article for the dean. Every time she sat down to work on it, something else came up: preschools were already filling up for the fall, so she had to visit three and complete the applications; she called half a dozen pediatricians before she found one who had experience with Russian adoptees; and she had to gather over-the-counter medications Mat might need when she went to Russia.

She thought about calling the dean to explain why she might not be able to finish the article in time, but she was afraid he might try to talk her out of taking on such a huge responsibility. The thought of being faced with reason terrified her, because the whole house of cards might come down under its weight.

In that spirit of instability, she walked out the door to meet Yulia and almost ran into Cokie, who had her hand raised, midknock.

"Thank God, you're here," she said, running a hand through her hair, which was now evenly blond and not far from platinum. "I need your help."

"What's wrong?" Lucy said, stepping back inside. As Cokie walked past, she smelled something that reminded her of the indoor pool at the YWCA. "Are the kids okay? Paul? Are you leaving him again?"

"No, no, everything's fine." Cokie took a deep breath. "I have to ask you something."

"Ask away," she said, glancing at her watch.

"Actually, what I need is a second opinion."

"I'm listening," Lucy said, though she was adjusting the strap on her sandal.

"Well, I had this idea, see, about writing this book. I think it's huge. Just huge. Let me just get my notes."

Cokie rummaged around in her large black purse and pulled out a school-sized spiral notebook.

"It's a budget guide to beauty after forty. Look at my hair, Lucy. I found it on the Internet. It's a mixture of lemon juice, honey, a smidge of bleach, and a couple other things. It's like magic. And then I found this place in Canada that sells Retin-A wholesale. And there's this exercise that tightens up the flab under your arms. Is it fantastic or what?"

"What does Paul say?"

Cokie hesitated and glanced again at her notebook.

"Paul isn't what I would call 'on board.'"

"So I'm supposed to talk him into it?"

"Just share your sincere enthusiasm. Don't you see how big this will be? Oh, you're not even forty yet, but just wait."

"You're not forty either," Lucy said.

"Thirty-eight and a half. Close enough. And frankly, after thirty-five, it's all downhill anyway. But you'll just have to trust me that this book will make money. I'm one hundred percent sure of it."

"You don't need Paul's permission," Lucy said, picking up her book bag. "Do you?"

"No, but I need to quit my job so I can write the book, don't I?"

"Do what you have to do," she said, looking at her watch again. "I'm sorry, Cokie, but I'm very late."

"So go already," Cokie said, stuffing her notebook back in her purse. "I'm going to thank you in the acknowledgments."

Lucy walked to her car, glancing back at Cokie, who was looking at her reflection in one of Lucy's windows and rubbing lipstick off her teeth. Cokie's obsession with her looks had a veneer of desperation so obvious that Lucy wondered how Cokie couldn't see it. But then again, she thought, no one sees themselves as others do. The tics, the fears, the neediness, the vanity—all of it could be laid bare in one conversation.

But years and years of self-assessment in mirrors and photographs gave you only the barest clue of how others perceived you: of how your mouth twisted slightly just before you smiled, of how you had a tendency to clear your throat before speaking, of how your hair flew out in back when you rode a bike, of how you peppered your speech with "you knows" when you were nervous, and how it seemed as if you were trying too hard when you wore lip gloss.

As she headed toward Yulia's office, she stuck a hand in her own mass of dark hair and wondered what she would do when it started turning gray, which could be any day now. She didn't want to get old, any more than the next person, but she hated the idea of coating her head with chemicals, the deception of it. On the other hand, everyone colored their hair these days, and they talked about it, too. So if you flaunted coloring your hair, could you stake a claim to honesty? It was all too complicated.

As Lucy walked down the corridor to Yulia's office, she saw a couple leaving, the woman holding a manila folder—the paperwork of lives in radical transition. Yulia was at her desk when Lucy came in.

"Please sit, Lucy. We have much to go over. Not too many clothes, just one nice suit—black one—for court appearances. Make sure you have suitcase with wheels. In carry-on bag, you need to bring all documents, including home study, birth certificate, passport, and visa. Bring three thousand, maybe four, in cash. I will give you time line, phone numbers for facilitator and *detsky dom*."

"Slow down," Lucy said, trying to take notes. "Don't you have this on paper somewhere?"

"You should have photos. House and family. List of questions from pediatrician, I-171H, I-864, and I-600. Here is name and address of hotel. Show it to driver."

Yulia handed her a slip of paper torn from the corner of a notebook.

"I thought I had another month to get ready."

"You must leave in three days. Here is number for Delta. Flight 62 still has seats."

"This is insane, Yulia. There is no possible way I can leave in three days."

"If judge agrees to adoption, Mat is yours," Yulia said. "But Russian authorities tell me when time is available for court appearance. We have no choice."

Lucy took a deep breath. No one needed to tell her that she was stepping into quicksand without anyone there to extend the traditional tree branch. She wondered if she had any sense left at all.

"Don't I need a tetanus shot?" she said. "Maybe the doctor can squeeze me in."

Yulia tightened her lips. "My apologies for your rushing. It was not intended."

"I just want Mat." Lucy picked up her purse and started toward the door. "Wish me luck."

"You don't need luck," Yulia said, "just cash."

"Do you treat all your clients this way?" Lucy said, unable to contain her frustration.

"Yes," she said, untroubled by Lucy's tone. "I do."

...

THAT NIGHT, Lucy couldn't sleep. At three in the morning, she lay there envisioning the earth as seen from outer space. She would be in the central part of the planet's dark side, and just about everyone in that longitude would be unconscious. There might be—what?—10 or 15 percent of the population awake, working in hospitals, thrashing in beds, walking beaches in worry, or robbing other people's houses. And tonight, she was one of these nocturnal few, desperate for a few hours' oblivion but unable to achieve it.

So she thought of Mat, a stranger soon to be her closest relative, a little boy who was likely playing in the middle of the day but would go to sleep that night completely unaware of how much his life was about to change. In a state between waking and sleeping, she imagined showing up at the orphanage and being told there was no such child, then searching for the photo in her bag but being unable to find it, and then calling Yulia from a pay phone on the street, only to get a message saying the number had been disconnected.

Her heart pounding, she followed the dream logic to its conclusion, in which she wandered through the somber Russian night, back to her hotel, where they had no record of her and couldn't find her luggage, and she would be stranded, orphaned herself. She woke up at five, sticky with sweat, and raced to the kitchen to check the paperwork on the dining-room table once again. Then she curled up on the couch and fell into a deep, dreamless sleep until the morning sun flooded the room, and she suddenly became fully awake, realizing there wasn't a minute to spare.

eleven

Lucy attempted to hang her carry-on on the hook inside the airport bathroom stall, but it kept slipping off, so she rested it on the floor, within reach of the bands of bathroom thieves who surely waited for such lapses. Rosalee was near the bank of sinks.

"So you'll call me as soon as you land, right?" Rosalee said in a voice that echoed through the bathroom.

"Ma, don't yell, I can hear you," Lucy said from inside the stall. "I'll try, but I don't expect my cell phone to work from there, and Yulia says the pay phones are impossible to figure out, even if you're Russian."

"So you'll call collect," Rosalee said, still shouting.

Lucy emerged from the stall with difficulty, hauling out her large carry-on bag and her raincoat and trying to keep her rain hat from falling off her head. She was overheated and sweating inside the layers she was wearing because Yulia had told her not to bring more than two bags. She pushed up her sleeves, washed her hands, and let the cool water run over her bare wrists as her mother looked in the mirror and etched in her lips with a liner, then filled them with red lipstick.

"I wear this color when I feel fat. Too many cookies around after the funeral," Rosalee said, turning the tube upside down. "L'Oreal's Red Letter Day. Draws the eyes up to the face. So how will I know you've landed safely?"

"I solemnly swear to land safely," Lucy said to her mother's reflection in the mirror. "And if anything happens while I'm there, the American Embassy will notify you."

"You know I won't sleep a wink until you're back home with your little bundle."

"He's four, Ma. He's a little more than a bundle."

"Oh, that reminds me," Rosalee said. "I bought a trundle bed for the spare room, so he can stay over. And Dad's going to buy out the toy store while you're gone. I told him I want a mountain of toys for my new grandson."

"My adoption book says we shouldn't overwhelm him with toys. He has to bond first."

"I say a few presents will help him bond. So there." Rosalee nudged her. "Try and stop me."

Lucy smiled and hitched the carry-on over one shoulder. She was numb with anticipation, desperately anxious, wanting to fast-forward time to a few months from now, when Mat would be a normal kid waking up in his tidy little twin bed with the fish-patterned sheets, and she would be a normal mother, picking up his toys and reminding him to throw his dirty clothes in the hamper.

"This is my son," she said under her breath.

"What?" Rosalee said.

"I better get moving. Yulia said to leave extra time to go through security."

When Lucy emerged from the bathroom, with Rosalee behind her, she was startled by the sight of Cokie, Paul, and the kids; her father; Angela and Vern; and Louis, all standing near the security gate with balloons and a large paper banner that read "Mazeltov!"

Cokie stepped forward as Lucy came toward them. She looked annoyed. "The guy at the flower shop said that 'mazeltov' meant 'good luck,' but I've since been told otherwise. I'm taking it back after you leave."

Cokie was wearing some sort of strong citrusy scent that smelled familiar—possibly air freshener. She tucked a small plastic bag into

Lucy's raincoat pocket, whispering, "Here's a little beauty trick for the trip. You'll wake up looking fabulous."

Paul came over and stood next to Cokie. "Good luck, Luce. Free meal for you and the kid at T.G.I.'s, soon as you get back."

Lucy looked at her watch. She had an hour before her plane left, but she wanted to get through security, the final barrier before the journey could truly begin. Her niece and nephews hugged her next, then Angela, and then Vern, who looked up at her: "Remember, I get to teach him baseball."

"Of course, Vern. We'll get him a little ball and bat as soon as we get home."

"And a glove," Vern said. "Don't forget the glove."

Her father came forward. She sensed some important shift in their relationship, one in which she had always been the protected child, the one who hadn't quite grown up. But now she was about to find out what it was like to be rewarded and terrified by parenthood, just as he had been. His hands were jammed in the pockets of his rain jacket. Lucy used to think he kept candy or mints or change in his pockets, but now she realized it was a pose of submission, an acknowledgment of the many things over which he had no control.

"My little girl, going to get her new son," he said, his lower lip quivering. "You be safe, sweetheart."

"I will, Dad. Don't worry, okay?"

"Oh, I'll worry," he said, smiling through watery eyes. "But don't you worry about me worrying."

Louis came forward next, putting an arm around her shoulders. She wished, then, that he was coming with her, if only for the company on the long plane flight. But then she would have had to send him home. She couldn't afford to let Mat see him yet, when their relationship was so new. And in the smallest corner of her mind, she anticipated her own jealousy. She wanted Mat to need her most, couldn't allow for the possibility that anyone else might bond with him first.

Yulia emerged from behind a large rectangular pillar, as if she had been waiting for the good-byes to be over but had lost patience.

"No time to waste," she said, motioning for Louis to get it over with. "She must go."

Louis took Lucy in his arms and kissed her, knocking off the rain hat as everyone else applauded. She flushed as she bent over to pick it up, aware that her entire family was grateful to Louis: for his attention, his persistence, his obvious affection for her. She knew what they were thinking, too: He was young, sure, but wouldn't they make a nice family when Lucy came back with her little son. And they could certainly have a few kids of their own. A new fantasy to replace the old one.

"Good-bye, everyone. Thanks for coming to see me off." Yulia took her arm and led her toward the security gates. "Good-bye."

Yulia squeezed her arm a little too hard as they stood in line, and Lucy shook her off. "What's with the death grip?"

"Just nervous."

"But aren't you supposed to be reassuring me?"

Lucy showed the security officer her driver's license, airline ticket, and visa and began piling her belongings on the conveyer belt. She could still see Yulia, who couldn't accompany her but appeared to be waiting for a last word.

"Wish me luck," she said.

"Remember," Yulia called through the gate. "No luck needed. Just cash."

Lucy looked around, hoping no one else had heard the invitation to mug her, then strode off down the concourse, relieved to be on her own, responsible—at least in part—for how all this turned out. She shifted her heavy carry-on bag higher onto her shoulder and lifted her chin, striding forward with a surprising degree of fake confidence until she stumbled over a slight ripple in the hideously patterned terminal carpeting. She caught herself, though, and kept going, certain that Harlan would say that fake confidence was better than no confidence at all.

LUCY FLEW TO JFK in New York and then found her flight on the departures board in the terminal: Delta Flight 62 to Moscow, 5:39 p.m., On Time. She boarded the plane and settled in for the long flight. As they flew over the Atlantic, she watched a movie, ate something that might have been chicken, flipped through the airline magazine, then attempted to sleep in her narrow coach seat, with her raincoat bundled up for a pillow. After an hour, she gave up and remembered that Cokie had stuffed something into her pocket.

She unrolled the raincoat and found the plastic bag, which contained an eye mask filled with a cooling gel. Feeling ridiculous, she tried it on, adjusted the elastic strap, and eventually relaxed, losing consciousness. When the plane landed in Moscow, she almost felt refreshed. She reset her watch to 11:10 a.m., then stood in the customs line for an hour, where an agent who spoke a little English directed her to the shuttle bus that took her to Vnukovo Airport for the flight to Murmansk.

With less than an hour before her next flight, she was afraid to wander too far from the gate, so she sat down in the shabby, poorly lighted waiting area, which reminded her of a bus terminal, and ate a granola bar from her carry-on while rereading the information Yulia had given her. The description of her hotel, which touted its "original coziness," made her smile until she read the descriptions of several other hotels and realized that they all claimed to have "original coziness." So much for original, and now she had to wonder about the coziness as well.

Lucy read, for the countless time, the section in her guidebook on Murmansk: population four hundred thousand . . . on Kola Bay . . . substantial downtown, several museums . . . the largest city in the world inside the Arctic Circle. She hoped she had enough warm clothes.

She reassured herself that the facilitator would be waiting for her at the Murmansk Airport, remembering Saint Anthony of Padua, who helped travelers. She could say nothing in Russian besides *do svidaniya*, which meant simply good-bye but sounded more dramatic and tinged with finality. Yulia had gone on the Internet and printed out a phonetic phrase guide, which turned out to be from a Web site for mail-order brides. Lucy had looked through the phrases on the plane and wondered about the desperate American men who found it useful to say things in Russian like "I thank my destiny for sending you to me," "My sincere greetings and best wishes!" or "Fly to me on wings of love."

Three hours later, after a nauseatingly rough flight, she landed in Murmansk. At takeoff, she had been reasonably sure someone would be there to meet her, but the bumps and vibrations had shaken the odds in her mind down to about fifty-fifty. She was the last in line to exit the cabin because everyone around her had unbuckled their seat belts and started unloading luggage from the overhead compartments as the plane was still taxiing toward the gate. When she stepped off the plane, her legs shaking, she spotted a rectangular piece of gray cardboard that said "Lucy McVie," held by a short, stocky, balding man who was scanning the faces of the passengers. She lugged her carry-on over to him.

"I'm Lucy McVie," she said, extending her hand.

"*Zdravstvujte*, hello," he said, ignoring her hand. "Yes, I wait for you, Lucy McVie. I am Lesta Petrovich, facilitator for Yulia Doletskaya."

"Lester?" she said.

"Les-TA," he said, emphasizing the second syllable. "And this is what you may call me."

"Got it," she said, relieved that she would be able to communicate with at least one person in this vast country with its unfamiliar alphabet. Following Lesta closely through the dim terminal—which smelled like an ashtray—Lucy feared that he might turn a corner and leave her alone in the maze of hallways. The last flight had left her feeling slightly dizzy, as though she had just stepped off an amusement park ride.

Lesta found a cart for her baggage, and they waited with the other passengers for a half hour at what Lucy presumed was the baggage area, until someone became impatient and opened a door that led directly onto the tarmac. All the passengers trooped outside to haul their luggage from a little train that had been abandoned a few hundred feet from the terminal. Lucy pointed to a large green suitcase, and Lesta crawled over the others to retrieve it. It took them another twenty minutes to find her smaller blue duffel bag, which was buried under a mound of flattened cardboard boxes in the last car.

Outside the terminal, the sky was almost indistinguishable from the murky gray inside the building. Lesta stored her luggage in the back of a battered blue sedan and held the passenger door open for her.

"You must be very tired, Lucy McVie," he said. "I take to hotel, and tomorrow we pick up paperwork."

"When will I go to the children's home?" she said, gripping the car door as Lesta drove through the airport, one hand on the wheel, the other holding a cigarette, swerving around cars stopped in the middle of the road. She felt around for a seat belt but couldn't find one.

"We call and set appointment," he said. "Tomorrow or day after."

In the time it took to drive from the airport to the hotel, about thirty minutes, Lesta gave her a short history lesson on Murmansk.

"You see the hills—here we say *sopki*—very different for Russian city, like your San Francisco, eh? In the ports, we have Northern Fleet and many nuclear-powered icebreakers. Outside city, we have Alyosha, giant concrete soldier built to celebrate hero of Great Patriotic War, who blew up Nazis and himself, too, with grenade. We also have beautiful St. Nicholas Church. Government made plans to tear down, but then we have perestroika—you know this word?—and church was saved."

After another few minutes of swerving around bicyclists, pedestrians, other cars, and various bits of debris in the streets, Lesta pulled up to the Best Eastern Arktika hotel. It was a white modern-looking building in the shape of a wedge of cheese. Lesta helped Lucy bring her bags into the lobby, which looked less promising than the exterior, with worn carpeting and a few uncomfortable-looking chairs. Still, it wasn't too expensive, and the Web site had mentioned a bar, a beauty salon, a coffee shop, a currency exchange, a gift shop, a restaurant, and a sauna. Lesta took her to the front desk to check her in.

"Here is your key," Lesta said, smiling. "Get some rest, and tomorrow I pick you up in lobby at nine. Restaurant is terrible, but you find something."

"Do you really have to go?" Lucy said, feeling suddenly very fond of Lesta, with his head the shape of a volleyball and his matching volleyball paunch. He had straight teeth with the exception of one canine that was turned sideways, and her eyes were pulled to the imperfection. She realized he wasn't as old as she had originally thought, just prematurely bald. "Let's get a cup of coffee."

"I'm sorry, Lucy McVie," he said. "I must get home. Wife is waiting."

"Just call me Lucy."

"Okay, Lucy McVie," he said. "Be in lobby at nine."

She went to her room, which was a double in standard, overused Holiday Inn decor—no sign of Original Coziness. She had requested a nonsmoking room, but everything, including the bathroom towels, smelled of smoke. She took a bath in the surprisingly large tub and changed into her nightgown. Then she made an attempt to call home through the room phone but gave up when she kept getting recordings in Russian. Her cell phone had no service.

She had no one to talk to, nothing to read that she hadn't already read twice on the plane, so she finally fell asleep out of sheer boredom. It was ten o'clock when she woke up, eerily alert. She paced the room, turned on the television, and watched ten minutes of *Seinfeld* in Russian, then she put on jeans and a sweater, thinking a glass of wine might help.

The lobby was empty except for a couple waiting at the front desk with two sleeping children draped over their shoulders like sacks of grain. Lucy found the dark-paneled lounge behind double doors of etched glass and sat down on a stool at the bar. A singer in a purple-sequined head wrap crooned Russian ballads into a microphone, with a single keyboard player behind her.

The ten or twelve other people in the bar didn't seem to notice her, and neither did the bartender, who was watching the singer. Lucy—who could be struck with ordering anxiety at McDonald's—had no idea how to get his attention without seeming rude, so she sat there self-consciously, until a slender middle-aged man with dark skin and a goatee sat down next to her.

"Hello," he said, extending his hand. "Calvin Olmstead. I'm gonna take a wild stab and guess that you're here to adopt."

"How did you know?" she said.

"First day?" Calvin asked. "You have that glazed look, that jet-lagged, can't-fall-asleep-but-I'm-exhausted kind of look. Don't worry, it gets worse."

"Worse?" she said.

"Well, it might. I meet a lot of folks like you."

"Do you actually live here?"

"I'm a tap-dance instructor. Remember *White Nights* with Mikhail Baryshnikov? They think I'm Gregory Hines or some crazy thing. I came over here with a production of *Tap* in 1997 and came back in 1998. Been here ever since. And they love me. I could teach seven days a week if I wanted to. Every housewife in Murmansk signs up for my classes."

Lucy kept nodding, wishing the bartender would look her way. She caught Calvin's words in snatches, intermingled with the purple-sequined singer's Russian ballad.

". . . one toe-ball-change away from Broadway, I swear, and then this kid named Savion Glover comes along, bringing in da noise and da funk, and I'm done. Over. Yesterday's news . . ."

"Davay nikag-da ne ras-ta-vat-sya."

". . . so when I came back, the recreation director in Murmansk was like, 'Calvin, whatever you need,' and I was like, 'Yeah, who needs that, traveling shows and bit parts, tapping till your feet fall off.'"

"Kak mee zshi-li drug bez dru-ga vse e-ti go-dee."

"And they love me here. They like old school, Gregory Hines. Hey, let's drink to Gregory Hines," Calvin said, looking for the bartender, who was watching the singer.

"To Gregory Hines," Lucy said, though Calvin wasn't listening, and she had no drink to lift.

The audience applauded politely as the singer finished and her keyboardist began to pack up his equipment. Lucy turned around to say good night to Calvin, but he was gone. She walked back to the elevator and stared through the lobby windows. It had to be close to midnight, but the sky had only dimmed a bit, as though it were dusk.

She looked at her watch, disoriented, until she remembered how close she was to the North Pole. Like Alaska. Land of the Midnight Sun. When she finally found her room again, she pulled the heavy curtains closed, collapsed on the bed in her clothes, and didn't wake up until morning, when she had about fifteen minutes to wash her face, brush her hair, change her clothes, and run down to the lobby to meet Lesta, her stomach still empty.

...

HARLAN LOOKS at Lucy and sighs as it becomes clear that they are stuck on the balcony for the night.

"I haven't told my mother yet," he says, as though this has been on his mind. "She hasn't been the same since my father died twenty years ago. Once I left for college, she bought a bunch of sweat suits and moved to Florida and let her hair go gray. She just sits around her little complex with the other widows, acting way older than she is."

Lucy thinks he must be exaggerating.

"She must have been a good mother, though, because look at you. You turned out fine."

"A pleasure to have in class."

"Of course you were."

"I wonder what happened to all those report cards."

Lucy thinks of the large trunk in her mother and father's room, stuffed with her and Paul's report cards and art projects and posters on the four basic food groups. Her past is almost too well preserved.

"I don't know how to tell her I'm sick," Harlan says. "I'm afraid she'll cry."

"I'd be surprised if she didn't cry."

"But that's what I remember most about my dad's death. She came home from the hospital and sobbed and wailed and screamed. It was pitiful. I couldn't sleep until they sedated her."

"That must have been awful for you."

"You have no idea."

And she didn't. In her experience, a mother puts her own needs after the needs of her children. A mother skips her annual trip to Atlantic City so she can watch her daughter's math team compete in the state finals. A mother lets her daughter borrow her new shoes for the high-school concert, shoes right out of the box. A mother on a diet sits with her daughter and eats a pint of ice cream when her daughter's college boyfriend dumps her.

"My parents would adopt you," she says, trying to make him laugh. "I'll have them call a lawyer tomorrow."

He smiles at her, but without mirth. The shadows under his eyes look deeper and darker in the yellow haze of the lights from the apartment parking lot.

"I want this to go away," he says, closing his eyes. "I want to go to sleep and then wake up and shudder because I had a terrible nightmare. That's what I want."

"That's what I want, too."

...

LUCY DIDN'T SEE Lesta in the lobby, so she ducked into the coffee shop and pointed to the coffeepot, sizing up the cup with her hands. The clerk handed her the coffee and took the five-dollar bill she left on the counter, smiling at her in a way that made her realize she should exchange some of her dollars for rubles. She was about to find the money exchange in the lobby when Lesta walked in the front door.

"Good morning, Lucy McVie," he said. "Big day for you."

"I hope so," she said, putting her wallet back into her purse. "What's first?"

"We go to Department of Education; then we set up appointment at children's home, maybe for today. Would this be fortunate?"

"Yes, very fortunate," she said. "Do I look okay? I didn't sleep well last night."

"Lucy McVie, you look fine. Nice shoes," Lesta said, looking at Lucy's plain black boots. Under her black winter coat, she was wearing a long vintage skirt with a muted flowered print and a white blouse, an outfit she had long ago picked out for her first meeting with Mat. They were conservative clothes, clothes a preschool teacher might have worn, meant to convey only one thing: trust me.

She took a sip of her coffee and asked Lesta if they could stop somewhere for a quick breakfast.

"You like Egg McMuffin?"

"I thought maybe something more Russian. What did you have this morning?"

"Cottage cheese and a little Cocoa Puffs."

"An Egg McMuffin sounds great."

Lesta swung through the McDonald's drive-through, ordered for Lucy, then continued on to the Department of Education, a gray institutional building that reminded her of the federal building in Baltimore, a bureaucratic monolith. The downtown of Murmansk, plastered with signs she couldn't even begin to decipher, had a few tall buildings and, above those, in the hills, street after street of what looked like identical apartment complexes.

Trees, she noticed as they walked from the parking lot to the education building, were a rare commodity. Efforts had been made, obviously in the recent past, to paint some of the downtown buildings in painfully bright colors—gaudy yellows, oranges, and blues. But a dark-gray soot covered most of the other buildings, continually replenished with exhaust from the flimsy-looking cars that darted between potholes and around pedestrians like insects.

A half hour later, they emerged from the Department of Education building with their paperwork stamped and an appointment to see Mat that afternoon. Lesta had asked her for a hundred dollars to give to the clerk, which apparently went into the clerk's pocket. But Lucy wasn't about to complain if it got her closer to taking Mat home. She'd hand out hundred-dollar bills to everyone she met on the street if that's what it took. She felt a cold sweat break out on her forehead, all the hours of anxiety and anticipation merging into a feverish peak. This would be the day she would meet her son, hear his voice, maybe even hold him and feel the warmth of his breath. She felt a sudden panic, remembering that her gifts for the children's home and her list of medical questions were back at the hotel.

"Do we have enough time to go back so I can get a few things?" she asked Lesta.

"Certainly, Lucy McVie. And when papers are signed, we celebrate. My wife to make chicken Kiev."

Lucy nodded and smiled, though her stomach was a little upset from driving around in Lesta's smoky sedan. He dropped her off at the hotel, and she ran inside, determined to call home before she had to dash out again. The hotel clerk seemed to understand the string of numbers she wrote on a piece of paper and placed the call to Rosalee and Bertie, handing her the desk phone and adding a note to her bill. She had expected to hear her mother's voice, but instead she got the answering machine and had to leave a message.

"Hi, it's Lucy. I'm here, everything's going like clockwork, and I'm going to meet Mat this afternoon. Wish I could hear your voices. I love you . . . Bye."

A surge of adrenalin propelled her up the stairs to the sixth floor; she was too impatient to wait for the elevator. She made a circuit of the room, stowing presents in an extra duffel bag she had brought and stuffing envelopes and a notebook in her purse. In fifteen minutes, she was ready and had to force herself to sit down to wait another half hour until Lesta was due to arrive. It was all too much.

Lucy closed her eyes and thought again of the ecumenical Saint Julian of Norwich—*All shall be well, and all shall be well, and all manner of thing shall be well*—who had written in the fourteenth century that God's mystery was found in one's self, in the depths of one's soul. Julian—who technically wasn't a saint because she had never been canonized—had had a famous vision in which Jesus put a hazelnut in her hand. "What is it?" she had asked, and he had responded, "It is all that is made."

The hazelnut. It was almost Lucy's. In that moment, the weight of her grief came to rest on her shoulders, which still ached from flying overnight in coach. It had been six months since Harlan's death, a time during which she had plumbed depths she never thought possible. But it was also when her watershed year had started—the year in which life would either flow uneventfully toward flat waters or rush joyously down a mountain stream—and she had found God's mystery in the photo of a small Russian boy.

It was a time during which she had waded in and out of grief and connected with a man who wouldn't let her reject him, no matter how confused she seemed. It was a time during which her Nana Mavis had died, pushing her mother into the matriarch role, aging her in ways that were sad but inevitable. It was a time in which her brother had been humbled and in which Cokie, losing it, had turned to her— of all people. It was a time she had, for once, put just about everything else ahead of her job, and might end up regretting it. It was the time Harlan—in his own unique way—had come back to her again.

She stopped in the bathroom, wiped her eyes with a piece of scratchy toilet paper, then took her duffel bag to the lobby to wait for Lesta. She was too nervous to eat anything, but she exchanged fifty dollars into rubles. She flipped through a magazine, checking the clock every few minutes, and heard what sounded like a dance class coming from the hotel ballroom. The staccato racket of metal on wood—it had to be Calvin and his Murmansk housewives—was almost unbearable. She paced the lobby, wondering if she would ever be able to find the children's home on her own. Then Lesta walked in.

"Lucy McVie, my apologies," he said, waving his hand. "Traffic."

"Lesta," she said. "You're here. I was going nuts."

"Nuts," he said, twirling a finger near his head. "I know this expression. In Russia we say, 'Your roof is sliding.'"

"I can't wait another second."

"Of course, Lucy McVie. We go."

On the way to the home, she had to open the window and lean out to prevent herself from fainting. She had no reserves, her nerve endings like electrical wires scraped bare of their protective coatings. She took deep breaths of the smoggy air and tried to pull herself together, for Mat's sake. A four-year-old would have no sympathy for her distress.

When Lesta stopped the car, Lucy saw that the children's home was just another institutional building on the edge of town. She saw no playground or bright colors, just another gray box with a small sign on the front. On the way over, Lesta had explained that children under four were kept in *dom rebyonka*, or baby homes.

Mat had been in a baby home briefly but went to this *detsky dom* when he turned four in March. Children who weren't adopted would stay at the *detsky dom* until seven, after which they would move to a home that would care for them and educate them up to the age of seventeen. Some of these homes had their own schools, and others sent the orphans to outside schools. Growing up in an orphanage was a social stigma in Russia, Lesta said, confirming what Yulia had told her.

"We Russians, you must understand, we like to suffer. It gives us something to complain about," Lesta said. "But children . . . left here . . . It makes me glad to think they go to better place."

Lesta carried her duffel bag to the front door. He rang the bell, and a woman in cleaning clothes opened the door, waving them into a dark entryway. The foyer, devoid of furniture and painted a bland off-white, smelled like vegetable soup. The floor was covered in green-and-white linoleum squares that Lucy could have sworn were identical to the ones in her elementary school back in the seventies.

When the director finally emerged, she greeted Lucy with a stiff nod. Her graying hair was cut close to her head, and she wore the kind of narrow black skirt that said she didn't sit on the floor with the children. With her excellent posture, she was a good head taller than Lucy, who could tell she liked being in charge. She said something in Russian to Lesta, who translated.

"This is director Zoya Nikolayevna Minsky. She say Azamat is sleeping now," he said, looking upset. "Best for us to come back in morning."

twelve

L ucy couldn't wait another day. She was here, doors away from Mat, wearing her white blouse and her trustworthy skirt. She had come all this way. Telling her to come back in the morning was like telling her to stop breathing. But Lesta shook his head, not even translating, as if to say, "Don't bother."

"Couldn't I just take a peek at him while he's sleeping? I promise not to wake him. Or we could wait until he's finished his nap."

Lesta translated this to Mrs. Minsky, who blew through her lips like a horse, which needed no translation. But as Lucy was gathering her things to go, the woman seemed to relent, pulling Lesta aside and speaking to him in a low voice.

Lesta touched Lucy's arm. "You peek. She say okay."

Mrs. Minsky led them down a long corridor, past a playroom for the children with a few toys and books on open shelves, and then opened the door to a spare dormitory with eight cots. The shades were drawn. All the children slept silently. She pointed to a boy with a blue wool blanket pulled up to his chin. Lucy took a wide step to an area rug on the linoleum to muffle her footsteps. She walked over to the cot and knelt down beside it, her heartbeat quickening as though she had just run a mile.

He was small; she noticed that right away. Certainly smaller than most American four-year-olds. The light-brown hair she had seen in the photograph had been shaved down to a short stubble on his round little head. His full lips were open, and he breathed softly through his mouth, slowly, deeply. As her eyes adjusted to the light, she could see the tiny veins that ran across his eyelids, the eyes moving slightly underneath as though he were watching her from inside a dream. He had a scrape, about a half-inch long, on the left side of his nose. His ear, the one she could see, was perfect and so lovely that she almost couldn't stop herself from touching it. This was the child in which she had invested so much, the one whose picture had allowed her to forget her grief for small, healing moments.

The hazelnut. All that is made.

She wanted him to stir, to open his eyes and see her there, devoted to him. She willed him to wake up, but he slept on, immobile. After several minutes, Lesta touched her on the shoulder and nodded toward the door. Only then did she become fully and guiltily aware of the seven other little boys breathing softly under their blankets. Would others come to kneel by their cots? Who decided, she wondered, which child went and which child stayed? Was there a complicated rubric, or did someone simply choose at random to send one child off to parts unknown while his little friends ate vegetable soup until they were seventeen?

Back in the spartan foyer, Lucy made another plea to wait until Mat woke up.

"But that would not be possible," Lesta translated, "because they have a lesson, then dinner, then bath time, then bed. There is no time for visiting."

"Then why did she make this appointment in the first place?" Lucy asked, but Lesta only shrugged. Lucy stood with her arms folded, trying to convey her frustration through facial expressions, which were completely inadequate. Then she saw, very suddenly, that this was a test, that the director was putting her in an awkward position to see how she would react. The director was *directing*, and it was her play. Lucy was an out-of-work actor brought on the scene to make a plot point. She could be replaced, or the scene could be cut altogether.

She picked up her duffel bag and smiled at Mrs. Minsky, who nodded in response.

"I'm looking forward to seeing Mat tomorrow," she said.

Lesta translated, and they left.

...

LUCY SAT AT THE HOTEL BAR with a glass of red wine that night and told her troubles to Calvin, who proved to be a surprisingly good listener.

"So she makes this appointment and then won't let me see him when we get there," she said. "I finally talked her into letting me peek at him while he was asleep. So I do know he exists. That's one worry to check off."

"Sounds like they're giving you the business."

"Let's just say his adoption may be a little unconventional."

"Hey, that don't surprise me. Nothing's conventional here. It's all about the back door and the cash. Russians love to stick it to Americans. Payback for the Cold War, one sucker at a time."

"Well, if she doesn't let me see him tomorrow . . ."

She couldn't finish the sentence because she realized she had no recourse. The only person who might take pity on her was Lesta, but she wasn't sure how far he could push her case. She got the impression that he just followed orders.

"Hey, have some of these," Calvin said, pushing over a plate of pierogi. "Heavy food interferes with my dancing."

Lucy took a bite of the pierogi, which held some kind of bland potato-like filling. She hadn't been impressed with Russian cuisine, what little she had seen of it. They all seemed to subsist on tea and cigarettes anyway, looking down their narrow noses at anything as prosaic as nutrition.

"So what are you gonna do?" Calvin asked, downing the last of his beer.

"I don't know," Lucy said. "I think I'll just say a few prayers and hope for the best."

"You religious and all? Well, put me down for a prayer or two. I could use the help."

Lucy laughed and ordered another glass of wine. She seemed to be living some parallel version of her life in which she sat in bars and drank with strangers. She found the company completely benign, just other lonely people looking for a laugh or a sympathetic ear. Why had no one told her that bars didn't have to be about getting picked up? And for what perverse reason had she discovered this on the eve of becoming a mother? Somehow she felt less sad about Harlan here, as if he, too, were off in some foreign country and would return with amusing stories about the price of bottled water.

Calvin, meanwhile, had called over a friend, another expatriate who had chucked an American nightmare for a Russian one. He was a ship's cook who had docked in Murmansk a few summers ago and decided to stay, picking up jobs in hotels and restaurants between ships. He reminded Lucy of a pug—a broad face with an underbite, all rolls and ripples underneath a straining sweatshirt, yet somehow sweet and unthreatening.

"Here's how I see it," the cook said, settling himself on a bar stool next to Lucy and taking a sip of his Budweiser. "Your *haves* in America got nothin' to complain about. Great health care, decent schools, five hundred channels, and pay-per-view to boot. But your *have-nots*? Not only do they miss out on the health care and the schools and the five hundred channels, but they have to look at it every day.

"Walk down the street and see the Hummers you can't have and the big house you can't have and the doggy bakery selling pastries you can't afford. I mean, when dogs are eating birthday cakes, there's something wrong with the values. The *values*, man. In Murmansk, we're all in the same boat together, am I right, Calvin?"

"Absolutely," Calvin said, clicking his second beer against the cook's bottle. "But you know what I miss?"

"What?" Lucy said, having no idea what a tap-dance instructor would miss most about the country of his birth.

"Toast," Calvin said. "Ain't no regular toasters here; everything's grilled or fried. Just give me a nice piece of toast. Whole wheat with a little butter on top."

Lucy left Calvin and the ship's cook to their discussion of toasters versus toaster ovens and went upstairs. They were right, of course. America seemed even more confused in the new millennium than it had when she was growing up. And yet, for the most part, its people had good intentions. They liked to see themselves as the benevolent hosts of the planet, mediating disputes and only bringing down the hammer when they had no choice.

She climbed into bed and tried to remember the features of Mat's little face, which had already blurred in the course of a few hours. The resistance she had seen in his photo hadn't been there as he lay sleeping. She hoped he would welcome her, couldn't wait to find out if her own good intentions—or foolishness or blind faith or wishful thinking—would be rewarded.

...

AFTER A QUICK BREAKFAST at the hotel café, Lucy asked the hotel desk clerk to call Louis as she waited for Lesta in the lobby. It would have been one in the morning in Baltimore, she calculated, but she had remembered at breakfast that she had never dropped her article off to the dean. She had forgotten about it in the rush to arrange her trip, and she wasn't sure exactly when she would be back. Louis answered the phone after three rings.

"Hello?"

"Louis? It's me. I'm sorry to call so late. I'm waiting for a ride over to the orphanage to meet Mat. We went yesterday, but he was sleeping. I did get to peek at him though, and he's exactly how I imagined him from the picture. Only smaller. I can't wait to see what he's like when he's awake."

"It's so nice to hear your voice." He yawned. "Sorry, I'm a little sleepy. I guess I passed out while I was reading. So when do you bring him home?"

"A few days, or maybe a week. I'm not sure. I'm worried, though. The director of the children's home wasn't exactly friendly when I met her yesterday. But he'll like me, right? Is there any reason he wouldn't like me?"

She hadn't intended to seek out comfort so blatantly, but now that her questions were out there, hovering across the Atlantic, Louis did what was required.

"Of course, he'll like you, Lucy; he'll love you. It's all gonna work out fine. Trust me."

The desk clerk glanced at her and looked at his watch. This phone call would probably cost another hundred dollars.

"So call my mom, okay, because I couldn't talk to her the other day, and I had to leave a message."

"I will."

"Oh, and I forgot to drop off my article to the dean. It's rough, but I'm hoping I can smooth it out and send it off to a journal when I get back. Would you go to my house—the key's under the plastic frog on the front porch—and bring it over to his office? It should be on my desk, right next to the computer."

"I'll take care of it. I promise," Louis said.

"Thank you. I can't believe I forgot about the paper. Yulia had me in a panic before I left."

"Lucy?"

"What?"

"I miss you. I wish I could—"

"I have to go," she whispered, because the clerk was looking her way again, as if she had tied up the phone too long. "I miss you, too. Bye."

And she did miss him, missed the comfort of lying next to him, his skin keeping hers warm, missed being part of a pair. But then Lesta showed up, grinning broadly, and she was back in the parallel universe. She found herself smiling, too, as she marveled at the circumstances that brought them together.

If Lesta had been American, he would have been one of those people who blended into the crush of humanity for her—a middle-aged married man with neither the looks nor the education to stand out in any crowd. She couldn't think of many situations in which they might become friends, have a beer together, go see a movie, discuss politics. But here, Lesta was more than just her candle in the darkness; he was the light itself. He could make her happy just by smiling.

"Why are we so happy?" Lucy asked.

"Because," Lesta said, opening the hotel door for her. "I call the director this morning, and she say everything good. No more problem. Just five hundred dollars."

"Five hundred dollars?"

"Yes, and you take Mat."

"Today? You mean I could take him home right away?"

"You must go to court hearing, get his passport and birth certificate, then you take him back to Moscow for visa. Five hundred dollars."

"But how did this happen? I don't understand."

"This is good boy, Lucy McVie. Healthy boy. No worry."

Nothing felt right about this new arrangement, but Lucy didn't know if she could reasonably object. She had the money with her; it wasn't that. And she could no more walk away from Mat now than she could walk away from her family, or cancel Harlan's e-mails, or turn her back on the saints. It just left her with that ripped-off used-car feeling again.

She followed Lesta to his car, got in, and gripped the door as he took off around a corner, wondering how he could distinguish the cloudy sky from the gray pavement and the grayish buildings and the soot-covered cars.

Before long, they were back in front of the children's home, ringing the doorbell. This time, Lucy was nervous but more resolute.

The cleaning lady answered the door once again and led them to the playroom they had passed on the way to the dormitory the night before.

The room smelled strongly of beets, and two of the four overhead lights were out, leaving the room in a kind of twilight, darker than it was outside. Lesta moved a rocking chair toward Lucy, but she couldn't sit down. She felt she might have to run to the bathroom if they had to wait too long. Other than the rocking chair, the room had only a small brownish rug and a children's table with three mismatched chairs. She wondered if this was where Mat had drawn his card on the blue construction paper.

Minutes passed, and they heard nothing. No sounds of children playing or laughing or even being scolded. She could only hope they were all on a field trip or out on a playground that couldn't be seen from the front of the building. Just when she was about to start searching the place on her own, the director came to the door holding the hand of the little boy whose face Lucy had examined countless times in a single photograph. He was here with her, finally, on the same continent, in the same country, the same city, the same room, within her reach. And he was awake. She had rehearsed this moment in her head a hundred times.

"Azamat," she said, getting down on her knees. His brown eyes took her in as though she were a piece of furniture. He wore a pair of blue sweatpants that were too long for him and a light blue polo shirt. One of his socks was white, or had been white and now was closer to gray, and the other was yellow. He wore no shoes. She looked at Lesta. "Does he understand who I am?"

Mat let go of Mrs. Minsky's hand and made a detour around Lucy to play with a small truck that was missing a wheel. It was a dump truck, and he piled some blocks in the back of it, then rammed it into the wall. He had not smiled since he entered the room, but he didn't appear to be afraid of strangers. He merely looked indifferent, focused on the truck and his opportunity to play without rivals.

Lesta went to speak to Mrs. Minsky as Lucy sat down on the floor and stacked blocks, watching Mat as her heart pumped so forcefully she imagined she could hear it. She found herself organizing the blocks into groups by size—straining to hear what Lesta was saying even though she could understand none of it—when Mat took the truck and slammed it into one of her block towers, sending the little cubes flying. This made him smile, and Lucy felt as though they had passed from strangers to friends. She smiled back and stacked the blocks again. They played their little game of stack and destroy until Lesta came over to speak to her.

"Excuse me, Lucy McVie, and young boy, yes, excuse me," Lesta said, clearly flustered. "The director is telling me that boy is, perhaps, not understanding his adoption."

"I was told his father terminated his parental rights. Isn't that what happened?"

Lesta went back to Mrs. Minsky as Mat stayed on his knees and slammed the dump truck into Lucy's towers of blocks. Lesta returned.

"Yes, this is the case. Termination of rights. He was brought into system last year, after his mother died. His father has a job with long hours and did not feel he could take proper care of him. This is not unusual here. His father came to visit him several times in baby home but has not been to visit since he came here. You explain, she say. Someday, he understands."

Mrs. Minsky bent down and spoke to Mat for a long time, curtly and without touching him. Then she pulled a little on his arm until he stood up and led him toward Lucy.

"This is your new mother," Lesta translated. "She will take you to America."

Mat looked up at Lesta, questioning with his eyes but saying nothing. Lucy could tell that Lesta's words had only confused him. Didn't they prepare him at all?

The director explained, through Lesta, that Lucy would attend a court hearing that afternoon and could pick up Mat immediately after. They would have his belongings packed.

"These are for you," Lucy said, handing the director a bag of new clothing for the other children and the other gifts her guidebook had recommended for the orphanage: mostly candy and over-the-counter medicine. Then she reached into her purse and took out five crisp hundred-dollar bills. She was embarrassed by the money, by what it said about Americans who could enter another country and walk away with one of its sons or daughters. At the same time, it impressed her, the power of these virtually weightless slips of paper, their undeniable persuasiveness.

"I was hoping to get a little more information about his health," she said, her voice steady, her fake confidence returning.

Mrs. Minsky took the money, folded it carefully, said something to Lesta, and then left the room.

"He is healthy, she say. Nothing but colds," Lesta said. "She goes to get medical records."

Mrs. Minsky returned a few minutes later and handed Lucy a sheaf of papers, handwritten in Russian. Lesta took them and flipped through the pages.

"Two ear infections. Bronchitis in March. Underweight. Normal reflexes," he read.

As Lesta tried to interpret the records, the director took Mat's hand and began to lead him toward the door. But he let go and walked back over to where Lucy was standing. She smiled at him, her lips stretched tight. It was a smile so eager to convey sincerity that she was sure it couldn't have looked more insincere. He stood for a moment, his face impassive. Then his lips formed the shape of an O, and his tongue emerged slowly, curled at first, then flattening out so he could give her the full effect of his rejection.

"Azamat!" the director said, yanking him away by one arm. "Nyet!"

Lucy sat down in the rocking chair as the director hauled a stoic Mat away. She tried to examine the worn linoleum, which shimmered before her as though it were under water.

"Lucy McVie?" Lesta said. "You okay?"

She didn't answer because she felt as if she had been pushed off a dock into a very cold lake and still couldn't catch her breath. The books she had read had made it seem as though orphaned children couldn't wait to be adopted. Then again, she couldn't guess what his life had been like before, couldn't imagine what Mrs. Minsky might have told him. And she, after all, was just some stranger who showed up one day and wanted him to love her. How could he understand that?

"I'm fine, Lesta," she said when her voice returned. "Let's go finish this."

...

ON THE SIXTEENTH OF MAY in the year of our Lord Two Thousand and Three, a judge created a family. It was a small family, just a mother and a son, but it was official. Lucy could only wish that some of her own family had been there to witness it, to whistle and cheer inappropriately, and to offer more than the polite handshake she received from Lesta. They left the courthouse and stopped at two government offices to gather Mat's birth certificate and his new passport.

"Well, Lucy McVie," Lesta said as they headed back to the children's home. "Congratulations. This go very smooth."

"It did?"

"Yes, this judge often question this paper or that paper. Now we get little Azamat, and tonight, chicken Kiev."

Lucy was relieved, but not as much as she had hoped to be. Even with her motherhood sanctified by a judge, she felt completely unmoored at the thought of taking Mat away from the children's home. Eventually, when he could speak English, she would be able to explain in detail why she was taking him away and why his father wasn't coming back. But right now, she couldn't smooth things over with words. Not her own words, anyway.

At the front door, she asked Lesta what she could do.

"You have toy?" he asked.

"But the book I read said not to bring too many toys, not to bribe a child for affection."

"What does book know?"

"Well, I do have one toy I was saving for the hotel," she said, digging through her purse. "It's a little bubble maker."

"Shaped like car?"

"Little boys like cars, don't they? Why didn't I know that?"

"No, bubbles good. Better than nothing."

Inside, they were shown directly to Mrs. Minsky's office, which wasn't much bigger than a closet, with a desk, three chairs, and a filing cabinet. It was noticeably devoid of toys or drawings. Mrs. Minsky had been at the court hearing and had made no objections to Mat's adoption. She motioned for Lucy to sit down and opened a file on her desk. She asked Lucy to sign a few more documents and put them back in the file, closing it.

"Do I have a copy of the termination papers?" Lucy asked.

"They are with your packet of materials from the court," Mrs. Minsky said as Lesta translated.

Lucy shuffled through the stack of papers, but most of the documents were in Russian. Some of them had English translations, but she sensed that Mrs. Minsky wanted to get on with it. Her day was all about schedule, Lucy could tell, and something like an adoption threw everything off.

"Just a few more questions. What can you tell me about him, his personality?"

Mrs. Minsky seemed to have trouble understanding Lesta's translation. They spoke for a while before Lesta turned back to Lucy.

"He is, she say . . . difficult."

"Difficult how?"

In reply, Mrs. Minsky released a torrent of Russian.

"Resistant to schedule, reluctant to do chores, prone to striking other children. He threw his potato once at the cook. But we attribute this to late arrival at children's home. Most children have been here since they were babies," Lesta translated as she spoke.

"Do you think he'll cooperate with me?" she asked. "Do you have any advice?"

"Be firm. He is very strong-willed. With stable home, stable family, he will improve. And now, we get your new son for you. You have toys?"

Lucy had a hundred more questions, but Mrs. Minsky was already standing, halfway out the door. Lucy dug out the small bubble maker, which had to be filled with bubbles. She was unwrapping the package when Mat was brought in, wearing a thin navy-blue cloth coat and a small red knit cap on his head. He was clutching a ragged stuffed animal that looked as if it might have been a monkey in better days. Lesta bent down to speak with him.

"I'm going to drive you to your nice new mother's hotel, where you will stay overnight in a big bed with television," he said in Russian first, translating for Lucy. "Would you like to come to my house for dinner tonight?"

Mat squeezed his toy animal and shook his head. The director, who might have intervened, was stuffing papers in a filing cabinet. Then Lucy tried, through Lesta.

"Tell him that I like his . . . um, monkey? And I have some bubbles for him."

Lesta translated, and Mat peered up at Lucy. She looked for a softening of his hard expression but didn't find it. Instead, he grabbed the bubble toy, which she had managed to fill. He turned a crank and sent a few dozen bubbles into the air, then ran out of the room yelling with the toy.

"Where'd he go?" Lucy asked.

"He go to show other boys," Lesta said. "Because the toy is only for him."

"Oh, great. Now we'll never get him out of here."

The director turned away from her filing cabinet. "Best to leave now," she said through Lesta.

They found Mat in the playroom, filling the air with bubbles, and Lucy tried to take his hand. He resisted, but she led him firmly toward the door as he shouted all kinds of things in Russian she was glad she couldn't understand. Once outside, the fresh air seemed to calm him down a bit, and she helped him climb into the backseat, sliding in next to him. As they drove away, he began to cry and mumble, hiding his face in the smoky upholstery.

"What's he saying, Lesta?"

"I cannot hear words, only crying."

She tried to put a hand on his shoulder, but he shrugged her off. They drove back to the hotel that way, Mat sobbing and Lucy turning every brain cell inside out for some clue about what to do next. She was terrified, completely at a loss for how to convey to Mat that she wasn't the enemy. She was no better than her mixed-up nation, invading another country without an exit strategy. What had she done?

thirteen

B y the time they returned to the Best Eastern, Mat had fallen into a fitful sleep punctuated by an occasional hiccup. Lucy carried him into the lobby from Lesta's car, his head bobbing against her shoulder. She was grateful to avoid dragging a screaming child through the hotel, but even more grateful for the chance to hold him, to support his slight weight and feel his warm breath on her neck. Lesta followed into the elevator and down the carpeted hall, holding her paperwork. He stood in the hallway outside the open door as she laid Mat down on one of the double beds and came back into the hallway to collect her papers.

"I wait here for you," Lesta said.

"For what?"

"For getting ready. The chicken Kiev."

"But look at him. He's exhausted. I think we better stay here."

"This is too bad, Lucy McVie. This mean many leftovers."

"I'm so sorry. Tell your wife I'm sorry, too. I just don't think we're up for it."

"You make flight back to Moscow. I take you to airport tomorrow."

"Thank you for everything. You've been so wonderful."

Lesta hovered, turning to go several times but failing, as though his feet were not cooperating. Lucy finally realized what was happening and ran back into the room for her purse.

"Here, Lesta," she said, handing him five bills. "I wish it could be more."

He looked down at the money in his hand, the last of the crisp hundreds she had withdrawn from the bank when she had emptied her savings account. He seemed pleased by what was there and nodded his head as she looked back to make sure Mat was still asleep. The fear she had felt when they left the children's home had subsided only slightly, leaving a film in her mouth. She longed to brush her teeth.

"Best of good luck for you, Lucy McVie," Lesta said from the hall.

She stretched her hand across the doorway, but Lesta wouldn't take it.

"No, no," he said, backing away. "Bad luck to shake over threshold."

Instead, she stepped out into the hallway, threw her arms around him, and hugged him tightly, and he hugged her back, kissing her quickly on each cheek.

"I go home now," he said. "Call when you know time of flight."

When he left, Lucy sat down on the edge of the bed to watch Mat as he slept, still buttoned into his cloth coat. His hiccupping had stopped, and he seemed to be in a near coma, too distraught to cope with consciousness. She rested her palm on his forehead, pressing it against the short stubble on his hairline. She imagined another time, maybe only weeks from now, when she would take him to Arnold's drugstore and scoop up a little bag of candy for him. If he was like Paul's kids, he'd go for the Gummi Bears or something else that adhered to the back molars. That's all she wanted for him, the opportunity to eat too much sugar like every other normal American kid.

Of course, her idea of "normal" was her own upbringing. So that meant being loved by people who had very little understanding of her accomplishments—the articles published in obscure journals, the fellowships, the teaching posts—but bragged about them anyway. It meant having a brother who threatened to beat-up the joker who pointed and laughed when her towering stack of books spilled all over the floor of the school bus. It meant having a father whose eyes watered every time he saw an American flag and who taught her that most people working for the government weren't crooks. It meant having a mother whose love comforted and smothered her at the same time. Could she be all those things for Mat? Would he let her?

She couldn't help but wonder, for a moment, what Harlan would have been like as a father. Before his illness, he once told her that he loved children, but only between the ages of five and eleven. "Before and after, they're self-centered and whiny," he had said. "If you get six good years out of them, you're lucky." She had responded that it's not the same with your own children, but he had shaken his head and grinned. "Six good years, as I say, if you're lucky."

Mat stirred as she took off his sneakers and cautiously unbuttoned his coat. She couldn't figure out how to remove the coat without waking him, so she pulled up the edge of the thin bedspread and draped it over him. It was past dinnertime, and she was starving. She thought about running down to the restaurant, but she couldn't risk the chance that he would be further traumatized by waking up alone in a strange room. She couldn't imagine trying to negotiate room service, if it even existed. Instead, she found another crumbled granola bar in her carry-on and ate that, drinking lukewarm water from a bottle she had brought on the plane.

She dared herself to be happy, but there were too many obstacles. She was hungry, tired, and unable to share her news. On the other hand, Mat was there with her, and within days they would be home. She took one last swig of the water, feeling the warm trickle run down her throat and into her stomach. She called the airline, arranged their flight for the next day, and then called Lesta. Then she brushed her teeth, curled up next to Mat under the blanket on the bed, and fell asleep.

In the middle of the night, she woke up at the sound of a heavy thud. Mat had rolled off the bed and was now lying dazed on the floor. She ran around the bed and tried to pick him up, but he scooted back on his rear until his head hit the nightstand. She reached for him, but the terror in his eyes stopped her.

"It's okay. You fell off the bed," she said softly, making a rolling motion with her hands.

He shouted some words in Russian and began to cry, clearly upset that she couldn't understand him. She finally noticed he was clutching the front of his pants.

"You need to use the potty?" she asked, realizing how many questions she had failed to ask at the children's home. She walked toward the bathroom, and Mat slowly followed, holding himself with both hands. He made it to the toilet and pulled down his pants, but he wasn't standing close enough, so much of the urine ran down the front of the porcelain bowl and onto the floor. She threw down a smoke-scented towel and turned on the water to have Mat wash his hands, but he was already gone. She left the mess in the bathroom and found him lying on his side on the floor, crying, wrapping his coat tightly around him.

"It's okay, Mat." She touched his shoulder, but he shrugged her away. She pulled the spread off the bed to cover him, tucked a pillow under his head, and curled up on the floor herself under a blanket. She could only hope he was young enough to forget all this miserable confusion, that he would eventually thaw under her patience and understanding. If they were very, very lucky, she thought as she drifted off, he'd just repress the whole thing.

...

BY MORNING, Lucy's back refused to bend in the ways it had always bent before. As Mat continued to sleep, one arm thrown over his face, she untangled her blanket, got on her knees, and stretched her aching limbs before standing up. She had never liked sleeping on the floor; even as a child during sleepovers, she had always begged for a couch or a chair, needing some kind of buffer, some platform for dreaming. She dragged herself into the bathroom, which smelled of urine, and pushed the towel into one corner. She was brushing her teeth when Mat appeared at the doorway, still in his coat, pointing into his open mouth.

"Oh, you're hungry," she said, relieved they had performed a simple act of communication. "Let's wash up and go get breakfast."

She left the bathroom, opened her suitcase, and found a little toothbrush kit she had brought for Mat, along with a new set of clothes: a pair of sturdy size-four jeans, a long-sleeved polo shirt, and a pair of small blue-suede work boots. She tried to get him to brush his teeth, but he threw the toothbrush on the floor.

"Okay, then," she said. "Let's get dressed."

Mat drew his coat closer around him and let out a high-pitched scream when Lucy tried to take it off. His face and ears grew bright red. Anyone passing by the room might think she was poking him with pins.

"Okay, okay. Leave it on," she said. "Let's just get something to eat. We'll worry about the rest later."

He stopped screaming but shook his head vigorously as she tried to put on the sneakers he had been wearing the day before. Instead, he kicked one across the room and pointed toward the blue boots, which she could already see would be several sizes too large. She put them on anyway and laced them as tightly as she could. He flapped toward the door, pointing again toward his open mouth.

"A little food, and we'll both be happier," she said. "Here we go, Azamat."

At the sound of his full name, he let out a string of Russian that she tried her best to interpret based on the tone of the words. She nodded along as they walked down the corridor, though she had no idea what he was saying, hoping she hadn't just agreed to take him back to the children's home, or to see his father, or to visit Disney World. She tried to hold his right hand as they stepped onto the elevator, but he pulled it away, jammed it into his left armpit, and stood in the corner, his wide eyes telling her as they descended that this was a new experience for him.

Once in the lobby, they entered the small café where Lucy had been getting her coffee and sat down at one of the two empty tables— the six or seven others were occupied by businessmen reading newspapers or by couples examining brochures. When the waitress came, Lucy pointed to a random assortment of items on the menu, hoping she had happened on something edible, and mimed the pouring of coffee.

She tried again to get Mat to take off his coat, but he refused, twisting the buttons on it until she was sure one would fly off, half wondering if that was his intention. When the food arrived, he went straight for the *blini* and began shoving the folded pancakes into his mouth with both hands. She had to pound him on the back more than once to prevent him from choking.

"Slow down, slow down," she said, afraid to take any food for herself. She sipped her coffee, which tasted like instant Nescafé, until he began to decelerate. "At least you're not crying," she said, fully aware that he couldn't understand her but unable to stop herself. "When we get back to the room, we'll pack up. Then Lesta will pick us up, and you'll get to fly in an airplane. Have you ever seen a real airplane?"

He kept eating, dismissing the foreign words as so much background noise. When he finally seemed finished, one of his blue boots fell off underneath the table. As she bent down to retrieve it, he kicked off the other boot, letting it drop on her head.

"Hey, mister," she said, allowing herself to sound just slightly stern as she emerged from under the table and tied the boots back onto his feet. Several of the businessmen looked her way, then went back to their newspapers. She thought she saw one of them smirking.

"I think it's time to go, Mat."

He looked at her quizzically, then knocked a half-eaten bowl of milky cereal off the table. It splattered all over her clothes and shoes, the bowl landing several feet away. A clerk from the counter came over, tsk-tsking and frowning, to clean up the mess, and the businessmen shook their heads. Lucy apologized profusely in English, reminding herself to look up the word "sorry" in Russian, because she sensed she would need it again. She left a big tip on the table and ushered Mat out of the restaurant and back up to the room, where she sat him on the edge of the bed to watch a children's show on television while she showered and changed. The television as babysitter. Now it made perfect sense.

Several hours later, they checked out of the Best Eastern, and Lesta picked them up in his blue sedan for the ride to the airport. She tried to use the drive as a final chance to explain to Mat, in Russian, how much she looked forward to being his mother. Her adoption guidebook had recommended bringing photos of her home and Mat's new room, but she hadn't had time to get all that together before she had to leave. Instead, she tried to describe them through Lesta.

"So your room has these nice yellow walls and your own big bed, and you have your own bathroom with fish wallpaper, shiny little fish right on the walls. Are you getting all this, Lesta? And there are lots of toys, and your grandmother is buying you a whole mountain of toys. Does that sound good?"

Mat seemed to perk up a bit at the suggestion of a mountain of toys. She regretted saying it, but it had slipped out, the need to please him causing her to run at the mouth. Despite all the warnings in the guidebooks, she had envisioned this warm bond, this instant rapport, Mat sitting on her lap and clinging to her all the way home. Now she just wanted him to like her a little bit, to refrain from screaming, to stop acting as though he'd rather go off with a passing stranger. Was the prospect of being with her all that terrible?

Lesta parked and led them inside the crowded airport terminal, helping them check their luggage and find the proper gate. He patted Mat on the head and gave him an order: "You be good boy." Mat held his monkey tightly and stumbled forward in his too-large blue work boots to pick up a cigarette butt from an ashtray in the waiting area. Lucy took it away and kept her hands on his shoulders, even as he tried to pry them off.

"All will be fine, Lucy McVie," Lesta said with a solemn expression on his face. "I enjoy the knowing of you."

"Me, too, Lesta," Lucy said. "I'm sorry I never got to try your wife's chicken Kiev."

"For this you come back to Murmansk," he said. "Someday."

As she nodded and smiled, Mat squirmed away. She saw him pick up an old tissue from another ashtray.

"I'll miss you, Lesta. You have no idea how much."

...

THROUGHOUT THE FLIGHT, Mat refused to stay buckled into his worn seat, the frayed upholstery of which barely covered the foam padding beneath. She took him to the bathroom three times, because he seemed to enjoy seeing the tiny sink and toilet, though he never actually went. The novelty and enormity of being on an airplane seemed to impress him enough to keep the screaming to a minimum, except when they were descending, and he did, at that point, apparently need to go to the bathroom. She kept an arm tightly across his seat belt and wondered if her eardrums might suffer permanent damage. When they landed, she was grateful for the exposed foam padding, which seemed to have absorbed the puddle Mat had produced. She hustled him off the plane before any of the flight attendants had a chance to notice the sharp odor emanating from seat 14A.

In the half-light of the airport bathroom, Lucy attempted to wrestle the wet pants and underwear off Mat's kicking legs to at least rinse them out a bit in the sink. He was small and light, but he was wiry and strong—much stronger than she could have imagined when studying his picture back in Baltimore—and he refused to cooperate. She finally picked him up and held his wet rear, pants still on, in front of the hand-dryer until her arms gave out. In the future, she told herself, always bring extra clothes.

Emerging from the bathroom, they followed other passengers to the baggage claim, winding through the smoky terminal and out into the cold drizzle of Moscow in May. They took a taxi to a hotel Yulia had recommended near the American Embassy, traveling through woods and countryside until the suburbs appeared with the same gray, apartment high-rises Lucy had seen in Murmansk.

As they made their way into the center of Moscow, she barely had a chance to look out the window and glimpse what she had only seen in pictures—the fantastical onion domes of St. Basil's Cathedral, the Kremlin, or the vast stretch of Red Square—because Mat had pulled a big wad of stuffing out of a gash in the vinyl seat of the cab, requiring her to stuff it back in. When she did glance up as the cab driver slowed to turn into the hotel's entrance, the first sign she saw was for T.G.I. Friday's, unmistakable even if the letters were different. She would have to tell Paul that even Russians—or at least their tourists—appreciated large hamburgers.

Mat followed her cautiously into the hotel lobby, which was smaller than the Best Eastern's but cleaner and decorated in bold floral fabrics. The bas-relief cherubs on the ceiling were gilded, as was every available surface on the furniture and moldings, as though the Western visitors who patronized the place would feel more comfortable if the whole place glittered with gold paint.

The front-desk clerk spoke to Lucy in English. After they checked in, she walked Mat up the stairs to the second floor and found their room, which blessedly smelled of Lysol and not smoke. The bellhop had already placed their luggage near a small brown armchair in the corner that looked just as battered and worn as Lucy felt. As she was on the phone to arrange for Mat's medical exam the next day, he climbed up on one of the double beds, burrowed under the floral covers, and fell asleep.

An hour later, it broke her heart to wake him, but they needed to get his visa photo taken before the shop nearby closed, according to her guidebook, at five. In the tiny lobby gift store, she bought a bag of lollipops, though strategically, this backfired. The photographer had to pull the lollipop out of Mat's mouth to take the picture, which left him howling, his mouth wide open in the picture they would have to use.

As they walked back from the photographer's shop, the city came into focus for brief intervals: a babushka in a bright blue apron sold grilled meats from a cart; an anemic-looking young man with a scruffy beard manipulated a marionette to a Fleetwood Mac song playing on a boom box; an elderly man in black socks and sandals shuffled down the street on the arm of a stunning woman in high heels, her lips red and full. Lucy tried to smile and nod at a few people, but they looked at her as if she were mentally unstable, so she concluded it was best to keep her expression fixed. Mat seemed to know this already. His face was unreadable, though his eyes opened a little wider each time he saw someone selling food.

The air had the gritty feel of Manhattan in the summer, thick with particulates she had no choice but to breathe into her lungs. Bicyclists fought for the street with taxis, Mercedes with tinted windows, cheap Russian tin cans, buses, and trams. The expensive cars, she noticed, seemed to push past the other cars as if sticker price dictated the right-of-way.

She stopped at a bookstore to buy a Russian-English phrase book for children, which had large type and drawings, and she grabbed a disposable camera as well, having forgotten hers. Then she spotted a toy store and decided to stock up on bribes for the long plane ride back home. Mat, who had been drop-kicking his monkey and following her reluctantly down the sidewalk, smiled when they entered the store. He jumped into a bright red car with pedals and drove it around as Lucy filled a basket with small rubber balls and blocks of clay and Matchbox-style vehicles. When she had paid, he refused to get out of the car, locking his hands to the small plastic steering wheel. She asked an English-speaking clerk to explain to Mat that the car wouldn't fit on the airplane.

"He say, 'No more airplane,'" the clerk told Lucy.

She said nothing else, just handed over the cash, and a few minutes later, Mat was pedaling next to her down the wide but busy sidewalk, a blissful expression on his face. When they came to a cross street, she stopped and took a picture: Mat smiling broadly from over the little steering wheel. It seemed necessary to preserve this moment, not only because it was sure to be brief and certainly not because she had acquired it through bribery, but because a photograph would distill the joy, fix it, and focus it in a way her memory could not. The look on his face, as she saw it through the tiny digital camera window, instantly changed her mood.

But just as quickly as her mood lifted, it plunged again. She gestured for Mat to get out of the car so they could cross the street, but he refused and stood up, turned the car around, and started pedaling in the opposite direction.

"Mat, Mat, Mat," she said, trotting along beside him. "We have to go the other way. The hotel is that way."

He looked at her as if she were someone he might have met once before but couldn't quite place and kept pedaling down the street. When he got to the curb on the other end of the block, he turned the car around and pedaled back the other way. She finally lost her patience.

"Okay, then, if that's the way you want it," she said. She reached into the car, worked his little fingers off the steering wheel, and pulled him out of it, tucking him under one arm. She slid her other arm under the car's plastic dashboard and lumbered across the street, dodging cars that failed to stop at the crosswalk. Mat writhed and screamed, and she came within inches of dropping him, but she held on, finding some preternatural strength, some shot of maternal adrenalin that allowed her to reach the other side.

Mat stopped screaming when she let him get back in the car, and in this way—contentment alternating with street-crossing meltdown—they made it back to the hotel, six blocks away. The clerks in the lobby, thankfully, said nothing as Mat pedaled across the carpeted floor, and into the elevator.

Once in the room, he pedaled as far as he could until he crashed into one wall, then turned around and pedaled back, crashing into the opposite wall. Lucy unpacked her cosmetics bag, trying to ignore the noise, until the phone rang and a clerk asked her in broken English if there was a problem.

"No, no problem," she said. "I'll take care of it."

She filled the bathtub with water, an attempt to drown out the crashing noises, then poured in a small packet of bubble bath she had found in her bag. She pulled Mat out of the car, and before he could get a good lungful of air, ran into the bathroom to show him the bubbles.

"Look, Mat, bubbles," she said, trying to make them sound exotic.

She blew into the bathtub and sent bits of bubbles cascading around them. In the warm, moist air of the bathroom, Mat's resistance seemed to falter. He finally allowed her to take off his coat, then his shirt and the pants from the plane, which were finally dry. Underneath, he was wearing new, overly large briefs, perhaps his parting gift from the children's home. His rib cage pressed against the skin of his torso in a way that looked painful, his constant hunger on display. On his rear, she noticed as he climbed into the tub, were two long pinkish marks, and she bent down to look more closely. They looked like scars. Her stomach seized up and she turned away, hanging her head over the sink. She felt light-headed and flushed. This poor, poor boy. No, her poor, poor boy.

As he played in the tub, she sat on the floor of the bathroom and tried to reconstruct what his short life had been like up to this point. He had been born into a harsh climate above the Arctic Circle, possibly beaten as a toddler, and then his mother had died. He had been abandoned by his father, transferred from one orphanage to another. And then she had shown up, taking him away from what was, if not comfortable, at least familiar. Was it any wonder he kept his fists up?

But then she noticed he was singing. The words were garbled, but the tune was familiar, and she finally figured out what it was. The song of the White Rabbit from the Disney movie.

He was pushing bubbles around and molding little mountains, singing the song over and over, or at least syllables that mimicked the song in English. She took a washcloth and rubbed his back before he could protest, discovering that his skin tone was about three shades lighter than she thought. She ran the wet washcloth over his hair stubble, careful not to get any water in his eyes. As the bubbles melted, she could see that the tub water had turned slightly gray.

With the water draining, Mat climbed out of the bathtub, and she wrapped a big white towel around his tiny body, which had barely enough fat on it to hold him together. She took a risk and whisked him up into her arms, but he cried out, so she put him down again, and he ran out of the bathroom.

She was picking up towels when he came back in, already dressed in the too-large pajamas she had laid out on the bed. He took her hand and pulled her up and out of the bathroom, half leading, half dragging her toward the television. So she found what looked like a children's show, propped him up in bed with some pillows, and pulled over the brown armchair to watch him watching the show. Next thing she knew, it was morning, Mat was sleeping soundly, and the TV was still on.

fourteen

Lucy tried to keep Mat on the doctor's examining table, but he kept climbing down, crawling under chairs, and finding used tongue depressors. The clinic had the familiarity of all things medical—white walls, white ceiling, metallic instruments, cotton swabs in a clear glass jar—but it startled her to see that patients smoked in the waiting room, and the floor looked as though it hadn't been cleaned for a week. She had washed Mat's hands in the small examining-room sink three times before the doctor came in without knocking.

His English was passable, enough to understand when she asked him to look at the scars.

"Year or two old." He shook his head but didn't seem surprised. "I cannot say for sure, but possibly beating. Could be with belt."

She swallowed hard. He was so small, and yet he would have been smaller when he was beaten. Completely helpless. Who could have done this to him? Nothing in her experience could explain the kind of white-hot anger that led to such injuries. But if the scars were a year or two old, they hadn't been inflicted by anyone at the children's home. The doctor cleared his throat.

"Boy is healthy," he said, signing her forms. Something about the doctor's face—a trace of freckles, maybe—had made her think of Harlan, and it saddened her, because she couldn't ask for his advice. Harlan had always found a way to put the world's ugliness in perspective. She imagined what he would tell her. Don't dwell on the scars. Move forward. Help Mat feel as safe as possible. And that, she realized, was all she could do.

...

THEY MADE their first trip to the US Embassy for Mat's visa on the morning after the doctor's appointment. She had checked and rechecked all the documents, and they all seemed to be there, though half of them were in Russian and could only be identified by a number on the top or by the color of the paper. She and Mat waited in a line outside the imposing US Embassy building, all white with gold accents, casting an aura of wealth and privilege.

She noticed that most of the others in line were men, husbands who had apparently left their wives back at the hotel with their newly adopted children, or facilitators being paid to drop off the paperwork. They all looked exhausted or homesick or just sick, even the Russians. She couldn't catch anyone's eye to even start a conversation as the line shuffled toward a large black door that was propped open and guarded by an American soldier.

Half the bag of lollipops was gone by the time they reached the window, where Lucy passed through her thick stack of documents and was given a ticket to return in the afternoon for the visa interview. It seemed like one of those archaic systems that had been set up decades ago and couldn't be changed because it had its own momentum.

Now they had three hours to kill. Enough time, she figured, to get to a place she had always wanted to visit and back.

...

IT WAS A SMALL Russian Orthodox church, not one of the spectacular cathedrals in which tourists regularly walked about, gazing upward and bumping into one another. The taxi driver had even shaken his head in disgust when Lucy gave him the address, copied from a 2001 issue of *Religion* onto a scrap of paper. This part of the city had not been scrubbed and painted for foreign guests; the steps and sidewalks were crumbling as though the concrete had been watered down.

The facade of the church was missing large swatches of its light blue paint, and the large iron door-pull swung loose as she yanked on it. One determined screw was all that kept it from falling off. She and Mat wandered through the sanctuary, which, unlike the exterior, had been beautifully maintained, all polished wood moldings and sparkling stained glass. Since it was tradition to stand through the service, there were no pews, so she found herself studying the frescoed ceiling. As they neared the altar, she saw the nook she had been seeking to the right. She had a lollipop at the ready, but Mat had become unusually quiet.

"See that," she said, pointing to a statue of a woman in a long cloak, her head surrounded by what looked like a sunburst. "That's Saint Princess Olga."

Mat climbed onto the bottom rung of a railing that separated the faithful from the shrine. He stretched out his hand but couldn't quite reach the votives burning in rows just in front of Olga's statue. Lucy stood behind him, ready to catch him if he fell.

"Olga was a real princess who lived about a thousand years ago," she said, hoping some of the spiritual message, the reverence in her voice, would find its way through. "She married a prince, but he was killed, and years later, she went to a place called Constantinople and visited a church that changed her completely. She became filled with light, and she wanted to spread that light to everyone she met. After that, they say she never got any wrinkles, and her blue eyes sparkled."

Mat stepped down from the railing and tugged on her coat, pointing to his open mouth, and she gave him a lollipop. "Holy Olga," who had a complicated history that included episodes of merciless revenge before her conversion, had always been one of her favorites, and she was hoping this visit would inspire her for the rest of her journey with Mat. But it wasn't enough to be filled with light, she realized. The coercive power of sugar could not be underestimated.

Lucy had asked the cab driver to wait outside the church, and she found him there, reading a newspaper. She and Mat rode back to the US Embassy, then bought grilled sausages from a wagon on the street. When it was time for their appointment, she handed over her interview ticket and passport to a guard, who asked to see her driver's license and then directed them to the second floor.

Mat was fading. He dragged his feet up the broad staircase and let his monkey bump off each step. At the top of the stairs was a wide hallway with a brocade couch against one wall and a small reception desk manned by a thin young American wearing a white shirt and a red tie with an American flag pin on it. He took their appointment ticket and nodded toward the couch.

"It'll just be a few minutes," he said. "Make yourself comfortable."

For some reason, this prompted Mat to throw himself on his stomach and wriggle under the couch with his monkey. He emerged with an unwrapped peppermint hard candy, which he popped into his mouth, dust and all, before Lucy could stop him. She sat down on the couch and rested her head in her hands, exhausted. A few minutes later, the young receptionist directed them to a small office down the hall.

Lucy had high hopes that they could make it through what was supposed to be a fifteen-minute process. It started out promisingly enough, with their American interviewer—a heavy blond girl with overly large front teeth—beaming at both of them and telling Lucy this was her last week in Moscow before she went home to Illinois. Springfield area. Did Lucy know Illinois? Ever been to Springfield?

But then Mat took a small glass giraffe from the woman's desk and refused to give it back. Lucy tried to trade him for a lollipop, but he made a face and ran out of the office, making her chase him back to the brocade couch. When she brought him back, he threw himself to the ground, and the figurine spun across the floor, the neck breaking cleanly in two. He screamed so loudly that several embassy employees ducked their heads into the office to make sure everything was okay.

The interviewer looked as if she was counting the hours, already on Illinois time. She flipped through the papers and pulled out the ones Lucy needed to sign, finally handing her the sealed visa package. As Lucy hurried back through the waiting room, she could only be glad she would never see these people again. She could just imagine the interviewer telling the story to her friends at a T.G.I. Friday's in Springfield.

...

THE NIGHT AIR keeps Lucy and Harlan awake as they discuss before and after his diagnosis.

"I was so much happier before," he says. "It was bad enough that the whole world convulsed a few weeks ago; now it's happening to me personally. Even if I'm cured, nothing will be the same. I had this outline, you know, these assumptions about my future. Now I can't predict anything."

"But now you can do something about it. You can treat it."

He ignores what she said.

"Predictability is definitely underrated."

He bends down, unties his laces, and kicks his shoes toward a corner of the balcony.

"What if I can't do anything?" he says. "What if I die from this?"

"You won't die," she says. "It might be rough going through the treatment, but you have your whole life ahead of you. I really believe that."

He rubs his upper arms below the sleeves of his T-shirt, and she hands him the blanket.

"Thanks," he says. "I wish I had your outlook."

"It's yours," she says. "I want you to have it. I insist."

"Lucy," he says. "It doesn't work that way."

He looks at his watch.

"It's one in the morning," he says, peering over the balcony. "Maybe I can climb down."

"Don't even think about it," she says. "You'll fall and break your legs."

"I don't really have the energy," he says. "It's sad, but now that I know I'm sick, I feel that way."

She calls out into the void: "Can anyone hear me? We're trapped on the balcony."

No response.

She calls again, as loudly as she can. She sees a light flick on for a moment in an apartment on the first floor. But then it goes off. She's suddenly exhausted, knowing that her bed is yards away but inaccessible. The glass looks too thick to break.

She looks at the lounge chair, which isn't wide enough for two people.

"At least we have the blanket," she says. "Let's put the cushions on the ground."

At another time, before Harlan's news, she might have fantasized about such a mishap, a chance to be alone with him, thrown together for warmth. Now it just seems cruel.

They spread out the cushions and lie down on their sides, draping the blanket over their midsections. It's a throw, not a full-size blanket, so it only reaches to Harlan's knees. She lies motionless, afraid to disturb him, but she feels his closeness as a revelation.

"Do you mind if I . . . ?" Harlan places an arm around her. She tries to relax, to welcome sleep.

"I'm sorry about the door," she says. "Try to get some rest."

His breathing has already slowed.

It occurs to her that he never asked the question he had mentioned when he first came over. Advice, he had said, was what he was looking for.

"Hey, what did you want to ask me about?" she says. But he doesn't respond except to snore, very softly, in her ear.

...

A RESTLESS EVENING passed with Mat driving his red car into the walls of their hotel room and Lucy scouring the phonetic Russian phrase book for words meaning "Get down," *ah-zheesh*, "Be careful," *asta-roe-zhna*, and "Don't touch," *nee troe-gee*.

In the morning, they took a cab to the airport for the trip home. They arrived an hour and a half before necessary, but the waiting area was already jammed with carry-ons and strollers and babies and toddlers—mostly adoptive parents just as desperate to get home as she was. She found a small space by the wall and made a little cushion of coats for Mat, who was momentarily interested in the crayons she had found in her bag when digging around for her paperwork to go through customs. She couldn't remember buying them. Maybe her mother, always thinking ahead, had put them there.

Another family arrived about a half hour later and propped itself against the same wall.

"Hi, I'm Lucy," she said, extending her hand to a harried-looking new mother with a baby girl who looked to be about ten months old and a toddler boy of about three. The father was attempting to read a battered section of the *Wall Street Journal*, but the three-year-old kept running off to crawl under the seats and take toys out of other people's bags.

"That's not yours," the father said, prying a wooden train out of the boy's hand. "Come sit with Daddy."

As Lucy wondered to herself why Mat wasn't doing the same, she turned back to check on him and saw that he was coloring on the airport wall.

"No, no, no, no, no," she said. "On the paper, Mat, only on the paper."

He answered this by running the crayon over his forearm and attempting to color the bottom of his shoes.

"I know he can't understand me, but I keep talking to him anyway," she said to the woman with the baby. "I guess it's hard to turn off that need to communicate."

"Look, no offense, but I'm not capable of carrying on a conversation," said the woman, whose baby was now asleep. "I haven't slept in a week, and I can't even form a thought much less a sentence."

"No, I understand," she said, and she did, while at the same time feeling humiliated. She glanced around and saw only couples, husbands and wives facing each other like quotation marks around their newly adopted children, defining them. In her noncoupled state, Lucy felt inadequate, defective, the only one in gym class without a partner for the square dance.

When she turned her attention back to Mat, he had half a crayon in his mouth.

"Yuck," she said, pulling it away. "We don't eat crayons. Here, have a Gummi Worm."

She had been saving these for the plane, but her options seemed limited. She could only hope he would sleep through at least part of the eleven-hour flight back to JFK. As he chewed on the Gummi Worm, the enormity of what she had done became suddenly clear. This boy was hers, hers alone, and in the legal sense no different than if she had given birth to him. There was no going back, no matter how ill suited they seemed for each other. And if she screwed this up, Mat would be the one to suffer for the rest of his life.

She had already considered the minor issues: no more lazy weekend mornings reading the newspaper; no more vintage clothing expeditions; no spontaneous trips to an art gallery or days on end spent researching a saint. And other things: no more frozen dinners for one, no more nights alone at the movies, no more fear of growing old alone. But it had never occurred to her that Mat wouldn't want to be adopted, that she would have to win him over with something more than his own yellow room.

What would happen, she wondered, on the day Mat came to her and asked why? Why had his mother died? Why had his father abandoned him? But most terrifying of all, why had she adopted him? What would she say? She could tell him she had always wanted a child. That much was true. But wasn't it also true that she had been lonely? That it gave her something else to think about besides Harlan?

She turned to Mat, who had found the bag of Gummi Worms and now had two or three in his mouth, their multicolored tails whipping across his chin as he chewed. The flight attendant had finally announced in Russian and English that it was time to board the plane. Mat, who seemed strangely compliant, stood with her behind two women cradling a baby with all four arms. She wanted to find out who had invented Gummi Worms and have him canonized.

As they neared the gate, though, Mat appeared to realize that they were at another airport. He tried to run away, yelling something over and over, but she caught him by the coat collar. She wanted to dig her Russian phrase book from her purse, but she couldn't find it without letting go of him.

"Can someone tell me what he's saying?" she yelled.

A flight attendant in a tight skirt and high heels approached them.

"He say he wants his car," the woman said.

Lucy gripped the flight attendant's arm with her one free hand before the woman could walk away. "Tell him, please, that his car is too big to fit on the airplane." She had left it inside the closet at the hotel.

The flight attendant tried to speak to Mat in Russian, but he was beyond hearing. His face was a vibrant red, and his screaming had bypassed words and become something primal. Lucy wanted to clamp her hand over his mouth—*make it stop, just stop, please, please stop*—but two hundred passengers were watching. Instead, she picked him up and took him to the farthest corner of the waiting room, where she let him throw himself on the floor and pound it with his little fists. The line moved forward slowly, inevitably, until only a few passengers were left.

"Are you finished?" she asked, and he responded by spinning on his elbow and kicking the wall. So she picked him up and carried him back to the end of the line as he thrashed against her carry-on and threw his head back at impossible angles.

"Let's just get through this, okay?" she said. "I'll buy you ten of those cars at home if you'll just let me get through this flight."

Though he understood none of it, Mat stopped struggling, probably due more to exhaustion than any attempt at cooperation. He allowed her to carry him onto the plane and fell asleep against her arm as they taxied down the runway, Mat in the window seat and Lucy in the middle, with an unlucky gray-haired man sitting next to her in the aisle seat.

"Thank you," she whispered to the patron of acute embarrassment, whoever that might be.

Lucy was still calming down an hour later when Mat woke up, refreshed and ready to begin wandering the aisle for trips to the bathroom, any one of which might actually be necessary. The bathroom trips were what she dreaded most, because Mat, unstrapped from his seat, was like a pinball launched into a maze of seats and flight attendants and drink carts and luggage. He seemed determined to bounce off all of them.

. . .

FLYING WITH A SMALL CHILD, Lucy discovered, was a perversion of physics, because time actually slowed down, moving at about one-fourth its usual pace. The flight seemed to take several days, interrupted only by small breaks when Mat would collapse into sleep, only to be awakened an hour later by engine noise or the screaming of another child.

When they landed in New York, she was covered with juice and chocolate stains, her clothes felt rough on her skin, her hair had escaped its ponytail holder and was frizzing around her head like some kind of novelty fright wig, and she was close to fainting from lack of food and water. Mat refused to hold her hand as they stumbled down the corridor to the gate.

Throughout the flight, she had been sustained by the image of emerging from the gate to find her family waiting for her, ready to shoulder her overstuffed bag and surround Mat with their inescapable love, a parachute of love that would descend on his unsuspecting head. But she had been dreaming in pre-September 11 time, and no one without a ticket was allowed at the gate.

She would have to take Mat through immigration by herself and bring her luggage through customs, with her parents waiting for what might be hours. She could only be glad that Louis wouldn't be with them, although he had offered. She needed time to remake, remold, wash and dress, and repair the damage.

The immigration process was surprisingly smooth, and they made it through, with Mat's passport stamped, in less than thirty minutes. Then she found a spot near the conveyor belt at baggage claim and waited as the minutes ticked by and nothing emerged from the fringed opening that separated the knowing from the unknowing. They had been at the airport for at least forty minutes. She felt dizzy and wondered if she could justify sitting on the ground when a woman yelled in her direction, "Excuse me, ma'am, is this your child?"

Mat had climbed to the top of the line of handcarts waiting in locked positions for the right number of quarters to release them. He was sitting in the wire basket on a cart at the front end on the row. Lucy ran over, paid for the cart, and pulled it out, then wheeled him back to where she had left her carry-on.

"You know," an older woman with carnation pink lipstick observed, "you really shouldn't leave your bag like that. Anyone could take it."

Lucy had almost nothing left, just a shallow well of shame to berate herself for losing track of the one thing she would always—always—have to remember. Mat dug around in the carry-on, probably looking for some candy, as the conveyor belt finally roared to life and began spitting out luggage that looked as if it had traveled halfway across the world and back again, kicked and abused the entire way,

She grabbed her large green suitcase off the belt—she barely had enough strength to pull it upright—and found her smaller duffel bag a few minutes later. She went through customs in a daze.

"Now let's get out of here," she said, aiming her rented luggage cart at a set of automatic double doors. American airports might have their flaws, she thought, but you could almost always count on the doors to fly open as soon as you approached them. Outside, she saw her mother—her blessed, blessed mother—jumping and waving, her bosom bobbing, in front of Bertie's double-parked car. Lucy turned the cart in their direction as Mat began climbing out of his seat.

"No, Mat," she said. "Just a couple more feet. Please don't get out."

"There's my grandson," Rosalee told the general population of the pickup area. "My beautiful little grandson."

Rosalee ran toward them, her arms outstretched, and tried to give Mat a kiss on the cheek. He released a scream that rivaled the planes taking off on the runway.

"He really doesn't like to be touched," Lucy said. "It'll take some time."

Rosalee nodded, then stared at her. "What on earth? You look awful. Just awful. Are you sick?"

"I don't think so . . . just incredibly tired," she said, glancing at her reflection in the terminal windows. The vaguely familiar person looking back was teetering as though she might collapse. She had a flashback to the night Harlan told her about his diagnosis, describing his loss of consciousness. She was there with him, suddenly, watching television coverage of the planes hitting the twin towers, over and over, until the signal was interrupted. A solid wall of static filled the screen, and then she was inside it, unable to move, surrounded by a wordless scramble of light and noise.

"Come on, baby," her mother said, helping her into the car. "Let's get you home."

fifteen

When Lucy woke up, twenty-four hours had passed since the plane landed. She was in her parents' bed, wearing one of her mother's voluminous nightgowns. She wandered dizzily into the kitchen, where Mat was sitting at the table eating a peanut-butter-and-jelly sandwich and drinking a glass of milk.

"Ma," she said, pushing hair out of her face. "I'm not sure he can eat peanut butter."

"Oh, please," she said. "He's fine."

"But he might have an allergy."

"He's already had three of those," Rosalee said, wiping some jelly off Mat's face with a wet paper towel. "We thought you'd never wake up."

"I feel like a train hit me," she said.

"Go take a shower. He's just taking a break from playing with his new toys."

"So the fabled mountain exists."

"He's been riding around the basement with his new tricycle. I can't understand his Russian, but I bought a phrase book, and he seems to understand me."

Lucy nodded and wandered to the bathroom, hoping the hot water from the shower would wash away her confusion. Could it be this easy? Did she lack some essential mothering instinct or display some deficiency Mat could sense, or was it just the mountain of toys? She stood under the showerhead, letting the water tamp down her overwrought hair, finding it hard to believe she had ever been in Russia, ever met a saint named Lesta, ever sat through the longest plane flight in history. Her mother leaned in through the bathroom door.

"Louis called. He's very anxious to talk to you."

"Thanks, Ma," Lucy yelled through the steam. She wasn't ready to face Louis. Their relationship was so new, so fragile, that it seemed certain to change radically with Mat in the picture. They would either break up or become an old married couple raising their adopted son. She couldn't think of any alternatives. When the water began to lose its heat, she finally emerged, wrapping herself in a pink towel. The door opened and Mat walked in, wearing a pair of shorts she had never seen before. He made his way to the toilet as if she wasn't there.

He used the toilet and flushed it. Then he turned around, reached up, and flicked the light switch on and off a few times without any expression on his face, then left.

"But you need to wash your hands," she yelled out the door in time to see his little head bobbing down the stairs to the basement.

A half hour later, dried and dressed in clothes that sagged as if her shoulders were the points of a hanger, Lucy discovered the true meaning of a mountain of toys. The basement rec room was filled with them, some still in wrapping paper, and Rosalee had draped the low-hung beams with streamers and wrapped them around the center basement pole. Mat was squatting near a collection of Matchbox cars lined up in a perfect row, and her father was lying on his side, belly resting on the floor. Mat would take a car and run it over Bertie's belly as if it was going over a hill, then line it back up. Her mother, on her knees collecting wrapping paper, put a free hand on Mat's head. He looked up and smiled.

"You realize he thinks he's staying here," Lucy said.

"We'll deal with that when the time comes," Rosalee said.

"But I don't have a basement full of toys."

"Well, take some of these or go shopping. Little boys need toys. That's all I know."

Lucy sat down on the floor with an old-fashioned wooden toy and began pounding pegs with a small mallet. Mat came over and grabbed the mallet.

"*Mah-yee.*"

"That means 'mine,'" Rosalee told her.

Lucy nodded and went upstairs to call Louis, feeling the need to speak to someone who actually wanted to speak to her. She dialed his home number.

"Hello," he said urgently, as if he'd been waiting for the phone to ring.

"Hi, it's Lucy," she said, unable to mask the fatigue in her voice. "I'm back."

"Are you okay?" he said, clearly worried. "You don't sound like yourself."

"I don't think I slept more than a few hours the whole time I was gone. You know how you feel when you're just starting to come down with something terrible? This is like that, only without the vomiting."

"So when are you coming back to campus?"

"I think I need to stay with my parents for a couple days, let my mom help with Mat. He needs some time to adjust."

"A little rascal, eh? Well, don't worry about your article. I took care of it. I miss you, Lucy."

"I miss you, too," she said. The words felt strange, as though someone else were saying them. "But this won't be easy."

"What won't be easy?"

"The transition. Having to be a mom all the time, and trying to get my work done, and . . ."

"I get it. I'm okay about it. Really," he said, and though his words said one thing, she heard another.

"I'm not sure you sound okay."

"I'm not much more mature than a four-year-old."

Rosalee yelled from the basement for Lucy to come watch Mat use his new mini-trampoline.

"Gotta go."

"Call me tomorrow."

"I will. Bye."

She hung up and returned to the basement to watch Mat jumping, literally, for joy.

...

THE HAGIOGRAPHERS were extremely annoyed. Lucy had missed a series of increasingly frantic e-mails from the Hagiography Society, asking if she could sit on a panel at the society's annual meeting. The last one—from someone given the task of submitting a printed program—was a keeper:

You could be in Antarctica and still check your e-mails once in a while. If you're not dead, you must be in a coma. If, and only if, you are dead, I apologize.

Lucy could have taken her laptop to Murmansk, but there had been too much to carry. So now her academic colleagues, of whom there were scant few around the world, were fed up with her. On top of that, her mother kept hinting that Lucy needed to bond with Mat more closely before she could take him back to her duplex. Louis kept calling, asking why she wouldn't let him visit, and she hadn't returned calls from Yulia, Angela, Paul, or Cokie. She was stuck in some sort of netherworld, webs of obligation crisscrossing so effectively that she couldn't move at all. This went on for several more days—Lucy moving slowly around the house in her mother's bathrobe—until Mat finally cut through all the angst. He started asking about his father.

"He keeps saying something," Rosalee told Lucy at breakfast. "Sounds like *pa-pa* or *pap-ya*."

Lucy flipped through the phrase book, examining the phonetic pronunciations. "Well, it's probably 'father,' although it could be 'pointe shoes.'"

"You need someone who speaks Russian to sort everything out for him, explain where he's going and why," Rosalee said. "This little boy is confused. He needs some help."

"You're right," she said. "I'll call Yulia."

Rosalee handed her the phone and waited for her to dial.

...

YULIA SHOWED UP AT THE DOOR a few hours later with a tiny kitten in her hands.

"You're kidding, right? You must be kidding," Lucy said. "Don't let him see it, Yulia. I'm allergic to cats."

It was too late. Mat had heard the doorbell and came up the stairs from the basement. He took the kitten from Yulia and began talking to it in a sweet voice Lucy had never heard from him before. Yulia threw her bags in the corner of Rosalee's dining room and sat down on the floor with Mat in a pool of sunlight that came through the narrow panes of glass on either side of the front door. Mat cradled the sleepy kitten in his lap as they began to speak in Russian. Lucy interrupted.

"What's he saying? What are you telling him?" she said.

"I say 'hello' and that I am Auntie Yulia, and I say 'Welcome to America.' And he says he is naming cat Dinah like in *Alice and Wonderland*, and I say 'It's a boy cat,' and he says 'Oh.'"

"Fine. Good. Just explain to him that I'm his mother now, and I'll be taking him to his new home in a few days. This is his grandmother's home. I don't think he understands that."

Yulia stood up, with some effort, and spoke to Mat quietly. He said nothing in return but stood up with the kitten and left for the basement.

"What did you say?" Lucy said. The tears were close, and when they came, there would be no stopping them. Where were the hugs, the lullabies, the small hand grasping her own? Mat would tolerate everyone as long as the toys kept coming, but they wouldn't become his family, just his suppliers.

"I told him to go play. We must talk first."

"We don't need to talk. I just need your help so he'll understand..."

"Why is it that you worry so much? He will adjust. I have seen it many times."

"But he's asking about his father, Yulia. Does he think his father is coming back for him?"

"Oh," Yulia said. Her weight shifted slightly, and she leaned against the door frame between the dining room and the foyer. "Did Zoya Minsky say anything about his father?"

"She said he'd been to visit him at the baby home several times but not at the children's home. His termination papers were with all the paperwork they gave me in court."

Yulia sighed heavily. "I'm not certain, but this may be why Zoya wanted more money," she said.

So Yulia knew all about the extra $500; Lesta must have told her about it. Then Lucy remembered the scars and told Yulia about the medical exam in Moscow.

Yulia's mouth turned down, and she showed her bottom teeth, which were crooked and yellow near the gum line. Lucy sensed disappointment but not surprise.

"This could be his father, but Mitya never told me this. This could be his day care, or a neighbor, anyone. Very sad," she said.

Lucy stared down at her hands. A trick of the light from the windows made it look as though she could see through her pink palms. She shook them, wanting the color back.

"He is safe now," Yulia said. "You passed through customs and immigration. You are legal parent. We go talk to him."

An hour later, Yulia left and Mat allowed her to give him a quick kiss good-bye. Lucy wasn't sure how much he understood, but the cat was now named "Bill." She also discovered that Mat liked Spiderman and bubblegum, and that he had never been to a restaurant before the hotel in Murmansk. She learned that he remembered a few things about his mother, and she wrote these down. He remembered that she had a red sweater, that her hair was very short, and that she would sing to him. Yulia also asked him, gently, if anyone had ever hit him. "Yes," he told her, "when I am bad boy." When she asked him about his father, he said nothing and turned away, back to his toys.

Later that afternoon, Lucy repacked her luggage and ran out to buy kitty litter, cat food, and some new clothes for herself and Mat, since both of them had been walking around for weeks in ill-fitting ones. That evening, she told Rosalee she was ready to take Mat home.

"I'm so happy for you, sweetheart," Rosalee said. "Happy, happy, happy."

Lucy just smiled and said, "I'm happy, too," though it wasn't happiness she felt. It was more like resolve, a determination to go through the motions of parenthood, until one day, she would stop remembering what it was like to be a nonparent and embrace what parenting seemed to be: experimental treatment that might or might not work, the results too far in the future to know.

The next day, Mat picked out a dozen of his favorite toys from the mountain, and Lucy crammed them into the trunk of her parents' car, along with her luggage. Bertie and Rosalee rode in the front seat, and she rode in the back after strapping Mat, with some difficulty, into his new car seat. They entered the Ellsworth campus through the front gates, the hot sun glinting off a modern aluminum sculpture in the shape of a giant paper clip. She had passed it hundreds of times before without wondering what it was supposed to mean, but now she saw it through Mat's eyes and found it utterly baffling.

"This is your new home," Bertie said, gesturing toward the lions on the pillars marking the entrance.

"Dad, don't say that," Lucy said. "He'll be pretty disappointed when he sees where we really live."

"This morning I taught him how to say something truly important for anyone living in Baltimore. What do we say, Mat?"

"Go O's," Mat said, thrusting his monkey in the air, and Bertie gave him the thumbs-up.

Lucy ruffled Mat's buzz cut. For the first time since he had stuck out his tongue in Murmansk, she could see the promise. She could see that it would take countless small moments like this one to bring them together, and that those small moments would build on each other, only to be torpedoed by larger moments of frustration and loss. Eventually though, the small moments would win out.

She could also see right then that she hadn't given Mat enough of a chance to deal with his own mourning: the loss of his mother and father, of course, but also the loss of words, sounds, experiences. She had removed him from everything that was predictable and familiar and expected him to embrace a new world before he had let go of the old one. Predictability, as Harlan had said, was definitely underrated.

When they pulled up to her duplex, Louis was on the porch. She looked at her mother, who, it was obvious, had called to let him know they were coming. In Lucy's mind, Mat's homecoming—his first view of his new room, his new life—should have been separate from her own with Louis. Now she had no choice but to merge them.

"Hey, welcome back. I bought some groceries," he said as Lucy and Mat came up the stairs. Hands behind his back, he bent slightly at the waist as if he were a butler. "And this, young man, is for you." He pulled from behind his back a large Spiderman action figure and showed Mat how to push a button on the back that made Spiderman's wrist fling out, as if he were about to let out some string.

Mat grabbed the Spiderman and ran inside as Rosalee slowly climbed the stairs, cradling Bill the kitten in her hands. Lucy kissed Louis briefly and turned to go inside.

"Lucy, wait," he said, taking her by the wrist. He kissed her again until she pulled away. She wanted to be the one to lead Mat around the house, introduce him to the rooms, give him the Tonka truck and the stuffed penguin.

"I'm sorry," she said. "I just feel like I need to be inside, helping Mat get adjusted."

But she had missed the moment she had dreamed about for months. Mat was already in his room, playing with the large yellow truck.

"Did he like it?" she asked her parents, who were admiring the room. "What did he say?"

"His little face just lit right up, didn't it?" Rosalee said, turning to Bertie. "He went straight for the truck."

"Straight for it." Bertie's hands were folded over his belly, and he rocked forward on the balls of his feet. "All boy."

Lucy tried to shake off her disappointment. She opened the blinds, grateful in the full disclosure of the sunshine that she had decided against the sponge effect.

"Tell Louis to come in and see how much he likes his room," she told her mother. "He helped me with the bathroom wallpaper."

Rosalee left but returned a few minutes later. "He's not here," she said. "And his car is gone."

"He left?" Lucy said.

She wandered back into the living room and noticed that Louis had left a gift on the dining-room table: a Felix the Cat clock with a tail that swung back and forth to mark the seconds. Its whiskers were the hands. She had almost forgotten she had told him about the spare key. In fact, the time they spent together—such a short time ago—had no bearing on her present reality. She felt postpartum, if that was possible, passionately wrapped up in the details of caring for a child. At the same time, she didn't want Louis to leave. She just wanted him to wait.

...

LATER THAT NIGHT, after Mat had put Bill the kitten to sleep in a cardboard box and had gone to bed in his new room, clutching his old monkey and his new penguin, Lucy sat down at her computer and reread all of Harlan's e-mails. She counted the days remaining—eight—until his June edition and realized that Harlan was one of the few people in her life who wasn't fed up with her. And then she wondered how much that mattered, given that he was dead.

Before going to bed, she resolved to win them over in order of priority. Mat would be first, then Louis. She would get in touch with the dean, hoping she still had a job, and then she would deal with Paul and Cokie—whom she hadn't had the energy to see since she got back—and finally, the hagiographers, who might be hardest of all. Yulia . . . well, she owed Yulia nothing but needed her services as a translator. That one she'd have to figure out as she went along.

She woke up early the next morning and slid her hands along the walls in the darkened hallway to check on Mat. He had seemed so tiny when she tucked him in the night before, almost lost in a twin bed that was twice as big as his cot at the children's home. She reached out to smooth the covers, then realized he wasn't there and felt the panic rising in her chest. She turned and, in the dim light, saw that the bathroom door was open. She found Mat on the floor, fast asleep on a towel with yards and yards of blood-spotted toilet paper scattered around him. A wad of it was bunched up near his face, apparently to staunch a nosebleed. He held his monkey tightly in his sleep.

She soaked a washcloth in warm water and gently wiped the dried blood from around his nose. He stirred and pushed the washcloth away, but his eyes stayed closed. Before he could wake up completely, she picked him up and cradled him in her lap, his stubborn little head resting warmly in the crook of her arm. Her throat hurt, a sense of shame coalescing there, because she had failed. He counted on no one but himself.

"Why didn't you come find me?" She rocked side to side, a sleep-inducing metronome. "I just want to help you, sweet boy . . . I only want to help."

sixteen

In the days that followed, Lucy trailed Mat around, half hoping for another nosebleed to show him how useful she could be. One morning she woke before Mat and made her way quietly to the kitchen to call Angela, whose special talent was to sweep away the cobwebs that prevented Lucy from thinking clearly. The tail on the Felix the Cat clock brushed a loose flap of wallpaper as she dialed the kitchen phone. Angela answered after the fourth ring.

"What time is it, six o'clock?"

"I thought you got up early for yoga."

"Not this early."

Lucy sat down with the phone at the dining-room table. She felt strangely awake, even before her coffee. She could see through the living-room window that the sun was up, spreading a soft orange glow around the complex.

"I'm sorry. I'm just having some issues with Mat. I'm not sure we're connecting enough," she said. "He treats me like a teacher, or maybe more like a babysitter."

"What are you feeding him? Is he eating?" Angela yawned loudly into the phone.

"He's eating a lot. I'm actually cooking dinner, Angela. Three things on the plate."

"If he's eating, sleeping, and playing, then he's okay. How's your place holding up?"

The rasp of the clock's tail against the loose wallpaper set Lucy's teeth on edge.

"It's falling apart, is that a good sign? The paint is chipping, and one of the baseboard covers is loose. You know my green desk chair? I've had it for ten years, and yesterday it fell to pieces. And the back of my couch already has this gray stripe across the back from where he runs his hand along the upholstery."

"Sounds normal to me."

Lucy didn't mention the rattling doorknobs or the lost remote control or that Mat had discovered a loose corner on the fish wallpaper in his bathroom and had ripped out a piece the size of a slice of pizza near the baseboard. With that in mind, she walked over to the cat clock and tore off the small flap of wallpaper brushing against Felix's tail. She felt relieved.

"So you think he's okay?" she said.

"I think he's adjusting. How's his English?"

"He's learning ten or twelve new words a day, and he's putting together some short sentences. I'm not a linguist, but I think it's amazing."

"Listen to you. You sound like a mother."

She did sound like a mother, but was that enough? An oral approximation of parenthood? It still felt more like taking care of Mat than parenting, supervising him rather than raising him. "Raising," when she thought about it, was such an interesting word to apply to a child, implying some sort of lifting action that she just didn't think she was getting. Literally he still wouldn't let her pick him up without screaming, and emotionally he stayed beneath the surface. Her little submarine.

"Did you hear about the kitten?" She opened a cabinet and found a box of animal crackers. She ate a lion, which tasted slightly stale.

"What kitten? Aren't you allergic?"

"Yulia gave it to him. And Mat has paid no attention to it since we left my mom's, so it follows me from room to room. I carry around a bottle of nasal spray and a box of tissues. Does Vern like cats?"

"I'm not taking your cat, but yes, Vern likes anything with fur. I let him have a guinea pig once, and the smell nearly killed me. What does Louis say about Mat?"

Lucy said nothing. She could hear Angela sigh into the phone.

"I guess I should call him," Lucy said.

"What happened? I saw him before you came back, and he was all excited to see you—said he bought you a clock or something."

Angela's words brought on one of those disorienting moments when Lucy realized her life was a topic of discussion among other people. She was always surprised that people cared enough to talk about her and simultaneously sure they didn't approve of her choices.

"I'm going to hang up with you and call him."

"I'd wait a few hours, but yes, you should call him. As for Mat, hon, I think he's fine. You have to tell me when I can come over and meet him. But next time you call, wait until six forty-five."

"Okay, and sorry again. You're the best."

She hung up just as Mat came down the stairs in his pajamas. He climbed onto a chair at the dining-room table and looked at her expectantly, as though his meal should have been ready and waiting for him.

"Good morning, sleepyhead," she said. "Want some breakfast?"

"Juice," he said, pointing at a purple plastic cup on the counter.

She smiled, feeling such pride in his language acquisition, although he still wouldn't address her directly, preferring to stick with naming inanimate objects. He appeared to think his yellow room, the hovering dark-haired woman looking after him, this kitchen, this home were transitory, not the end of a journey, and she didn't know how to convey the message except to be there, day after day, crafting the meaning of family for both of them until it became as natural to him as the language.

Two scrambled eggs, a piece of toast, and a cup of orange juice later, he climbed down from the chair and went to the living room to play with his Matchbox cars, running them around a plastic mat with roadways imprinted on it. The kitten wandered into the kitchen, and

Lucy filled a bowl with water. Her nose began to itch and she sneezed, upsetting the bowl before she could place it on the floor. She threw some paper towels on the floor, refilled the bowl, and went back to the phone to call Louis.

"Can we forget the other day?" she asked when he picked up the phone. "I'm asking you to block it out, forget it ever happened."

"You've waited a week, Lucy. It's already in my long-term memory." He sounded only slightly annoyed with her.

"I'm sorry. I was just so conflicted, because as much as I wanted to see you, I needed to be inside with Mat. I don't know why it mattered to me so much, what he thought of his room . . ."

She paused, giving Louis a chance to say that he understood, but he remained quiet. She would have to give him more, peel back the layers until he found her sufficiently exposed. She sneezed into the phone.

"Can we just go out and talk about all this?" Louis finally said. "I hate the phone. Do you have a cold?"

"Allergies. I'm not sure I can leave him yet. We're still adjusting."

"Just go out with me tonight, and I'll give you as much time as you need. Don't you think that's fair?"

Something in his voice told her she couldn't turn him down without sending him away for good. She had a sudden image of him standing with Ellen in the tulip garden, smiling from beneath her newsboy cap.

"All right. I'll call my mother. I'll meet you somewhere."

"Good. Seven o'clock. You know that French place on South Charles Street?"

"You can't afford that place."

"Meet me at seven."

"I'll be there."

AFTER CALLING HER MOTHER to babysit, Lucy looked outside and saw a stunning blue sky that told her to get away from the phone. Fresh air had never seemed important to her before, but now she saw why parents needed to shoo their kids out the door. Her reason told her otherwise, but she actually sensed a depletion of oxygen when Mat got bored with his Matchbox cars and started running around the living-room couch in circles. She decided to find a playground.

They started their search near the campus, but teenagers clearly ruled the nearby playgrounds, mostly skateboarding boys with terrible posture and sullen girls with facial piercings. Lucy got on the beltway and drove toward an exit where she had seen a spectacular playground from the highway. It was one of those elaborate wooden structures with towers and rope bridges and swings and slides. Another new concept: "playscape," suitably big enough to explain its semantic connection to "landscape." As they approached the entrance, she realized she knew nothing about the protocol. Was she supposed to follow Mat around so he didn't get lost in the maze, or was she supposed to find a bench and stay there so he could find her?

She decided to follow him for a while, but she lost him as soon as he disappeared into one of the tubular slides. She caught a glimpse of him entering a bright red tube but didn't see him come out the other end.

A blond woman wearing flowered overalls approached her as she peered into one end of the tube. "Did you lose one? That red slide branches, and the other part comes out near the rope ladder."

"Thanks," she said, "I'm new to this."

The woman smiled as though it were obvious. The other mothers wore T-shirts with jeans or shorts or overalls that were adult-sized versions of the overalls on their children. Lucy looked down at her short-sleeved sweater, peasant skirt, and leather sandals and felt as if she were back in Russia, so obviously was she a foreigner. The other mothers had insulated bags with juice boxes and snacks in individually rationed baggies or plastic containers. They brought magazines and cameras and water bottles and bags of extra clothes. She wondered if there were instructions on the Internet.

And what did you talk about with the other mothers? The weather? Harlan had always been good at the kind of chatter meant for complete strangers. She once stood in line with him at the DMV and watched him write down a recipe for Swedish meatballs from a truck driver wearing an IKEA sweatshirt. The previous summer, when his hair was gone, Harlan had discussed chemotherapy with a breast-cancer survivor as they waited at the Inner Harbor for the fireworks on the Fourth of July. But he wasn't there to help Lucy, and she felt his loss again, a surge of grief that subsided only when she heard someone yelling.

"Someone get him down. He shouldn't be up there."

In the fraction of a minute that Lucy had lost sight of him, Mat had climbed along the outside of one of the tubular slides. He was perched three-quarters of the way up and couldn't seem to go up or down. She looked around for help, but everyone else was immobile, staring at Mat as though their collective vision could keep him from falling. So she ran over, hitched up her long skirt, and began to shimmy up the outside of the tube, bracing herself on the plastic ridges that surrounded it every three feet or so. The hot plastic scorched the bare skin of her legs and gave off a petroleum smell that made her eyes water. What she would do when, and if, she reached him was still a mystery.

"It's okay, Mat. I'm coming. Just stay where you are."

She could hear him whimpering as she inched closer. Her sandals had a slick bottom, and she finally kicked them off to grip the tube with her bare feet. Mat emitted little yelps of fear that struck her right in the center of her chest, the very place where the loneliness had started before Harlan died. When she reached him, she grabbed a fistful of his shirt, and he looked at her, terrified, searching her eyes for reassurance that they both wouldn't fall twenty feet to the ground.

"Just hold still, buddy," she said, trying to keep her voice calm. Every mother and child on the playground had gathered below the tube to look up, shielding their eyes against the sun. She yelled down to them, "Could someone call 9-1-1?"

She told Mat the story of "Goldilocks and the Three Bears," stopping every so often to wipe the sweat from her top lip on the sleeve of her shirt. She was fairly sure he wasn't following the story, but he seemed to quiet down, the words binding him in place. By the time she reached the third bowl of porridge, a fireman had propped a ladder against the slide. He took Mat down first and then helped Lucy climb onto the ladder. Once on the ground, she dropped to her knees and held Mat to her, close against her chest, refusing to let him pull away.

"Blessed, blessed ground," she said, touching the playground's dusty surface with one hand, still hanging onto Mat with the other. "You're all right. Everything's all right." She gripped the back of Mat's head and pulled his face down to her shoulder. She couldn't sort out what she was feeling: fear, anger, shame, all three at once.

"I'm sorry, Mat. I should have been watching you." When she loosened her hold on him, he avoided her eyes and ran toward the fire truck where the firefighters were letting children take turns climbing into the driver's seat. She walked over, still trembling, and thanked two of the firemen profusely. They accepted her thanks, nodding along and smiling, but they seemed to be eyeing her skirt and her bare feet and her mass of unruly hair and adding that impression to the circumstances. She hadn't watched her child very carefully, had she, or they wouldn't have been called in. *An amateur.*

One of the firemen hoisted Mat into the fire truck to ring the bell. She watched him there, blithely clanging away, unfazed by the terror of five minutes before. The adrenalin rush had left her completely spent. When the fire truck left, she retrieved her sandals, circled the playscape, and coaxed Mat back to the car with the promise of some candy she now kept in the glove compartment. She drove home shaking and exhausted. They had been gone for less than two hours.

Lucy turned on the television and played Mat's favorite DVD about construction equipment, then she filled up the tub for a hot soak. She looked in the mirror and saw that her eyes—already red-rimmed from the cat allergies—were puffy and irritated from the playground dust. The aftermath of fear lingered there as well. Mat could have broken his neck. She would have to stay within three feet of him until he was old enough for college.

Before getting into the tub, she ran downstairs to the kitchen and found some cucumbers in the vegetable drawer, grateful that Louis had stocked the fridge. She cut some thin slices, put them on a paper napkin, and brought them into the bathroom, resting the napkin on the side of the tub. She added some bubble bath, then sank into the warm water, slipping down until there was nothing above the water but the tip of her nose and her lips. She rested there, eyes closed, her muscles still recovering from gripping the tube.

The discipline of preventive worry had always helped before. If you worried long and hard enough about unpleasant possibilities—dying in a car crash, losing a limb to frostbite, being trapped in a house fire—you stopped them from happening, because what were the chances that your worry would be justified? But with Mat, her capacity for worry wasn't long or deep or broad enough to encompass the myriad ways he could put himself in permanently disabling or life-threatening situations. She could worry for eighteen years straight and never cover it all.

She heard a noise and opened her eyes.

Mat was sitting by the tub, munching on one of the slices of cucumber she had planned to use on her eyes. He reached for the other and treated her to a rare smile.

"You like those?" she said. "I'll get you some more when I get out of the tub."

He nodded. He seemed content just to sit there in the warm steam of the bathroom, letting her talk to him in her strange language. Nothing like a near-death experience to bind two human beings together, she thought, although she could never go back to that playground again.

...

ROSALEE ARRIVED to babysit as Lucy was feeding Mat his dinner of macaroni and cheese with a hot dog. All her lofty ideas about buying only organic food had evaporated in the first week when she discovered he wouldn't eat cooked vegetables except for potatoes. Most of what he liked had some relationship to pork or sugar.

Rosalee placed a white cardboard box tied with string on the counter.

"Butter cookies," she whispered, "for after dinner."

"Nana," Mat said when he saw Rosalee. She clapped her hand over her heart.

"He's a genius, this boy," she said.

"He's picking up a dozen words a day," Lucy told her. "I think it's incredible."

"Nothing short of spectacular," Rosalee said, opening the refrigerator to search for one of the diet sodas that Lucy kept in supply for her. "Have you heard about Cokie?"

Mat got up and went straight to the cardboard box.

"Cokies," he said.

"Cookies," Lucy said. "What about Cokie?"

"Cokies," Mat said again.

"No, hon, cookies," Rosalee said. "She already has a publisher for her beauty book. She had a friend who knew someone in the publishing business, and she gave him the outline, and now she has a contract. Apparently she's tapped into a very hot market."

Lucy cleared Mat's plate as Rosalee cut the string on the box of cookies. The whole story reminded her of a long discussion she had had once with Harlan about the conflict women feel about being viewed as attractive.

"It all boils down to how hard you want to try," she had told him. "Pretty much anyone these days can have long blond hair. Thinness is tougher, but it's attainable if you work hard enough. If you wear a short enough skirt, or a tight enough sweater, you can be noticed. But most women start to resent the effort. And what's the point? Do you want that kind of attention from every male who passes by? At the same time, if you swing too far in the other direction—skip the makeup, wear sweats, tie your hair in a knot—people assume you've lost it completely."

"So very attractive women, in your opinion, are trying too hard?" Harlan had said.

"Not necessarily. But we all have a limit, and it's based on a complex formula of upbringing, financial status, natural resources, so to speak, self-esteem, and cultural pressure. Do the women in the African bush think they're beautiful? Do they care if they're not?"

Harlan, as usual, had brought her back from her flights of abstract theory.

"It's different for men. We all think we're attractive."

Rosalee rummaged through the box of cookies and pulled out one with a chocolate-coated bottom and handed it to Mat, who stuffed the entire cookie into his mouth.

"So how's Paul taking it?" Lucy asked. "Chew, Mat, chew."

"He's trying to talk her into using the book money as a down payment on a T.G.I. Friday's franchise. He's seen the numbers, of course, and he says it's a foolproof investment."

"Seriously?" and then to Mat, "Do you want some milk?" and back to her mother, "What does Cokie say?"

"So far she's resisting. He told me she went out and bought herself a Prada wallet the other day. Five hundred dollars. And when he asked her about it, she said she deserved it. She said it would keep its value better than the five hundred dollars' worth of Legos in the basement. So I guess she does have a way with words."

THE PINK LINEN NAPKINS at the French restaurant were folded into the shape of swans. Lucy held one up and examined the folds, trying to figure out how it had been constructed.

"See, this is the kind of thing I won't be able to explain to Mat. Only Americans would use origami on napkins and try to pass it off as French." She was nervous, or maybe just tired from the playground incident. Aside from the ridiculous swans, the restaurant had an unwelcome formality to it. She felt like a child trespassing in the adult world as she tilted her head to examine the crystal chandelier above their table. Why had Louis picked this place?

Louis shook out his swan and put it on his lap. He had worn a tie and a jacket but still looked like the youngest person in the room, except for the teenage busboy who came to fill their water glasses. He looked uncomfortable as he glanced around.

"Someone told me the food here was great," he said in a low voice. "But this isn't what I pictured."

"Who told you it was great?"

"It doesn't matter."

"Louis, who?"

"Ellen," he said. "But that was . . . before you and I . . . we never came here."

Lucy could picture Ellen in a place like this, ordering waiters to and from the table, sending back an undercooked entrée. Lucy had never sent anything back. It had always made her feel uncomfortable to be treated with the forced deference of the tip dependent. She wanted everyone to be friends, equal, right down to the guy at the car wash who took her money and put her antenna down. But Ellen would have enjoyed it. Of this, Lucy was somehow sure.

As Louis scanned the wine list and ordered a bottle of merlot, she realized how little she knew about him—his family, his childhood, his politics. It felt as though their relationship had been thrown into reverse, and here they were on the awkward first date.

"So tell me about your parents. Were they Republicans or Democrats?" She sipped the wine, which left a bitter taste on the back of her tongue. "I had one of each, which is kind of funny because—"

"I thought we could talk about Mat." He fiddled with his salad fork as the waiter placed a basket of French bread on the table.

"Well, today I took him to a playground, and that was a disaster—"

"No, about me and Mat. You let me stew for a whole week, Lucy. It wasn't what I expected when you came back. I know we never really talked about it, but I thought you'd let me help."

She buttered a piece of bread, wondering herself why she didn't want his help. If anything, she could use more help. She bit into the bread, which was slightly stale.

"Why do you think I adopted him?"

"Why?"

"I'd really like to know how it looks from your perspective."

"Because you wanted a child, because you're a good person."

A good person. The words stuck in her throat along with the stale bread, which had formed itself into a large pill.

"But see, that's what I'm struggling with. I didn't do it because I'm a good person, Louis. In fact, I'm still not sure why I did it. I mean, I wanted a child, but I think I did it more to stop up the holes—the holes in my life, not Mat's. Does that make any sense?"

"You're being too hard on yourself. The end result is that you're giving him a better future. That's what matters."

She placed the half-eaten piece of baguette on her bread plate. Was the end result all that mattered? Was it really that important to understand her own motives? She pictured them as a tangled ball of yarn that might take years to unravel.

"I still have this guilt that maybe I didn't have my priorities straight. So that's why I need to be so careful now. I can't afford for Mat to get confused, because I think he's finally starting to understand that we're in this together. I'm trying to turn it around now, to fill in the holes in his life."

"So you're saying I'll confuse him."

"I'm saying I need a little time to figure it all out. It's so new still. I don't have a handle on him yet."

Louis paused as the waiter came over to take their orders. Neither of them had looked at the menu, so they asked for more time. The waiter filled their wine glasses and slipped away noiselessly.

"I'm sorry," Louis said. "I shouldn't be pushing you. Take as much time as you need."

She was pleased at first, until she glanced up from the menu and saw the expression on his face, which didn't match the generosity in his voice. He wanted to understand, but he didn't. She could tell by the way he shifted in his chair and glanced back at the chandelier, as though patience were a virtue he could find among the winking crystals that dangled over their heads.

She ordered the filet mignon, medium, and ate it anyway when it was served rare.

...

LOUIS WALKED HER to the door after dinner. She stood on the small porch, feeling her second glass of merlot in an unpleasant tightening of her forehead. It was a warm night, the air slightly humid. The stars looked dim and unfocused, as though some gauzy material floated between earth and sky. "That was wonderful. Really wonderful," she said. "Thanks for being so patient with me."

Louis said nothing, then kissed her with an urgency that told her he wanted something more. Slowly, he backed her up against the door and kissed her again. *More. More. More.* She could hear it in his breathing. Did it always have to be more? Was she the only one who sometimes wanted less, so she could hold what she had with two hands and examine it from all sides?

"Let's go inside," he said.

"My mother's in there. And Mat. I think you should go."

She felt a little feverish now, weakened, her skin overly sensitive. She needed to sleep for at least two and a half days. He pushed her hair off her face and kissed her cheek, but it was a dismissive gesture, without kindness or affection.

"Bye, Lucy."

As Louis turned and walked down the steps, she noticed in the glare of the porch light that the jacket he was wearing still had a transparent size sticker on the back. She went inside, past the couch where her mother was snoring with her mouth open. She climbed the stairs. As she passed Mat's door, she peeked in and saw him sprawled across his bed, one arm thrown over his head.

Inside her bedroom, with the door tightly closed, she unbuttoned her blouse and slipped out of her skirt, putting on a nightgown. She threw herself on the bed, without getting under the covers, and fell instantly asleep. She had no idea how much time had passed when she felt a tug on the comforter. Mat stood on her side of the bed, staring at her without saying anything. It was as if he was checking on her, making sure she was still there. She didn't know what to make of it.

She brought him back to his bed, returned to her room, blew her nose, rubbed her itchy eyes, and fell back into a restless sleep until Mat woke her up—again—at six thirty. She threw on a robe in a sleepy daze, followed him to the kitchen, and burned two slices of toast before she remembered to turn down the dial on the toaster. Her first sip of coffee brought her back into consciousness, and she thought of Louis and the sticker on his jacket, which made her sad. As Rosalee came into the kitchen, all showered and dressed for church, Lucy sneezed violently four times in a row.

"That's it. I'm taking the cat," Rosalee said. "Mat can visit Bill at our house. You'll have nothing left of your nose if he stays here."

When her mother left with Bill and his bag of supplies—a transition about which Mat said nothing—Lucy made a mental apology to Saint Gertrude of Nivelles, the seventh-century abbess who was the patron saint of cats. Gertrude, she suddenly recalled, had died at the age of thirty-three, which made her think of Harlan, and she found herself wondering what he would have thought of Louis. If she could ask him now, would he encourage their relationship as part of her mission to find joy? Or would he say that Louis was too young, or too impulsive, or too needy. She felt sure he would have an opinion.

Mat yelled from the living room, but she couldn't understand him. She walked in and found him trying to reach one of his small cars—a little black pickup with red-flame detailing—which had disappeared under the couch. She reached under the couch, pulled the truck out, and handed it to him, but he barely glanced at her.

"We say 'thank you,' Mat, when someone helps us," she said in a firm voice. The coffee had succeeded in waking her up but also in defining a headache of such intensity that she pictured it as a thick rubber band tightening around her skull every time she moved.

Mat looked up with an expression of slight surprise.

"My car," he said, holding it up for her.

Lucy noticed that his fingernails needed clipping. No one had told her how many small tasks would fall under the heading of "basic grooming," for which a child had no awareness and took no responsibility. Bathing, hair combing, nose wiping, rear wiping, finger- and toe-nail clipping, earwax removing, eye-crust cleaning, tooth brushing . . . the list was endless. She felt a tiny pinch of resentment.

"I know it's your car, but I helped you get it from under the couch. So you should say thank you. Just two small words: 'thank you.'"

She could tell he understood the gist of what she was saying but hadn't yet decided whether to cooperate. He stood there, the tops of his ears getting red, then fired the miniature pickup at the wall, where it left a black mark and small dent. Lucy grabbed his upper arm and marched him up the stairs to his room. She shut the door and spoke through it.

"You can stay in there, mister, until you decide to cooperate. We do not throw cars against the wall."

She ran back down the stairs, her heart pounding, and poured herself another cup of coffee with a shaking hand. Then she called Angela and cried.

"Honey, you did what you're supposed to do," Angela said. "You're the parent, not his friend. You can't worry so much about him liking you. Eventually, if you do your job and teach him how to survive in this world, he will love you for it. 'Please and thank you' are non-negotiable. Don't you think you deserve that much?"

Lucy saw, in that moment, what Harlan had been trying to say to her. It wasn't just a matter of capitulating to the whims of a four-year-old for some momentary peace, but a decision to focus on eventual outcomes. She needed to move ahead of the obstacles, to see them for the temporary roadblocks they were, instead of letting them knock her off her feet. It required a toughness and a sureness of foot that she wasn't sure she had. But then Mat came downstairs from his room. He stood in front of her, his face streaked with tears. The receiver fell out of her hand as he spoke in the direction of her knees.

"Thanks . . . you."

seventeen

M^{y Lucy,}

It's June now, when all teachers remember why they became teachers: to have the summer off. Ending an academic year has a way of resetting the clock, and I'm hoping you've reset yours, Lucy. I hope you're barreling along now, full steam, because everything is ahead of you. You get to fill in the blank squares on your calendar, and it doesn't matter if it's jury duty or a root canal or bunion surgery; it's life, and you get to live it.

If you can bear with me, I have the need to get philosophical.

What's your average life span now? Seventy-five, eighty years? In your thirties, you're still riding up that arc, reaching for something you hope to achieve. A few people manage to buck expectations and stay productive on the other side. Frank Lloyd Wright, if I remember correctly, designed some of his most impressive buildings in his seventies and eighties.

The sad part of my way-below-average life span—other than the obvious—is knowing that everyone will look at what came before my illness and view it through that lens. Why did the poor guy bother with all that education? It's too bad he didn't get married and have kids early, leave something of himself behind. If he had known when his life would end, he never would have fill-in-the-blank.

Why am I telling you this, other than to grovel in self-pity? It's to make sure you know that you can't take the arc for granted. And to tell someone—or maybe just to remind myself—that my shortened arc doesn't erase or even alter what came before. I refuse to believe that.

I often think about the time earlier this year, after my second brush with death, when I had a short remission and even allowed myself to imagine being well again. I truly enjoyed that trip we took to Hershey Park, when we rode that embarrassing little factory ride and ate chocolate and watched the kids on the roller coasters, and I pretended I was a normal person who had my calendar filled all the way through Christmas. It was a nice fantasy, and it's those kinds of memories that sustain me now. I want you to have more memories like that, even if they're with someone else.

That little interlude almost made it more difficult when the tumors began to grow again. I never told you this, but Dr. Singh gave me the number of a hospice a few months ago, when I was at my lowest point. A week later, he called me to say I was eligible for the phase 1 trial. But it was always a long shot just to get me ready for a bone-marrow transplant, which was another long shot. I agreed to the experimental stuff in part because all these doctors wanted so badly to give me another chance and in part because of you. I didn't want to let you down. We have one of those rare connections, Lucy. I'm my best and most comfortable self in your presence, and you've made it clear how much you want me to stick around. But after they chemo'd me into the ground for the umpteenth time, the color just drained away. I couldn't do it anymore. As hackneyed as it may sound, there's no point in fighting the battle when you don't think you can win the war.

I regret, sometimes, that we didn't spend a lot of time together before my illness. If we had, if Sylvie had never been in the picture, I'm sure you would have better memories of me. Back in the day, I was a lot of fun. If I thought I could become that person again, I would force myself to wait, to see if medical science might catch up to my disease, as you so strongly advocate. But that person is gone, Lucy. I don't know if he was suctioned out the first time they tested my bone marrow, or if

*he was blasted with toxic chemicals during my last chemo treatment,
but he's not coming back.*

*It might seem a little contradictory for me to advise you to move on
when I'm inserting myself into your monthly chores with these e-mails.
I only want to remind you that you have a long, long story that's yet
to be told. I need to think that you'll propel yourself ahead instead of
dwelling on the past.*

Love, as always,

Harlan

Mat was calling her from the other room, but Lucy stayed in her
chair, holding the words in front of her, letting them float in and
out of focus.

She had no idea that Harlan's doctor had given him the number
of a hospice before he started the experimental treatments. She
couldn't imagine what he did with that information or which part of
his brain had tried to cope with the idea that no one could help him
anymore. And yet, when the chance came for the phase 1 trial, he had
agreed, not because he thought it would help, but because his doctors
weren't ready to give up and because Lucy had wanted to prolong his
life. Maybe they had all just pushed him too far with their positive
reinforcement and their desperate hope. He was the one living it,
and they couldn't have known—not even his doctors—what he was
feeling inside.

She went back to the top of the e-mail, to the arc. So that's what
happened when you knew you were dying; you sought patterns
to make sense of it, to give it some shape that could be replicated,
described by a mathematical equation. And that might explain the
e-mails, too, the need to pass along something learned, something
others could put to use, like those parents who started organizations
against drunk driving or to prevent choking hazards or to require
fences around swimming pools, so that their child wouldn't have
died in vain.

She read the e-mail again, still lost in the words, which she could hear being spoken as though Harlan himself was standing by her side. His voice had been fading, but this note brought it back with all its resonance.

Just as she closed her eyes, Mat came in on all fours, pushing his Tonka truck until he was close enough to tug on her leg.

"Cokie," he said.

"Just a minute, Mat." She could let him wait now, had finally realized that her constant ministrations and availability only diminished her in his eyes. She had grown more opaque, holding her need to be loved like a hand of cards, close to her chest. And it was working. More and more often now, Mat came to her.

She turned back to the computer as Mat ran the Tonka truck under her chair. When he stood up next to her and stared at the computer screen, she felt somehow that he was reading Harlan's e-mail, though she knew it wasn't possible. She closed it quickly, as though she were hiding a love letter.

"One more minute," she said, glancing back at the e-mail directory. A new e-mail had arrived, apparently while she had been communing with Harlan's ghost. This one was from Dean Humphrey.

Lucy,

While I appreciate your work on this piece—and it's a good one—I don't remember discussing a joint effort with you. Please call me as soon as possible to explain Louis Beauchamp's role.

Dean

She read it again. *A joint effort?* She had hoped to scrape by with the article, just buy herself another year so she could settle in with Mat and get her academic life back on track. What did Louis have to do with it?

Mat tugged on her sleeve, and she got up, following him downstairs to the kitchen. She handed him a cookie and spread some peanut butter—he never seemed to get enough—on a slice of bread.

She had to call Louis. She opened the refrigerator for some milk and saw that she would have to go shopping again: bread, eggs, orange juice, cheese, apples, more peanut butter. What did it mean? *A joint effort.* Louis was supposed to walk the article from her desk to the dean's office. Was Dean Humphrey upset that she hadn't delivered it personally? She bent down to get a new sponge from under the sink. She needed dishwashing detergent, too. And more cookies. How could such a small boy consume so much?

"*Kotka?*" Mat said, which surprised her, because she hadn't heard him use a Russian word in at least a week. She picked up her Russian-English dictionary, which was on the counter near the kitchen phone, but she didn't have to look it up because she noticed that Mat was pointing at the cat clock, its tail incessantly swinging.

"Cat? Are you looking for the cat?" She wondered if he had just noticed it was gone. "The cat is with Nana."

"Nana?" he said.

"Nana has *kotka*," Lucy said, picking up a piece of paper and a blue crayon to draw a primitive sketch of her mother's living room. She drew the cat, placing him on the floor near her mother's couch. She had started to add some exaggerated whiskers when the phone rang.

"Hello." She held the phone with her shoulder so she could delineate the cat's paws. She had never been particularly good at art, but she was quite pleased with her drawing. At least it was identifiable as a cat.

"Lucy, this is Yulia. You are with Mat?"

"He's here. What's wrong? You sound upset."

There was a pause on the other end of the line, a pause so blatantly awkward and long that Lucy felt it physically. An abdominal cramp nearly caused her to double over.

"It's Mat's father, Vasily. He is here. He called from JFK. He is renting car to drive to Baltimore. He wants to see his son."

Lucy dropped the crayon, which hit the counter and rolled to the floor. This was both impossible to believe and the inevitable result of Yulia's manipulations, as well as Lucy's own complicity. A faint whine in her ear grew louder until she could barely hear herself when she spoke.

"He doesn't have a son anymore, Yulia. He signed the termination papers. He's my son now."

"I'm afraid this may not be true," Yulia said, sighing deeply. "Vasily says he never signed any papers. Zoya Minsky apparently signed for him. He says he agreed to the adoption but never sent paperwork. Now he has changed his mind."

"Changed his—how is that possible?" Mat was on the floor, retrieving the crayon. Lucy took the last few chocolate chip cookies out of the bag, gave him a small stack, and took the phone into the closet, closing the door.

"I'll get a lawyer. I'll get a restraining order. He gave him up, Yulia, stuck him in that dark, sad place, and now he wants him back? And he probably beat him, too. Do you know how hard you have to beat a child to leave a permanent scar?"

The musty coats in the closet brushed her face, closing her in. She reached around and pulled the chain on the light switch; the bare bulb half blinded her as she shifted the phone to the other ear in the absurd hope that it would change what Yulia was telling her.

"All this I know. But if Vasily didn't sign, as he says, then you may have trouble for taking Mat out of his home country."

"I'm the one? I'm the—" It hit her now, everything she had feared and tucked into small hidden corners of her brain whenever Yulia made her excuses. Lucy realized she was on her own now, and she vowed that no one would take Mat away, not after she and her family had chipped away at his brittle exterior enough to see the vulnerable little boy beneath. She hung up on Yulia and emerged from the closet, wiping her face before Mat could see her tears.

"More cat," he said, handing her a blank sheet of paper.

She drew him another cat with a curious calm, her hand perfectly steady as her mind raced into dead ends, all involving extended courtroom scenes that dissolved into Mat being torn from her arms. Mat's father was driving down from New York, could be at her door within hours. She had a shocking image of Mat being dragged into a car with dark-tinted windows.

"Come on, sport," she said, faking a smile. "We're going for a ride."

Lucy strapped Mat into his car seat, then ran back into the house to throw some of their clothes into a large plastic garbage bag. She grabbed his monkey and his penguin and dropped her keys twice before she could finally lock the door. The sky was so heavy with dark clouds that it looked as if one might be crowded out, dropping directly on them. Before getting in the car, she took out her cell phone.

"Ma, it's me. I need your help, and I need some money."

A half hour later, Lucy pulled into Paul and Cokie's driveway and rested her forehead on the steering wheel. A drop of blood fell onto her bare leg, just below where her shorts ended. She touched her mouth, and her fingers came away red from where she had bitten the inside of her lip until it was torn.

Rosalee and Paul both emerged from the house. Rosalee took Mat out of his car seat as Paul gently opened the driver's door as though Lucy were an invalid and might need help walking. She found a tissue, blotted her lip, then followed Paul into the cavernous foyer.

Molly was the first to spot Mat.

"Hey there, buddy. I'm your cousin Molly," she said, kneeling in front of him. Mat backed away from her to stand behind Lucy. Then Sean and Jack came in with a soccer ball and rolled it toward Mat, who kicked it back.

"Would he go with them to the backyard?" Paul asked. "I think the rain will hold off for a while."

"I'm not sure," Lucy said, afraid to have Mat leave her, even for a few minutes. But when she turned around, Mat was already gone. She saw him running down the hallway behind Jack toward the back of the house. It struck her, painfully, that he probably missed playing with other children. She had kept him to herself, except for the one disastrous playground visit. She looked up, wishing the foyer didn't have such a high ceiling. A smaller space would have helped her feel less exposed.

Cokie came down the sweeping staircase, pausing just long enough in front of the ballerina painting to make it appear to Lucy that she was one of them: tall, slender, her hair now evenly and professionally blond.

"C'mon." Cokie herded them from the foyer into the kitchen, taking charge with the authority of her newly minted success. "Let's all take a deep breath and figure this out."

Bertie emerged from the bathroom pale and weak, to join them around the kitchen counter. Lucy couldn't bear to look at him, knowing her own face was just as drained, just as terrified. Rosalee spoke first.

"You can't go home, that's a given. He'll look there first. Then he'll probably come to our house. Yulia knows where it is."

Paul interrupted. "Whose side is she on, anyway? Did you get the impression that she's okay with her brother-in-law taking him back?"

"She just sounded"—Lucy tried to think—"resigned, like she couldn't do anything about it."

Cokie put a coffeepot on the counter and took mugs from the cabinet, grouping them near the pot. Lucy wanted to swipe them all to the floor, because coffee was what people drank during dramatic family discussions on television, in soap operas, consulting their cups as if they held all the answers. But there wouldn't be any answers inside her cup, and she knew she couldn't hold one without shaking.

"Stay here," Paul said. "We have room."

Lucy nodded, grateful for the offer, though she couldn't accept it. She wrapped her arms around herself, warding off the chill from the air-conditioning, or was it from inside her, cold dread penetrating something central, her liver or her spleen. Vasily would find them here. The spaces were too large, too open, the ceilings too high. Yulia would be convinced, or forced, to reveal things. Vasily would find out that Lucy had a brother and look him up on the Internet. If she knew anything about Mat's father, she knew that he was a *sobaka*. A dog. Yulia had told her as much on the day of her fingerprint scan.

"I have to leave." Her breath became shallow. "I need to get out of here, get a head start before he figures out where we might be."

Rosalee slipped off her stool, left the kitchen, and came back with her purse. She handed Bertie an ATM card.

"Get whatever you can," she said.

"Let's go," Paul said, and Bertie followed him into the hallway, shuffling as though he had aged ten years.

Lucy hated taking their money, but she had only a few hundred dollars in her own checking account and wasn't due to be paid until the following week. She looked down at the car keys in her hand. She was gripping them so tightly her skin had turned white.

Canada. Montreal. The Grey Nuns would take them in, hide them until Mat's father gave up and went home. Saint Marguerite would guide them to safety. Cokie placed a cup of coffee in front of her.

"Lucy," she said. "Are you okay?"

Lucy looked at her, seeing for the first time the spidery lines branching around Cokie's eyes.

"I have a plan," Lucy said.

"What is it?" Rosalee asked, peering out the kitchen windows at Mat in the backyard. She rattled her spoon in her coffee.

"It's somewhere safe. I'll find a way for you to let me know when Vasily leaves."

Rosalee kept her eyes trained on Mat, still fiddling with the spoon.

"Ma, look at me."

Rosalee turned her wide brown eyes toward Lucy, who had expected to see resentment—because it must now be clear to her mother that she hadn't checked out the agency thoroughly enough, had rushed headlong off a cliff without regard for the people standing on the rim shouting warnings. But there was only fear.

"Don't let anyone take our baby," Rosalee said. The mug dropped from her hand, splattering the floor and the cabinets with coffee, and the spoon bounced away, landing near the sink. Cokie grabbed a roll of paper towels from the dispenser and unspooled them onto the floor. They were still wiping down the cabinets when Paul and Bertie returned.

Paul laid a thick white cash envelope on the counter, and Bertie placed another one on top of it.

"That should see you for a couple weeks," Paul said. "We can always send more."

"I should get going." Lucy looked out the window and saw the boys kicking soccer balls. Mat kicked a ball that bounced off a tree and ricocheted back to hit him on the forehead. She almost ran out until she saw that he was laughing as Sean rubbed his own head and threw himself to the ground.

"Thanks for the money, really. I'll pay you back." As she walked out the back door, they all followed: Rosalee, Bertie, Paul, and Cokie, moving almost as one as Lucy approached Mat and took his hand.

"Thanks, guys, we'll see you soon."

Mat pulled his hand away from Lucy and ran back toward one of the soccer balls. She turned around, imploring her little knot of supporters to help.

"Get in your car, Lucy," Cokie said, taking charge again. "We'll bring him out."

Lucy followed the slate path from the back of the house around to the driveway. The rain clouds had merged into one thick layer, a vast gray mattress above her head. She kept blinking, but the path blurred in front of her, the colors merging and re-forming into an abstract mosaic. She got into the car and stuffed the envelopes of cash into her purse, peeling the keys from the palm of her left hand, which was pockmarked as though she had been gripping a grenade.

Rosalee emerged first, then Bertie, then Cokie, followed by Paul, who was carrying Mat upside down by his ankles. Mat's mouth was hanging open, and Lucy couldn't tell if he was laughing or crying. Paul flipped him right side up. Oh, good. Laughing. But then crying, no howling, as Paul strapped him into his car seat.

Her parents leaned into the driver's-side window to kiss her good-bye as Paul closed the door on Mat's screams, which trapped them in the car with her, giving them extra volume. She was almost grateful for the screaming, which hastened her exit, left no time to rethink. She backed down the driveway.

"I know, I know," Lucy said over and over, although she realized she couldn't know, could never put herself completely inside his confusion, just as she could never put herself inside Harlan's pain. As they made their way toward the interstate, the mantra either calmed Mat down or annoyed him so much that he fell asleep. She drove north on I-95, her foot bearing down on the accelerator, easing up only when she saw she was approaching eighty. She couldn't afford a speeding ticket.

The rain finally started as she drove across the Delaware Memorial Bridge, with its central towers spiraling above her and its elegantly curved supports, both rigid and fluid at the same time—one of those feats of engineering indecipherable to a student of religion but which seemed to have some spiritual meaning all the same. In the mood that overcame her, she saw tragedy there, the reaching, reaching, reaching, and the inevitable return to earth. Harlan's arc. The rain pounded on the windshield, and the wipers whipped a reprimand back and forth: *your-fault, your-fault, your-fault.*

She couldn't comprehend how her life had imploded in the course of one morning. As she passed the Welcome to New Jersey sign, it occurred to her that she might never be able to go back. What if Mat's father stayed here, ignoring the return date on his visa? Or what if he returned to Russia, and she came back to Baltimore, and then Yulia ratted her out? What would prevent him from getting on a plane again? Doubts pelted her like the rain on the roof of the car. What if there was no God, no saintly intercession, only you and your half-blind choices and the random collision of events in the universe and, in the end, only death? She fought it, but the doubts crept into her brain, prying up the boards of faith she had so carefully nailed down.

As the rain let up, a slice of blue sky emerged on the eastern horizon. Then Mat woke up and said, "Potty."

She had to drive for another fifteen minutes before reaching one of the Jersey Turnpike's enormous rest areas, and in that time she nailed down the boards again. She couldn't afford to stop believing that something beyond her own feeble capacities guided her through this life. She couldn't live without allowing for the possibility that Harlan's soul carried on, someway, somehow. She took Mat out of his car seat and held one of his hands as he gripped the front of his pants with the other. They ran through the parking lot and made it to the toilet just in time.

"One disaster avoided," she whispered as she and Mat stood inside one of the long line of bathroom stalls. After she washed his hands, the two of them waited at McDonald's for a Happy Meal. Here was the promise of America: happiness right there on the menu for the low, low price of $2.99. If she could drive straight through, they could be in Canada tonight, where happiness might cost a little more. Mat was talking to himself in Russian, which she hadn't heard in a while. Then he became agitated, pulling on her arm. He was repeating a phrase, which Lucy finally realized was in English.

"No airplane," he said again and again.

She looked around. The rest area didn't look anything like an airport to her, but to Mat's eyes, it must have been similar enough, with its food stalls and large bathrooms and extensive parking lot.

"No, Mat, I won't take you on another airplane for a long, long time," she said. "We're not leaving."

But they were leaving everything that was just becoming familiar to him—his room and his toys and his grandparents. They were leaving with no guarantee that they could ever return. She took the Happy Meal from the counter and found a table, spreading out the hamburger wrapper and french fries for Mat. Then she thought of Vasily, Mat's father, and how he had traveled all the way from Russia. If he was a child beater with no interest in raising his son, then why had he come all this way? She opened Mat's milk carton, inserting the straw.

Was there even a chance he genuinely loved his son? And if he did, would he ever give up trying to find him?

Mat ate his french fries methodically, dipping each into the tiny paper cup of ketchup she retrieved for him from the condiment bar. Then he ate a few bites of his hamburger and reached into the Happy Meal box for the toy. It was a purple plastic sound maker. One end was a whistle and had knobs that made various clicking sounds. He played with it as she held the hamburger up to his mouth for a couple more bites.

What if Yulia had been misinformed about Mat's history? What if Mat was placed in the orphanage without Vasily's consent? On the other hand, who was this Vasily? How would she even know if he was Mat's real father? She looked at Mat, who was spinning the sound maker on the table, which meant it could fly off into someone else's Big Mac at any moment. Mat would know, she realized. He would recognize his father, even after months and months without contact.

She cleared the wrappers and half-full milk carton from the table as Mat ran to pick up his sound maker, which had skidded under another table. She suddenly felt so empty, so drained, that she had to stand in line again to order a Filet-O-Fish so she wouldn't faint. Mat stood next to her in line, looking up, worry playing around his eyes. He sat quietly as she ate her sandwich.

"Follow me, Mat." Her strength had returned just enough to contemplate getting behind the wheel again. She stopped near the front door of the rest area and bought a Coke from a soda machine for the drive home.

She would have to find out for herself what kind of father Vasily was, his motives for sending Mat away and suddenly wanting him back. If she didn't, she would dread that phone call, that knock on the door, for the rest of her life.

...

LUCY OPENS HER EYES, aware that the blanket has slipped down, leaving her shoulders exposed. She pulls on it gently, and Harlan stirs, his arm pulling her closer. She closes her eyes again and shifts minutely, trying to ease the pressure on her hip bone.

His mouth is near the back of her neck, where her long hair is pushed away. She feels the heat of his breath. Then she feels his lips graze her skin. It's not a kiss exactly, maybe just inadvertent touching, which can happen when two people sleep so close together. She wants to turn toward him, but she's afraid. What if he didn't mean to touch her? She rests a hand on the cold cement floor to make sure she's awake. She has wanted this for years, but not this way, not as the result of his fear.

He kisses her neck again. This time she is sure it's a kiss, but she holds her body still. She wants to give him time, to make sure he wants her, not just because she's sympathetic and inches away.

She waits for several minutes, but there are no more kisses. She feels him move and turns toward him.

Harlan is on his back now. He is snoring softly as the sky behind the pine trees begins to lighten. She watches the sky as it takes on the subtle orange and pink gradations of a peach.

He opens his eyes and blinks a few times, disoriented. She leans forward to see if he will meet her halfway.

"My back," he says, groaning.

"What's wrong? Is it bad?" she says.

He rolls over onto his side and struggles to sit upright.

"Just stiff, I think," he says, twisting at the waist. He staggers up, stumbling over the cushions, then drapes himself over the balcony, letting his feet come just off the ground. He balances on his stomach, letting his arms dangle over his head.

"Be careful," she says. "You'll fall."

"It feels good," he says. "Gets the kinks out."

She sees a newspaper deliveryman walking up the sidewalk and asks him to call the super. "We're locked out," she says. He nods.

Ten minutes later, the super lets them back inside the apartment, where she shakes off her chill. Harlan follows her to the kitchen as the super lets himself out, promising to come back later to fix the lock on the slider.

"I had this problem last year on C block, but never on B," he says. "You're the first."

"Lucky me," she says, turning to Harlan. "Coffee?"

He looks at his watch.

"I guess I have time," he says. "I have to pick up Sylvie at nine."

The name, this time, is like the slip of a knife.

. . .

IT WAS ALMOST DARK when Lucy pulled into her complex and saw Louis sitting on her porch. The rain had stopped, and the sky was now a dusty gray that reminded her of Murmansk. Louis stood up and held the door open for her as she carried a sleeping Mat inside and up the stairs. She deposited him on the bed, pulled a blanket over him, and left, leaving the door ajar. When she came back to the living room, Louis was on the couch, his head in his hands.

"There's something I should have told you the other night," he said, looking up. "It's about your paper."

She stood in front of the fireplace, nodding for him to go on. There was no sign that Vasily had been there, no note on the door, no phone message. She allowed herself to hope that Yulia had been wrong, mixed up, or that she had somehow convinced her brother-in-law to go back home and leave Mat with her.

"It's like this," he said, taking a long breath. "The word was out after you left for Russia that they might not renew your contract. So when you asked me to deliver the paper to Dean Humphrey, I read it, and I thought you were right. It was rough. So I smoothed it out, rewrote it in parts. Actually, I rewrote most of it. I didn't add any new information, but I realized that, ethically, I had to add my name as a secondary author." ✦

As he said the words "secondary author," her eyes fell on a tiny hole in the thin fabric of the gray T-shirt he wore. She could focus on nothing but the hole, which was on the seam of his right shoulder. It didn't seem possible that he was telling her she might lose her job on the same day she had been told she might lose Mat and had almost ditched her life at Ellsworth and made a run for Canada.

"You were concerned about the ethics of it?" she said, finding her voice. "Well, ethically, you had no right to touch that paper. I didn't even ask you to read it."

"But I had no way to get in touch with you. I thought you might lose your job if you turned it in the way it was."

The way it was. She took his words as an accusation, as though her efforts reflected poorly on all students of religion.

"I still might lose my job, as if that matters anymore. The dean wants to know why your name is on it, and I don't blame him . . . Why didn't you say something the other night?"

Louis sighed. "I tried. I did. I almost had it out a few times. I'm sorry."

She didn't care as much about the paper as she did about Louis's smug assumption that she needed his help. But none of it mattered anymore. She came close to telling him about Mat's father but decided he would just start telling her what to do. Her copy of the *Saint Blaise* biography was on the side table near the couch. She grabbed the book, opened the front door, and pitched it as far as she could. It bounced a few times, then landed on the grass, its pages spread open to the murky sky.

"I didn't ask for your help. I'm thirty-eight years old, and I take responsibility for my own mistakes."

He appeared to be working on an addendum to his explanation, so she waited. He stalled, tugging on the short sleeves of his T-shirt until they were almost down to his elbows. The hole grew bigger.

"I didn't think it through. I just wanted to help."

"Did I appear to be so incompetent that I couldn't help myself? Am I so clueless that you had to step in and show me the way? Is that what happened? Did it ever occur to you that I would have taken care of it when I got back?"

He mumbled something she couldn't hear.

"I really don't need this right now," she said.

He got up slowly and walked to the front door, looking back at her.

"I just wanted you to have another chance, and I thought it would take the pressure off, so you could focus on Mat. Doesn't that count for something?"

"Go home," she said. "I can't talk about this anymore."

She watched as he went down the porch steps, struck that people interceded in her life so much more frequently than the saints and without her asking. Even Harlan fit into this category, deciding that she needed his advice even after he was dead. When Louis reached the *Saint Blaise* book, he picked it up, closed it, dusted the dirt off the spine, and placed it back on the grass. Then he walked off in the direction of the library spire without looking back.

eighteen

L ucy woke suddenly from a fitful sleep. Just before she went to
bed, she had spoken on the phone for an hour with her mother,
who had wanted her to drive back to Paul and Cokie's in case Mat's
father showed up in the middle of the night. She squinted at the digital clock and saw that the first number was a five, the second was a
zero, and the third was an eight, sharp-edged and red. She wanted
the rounded eights of her youth back, the eights that represented
infinity, which didn't have corners.

She began to drift off again, swirling around on the endless loops
of a rounded eight, but some noise kept her from sleeping, drove
out all thoughts of past or present numerals, hammered into her
consciousness like a nail, and triggered the memory of all that had
happened the day before. Someone was knocking at the door.

She slipped her legs past the cool edges of the sheets and put her
feet flat on the floor. The knocking grew louder, and she grabbed her
robe, hoping Mat wouldn't wake up. Downstairs, she peeled aside the
curtain at the window closest to the door, expecting to see a hulking
Russian man dressed in black. Instead, she saw only Yulia, who was
using the curved wooden handle of her umbrella to rap on the door.
She wore a raincoat and men's dress shoes that were way too large for
her feet, the laces dangling. Lucy let her in.

"I hope you're here to tell me your brother-in-law went back
to Russia."

"I wish it were so," Yulia said. She slipped her feet out of the men's shoes and took off her raincoat, draping it over the back of the couch. "He called last night from Atlantic City, where he stayed with friend he used to know in Russia. He will arrive this morning, so we need plan. I call you many times yesterday, but no answer, so I come as early as possible to give us time."

Lucy didn't want to plan. Planning would acknowledge that Mat's father had some leverage. In the hours that had passed since she turned around in New Jersey, she had become convinced that the law would protect her. No court would hand Mat back to a father who put him in an orphanage. She crossed her arms.

"If you think he's going to walk in here and take Mat, you're wrong," she said. "I'll call the police."

Yulia pinched the bridge of her nose. "Do you have coffee?" She followed Lucy to the kitchen and sat down on a stool at the counter.

"Vasily did not sign papers," Yulia said, fiddling with a crayon Mat had left on the counter. "He says he can prove this."

"I don't care if he didn't sign the papers. You said he was a dog, Yulia. A dog. How could you let him take Mat?"

"Maybe he just wants money. So we offer him money to sign papers and go away."

Mechanically, Lucy placed the filter in the coffeemaker and filled it with coffee grounds. She pushed the button, then realized she had forgotten to put in the water. When she filled the reservoir, the pot hissed.

"You think that's all he wants?"

"I meet him only once, at Mitya's wedding. But she wrote letters, so I know that he buys many things—iPod, stereo, game system."

Could it be that easy? If she managed to scrape together a few thousand more dollars, would he just go away? She was back in the used-car lot, finding out she would have to shell out far more than she thought for a car that actually ran. She felt a tug on her robe and looked down, thinking she had caught it on the edge of the counter.

It was Mat, and now it was too late to pretend to Yulia that she had hidden him away with a distant relative.

"Well, hello," she said. Mat looked up at her, his eyes half-closed. "Did we wake you up?"

Yulia sat up with a start, her too-long bangs falling across one eye. She brushed them away.

"Look at you, Azzie," she said, as though she had forgotten that he was the object of all her scheming. "His face has filled out. He looks so much like his mother."

Envy, with all its irrational force, hit Lucy like a slap. *She* was his mother, not some careless young Russian woman who didn't know enough to stay out of the way of a speeding car. She wanted to push Yulia off the stool, shove her out the door, and lock it behind her. But then she looked at Mat, who was rubbing his eyes. She noticed the altered shape of his cheeks, the glow of sufficient calories and vitamin-packed cereals and juices. Was it his fault he looked like his mother? She poured him a cup of orange juice.

"How much should I offer him?" she asked Yulia, handing Mat the cup. He took a sip.

"Let me talk to him, try to find out what he wants, and then I call you. Stay here."

Yulia slugged down a half cup of coffee in one gulp, tousled Mat's hair, then grabbed her raincoat, slipped on the men's shoes, and left.

...

"WHAT ARE YOU talking about? You can't be serious."

Angela stood on the porch watching Vern toss a white plastic baseball to Matt on the tiny patch of grass in front of Lucy's duplex. They had shown up a few hours after Yulia left, Angela barging in with a gift bag for Mat stuffed with a plastic baseball bat, a mitt, and a dozen plastic balls. "We decided not to wait for an invitation," she had said.

"His father is here? In the US?" Angela went on. "Why on earth would he be here?"

"I wish I knew. Apparently he didn't sign the adoption papers. Yulia thinks he wants money. And if that's all he wants, I'll hock my furniture, my car, my parents' furniture, and their car. But would he come all this way just to ask for money, when he could have bribed me over the phone? It would have cost him a fortune for the plane ticket."

Lucy flipped through her mental Rolodex of saints for one who could deliver her from this mess. She could have called on three or four, but it seemed more prudent to direct all her energies to one, and she settled on Saint Rita of Cascia. Saint Rita took on desperate cases, like Saint Jude, but Lucy reasoned that Saint Jude, being better known, got many more requests. There was a shrine to Saint Rita in Philadelphia, just a few hours away.

Angela pinched her hard on the arm. "Why are you standing here? You should be on the phone with a lawyer."

She was right, of course. It was possible that Mat's father had no legal standing, even if he hadn't signed the papers. She ducked into the house for her cordless phone, came back to the porch, and let Angela dial the lawyer who had handled her divorce.

Mat opened his tiny glove and caught a ball that Vern had tossed from about four feet away. Mat grinned, holding up the glove for her to see. Lucy's heart shifted in her chest, almost crowding out her lungs and stifling her breath. She wondered if he felt even a fraction of that love for her.

"Here, talk to him." Angela handed her the phone.

Lucy condensed her story as much as possible but got across the point that Mat's father hadn't signed the termination papers and might want his son back. The lawyer said he'd look up whatever case law or statutes he could find and call her back. She put the phone down on the porch railing as Angela put her hand on the middle of Lucy's back, holding it there, propping Lucy up as she watched her son discover the thrill of baseball.

"He's not going anywhere," Angela said. "You got the fish wallpaper and everything. He belongs with you."

Lucy found a hangnail on her right thumb and tore it off, leaving a patch of raw skin.

"Not that many weeks ago, we were complete strangers," she said. "When I look at him now, I find that so hard to believe."

Lucy rested her forearms on the porch railing as Mat crawled into the hedges to look for the ball. The waiting was torture, a form of physical abuse that affected not only her stomach but her head, her vision, her muscles, her nervous system.

The phone rang.

"Lucy, it's Yulia."

She almost dropped the phone into the bushes but caught it before it fell. Denial was the only acceptable path. She could speak to Yulia if she convinced herself that Vasily was on a plane back to Russia.

"He wants to see Azamat."

"Absolutely not."

"He says he will meet with you first, then see his son. If not, he says he will call Russian Embassy."

Lucy still had the lawyer in her pocket, researching the case. She could meet with Vasily, size him up, stall.

"Does he speak English?"

"You come to my office at noon. I translate."

Lucy had the feeling Vasily was standing over Yulia's shoulder, threatening her. She pictured him as a bully, a man who didn't let women tell him what to do. She imagined the coarseness of his features, the fleshy neck, the ruddy skin. He would have meaty hands, like a butcher's, and large pores on his face. Black, shapeless clothes and thick-soled shoes.

"I'll be there, but I'm not bringing Mat." She could hear Yulia turn away from the phone and speak in Russia.

"For now, he says this is okay. We see you at noon."

...

LUCY SENT MAT off with Angela and Vern, who wanted to take him to a video arcade. Then she went inside, took her black suit from the closet, and slipped into the jacket, which was too big. She started to take it off but changed her mind, sensing some residual power in its fabric. She wrapped the jacket around her, over her jeans, and fastened a thick black leather belt around her waist.

On her way out, she stopped in Mat's room, returned the stuffed penguin to the bed, and smoothed the comforter. Then she kneeled down and put her face on his pillow, breathing in the slightly sour little-boy scent lingering there. He had only been gone for ten minutes, but she missed him already. She ran her hand under the pillow and wondered who would tuck the tooth-fairy money under his sleeping head when he lost his first tooth. Would it be her? His father? Or no one at all?

She stood up and brushed off her knees, taking the stairs slowly. She passed through the living room, trailing her fingers over the dark swath on the back of the couch. The house was so empty without Mat, quiet and still, funereal. Was it possible she had ever lived there alone?

Before she left, the phone rang again. This time it was the lawyer.

"Basically, you don't have a lot of options," he said, and she listened, nodding. "If he can prove this is his son and that it's not his signature on the papers, then someone is in a whole mess of trouble."

Not someone. Her. And it wouldn't matter that her heart was in the right place or that she simply wanted to believe in something so much that she let it block out all doubt.

...

THE DOOR to Yulia's office was open. Lucy could see the strip of fluorescent light from all the way down the long corridor. It grew wider as she neared the door, and she slowed her pace, halting completely about five feet away. A man appeared in the doorway: a thin man, early thirties, with a scrawny beard, pale blue eyes, and eyelashes so light they gave the impression he had just come in from the snow. He was wearing a green jogging suit with a white stripe down the arms and legs. Lucy thought he might be the janitor.

"Lu-cy McVie?" he said.

He opened the door a little wider, and Yulia motioned from where she was standing behind her desk for Lucy to come in. She wore an expression Lucy had never seen before—an expression of powerlessness—and her hands were moving here and there in a way that suggested she had no control over them. One hand pulled on her earlobe as the other twisted the swiveling office chair back and forth.

The man in the jogging suit half sat, half leaned against Yulia's desk. It took Lucy a few seconds to realize that this was Vasily. This was Mat's father. And he wasn't a hulking brute but a man of below-average height who looked as though he needed a drink. She moved into the office and stood three or four feet away from Vasily, waiting for him to look up again. But he kept his gaze trained at the floor, his arms crossed, until Yulia left her position behind the desk, shut the door, and then came back to stand between them, as if they might throw punches at each other.

Vasily spoke in Russian to Yulia, who translated for Lucy.

"He wants that you hear his story," Yulia said. "Please sit down."

Lucy moved hesitantly toward the pumpkin slip-covered couch but couldn't bring herself to sit down on it. Instead, she balanced on the couch's arm and looked at Vasily, who still wouldn't look at her. His eyelids looked heavy, and his pockmarked skin told the story of teenage acne. He turned to Yulia and began speaking in a low voice as she paced from one end of the small office to the other and translated.

"He says Zoya Minksy sent him papers many months ago. He was very busy with business meetings and so forth and could not take the time to find witnesses and such. Then he could not find the papers, so he calls Zoya to get new papers, and she tells him his son has left for America. When he realizes this, he makes a plane flight to come to America, because he has been defrauded, and he lets no woman do this to him."

Vasily glanced at her then. He had an insecure-looking face that suggested poor nutrition and chain-smoking and the bitterness of a man who had never lived up to his own expectations.

"How do I know this is even Mat's father?" Lucy asked Yulia. "What if this is some con artist who heard about the adoption? You said you only met him once."

Yulia translated, and Vasily jumped up, pulling his wallet from a pocket in the sagging pants of the jogging suit. He opened it and pulled out a picture, thrusting it at Yulia, as though she had questioned his identity, not Lucy. Yulia took the picture and carried it over to Lucy, holding it open on the palm of her hand. It was Mat, at least a year younger, on the right, and his mother, Mitya, in the middle, with the short brown hair Mat had described, and this man, Vasily, on the left, sitting on the steps of what in America would be called a tenement.

None of them was smiling, and yet Lucy could tell that it had been a rare moment of family unity preserved on film. In the picture, Mat's little arm was resting on his mother's leg, as surely as if he were still an extension of her body. Mitya had her arm around Mat, and Vasily was leaning back with his elbows on the step behind him. The picture meant Lucy couldn't deny that Vasily was Mat's father, but she could see that he had held himself apart from his wife and son. She looked away.

"He brought his son to the children's home, Yulia. Ask him why he did that in the first place."

Yulia translated, and Vasily answered.

"After Mitya died, he say, he was very busy with work, with electronics store he manages. He work many hours and could not find good woman to watch his son and cook and clean for them. His parents are dead, and Mitya's parents—my parents—also dead. Nobody lives long in Russia anymore. So friends, er, people he knows, tell him he must give his son to the children's home and forget him. So he does this, because it is not a man's job to raise children."

Vasily pulled at the few strands of hair in his beard as Yulia translated for him, her hands darting around as she spoke as though she were Italian. Lucy heard the words, but they refused to form any meaning, bouncing through the air like particles of dust that settled on the desk or on the floor. She remembered sitting on the pumpkin couch for the first time, and the exact moment Yulia had handed her a picture of Mat. She made fists and dug her knuckles into her thighs hard enough to cause a dull pain.

"Ask him about the scars, Yulia. Ask him to explain why his son was beaten."

As Yulia translated, Lucy stood up and went to the single office window, peering through the plastic blinds at the sun baking the cars in the parking lot. The air-conditioning in Yulia's office was either too weak or not working, and she felt a trickle of sweat run down her back beneath the black jacket.

"No," Vasily said, and she turned. He opened his hand, palm up, and she thought he might make a run at her. He spoke rapidly in Russian, and Yulia nodded, finally holding up her hand to interrupt him.

"He say he only spank Azamat like this, with open hand. This is to make him better boy, for discipline."

"Then why does he have scars on his backside? The doctor said they were old scars. They weren't made at the orphanage."

When Yulia asked the question, the tops of Vasily's ears turned red. He spoke to Yulia with evident anger, and she translated that he disliked being accused of beating his son. He said that Azamat had climbed out of his crib when he was two and struck himself on the corner of the radiator. The stitches he needed must have left scars.

Lucy had been prepared for him to defend his beatings. She hadn't expected another explanation, especially one she had no way to disprove. If she hadn't rescued Mat, then what had she done? She felt as though a wall on which she had been standing was crumbling beneath her feet. She hated this person, this Vasily, for his simplicity, his explanations. Because she had taken Mat away, she wanted him to live up to his side of the equation. The magnitude of her generosity, her sacrifices, had to offset his pettiness, his selfishness, his anger.

"What does he want, Yulia? Does he truly want to take Mat back to Russia? To raise him? Does he understand what it means to raise a child, to lift him up? Does he know his son anymore?"

Yulia and Vasily spoke in voices so low that Lucy strained to hear, as if she could understand the words. Vasily looked at her, opening his snowy eyelashes. What she saw there was resentment, perhaps anger that something had been taken away from him. But she also saw stubbornness. She saw that he wouldn't go away until he got what he wanted.

"He wants to see his son, talk to him."

Lucy cried then, telling Yulia to explain how much she loved Mat, how she couldn't bear to part with him. She offered money, told Vasily to name his price, but he turned toward the desk with his hands in his pockets and stared at the dusty Beanie Babies on Yulia's computer. He made no response.

She nodded, looking down at her hands again as if she might be able to see right through them. She felt fragile, transparent again, as it became clear that Vasily would not give up and even more clear that she had no right to keep Mat from seeing his father. She stood up and found a piece of paper on Yulia's desk to write down the beltway exit to the playground where Mat had nearly killed them both on the slide. She wanted Vasily to see what a climber he was, how hard it was to watch him.

"We'll be at the playground this afternoon, at four."

As Lucy turned to go, Yulia mouthed the words "I'm sorry."

Lucy left the office, feeling her way along the walls as though she had been blinded. She drove home without feeling the steering wheel or the seat beneath her, surrounded by a halo of numbness. She couldn't ask a saint to intervene because she didn't know what was right, what was best. When she reached the duplex, she rested her forehead on the steering wheel and asked herself, what would Harlan do? She didn't know the answer.

It was one thirty. Only two and a half hours left, and Mat wasn't even home. She threw her purse on the floor and ran to the kitchen to call Angela's cell phone, telling her to bring Mat home as soon as she could. Then she called her mother and gave her the news.

"Get back in the car and run," Rosalee said. "You are his mother. This man abandoned him. He can't be allowed to change his mind."

"If I run, this will never end, Ma. I'm trying to do the right thing. I'm thinking about Mat. If he shows any fear at all, I won't let his father get near him. I promise. And we only agreed to a meeting, nothing beyond that." She said the words to comfort herself more than to comfort Rosalee.

"Where are you meeting him?"

"This giant playground off the beltway. But don't come. That'll just make things harder for Mat." She thought of him now, blithely riding in a car with Vern and Angela, no inkling that his father was so near, that his life could shift again, the seismic plates over which he had no control moving him back to the other side of the world.

The language would come back to him quickly, she knew that. In another few months, she would fade from his memory until there was nothing left but vague images: the stuffed penguin, the taste of peanut butter, a room painted yellow. It was what Harlan had feared most: being forgotten.

She heard a car pulling into the parking lot.

"Mat's here," she told her mother. "I have to go."

Angela opened the door, and Mat came into the duplex first, holding an enormous wad of cotton candy. Vern followed, carrying a plastic bag full of small stuffed animals.

"He's a little sticky," Angela said. "Man, you've got a hot one. He never stops moving."

Angela refused to look at Lucy, bringing Mat to the bathroom to wash his hands. Lucy stood in the living room smiling stupidly at

Vern, finally taking the bag of toys from his outstretched hand. When Angela returned with Mat, she looked at Lucy and began to cry.

"No." Angela pressed her fingers into her eyelids. "This is all wrong."

"Vern," Lucy said. "Would you play with Mat for a minute?" Angela followed her to the kitchen and watched as Lucy leaned over the sink to splash cold water on her face. She dried it with a paper towel.

"I agreed to let him see Mat, that's all," she said. "Then I'll know what to do."

"Why does he deserve a second chance?"

"I'm not sure he does. But he came all this way, so I'm also not sure he doesn't. I can't spend the rest of my life wondering if I took a child away from his father for all the wrong reasons."

Mat came into the kitchen to show Lucy his arcade winnings, and she ran a hand lightly across his forehead, just as she had seen Cokie once do with Sean. He seemed not to notice, and she realized he was gradually abandoning his aversion to being touched. She wanted to hold him then, to rock him like a baby and beg him not to leave her, because the act of his leaving would wrench open the void again, letting the mist of her yearning back in.

"Look at this alligator," she said, holding it up. "Did Vern win it for you?"

"He won it all by himself," Angela said. "The boy is a Skee-Ball prodigy. Hey, Vern, put your shoes back on. It's time to go."

"Thanks, Angela," Lucy said, walking her to the door. "For everything."

When Angela and Vern left, Lucy sat down on the couch, wondering if she should begin preparing Mat for what might happen next. Should she get him to talk about his father? Should she question him again about the scars? Before she could decide, he pulled a stack of books from a magazine rack next to the couch and climbed onto Lucy's lap. He rested his head against her shoulder, held up a book on construction equipment, and said, "You read." The weight and warmth of his little body was an offering she had almost stopped hoping to receive. It filled her, made her whole, and she would never forget it, even if he forgot her.

She read the construction book six times—at the last page, he would flip to the front and say "again"—and then she took out her camera, snapping pictures of him from every angle, trying to capture his true nature in a photograph that might have to sustain her for years to come. When he tired of smiling, she took him into the kitchen and fed him peanut-butter crackers with milk, watching the minutes tick by on the cat clock, which sent them into the terrifying future with every indiscriminate swish of its tail.

When it was time to go, she packed a water bottle and some snacks and a hat for Mat, in case there was too much glare on the playground. She drove in silence. If Mat ran to his father, embraced him, cried tears of joy, she would have to give him back. If he showed any fear, she would fight for him, offer more money, beg, plead, insist. If he showed no emotions at all, well, she would figure out what to do when the time came. There, a plan.

She pulled into the playground parking lot at 3:45, finding a space in the sea of minivans that belonged to mothers who wondered when they would ever be free of obligation, just when she might be forced to relinquish hers.

As she and Mat walked toward the entrance, she recalled the fear of the slide debacle and noticed the metallic taste in her throat, though maybe that had more to do with her new fear. Mat climbed onto some old tires and grabbed a rope hanging from a thick wooden beam, letting himself swing in a wide circle. Lucy sat on the pile of tires and rubbed her sticky palms on her knees. It was a warm day, but her armpits were cold with sweat. She glanced at her watch: 3:50.

At 3:55, she began looking around obsessively as Mat moved to a ladder that ended in a cone-shaped structure with a floor. A modern tree house. At 4:05, her mother emerged from behind a rocking wooden ship.

"I thought he was supposed to be here at four," Rosalee said.

"I told you not to come, Ma." Lucy looked around again. She caught a glimpse of a stout woman who could have been Yulia but turned out not to be. She looked at her watch again. Six after.

"How could I not come? We drove around the entire beltway to find it," she said. "Your father's in the car, and Paul and Cokie are in that submarine over there. We couldn't let you do this alone."

"Nana," Mat said as he slid down a connecting slide.

As Paul and Cokie emerged from the submarine, Mat ran to a wooden structure that resembled the Eiffel Tower. He climbed up to the first platform, then began to cry. They all ran to him.

"What's wrong, Mat?" Lucy said. He sat down, legs dangling, on the platform, which was about the height of Lucy's shoulders, and held out his hand. A small splinter protruded from the side of his index finger, and Lucy pulled it out, pinching it tightly with her fingernails. Then he did something he had never done before. He held out his arms. Held them out to her.

She lifted him off the platform and held him as he wrapped his legs around her waist. Then Rosalee hugged him from behind, and Paul and Cokie each took a side. Bertie, who by that time had emerged from the car, came over and threw his arms around Lucy. They stood there, one tangled mass of humanity, until Lucy couldn't breathe anymore. She looked at her watch again as they all separated and she put Mat back on the ground. It was 4:15.

"Where could they be?" Yulia wasn't known for her punctuality, but wouldn't Vasily have been impatient to see his son? Lucy had half expected him to be there waiting when they arrived. She felt Mat pulling on her hand toward the swings.

"Mama, you push," he said.

She turned to her father. "Did he just say . . . ?" but she didn't wait for his response. The word rose up around her like a shawl, wrapping her in warmth. But why now, why this connection when she might have to watch motherhood slip away? She glanced again at the time—4:23.

At 4:37, she called Yulia on her cell phone. Angela and Vern had arrived by then, having discovered where she was by calling Rosalee's phone. Lucy's anguish grew with each passing minute. It was cruel to keep them waiting.

"Lucy," Yulia said, sounding breathless on her end of the line. "I am just now calling your number."

"We're waiting here on the playground, Yulia. Where's Vasily? I thought you'd be here at four."

"But this is why I was calling," she said. "Vasily is gone."

"He's gone? I don't understand."

"He tells me he needs to go for coffee, but then he doesn't come back. He does not answer his phone."

Yulia sighed, and Lucy let her go on. "Before he left, I had long talk with him. I tell him what he must do to be good father to Azzie. I tell him you are good mother. Maybe he goes back to Russia."

Lucy looked at her family and friends, all hovering around Mat, and picked up the insulated snack bag. She should have been relieved, but now the question was out there, open-ended. Maybe he went back to Russia, but maybe he didn't, and that "maybe" would hold her hostage until she knew what happened to Vasily.

nineteen

Lucy shifted on the squeaky leather couch in the dean's office, waiting for him to finish a phone conversation. She rubbed her fingers against the leather, testing its thickness. She was no longer worried about saving her job, but she felt compelled to meet with the dean when he called. What had consumed her just a year ago—her classes, her saint research, her academic standing—seemed like . . . work. The only thing that mattered now was keeping Mat.

The dean hung up the phone. He tilted back in his chair and looked at her, widening his eyes, his reading glasses balanced on top of his head. She sensed he was sincerely puzzled by her behavior.

"So, give me the story," he said. "And I mean all of it. Why didn't you tell me you were adopting? I only heard about it yesterday from Angela."

"I'm not sure." And she wasn't. Why had she assumed he wouldn't be sympathetic? She watched him shuffle through some papers on his desk, looking for her article, she supposed. "I guess I thought you'd be worried about whether I could do my job."

He held up the paper and put on his reading glasses.

"You could have tried me. What I don't like is surprises, like the one I got when I read this."

He set the paper down on the desk, flicking off some unseen speck on its cover.

"I was just as surprised as you were." Lucy told him what had happened leading up to Vasily's disappearance, including her trip to Russia and how she had asked Louis to deliver the paper. "Louis was trying to help. I mean, I threw it together, to be honest with you. I was hoping you'd give me a chance to rewrite it when I got back."

The dean put his open hands together, a prayerful pose, then sat for a moment with his index fingers touching his nose. She had never been in the principal's office for punishment, but she imagined this is how it might feel.

"I'm going to cut you a break, Lucy," he said finally. "You have the summer to get your act together. I'll give you one less course to teach in the fall, but you'll have to show me you can handle the work as well as your research. The article, by the way, is very good. I think you should submit it to the journals, with Beauchamp's permission, of course. I don't condone what he did, but the circumstances were unusual, to say the least. I hope it works out with your son."

Lucy nodded and worked her way to the front of the leather couch, putting her weight into the black pumps she wore to such meetings. "Thank you," she said.

The dean walked her toward the door, and she whispered another "thank you" as he closed it gently on her words.

...

BACK AT HOME, Lucy called her mother and told her to bring Mat home. Though her parents preferred to think Vasily was long gone, they had agreed to help move Mat from house to house a few times a day in case he showed up again. She had just opened a new *Religion* journal to the table of contents when the doorbell rang. She peeked through the curtains and saw that it was Louis.

"Lucy, I need to talk to you," he said through the door.

She sat down on the floor, her back against the wall, and said nothing. When he spoke again, she touched the door, which vibrated slightly with the sound.

"Angela told me what happened with Mat. I can't believe it, Lucy. You could have lost him."

Could have lost him? Everyone else seemed convinced that Vasily had left for good, but she had none of their confidence, and nothing, not even Harlan's death, had caused her as much distress as the thought that he might come back.

"Are you okay? What can I do?" Louis said. She could hear that he wanted to be part of the story, felt left out, but she wasn't sure how much sympathy he deserved.

"You've done more than enough," she said, finally opening the door. She wasn't angry about the paper anymore. She even understood, intellectually, why he had interfered, but he should have confessed right away. It seemed like a cardinal relationship sin among people who worked together: *thou shalt not withhold job-related information.*

Louis walked past her, straight to the kitchen.

"Sit down," he told her. "You need something. Tea? Water? Seltzer? Have you eaten today? I could go get some takeout."

Louis put a glass of water and an apple on the table, and she sat down. When she made no move toward the apple, he got a knife from the kitchen and peeled off the skin, cutting it into wedges, placing them in front of her on a napkin.

She arranged the apple slices into the shape of a flower. "I spoke to the dean. He says we should submit the article."

Louis ran his fingers through his hair, shifting in his chair until he looked as if he might slide off. "He told me the same thing. That was the last thing I expected him to say."

She bit into one of the apple slices. It was sour, a McIntosh out of season.

"When did you talk to him?"

"He called me today. He wanted to remind me of my ethical responsibilities toward informing colleagues when I stick my nose in their work. But he also wanted to tell me about a job."

"At Ellsworth?" she said.

"UMass."

This was how things went in academia. She knew that. Graduate students rarely found jobs at the institutions that granted their degrees. They went elsewhere. But for some reason, it had never occurred to her that Louis might leave. For that, she blamed herself—her own insular mind-set these days—but she also blamed him. Surely he had given her the impression that he wasn't looking around.

"The religion department here is pretty small," he said, pointing out the obvious. "So I have to think about it."

"Of course you do," she said. It now seemed inevitable that he would leave. How could she not have seen that coming? On the other hand, their relationship couldn't be repaired anyway. He had damaged the framework, delicate to begin with.

"I've been meaning to ask you something," he said.

"Go ahead."

"Your friend, Harlan, the one who died last year. What's with these e-mails?"

"What?"

"I saw one printed out on your desk when I was working on your article. I'm sorry, but it caught my eye. How is he sending you e-mails?"

"He wrote them before he died," she said, uninterested in his response. She looked down at his feet and saw that he was wearing flip-flops, like the students did. She wanted him to be six years older instead of six years younger. Then he might be able to help her instead of sitting there with his unlined face full of misdirected concern. "They've been coming on the tenth of every month since January."

She had never discussed Harlan with Louis before. He had known about their friendship, of course, of how she cared for Harlan during his illness, but he had never asked her why.

"Wasn't it hard on you that he ended his life the way he did?" Louis asked.

"Why are we talking about this?" Harlan had become a cottage industry, of sorts, inside her mind. She wanted to silkscreen his words on T-shirts and sell them, but only to a small but devoted following.

"At the time, I thought it was selfish, what he did," Louis said. "You could have been the one to find him."

"It wasn't selfish," she said. She rolled up the napkin around the apple slices, bunched it in her hand. "He wanted to spare me, and everyone else, watching him waste away. I can't put myself in his place. Neither can you."

"He loved you, though. I could tell from what he wrote," Louis said. "Did you love him?"

She looked at him, unsure of whether he wanted the truth, then slowly nodded. There was no point in lying. She got up and threw the apple slices away.

"Good-bye, Lucy," he said. "I'll be in touch."

She walked him to the door and watched him go.

...

LUCY HANDS HARLAN a cup of coffee.

"You never asked your question," she says. "The one you came over to ask."

"That's right," he says, blowing on the coffee. "I never did."

She takes her cup to the counter and sits on a stool. She pushes her hair aside and rubs her face, certain that it's creased and distorted, speckled with migratory mascara. She feels frumpy, imagining Sylvie with her freshly brushed smile emerging from the train.

"It's a weird question," he says.

"Just ask it," she says, irritated now, having forgotten for a moment why he came over in the first place.

He sits down on the other stool, holding his mug as though it's something precious, an ancient artifact or a piece of antique porcelain.

"When two people should be together . . ." he says, trailing off.

She says nothing, for once leaving the void unfilled.

"When two people are meant for each other," he says, trying again, "can they still misunderstand each other? Can they still find it hard to explain what they need?"

She imagines him waiting at the platform for Sylvie, preparing to tell her about his illness, bracing for her response.

"If you want me to be honest, I think love transcends that. Two people, if they're meant to be together, shouldn't find it hard to explain what they need from each other. That's what I think."

"I see," he says, putting down his mug. He gives her a look she can't quite interpret. She detects sadness there, or disappointment, as though she has given him the wrong answer. "I guess you're right."

As he leaves, glancing at his watch, she wants to ask him a question. About the kiss. But he looks preoccupied, as well he might be. And so she says nothing. Only good-bye.

. . .

COKIE HANDED Lucy a bag of pretzels, and she emptied them into a large bowl from a Tupperware set kept in its original cardboard box in one of her mother's lower cabinets. The box was so old it was soft, almost like cloth. It had been in the kitchen for as long as Lucy could remember, and she found comfort in its familiarity. She allowed herself to think, for the first time, that Vasily might not resurface. It had been four days since he was supposed to meet them on the playground, and Yulia hadn't heard from him. The anxiety lessened with each hour he stayed away.

Paul came in and wrapped his arms around Cokie from behind, kissing her hair. "Can you believe Molly's twelve?" he said.

"No, I can't," Cokie said, taking a pretzel. "I told her she had to stop having birthdays. Twelve is enough."

Paul was still working on his wife to purchase a T.G.I. Friday's franchise, and Lucy had heard that Cokie was beginning to cave.

They both had that entrepreneurial drive, a divining rod for making money that Lucy had never possessed. They didn't worry about how they made it, either; they didn't torture themselves about whether the world needed onion rings or mozzarella sticks, or whether they needed a flat-screen television. It was there, so it was theirs. A part of her envied them for lacking a sense of moral ambiguity.

"So what's the story with Louis?" Paul said. "I haven't seen him around lately."

Lucy had just taken a can of frozen lemonade out of her mother's freezer and dumped it in a pitcher. Paul waited as she let the water run until the pitcher was full.

"He took a new job," she said. "He's moving to Massachusetts."

From the kitchen, she could see across the hall to the door of the lunchbox room, which her mother kept locked when Mat was around.

"That's too bad," Paul said. "He seemed like a nice guy."

A nice guy, which was all they ever wanted for her. Maybe it looked simple from their perspective: Combine one lonely woman with one nice guy. Mix. Bake. Test for doneness. Decorate and top with plastic bride and groom. She couldn't blame them for wanting her family to have three members instead of two. But at this point, all she wanted was a little reassurance that her tiny family wouldn't be reduced to one again.

"He was," she said. "Very nice. He wants me to come visit, but I'm not sure I will. I don't think it would have worked out anyway. Hey, I brought that money you loaned me. Let me get it."

Paul shook his head. "Keep it," he said. "Start a college fund or something."

Lucy began to protest, but Paul ignored her and took the bowl of pretzels into the dining room. She went out the back door to check on Mat and keep her father company at the grill. Mat was playing in the backyard with Molly, who was giving him piggyback rides.

Bertie flipped a hamburger. "Mat's not going back to Russia, sweetheart. He's staying with us," he said.

Lucy squinted into the sun, trying to catch a glimpse of Mat as Molly rounded a tree. "I wish I could be sure, but until I hear that his father went back, I'm not going to sleep much."

"How are you holding up?"

"I'm okay," she said as Bertie put his hand on top of her head, resting it gently on the dark curls. "But you realize, there are no guarantees. I still don't have Vasily's signature."

In the past few days, she had made calls to the State Department and to Maryland's congressional offices, only to hang up when the person on the other end asked for her name, terrified to provoke an investigation of her paperwork when Vasily might never come back.

"The way I see it, you're getting a second chance," he said, and she nodded.

Not everyone, she thought, finds the cure—the sun-dried tomatoes that shrink the tumor or the boy who is the hazelnut, all that is made. With Mat in her life, everything seemed more concrete—full of dirt and tears and raw emotions—and at the same time, more mysterious, the *how* of their coming together now less important than the *why*. If Vasily came back, she would never have the time to figure it out.

"Tell your mother the hot dogs are three minutes to perfection," Bertie said. "For the hamburgers, more like five."

She hugged her father and went inside.

It was a vividly sunny day, less humid than usual, but they ate their picnic food in the dining room because Mat was afraid of bees. When Rosalee brought out Molly's cake with its lighted candles, they all sang "Happy Birthday" slowly, enunciating carefully, so Mat could catch the words. He seemed fascinated by the whole ritual, particularly the candles. After Molly blew them out, Rosalee lit them again so Mat could try it. Then he ate his cake and asked for seconds. How American he was becoming, Lucy thought, already addicted to sugar.

After the party, she drove back to the duplex and walked up the stairs, carrying a sleeping Mat. She wondered where Vasily was now, picturing him in some rundown apartment in Russia, wanting to make it so. But it wasn't so. After she tucked Mat into his bed, she listened to a message on her answering machine. It was from Yulia.

"Lucy, I hear from Vasily. He goes back to Atlantic City to think about his decision, but now he is to return. He wants to talk. Call me back."

twenty

D*ear Lucy,*

I know you're not expecting this e-mail until July, but I only have one more thing to tell you, and that is how much I love you.

I certainly had feelings for you soon after we met, a gentle crush that I thought would pass in time. To be honest, I thought it was no match for Sylvie and this life she imagined us having together, so I stopped myself from acting on it.

After you and I both moved to Ellsworth, though, I realized that I needed to break off my engagement and have an honest talk with you, but I hated to hurt Sylvie, and I saw no need to rush. I also wasn't completely sure how you felt about me. Then the planes hit the towers, and everything changed. Strange how that event is so intertwined with my illness, as if one precipitated the other.

The night I told you about my diagnosis, when we were locked out on the balcony, I finally reached out, tried to kiss you. You didn't respond, never mentioned it, and that hurt. Later I came to realize how unfair it was to hit you with that on the same night you learned I might not have a future. Maybe you just didn't know how to react.

So why am I telling you this now? I've debated about taking it with me to my grave on the hillside, but as I've written these e-mails and thought about the last year of my life—to which you virtually donated a year of your own life—I thought you'd want to know. If you loved me the way I hope you did, you'd certainly want to know.

Do you remember how you responded to my question that morning, when the super finally let us inside? You said you thought two people, if they were meant to be together, would understand each other. But you and I never really did, at least not on the same day. When Sylvie got off that train, I sent her right back to New Jersey without telling her about my cancer. I told her there was someone else, and even after she learned I was sick, I kept her at a distance because I didn't want her pity; yours was the only pity I could tolerate. There are times I wish I had been more honest, and other days I'm sure I did the right thing in trying to spare you even more grief.

Dr. Singh was the only one of my doctors who refused to give odds. He used to say: I'm not going to give you numbers, Harlan, because you'll fixate on them and talk yourself out of any hope. But I didn't talk myself out of hope, Lucy; I talked myself into taking control, into choosing a full life for the person I'm leaving behind, not a life spent in the shadows of a disease that would always hang over our heads.

Chemo brain is making it harder and harder for me to explain myself, or even to type. It takes me a long time to correct all my mistakes. I still haven't told you the story behind my grandmother's banjo accident, and I want you to hear my voice while I'm telling it, so I'm going to record it on an audiotape and fix it to the underside of her table. Maybe you already found it.

This is my final message, Lucy. I don't have much more to say except that I love you. In my eyes, you're nothing less than one of those saints you admire so much.

Yours always,

Harlan

In the flurry of phone calls that followed Yulia's phone message, Lucy hadn't checked her e-mail. When she did, she found an unexpected one from Harlan, weeks before the next one was due to arrive. She put her face down on the keyboard to feel closer to

Harlan, grateful for the distraction because it helped block out the choking rage she felt when she thought about Vasily. She could only get through the day by believing that he could still be persuaded, or bribed, to leave Mat with her.

So there it was. Harlan had loved her. He had loved her and had ditched the beauty queen, and she had kept him at arm's length because she thought he was confusing his gratefulness for affection, like a wounded soldier falling for his nurse. How could she have assumed his question was about Sylvie, when he was asking about her? He was right. They never really understood each other, at least not on the same day.

Lucy read through the e-mail again, stopping on the paragraph about Dr. Singh. *I didn't talk myself out of hope, Lucy; I talked myself into taking control, into choosing a full life for the person I'm leaving behind.* The implications of that sentence, the confessional tone, were too disturbing to ignore. She lifted up stacks of papers on her desk and pulled out the drawer in search of her address book. When she finally found it, it took her several minutes to locate the phone number on a page of Harlan's many doctors.

She dialed Dr. Singh's number and left a message with his answering service, requesting that he return her call; then she put her head back down on the keyboard. A few minutes later, Mat was standing by her chair, poking her in the arm with one finger as if he thought she was asleep. She sat up, feeling the indentations of the computer keys in her forehead.

He took her limp arm and pulled her along until they reached the living room, where he guided her to the couch.

"You read, Mama," he said, handing her his picture book about construction equipment.

She turned to the first page, then closed the book. "Just a minute, honey. I have to look for something."

She went to the dining-room table and crawled under it. Mat crawled under after her, holding out the book again. "You read."

She ran her hands along the wooden supports on the underside of the table until she found a small bump sealed with duct tape. She pulled off the tape and found a tiny audiocassette and a gift-card-sized envelope with "For Lucy" written on it. She stayed under the table, staring at the envelope, until Mat pulled her arm again and led her back to the couch.

With her arm around Mat, she read about bulldozers, front loaders, and cranes—barely seeing the words—as she tried to remember if she had ever unpacked the small tape recorder she had used in graduate school to record an occasional lecture. And if she still had it, did it work? What kind of batteries did it take? Did she have any new batteries? At the end of the book, before Mat could say "again," she stood and grabbed her purse. "Let's go for a ride."

Lucy clutched the minicassette in one hand on the way to the office-supply store and, once there, clutched Mat with her other hand, worried that both might disappear if she let go of them. The first employee she stopped led her to a crowded aisle and pointed out which recorders used that kind of tape. At the counter, she bought the batteries, checking the package three times to make sure she had the right size.

Back at home, she fed Mat lunch, silently urging the cat clock to slow down. Angela was due to arrive to take Mat for an hour so Lucy could examine his paperwork again and weigh the risks of another call to the State Department, but she hated to let him go. She still didn't know what Vasily wanted, why he had left, or why he was coming back. He was both the poison—the only one who could take Mat away—and the antidote—the only one who could sign the papers that legalized her motherhood.

As Mat chewed slowly on a brownie, she took the small envelope from the kitchen counter and opened it. Inside was an old picture of Harlan, taken before his illness. He had a full head of hair and a broad smile. He looked tan, his freckles glowing, literally the picture of health.

She stared at Harlan's picture, wondering when it was taken, and remembered details about him that she had forgotten during his illness. Back when he had hair, one of his eyebrows was slightly thicker than the other because of a chicken-pox scar, which altered the symmetry of his face just enough to make it interesting. She ran her finger over the picture lightly so as not to leave a smudge. She had loved his freckles. They gave him the air of someone who stayed connected to childhood, who couldn't take himself too seriously. This was a man who found humor in the Crusades, who had dreamed of her as Eleanor of Aquitaine.

She looked up and realized that Mat had finished lunch and slipped out of his chair. She helped him fill his small backpack with Matchbox cars, and when Angela arrived, he pulled the backpack over one shoulder. He waved to Lucy a little forlornly, as if he might even miss her.

"You'll be back soon, buddy," she said. "Vern needs you to help him play baseball."

He reached toward her with both arms. Harlan's picture slipped out of her hand as she pulled him off the ground. He rested his head on her shoulder until Angela tapped him on the back and told him Vern had a new Matchbox car for him.

When they left, Lucy retrieved Harlan's picture from the floor. But before she could begin sorting through Mat's paperwork, the phone rang.

She picked it up with dread, certain it would be Yulia relaying demands from Vasily, but it was Dr. Singh. She had forgotten him almost entirely in the period of her deepest grief because he had existed only in the context of Harlan's illness. Now she remembered that he was businesslike, not completely humorless but lacking in vitality, as though he never got enough sleep. He had been the only doctor to come to Harlan's funeral.

"Lucy? This is Dr. Singh. My office said you called."

"I did," she said, not sure what she should be asking. "I . . . I have some insurance forms left to fill out for Harlan Matthews, and

I was wondering if you could answer some questions for me. I have medical power of attorney."

"I remember you, and I remember Harlan very well. Let me just open the file."

Lucy listened intently to the doctor's footsteps, the sound of tapping on a keyboard, the push of a button, and the dull hum of her line being transferred to a speakerphone.

"It's all here," the doctor said. "So unfortunate that he decided to stop his treatments. What is it you need to know?"

She pulled the phone away from her ear for a moment, confused. Then it suddenly made sense, what Harlan had said about choosing a full life for the person he was leaving behind. She phrased her question as a statement.

"So you're saying that his experimental treatments were working?"

"He had an ugly time ahead of him, as I'm sure you know, but we were seeing a reduction in his primary tumor. He decided not to continue. I'd be surprised if the insurance company had any complaints."

She paused for a moment, uncertain if she really wanted to know why Harlan would walk away from a treatment that might have helped him.

"They want to know why he stopped the treatments," she said finally. "They're settling his final bills, and they want to know why he started the treatments only to stop them."

Dr. Singh waited a moment, and she could almost hear him gathering his thoughts.

"What really seemed to bother him was the constant threat of a relapse, knowing that even if he saw a remission, it likely would be temporary. Of course, he wasn't looking forward to the side effects of another round of intensive chemo. His liver was pretty much shot before we even started, so that was a factor. The infertility troubled him, too, although that seemed like a minor issue from my perspective."

She pressed on.

"So were you surprised that he chose not to take advantage of the time he had left?"

"Oh, it wasn't much, mind you. We might have prolonged his life a year, two at the outside, but who knows what medical science might have come up with in the meantime. That's what I kept saying."

Two years? Had Harlan taken two years from his already short life and tossed them away like garbage?

The doctor continued.

"In my experience, most patients will deal with just about anything for the chance to live a little longer, but Harlan had a fairly unusual perspective, so I wasn't entirely surprised by his decision. He didn't see the point of dragging it out. He used to say it wasn't fair to those who had to watch him deteriorate."

Not fair to me, Lucy thought. *Only me.* She hung up the phone while the doctor was still talking, seeing no point in pretending that she cared enough to say good-bye. He couldn't resurrect Harlan, and he couldn't prevent Vasily from coming back. Those were the only two things that mattered.

...

TWENTY MINUTES WENT BY before Lucy became aware that she had been sitting in the same position, her hand still on the phone. She felt numb, bound inside a dream.

It didn't seem possible, but Harlan might have had two more years to live, and he had chosen to spare her the pain of watching him live—or more accurately, "not die." She wondered briefly if this was her punishment for assuming she could have saved Harlan—or Mat, for that matter—when neither one had asked for salvation.

Outside, visible through one pane of her bedroom window, was the library spire. She got up, walked down the stairs, and passed through the living room. She opened the front door and went outside, walking down the short steps of her tiny front porch without any shoes. The summer sun had been relentless, blaring down for days without a cloud to temper its heat, so the ground was baked into a hard, almost colorless cement relieved only by the straw that once was grass. Lucy stepped over *Saint Blaise*, still on the ground, and traversed the burning black asphalt of the duplex parking lot, turning toward the library spire, though she couldn't see the tip of it, which disappeared into the glare of the sun.

She walked in as straight a line as possible, not feeling the soles of her feet, across curbstones and driveways, watered lawns and sidewalks, gravel pathways and wood-chipped flower beds until she stood in front of the library. A few summer students passed by on the sidewalk, glancing at her bare feet. She climbed the library stairs, holding tightly to the railing, and opened the door. The air-conditioning surrounded her, beckoning her onto the cool, clean tiles of the central hall, with its thirty-foot ceilings that commanded all who entered to look up and worship the words that lived there, hidden in stacks that went high into the sky as well as deep into the earth.

The library had been their common ground. Before Harlan got sick, in their first few weeks at Ellsworth, they had both come here to work, like students, because neither one had liked the solitary confinement of their offices. But they also came here to see each other, to crouch near the other's pile of books and whisper conspiratorially about a mutual student or Dean Humphrey's latest edict.

"That's probably bogus, you know," Harlan would say, picking up Lucy's copy of *The Letters of St. Bernard of Clairvaux*. "The author's a major-league idiot. He wears this incredibly pretentious, very long goatee. I met him at a conference once, and it was all I could do to stop myself from pulling it."

"So a bad goatee makes him a bogus authority on Saint Bernard."

"It doesn't speak well for his judgment. That's all I'm saying."

Lucy let her feet absorb the cool of the tiles, then walked two floors up a wide central staircase that led to a hallway with four doors. At the smallest door, she reached up and felt along the top of the frame for a key, which Harlan had learned about through a librarian who worked the night shift.

She climbed a narrow spiral staircase up to the bell tower, ducking under beams and brushing away cobwebs. In the small room that housed the bell, there wasn't much room to maneuver around the antique machinery that activated its tolling. She stumbled over metal rods and gears and found her way next to the bell, which came up to the top of her head, and laid her left cheek against its smooth surface. The cold shocked her for a moment, then filtered through her body, along her torso, and into her legs.

She remembered the night Harlan had showed her the key and led her up the stairs to the tower, at the peak of her hopes that he might begin to view her as more than a friend. They had laughed at the bell, such a squat, primitive thing, and climbed over to the balcony of the cupola to view the campus at night, spread out before them with the precision of a map, talking as they always did. So much talking.

She thought, then, that he might kiss her, or touch her hand, break through the barrier named Sylvie that stood between them. But they had forgotten to look at the time, and the bell's automatic timer went off at ten o'clock. The first clang had been deafening, and they had run down the stairs, hands over their ears. When they reached the hallway, a janitor standing with his mop had given them a reproachful look, and they had left the library, gone their separate ways, somehow chastened.

Lucy spread her arms around the bell, then turned to her other cheek as though finding a cool spot on her pillow; tears ran down, leaving tracks on the tarnished metal. She turned her head again and banged the bony part of her forehead against the bell, over and over, eliciting a dull thunk that had the effect of calming her.

She left the bell's side and climbed over the low partition to the balcony, which jutted out only a few feet from the bell tower. The railing surrounding the balcony came to just below her hip, and she leaned against it, stretching toward the moon, which floated, impartial and ghostly, behind the arts center. If someone were so inclined, she thought, it wouldn't take much to climb over the railing, just the activation of a few large muscle groups. Then it would be a question of whether to crouch and spring out or to fall passively, eyes open and expectant. The earth would receive such a person without shame, rushing up to greet her, welcoming her back into its womb.

The quad was empty, as far as she could see. The summer session drew a few students, but by late afternoon, they were usually holed up in the air-conditioned student center. A bird flew by, just inside her field of peripheral vision. It looked like a hawk, although she couldn't say for sure. She had the sense that she was alone on campus, that an evacuation alarm had sounded, and she had failed to hear it.

"Har-lan," she yelled, feeling as though she could watch the word itself drift over the trees and beyond, to a place where it would be received, a place that would send a response. But she heard nothing, not even the wind or a dog barking or a car passing by.

Acknowledgment was what she wanted. Acknowledgment that she had tried, in the best way she knew how, to keep her friend from dying and to enrich the life of one small child with the love, the yearning that had to latch onto something. Would no one acknowledge that she had tried?

She remembered then what she and Harlan had talked about when they had stood on the balcony of the bell tower.

"Look at this," he had said. "It's so beautiful, right? The lights and the trees in the distance, the stone chapel. But I just read this article on how we acclimatize to beauty, even to happiness. If you saw this every day, you'd stop noticing the beauty. Instead, you'd notice the flaws: that plastic bag or that junker car over there under the streetlight. They've actually studied people who win lotteries, and it's the same thing. They're happier for a few months or a year, then they acclimatize to having money, and they slip right back into the same level of happiness they had before they won. Strange, huh?"

She looked down at her hands on the balcony railing and wondered if she had acclimatized to sadness, to a state of wondering what could have been with Harlan. It had been there for so long, since even before he died, that she failed to notice it anymore. She had carried the burden of his death everywhere, afraid that if she put it down, he would be forgotten.

But that had to change. It would change, was changing—no, had already changed. She looked toward the bell and thought of Mat, who would have climbed inside it or banged on it with his small fists, determined to make noise. She thought of how he was softening around the edges and finding his place. She thought of his perfect ears and the way his breath smelled of peanut butter and how he studied the pictures in his books, forming new words, absorbing a new lexicon. She thought of his stubborn streak and his need for sugar and his terrifying aptitude for putting himself in physical danger.

Mat needed her, and unlike Harlan, she still had a chance to protect him. With the campus so quiet, she could hear the sounds of water rushing inside her head, sending her over the falls toward the frothing, churning pool beyond where life flourished. Adrenalin moved in, dissolving the dreaminess. Her feet hurt, and she noticed that her shirt was soaked in sweat. She turned her back on the new moon, climbed back over the partition, and walked down the stairs, striding numbly across the cool tiles, back across the white-hot sidewalks and parking lots and the dried-up patches of grass.

She wouldn't let Vasily anywhere near Mat. She would call more lawyers, the United Nations, the media. She didn't have to listen to what Vasily had to say any more than she had to torture herself over caring about Harlan and wanting him to live.

When she entered the parking lot near the duplex, she crossed it without looking either way for cars. She approached her little porch, climbed the stairs, opened the front door, and walked through the living room, now truly "lived-in," with its toy-strewn floor and book-covered coffee table. She headed toward the kitchen drawer that contained Mat's thick file of papers and his passport, wanting to see it and hold it as proof that he had legal status in his new country.

She was rifling through the papers when the doorbell rang. She unlocked the door and let Angela in. Mat was in her arms, draped over one shoulder, fast asleep.

"I dropped Vern at home," she said. "Look at this boy. When he crashes, he crashes."

Lucy carried Mat upstairs and tucked him into his bed. She was on her way down the stairs when the doorbell rang again. She assumed it was her parents, who had planned to hold vigil with her as she waited for Yulia's next call. Instead, she found Yulia on her tiny porch, and with her, Vasily, in the same green jogging suit he had worn the first time they met, the same sullen look on his face. Lucy appraised his physical strength, deciding that she was the stronger of the two, given his pallor and his rail-thin frame. She wanted to keep them out on the porch and moved toward the door, but Yulia pushed past her, pulling Vasily inside with her.

"Vasily has something to say," Yulia said.

Angela came out of the kitchen, and Lucy could sense the heat from ten feet away.

"He can say what he wants," Angela said. "He's not taking that boy, and I'll pin his scrawny rear to the ground if he tries."

Lucy moved toward the staircase, feeling the need to block it, when Yulia moved forward again, thrusting out the tote bag.

"Please," she said. "Please look."

"Tell him this, Yulia," Lucy said, ignoring the tote bag. "Tell him he had the chance to see his son, and he decided to drive to Atlantic City instead, and that tells me everything I need to know. Tell him to go back to Russia and let us get on with our lives."

Yulia said nothing to Vasily, who stood near the door and put his hands in the pockets of his warm-up jacket.

"Please let him explain," Yulia said.

"Why should we let him explain?" Lucy said. "He didn't think about Mat's future when he packed up his things, took him by the hand, and brought him to an orphanage. That he can't ever explain."

Yulia shook her head in frustration, opened the tote bag, then thrust a sheaf of papers toward Lucy, who was still blocking the staircase.

"The termination papers," she said. "They are signed. I tell Vasily that you are good mother, that you have family to help you. I tell him that this country gives him everything he could never hope to have in Russia. He decides that his son is better to stay here. He calls Zoya Minksy for new papers and waits for FedEx at his friend's house in Atlantic City, because he has no money for hotel. Now he brings you papers. This is why he came."

Lucy took the papers from Yulia and sat down hard on the bottom step of the staircase. She flipped to the last page and stared at the signature: *Vasily Andreyevich Panachev.*

"Thank God," Angela said. "Now get him out of here, before he changes his mind."

Yulia spoke to Vasily in Russian, and he nodded, thrusting his hands deeper into his pockets. He turned as if to go, but Lucy stood up and walked over to Vasily, who seemed to shrink into the wall. She opened her arms and pulled him toward her, sobbing into his shoulder. He seemed unsure of how to react and stood stiffly in her embrace as she whispered words he couldn't understand: "Thank you, thank you; I'll take such good care of him. Thank you, thank you."

When Lucy let him go, Vasily said something to Yulia, which she then translated. "Is it possible, he asks, to see his son one last time? He has come all this way."

Angela opened her mouth to speak, but Lucy held up her hand.

"He's sleeping," she said. "I'm sorry, but I'd hate to wake him. And I'm not sure it's a good idea. He might be confused."

Yulia translated, then Vasily spoke to her again.

"Okay for him to peek? To take one last look. He promises not to wake him."

Lucy hesitated, wanting Vasily to leave so that she could call her parents, her brother, her friends. But then she looked at his face and, without words, understood what he was saying: I'm leaving him here;

you owe me that much. She put the papers down on the couch and motioned to Vasily, leading him toward the stairs.

"Lucy, I wouldn't . . ." Angela said, but Lucy ignored her. She let Vasily follow her up the stairs and down the hall to Mat's room, where the door was slightly ajar. She opened the door a little wider and slipped through as Vasily came in behind her. Then she stood aside as he knelt by the bed and stared at his son, who slept as if he were awake, eyelids moving, breath audibly passing through his open mouth, fists curled. Vasily reached out a hand as if he couldn't stop himself, but he only waved it over Mat's forehead—a blessing perhaps, or a wish or a hope for his future, or a gesture of apology, or all those combined.

Air escaped from the back of Lucy's throat, an involuntary rasp of sympathy, because she could have been the one saying good-bye. Mat stirred, rolling over to one side and tucking both hands under his cheek. Vasily stood up, bowed formally over his son in a gesture that seemed to reflect his resolve, and turned to go.

Back downstairs, Yulia smiled and patted Lucy's hand. As they moved toward the front door, Vasily said something to Yulia, who turned and translated for Lucy.

"Vasily says he hopes you keep him informed of his son, and that you come visit Murmansk again someday, if he wants to meet his father."

"Of course," Lucy said. "Tell him I'll send him cards and pictures and drawings. He won't be forgotten."

...

THREE MONTHS WENT BY, Lucy's watershed year drawing to a close, and she still hadn't listened to Harlan's cassette tape, nor had she revisited any of his e-mails. Her relief about Mat had blunted her anger, but she still resented Harlan for lying to her. She wished he had been honest about why he was giving up. At the very least, she would have tried to understand.

Mat had started preschool and, with the exception of a minor biting incident, seemed to be adjusting well. Then one Saturday in early November, she realized while cleaning the bathroom sink that she hadn't thought about Harlan for at least a day. Her sense of loss had kept her company for so long that she felt guilty about watching it fade from inattention. Mat was napping, so she went to her room and found the cassette tape and the recorder. She cut through the packaging and loaded the batteries, inserted the tape, and adjusted the volume. And then . . . Harlan's unmistakable voice.

Look at my picture while you're listening to this, Lucy. I want you to remember me as I was before—the good-looking boy. (He laughs.) So my grandmother's story, which I never told you in person because it chokes me up every time . . .

It all happened the day I turned five.

My grandmother had made me a chocolate cake, and it was there on the middle of the dining-room table, calling to me, at her house in Louisiana. My parents and I and assorted other relatives were sitting around the table—your table now—listening to my uncle Reston play the banjo. He could play, Uncle Reston. He would bend his head over the strings and pick so fast you couldn't see his fingers move.

After waiting and listening to Uncle Reston, I apparently decided it was time for cake, or so the story goes. So I stood up on my chair and reached toward the cake in the middle of the table. As I stood up, the chair slipped out from under me, so my grandmother lunged to stop me from falling. Uncle Reston lunged too, banjo and all, and the handle flew up and cracked my grandmother right in the face as though she'd been hit with a baseball bat. Her nose was broken, and she lost the vision in her left eye.

Now, you might say, that's a terrible accident, but worse things have happened, and I would agree (I'm a case in point). But what you don't know is that my grandfather had died a year earlier, and my grandmother's taxes were already in arrears. She made her living as a seamstress, but she couldn't sew anymore because of her injuries, so she lost the house to foreclosure. The only thing salvaged was the dining-room table.

But just so you know, things improved for my grandmother. She moved into an apartment building, taking only her clothes and the table. She was down, Lucy, but she had her faith, just like you have yours. A few months later, she met a retired insurance salesman, fell in love, and got married again. The two of them had twelve years together. She died in 1987—I miss her still—and he died a few months later. The table went to my mother for a few years, but she gave it to me after she moved into her Florida condo. She said it didn't go with the decor.

So take care of it, Lucy. If you have any kids, just cover it up with newspaper for ten or twenty years. There's no reason it shouldn't last another hundred years, no reason at all. It's a tough old table, and it wants your stories, too.

Good-bye, Lucy . . . I hope you enjoyed hearing about the table . . . I love you.

She turned off the tape recorder and smiled. It was all so absurd, Harlan's grandmother and the banjo. It brought back memories of Harlan's sense of humor that had long ago evaporated. His throat had been sore when he recorded his message; she could tell by the strain and thickness of it. At the end, it had seemed that every part of his body had been forced to join in the suffering. But he had managed to sound as if none of that bothered him. He had choked up only when he spoke of his grandmother's death, wanting to provide the image of a little boy lunging for a cake so that Lucy could balance it with the cane-dependent invalid emptying his savings account.

She had sat down at her desk to reread Harlan's final e-mail when Mat came into her bedroom with his hair pushed into little devil horns from his nap. Framed on her desk was the picture of him driving his red car in Moscow, eyes gleaming, and he pointed at it.

"Car."

"Yes, that was the car you left in Moscow. We'll go back there someday."

Mat reached over her arms to type on the keyboard and hit something that brought up the prompt asking Lucy if she was sure she wanted to delete Harlan's e-mail program. She pulled Mat's hands away from the keyboard and stared at the question: *Are you sure?*

Then she reached for the mouse and clicked on Yes. Even though she knew no more e-mails were coming, it felt right to say yes, it's over.

She realized now that Harlan had never accepted her commitment to him, never understood that she would have been grateful to preserve what was left of him, because even a fragment of Harlan was better than no Harlan at all. At the same moment, it took her aback to realize that she could be just as self-centered as any child. She had cared for Harlan out of love, but she had also wanted the reward of a grateful Harlan, a Harlan who recovered and would never forget her devotion. She had wanted him to live because she needed him, more than he needed her. The truth of it hurt, but she couldn't change it. All she could do was take a little of his advice into the next phase of her life. She stood up and turned off the computer screen.

"Let's go somewhere," she told Mat, who ran to his room to get his sneakers.

It was cool outside, but not cold, the November sun shimmering behind a milky haze of clouds. They stopped at a Friendly's in the western suburbs and ordered from the takeout window. Lucy decided on a vanilla Fribble in honor of Nana Mavis, and Mat had soft-serve chocolate. His face was the picture of concentration as the thick ribbon of ice cream curled into the stubby waffle cone, as if something might go wrong if he didn't supervise carefully.

"Thank you," he told the clerk who handed it to him, and she felt a surge of pride. A mother's pride.

When they got back into the car, she wrapped Mat's cone in layers of napkins and drove west again, letting the car take her to a place she felt she needed to go. They parked at the bottom of the hill, and she held the chocolate cone as Mat unbuckled his own car seat. He was, she had discovered, remarkably adept at removing anything that might restrict his movements. They climbed the hill and found

Harlan's headstone. Grass covered the soil, erasing the outline where his grave had been dug the previous November, when her watershed year had truly started.

Mat's cone began to melt down his arm, and she cleaned him up with the extra napkins she now remembered to take. She sat down on the grass, cross-legged, and Mat found his place in her lap.

I know, Harlan. I know that you could have continued with the experimental treatments, and it breaks my heart that you couldn't tell me why you were stopping. But you were right; it was your decision. I'm sorry if I pushed you too hard. What I see now is that you feared your illness, while I feared your death. And what I really feared was how much I would miss you.

I thought I'd introduce you to my new son, Mat. I wish you could see him. He's so beautiful. He's a handful, of course, but he's worth it. I also wanted to thank you for the tape, and for your e-mails. I'm working to find this titanium core you say I have. I'm trying to be the strong one, allowing you to open the door for me. You may not have realized it, Harlan, but grief was your gift to me. Grief is what led me to Mat, and he's the reason I can put it behind me. For that, I can't thank you enough.

I only regret one thing, and that's never telling you when you were alive how much I loved you. But I think, somehow, you knew.

She paused and looked toward Mat, who had gotten up from her lap. He wandered over to the Virgin Mary statue, resting one chocolate-stained hand on her head as he crunched the edge of his waffle cone.

"Poor Mary," Lucy said, standing up and wiping off the ice cream with napkins.

She shoved the statue back a bit, centering it once again on its pedestal. Then she bent down and put her arms around her son, conferring on him the family legacy of happiness that she had so long resisted but was now, unmistakably, her own.

acknowledgements

I will be forever grateful to Lindsay Guzzardo, my warm and wise-beyond-her-years editor, and to Jessica Regel, my extremely talented and ever-optimistic agent. Jennifer Lonas, it should be noted, did an outstanding job copyediting the manuscript.

I must thank the Connecticut Commission on Culture and Tourism for supporting me with an Artist Fellowship and the Faulkner Society for honoring me with the gold medal for best novel in the 2006 William Faulkner–William Wisdom Creative Writing Competition.

To my friends, family, and early readers, I can honestly say that you fueled me with your enthusiasm. I must mention a few of you: Theresa Sullivan Barger, Karen O'Brien, Mary Ann Schoenberger, Nancy Schoenberger King, John Schoenberger Jr., Colleen Porth, Beth Papermaster, Michelle Souza, Mary Collins, Steve Courtney, Sally Lynch, Laura Giannone, Susan Fabry Daniels, Kristin Higgins, Deborah Hornblow, and Tima Smith. I am very grateful to Rebecca Homes for sharing her adoption story and to Dr. Michael Isakoff for his medical expertise.

I would also like to recognize my dear friend and former *Baltimore Sun* colleague Dan Reese, whose all-too-brief life inspired everyone who knew him.

Finally, I would like to thank my family. My parents, to whom this book is dedicated, never once told me that writing a novel wasn't an entirely realistic goal. My wonderful husband, Kevin, has worked tirelessly to support our family while allowing me to pursue a dream. I'm also truly grateful to my children—Andrew, Jenna, and Claire—whose love and support and dinnertime jokes managed to turn all the ups and downs of the writing process into a joyful ride.

about the author

Photograph © Shana Sureck

Susan Schoenber is a writer and editor who lives in West Hartford, Connecticut, with her husband, three children, and a dog named Jackson. *A Watershed Year*, which won the gold medal in the William Faulkner–William Wisdom Creative Writing Competition, is her first novel. Her short stories and essays have appeared in *Inkwell, Village Rambler, Bartleby Snopes, the Double Dealer*, and *Reader's Digest*. A longtime journalist, Susan has worked for the *Baltimore Sun*, the *Hartford Courant*, and many other publications. She reads a lot, runs, and plays the piano when she's feeling nostalgic. Please visit her Web site at www.susanschoenberger.com.

a conversation with

SUSAN SCHOENBERGER

Q. What inspired you to write *A Watershed Year*?

A. The first chapter of *A Watershed Year* started out as a short story called *"Intercession,"* which was published in the literary journal *Inkwell.* I wrote it several years after a friend and *Baltimore Sun* colleague of mine died of cancer, and in a sense, it was my way of coping with that loss and weaving an emotional truth into a fictional story. When I decided to expand the story into a novel, I found that I couldn't abandon Harlan's character, so I came up with a way for him to continue his presence in Lucy's life.

Q. What led you to a story about adoption?

A. I have a number of friends who have adopted children, and I've been privileged to witness how their families have adapted and grown in ways that are different from my own but no less beautiful. I'm inspired by the bravery of the decision to bring a child into a family and create a bond that's every bit as strong as a biological one.

Q. How did the story take shape? How long did it take you to write it?

A. The story took shape in fits and starts over a period of three to four years. I wrote a complete draft in 2004, not really knowing how the story would end. Over the next few years, I rewrote extensively and reshaped the plot, adding and subtracting details along the way. Even after the novel won its category in the William Faulkner–William Wisdom Creative Writing Competition in 2006, I continue to edit and add to the story. I wish I could say it came to me in one piece, but it was a very arduous and circular process.

Q. Are the characters based on anyone?

A. Other than Harlan, whose essential nature is similar to that of my late friend, and Nana Mavis, who is based on my unforgettable grandmother, Deloris Walsh, the characters are not based on anyone in particular. On the other hand, I can see pieces of myself in pretty much every character. I have Lucy's obsession with categories and Cokie's exasperation at what it takes to raise children in today's society. I have Paul's pragmatism and Mat's impatience. It may sound contradictory, but I'm none of them and all of them.

Q. Tell us about your writing process — where and when do you write? Do you listen to a certain type of music? Do you work from outlines?

A. I write mainly in the morning in a small office surrounded by books that inspire me, but my writing time is not my only work time. When I go for a run, I skip the iPod and think about my characters instead. I jot down notes everywhere I go, and once I solved a plot problem in the middle of a sit-up. I didn't use an outline when I wrote *A Watershed Year*, but I'm trying to use one for my next novel. Unfortunately, I keep rewriting the outline.

Q. What kind of research did you do for this story?

A. I did extensive research on the saints, on the adoption process, and on Russia. I have a whole shelf of books devoted to topics I needed to learn more about. I think my background as a newspaper reporter and copy editor served me well. At different points in the writing process, I interviewed a doctor about how Harlan's cancer would have progressed and a court clerk about the technicalities of adoption.

Q. Have you traveled to Russia? Why did you choose Russia as the country Lucy adopts from?

A. I haven't traveled to Russia, but I've always been intrigued by that country, and I hope to see it someday. I wanted Lucy to complete the adoption in one trip, so that limited the places I could choose from, even inside Russia. I decided on Murmansk because it's not as well known as other Russian cities, and it provided more of a blank canvas for letting the story run where it needed to go.

Q. What themes in this story do you hope will resonate most with readers?

A. I hope readers will wonder how they might have behaved if they had been in Harlan's circumstances, and I hope they will appreciate how Lucy grows as a person when she takes responsibility for Mat's future. Beyond that, I just hope they enjoy the story.

Q. What are you working on now?

A. I'm working on a new novel about a financially strapped weekly newspaper editor and her two siblings, both of whom are also in financial distress. The newspaper editor helps take care of a woman who has lived most of her life in an iron lung after having polio as a child. They story is mainly set in upstate New York, which is where I grew up, and it involves a cast of characters with the best intentions who make some pretty terrible decisions. I'm in love with it right now, but I'll probably rewrite it half a dozen times before it's ready for an audience.

questions for discussion

- *How would you define the role of the saints in Lucy's life?*

- *In what ways did the time frame of the story, pre–9/11 to several months after the start of the war in Iraq, impact what was happening in Lucy's life?*

- *Should Harlan have confessed the depth of his feelings for Lucy before he died? How do you think Lucy would have reacted?*

- *How would you have dealt with Yulia and her unconventional approach as an adoption agent?*

- *What do you think of Harlan's decision to discontinue his cancer treatment, even though he was getting better?*

- *What do you think the wallpaper for Mat's room symbolized?*

- *How did you view Mat's initial indifference to Lucy? What do you imagine he was thinking?*

- *Did you sympathize with Vasily? Do you think it was right that Mat stayed with Lucy, or do you think he should have gone back to Russia with Vasily?*

- *Did you believe Vasily's explanation regarding the source of Mat's scars? Why or why not?*

- *Was Louis as innocent as he seemed regarding Lucy's academic article?*

- *Given the emails and the audiotape under the dining table, do you think Lucy could receive more messages in other forms from Harlan?*